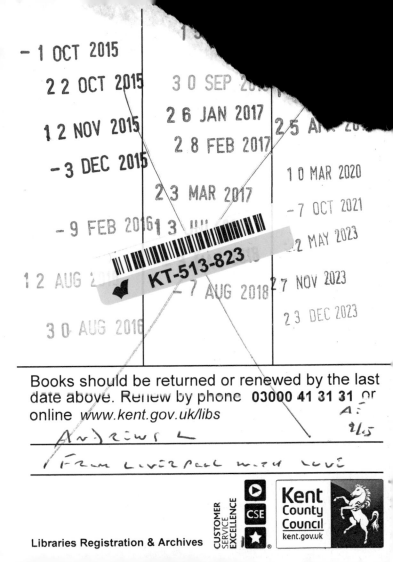

Books should be returned or renewed by the last
date above. Renew by phone **03000 41 31 31** or
online *www.kent.gov.uk/libs*

Andrews L

From Liverpool with Love

Lyn Andrews was born in Liverpool in 1943. Her father was killed on D-Day when Lyn was just a year old. When Lyn was three her mother Monica married Frank Moore, who became 'Dad' to the little girl. Lyn was brought up in Liverpool and became a secretary before marrying policeman Bob Andrews. In 1970 Lyn gave birth to triplets – two sons and a daughter – who kept her busy for the next few years. Once they'd gone to school Lyn began writing, and her first novel was quickly accepted for publication. She has since written a further thirty-six novels.

Lyn lived for eleven years in Ireland and is now resident on the Isle of Man, but spends as much time as possible back on Merseyside, seeing her children and four grandchildren.

By Lyn Andrews

Lyn Andrews

From Liverpool With Love

headline

First published in Great Britain in 2014 by
HEADLINE PUBLISHING GROUP

First published in paperback in Great Britain in 2015 by
HEADLINE PUBLISHING GROUP

1

Cataloguing in Publication Data is available from the British Library

ISBN 978 0 7553 9975 8

Typeset in Janson by Avon DataSet Ltd, Bidford-on-Avon, Warwickshire

Printed and bound in Great Britain by Clays Ltd, St Ives plc

HEADLINE PUBLISHING GROUP
An Hachette UK Company
Carmelite House
50 Victoria Embankment
London EC4Y 0DZ

www.headline.co.uk
www.hachette.co.uk

Grateful thanks go to Nicola Morgan, who suggested the title for this book, my agent Anne Williams, my editor Marion Donaldson, my copyeditor Richenda Todd, Jo Liddiard, Caitlin Raynor and all members of the sales, marketing and publicity departments at Headline – you all work so hard on my behalf.

Lyn Andrews
Isle of Man, 2014

Chapter One

———◆———

Liverpool, 1922

'THERE'S NOTHING ELSE I can do, Ada! I'm at my wits' end! We're destitute!' Ellen Shaw shook her head as tears once again filled her eyes. It was so painful and shaming to have to admit it.

Ada Ellis, her close friend and neighbour, could only sadly nod her agreement. Everyone was poor in Gill Street; times were hard, work for dock labourers such as her husband Fred was always in short supply and with six mouths to feed it was a constant struggle to make ends meet. For poor Ellen, although she only had young Jane and Alfie, the daily battle against poverty had finally come to an end. She had been defeated. It was now nine months since Ellen's husband Eddie had been killed. He'd slipped on oil spilled on the deck of the ship on which he'd been helping to load cargo, tripped over the hatch cover and fallen head first into the partially empty hold to his

1

death. They'd all been devastated by the news but Ellen had been utterly distraught. Oh, there had been great regret expressed by everyone at the tragic accident, condolences received from the foreman and bosses, even a letter from the owners of the ship, but there had been nothing in the way of compensation for Ellen.

Ada put her arm around her friend as a gesture of comfort but there was very little else now she could do to help. 'You'll stay and share the bit of scouse with us,' she stated firmly, thinking that at least from now on Ellen and her family would get three meals a day, which might help put some weight back on her friend's thin frame.

Ellen could only nod as her sense of despair deepened. She felt tired, so very, very tired.

As Ada busied herself with the pan of vegetables that had been simmering on the range and instructed her family to 'sort themselves out' and 'get up to the table', she glanced surreptitiously around her kitchen. She didn't have much to show for fourteen years of marriage, she mused grimly. What furniture there was was scratched and battered from constant use and it hadn't been new to start with. No lino or matting covered the flagged floor, only a cheap brass spill jar sat on the mantel above the range and there were no curtains at the window overlooking the tiny yard at the back of the house. She sighed. Both she and Ellen looked far older than their thirty-two years, she thought, and living in Gill Street didn't help. It was a slum. The houses were old, decrepit and damp and should have been pulled down years ago but it was all they could afford and she counted herself fortunate to have these few rooms she called 'home'.

As she carefully ladled out the meatless stew she thought how attractive, how relatively carefree and happy she and Ellen had been when they'd first become neighbours. Joe had been a baby then and Ellen, newly married, had confided how delighted she was that they had been able to rent the house rather than having to live with relatives or in a couple of cramped rooms. They'd quickly become friends. In those days her hair had been dark and glossy; now it was dull and liberally sprinkled with grey. Ellen's had been a fiery auburn, like burnished gold, but it had thinned and faded to a dull brown. They'd had fresh complexions and eyes bright with eagerness for life but time and grinding hardship had taken their toll on them both.

As the noise level in the room increased she banged the ladle down hard on the top of the range. 'In the name of God, will you lot behave! Emily, luv, give our Sonny a piece of bread to keep him quiet,' Ada instructed her daughter before turning her attention to her second son. 'And you, Danny Ellis, stop shoving Alfie! There's room enough for the two of you on the end of that bench.' Her voice was harsh with tension for this would be the last time Ellen and her family would sit with them.

It was all rather cramped as they gathered around the table but ten-year-old Emily obediently handed her three-year-old brother a crust and he immediately stopped whining. He'd been christened Albert but for some reason best known to her mother was always called 'Sonny'. 'Don't go cramming it all into your mouth or you'll choke,' she instructed him.

Jane, Ellen's daughter, smiled at her friend before scowling at her brother Alfie, who was still engaged in a jostling match with Danny Ellis at the end of the table. She and Emily were the same age and had played together since they could walk and she'd miss seeing her every day. 'You heard what Aunty Ada said, Alfie. Stop it! Hasn't Mam got enough to put up with without you acting up and making things worse?'

In return she received a glowering look from her unruly brother.

As Ada placed a large plate of dry bread in the centre of the table the boys settled down and Ada smartly slapped away the eager hands that shot out to grab at the thickly cut slices. 'Have some manners! You lot can just wait your turn! Fred, luv, you first,' she instructed her husband, 'and Ellen, take a thick slice to mop up the gravy. It's "blind scouse", I'm afraid,' she added. The few pence she'd had left from the housekeeping hadn't stretched to any meat.

'I'm so sorry it's come to this, Ellen,' Fred Ellis said gravely as he surveyed his neighbour's little family, and he felt frustration and resentment surge up in him again as he thought how little he could do to help. 'It's not right, not right at all! There should be some . . . compensation for a man's life; his family shouldn't be left to suffer like this.'

Ada nodded her agreement. 'They don't care, Fred, everyone knows that. All they're interested in is their profits. No one cares for the likes of us. Even the Liverpool City Fathers aren't interested. They're happy to let us live in these . . . hovels while they live a life of comfort in their fine, big houses in Rodney Street and Abercromby Square.'

'At least it's somewhere of your own, Ada,' Ellen reminded her, trying not to think of the house next door which after today she would have to leave.

'So, you're going tomorrow?' Fred said quietly.

Ellen nodded. 'That's when they said I should and there's no point in putting it off, Fred. We . . . we'll have to leave very early.'

The air itself seemed heavy and laden with gloom, Ada thought despondently. 'Well, at least you won't have far to walk, Ellen. Brownlow Hill is just at the end of the street.'

Even the name of the street conjured up an image of despair, desperation and humiliation, Ellen thought, for everyone in the city associated it with the workhouse. And tomorrow morning that was where she would take her children. It had come to a choice between living in utter destitution or throwing herself and her family on public charity: the workhouse. She had nothing now, not even a bed to sleep on. Over the months she had been forced to sell everything just to keep herself and her kids from starving. Without Eddie's wage and being unable to find work herself, she had sunk deeper and deeper into debt and poverty until she had been forced to come to the decision to throw herself on the mercy of the Parish. Oh, Ada had helped as much as she could but they had very little themselves for often Fred didn't get work. Many was the time both he and her poor Eddie had stood in all weathers, like cattle in a pen, waiting for the foreman to pick them for a half-day's work and many was the time they'd been disappointed and come home with nothing.

Everyone had finished and so, wearily, Ellen got to her feet. 'I'll help you clear away, Ada, it's the least I can do after you've shared your meal with us,' she said as she began to gather up the empty bowls, aware that there had been little enough of the stew to start with.

'I'll put the kettle on and we'll have a cup of tea,' Ada said firmly, trying to put off the moment when she would have to bid her friend goodbye, for unless a miracle happened she knew that once inside those dreaded gates there was little chance of Ellen coming out again. You had to have a job and a place to stay or at least someone who would vouch that you could support yourself before they let you leave.

To hide his sadness and resentment Fred busied himself building up the fire with some bits of a broken packing case he'd brought home and what coal there was left, for the nights were getting colder now. Eddie Shaw had been a good mate, he mused, a hard worker, and a man who didn't spend what little he had on drink, like some. He hadn't deserved to die as he had but there were often accidents on the docks. Men were maimed or killed and little was done about it. Oh, the union was trying to make a difference but as far as he could see it wasn't having much success. Both he and Eddie had fought in the Great War and been fortunate to have survived and they'd been promised a 'land fit for heroes' but that hadn't materialised. Nothing had changed for the likes of them.

Emily and Jane sat on the floor as near to the fire as they could, while Joe, Ada's eldest son, who was thirteen and considered himself to be more serious and responsible than his siblings, attempted to keep Sonny amused stringing bits of old newspaper together on a piece of twine.

'Will you have lessons in . . . there?' Emily asked tentatively, curling her toes appreciatively at the heat now emanating from the fire. Like her mother she had dark hair and eyes but was pale and slight and generally quieter than her brothers. She glanced at her friend, who was the image of her own mother when Ellen was young.

'I don't know. Mam says I might have to work, I'm old enough,' Jane replied. She really didn't want to have to think about what tomorrow would bring – not yet.

'Work? Doing what?' Emily probed.

Jane shrugged her slim shoulders and frowned. 'Housework, cleaning, helping in the kitchen, things like that, I suppose. Still,' she added, 'our Alfie will probably have lessons, which should be a bit of a relief to Mam.'

'They might even manage to drum something useful into his head, which is more than the teachers at our school seem to be able to do – he's hardly ever there for a start,' Joe commented, having heard Jane's remarks. He felt heartily sorry for both Ellen and Jane but Alfie Shaw was a different kettle of fish altogether. He always seemed to be in trouble of some kind. His poor mam had been so worried of late that he was certain she hardly knew where Alfie was or what he was up to most of the time. And he was a bad influence on Joe's brother Danny, who was easily led. 'At least he'll be away from the likes of Jimmy Cobham and Richie Corrin,' he added, naming two of the other lads in the street who were hooligans of the first order and – in his Mam's opinion –destined to end their days in prison. They called themselves the 'Gill Street Gang' and Alfie was proud to be one of their number. Joe personally thought it a daft name for a gang.

Sonny had become bored and had started to rub his eyes and grizzle, a sure sign he was tired, so Emily reluctantly rose to her feet.

'Shall I get him to bed, Mam?'

Ada nodded, loath to have to finish her conversation with Ellen.

'Will you mind very much being . . . in there?' Joe asked Jane a little hesitantly as his sister picked up the toddler. Instantly he regretted the question as Jane bit her lip. 'I . . . I . . . mean . . .'

'I don't want to go, Joe. None of us do but . . .' Jane began. If the truth be told she was afraid, for she'd often passed the soot-blackened walls of the workhouse and always thought it seemed like a prison. And in many ways it was: you were only ever allowed out to work, not to see the outside world or visit friends and relatives you'd known before. The thought filled her with panic.

'It might not be too bad,' Joe said quickly, for he could see she was getting upset. 'At least you'll be warm, and you'll get fed, Jane. Your mam won't have to worry about finding the money for the rent or coal or food,' he reminded her, trying to find something to cheer her up, for he had glimpsed the apprehension in her eyes.

She looked down at her shabby old brown dress, which was far too short now. 'And clothes, Joe. I heard they give you clothes too, but I wish . . . I wish Da hadn't died. Then we wouldn't have had to go.' She missed her da terribly and hadn't yet fully got over the shock of his death, let alone the grief.

Joe nodded. He knew how hard it was for a family to survive without a breadwinner, and he was already wondering what he would do when he left school in a year's time time. Would he find work? He hoped so for whatever he earned would help his mam, but there was nothing Jane could do to help her mam keep them out of the workhouse; she was too young.

Both Ellen and Ada had overheard some of their conversation and as Ellen finished her tea she sighed heavily. 'He's right you know, Ada. In a way it will be a relief. I'll not have to worry myself sick every minute of the day and night about trying to provide for them, but . . . but . . . I never thought it would come to this. It . . . it's so humiliating, everyone knowing that I've failed, and whispering about what happened to "poor Ellen Shaw". I felt so bad when that assessment officer came to see me, as though I'd done something really wrong – criminal almost.'

Ada reached across and took her hand. 'Don't talk like that! You haven't failed, Ellen, luv! How were you expected to cope with no money coming in?'

'I . . . I suppose I could have tried harder to get work – taken in washing, gone out cleaning . . . anything!' Ellen said wearily. Oh, life had become so hard without Eddie and she felt so lonely and lost without him. She knew she would never really get over losing him.

'You haven't got the room or the . . . facilities for doing laundry, even if we knew people well off enough not to have to do their own, and you know how difficult it is to get work of any kind when you've young kids, Ellen,' she stated, thinking that her friend was so undernourished that going cleaning could have killed her. Her health and strength had failed since Eddie's tragic accident but wasn't that only to be expected when she existed almost entirely on bread and weak, milk-less tea?

Reluctantly Ellen got to her feet. 'Well, Ada, luv, I'd better go. Thanks for . . . everything. I don't know what I would have done without you.'

Ada hugged her, tears springing into her eyes. Oh, she'd miss Ellen so much. 'You know I'll be thinking of you, Ellen, and you'll only be around the corner. Try and get word to me, let me know how you are all getting on? And maybe after a while they'll let me come and see you.'

Ellen could only nod for there was a large lump in her throat.

'Right then, Jane, Alfie, come here to me,' Ada instructed briskly to hide her emotions. 'Now, lad, you make sure you behave yourself and Jane, luv, you help your mam as much as you can. You'll be all right now, you'll . . . cope.' She hugged both children in turn before turning to her own three. 'Joe, Emily and Danny, you come with your da and me to the front door. They have a very early start in the morning so . . .' She faltered; she just couldn't say the word 'goodbye'.

Both Ellen and Jane turned to wave to the little group standing on the worn step of the house next door before they went into their cold, dark, dismal lobby. Alfie just shoved his hands deeper into the pockets of his old jacket and scowled. He wasn't looking forward to tomorrow but he was determined that whatever lay ahead, he wasn't going to let it get him down. He missed Da; he'd always been able to rely on his father even if he couldn't hide his frequent misdeeds from him the way he could his mam. Lately he'd more or less done as he pleased, and she'd not noticed. Yes, he'd miss his mates but he wouldn't be there forever; one day he'd get out and find his friends again, then he'd go back to suiting himself.

It no longer felt like home at all, Ellen thought miserably as she pushed open the door to the kitchen. There was no money for the gas so it was dark; the range was cold and empty and beginning to rust; the only furniture left was an old rocker and a straw-filled mattress on the floor. The room smelled damp and she knew she wouldn't sleep. She'd sit in the chair and doze until dawn came and it was time to leave. There was nothing to pack; they had no possessions now.

Jane lay curled up on the lumpy mattress beside her brother. With only one thin coarse grey blanket covering them, she was cold. She had promised herself she wouldn't cry but it was so hard to fight down the sobs. She was leaving everything that was familiar and the people she knew and loved and the world seemed a very dark and fearful place. But she still had her mam and Alfie, she reminded herself, and, she told herself firmly, somehow they *would* cope. Finally, Ada's words echoing through her head, she drifted into a restless sleep.

Chapter Two

⬦

IT WAS THE MOST soul-destroying, *final* sound she'd ever heard and one she would always remember, Ellen thought as early next morning the great iron gates of the Brownlow Hill Workhouse – opened for them by a uniformed gatekeeper – closed behind them. In the cold, misty, grey October dawn the bulk of the four buildings seemed to loom ominously over them and she shivered involuntarily beneath her woollen shawl. Jane, clutching her mother's hand, felt the movement and shrank closer to Ellen, tightening her grip. Even Alfie was subdued as he stared around at the large, soot-blackened two-storey buildings, which had such a grim reputation.

A porter appeared from a door in the gatehouse, shrugging on his jacket. 'You expected, missus?' he asked curtly.

'Yes. Mrs Ellen Shaw. I . . . I'm to see Mrs Florence Stanley, the matron.'

He nodded. 'Come with me then.'

They followed him into one of the buildings, down a long,

narrow, cold passageway painted dark green and lit by spluttering gas jets and Ellen felt her spirits sink even further. It all looked far more depressing than she had imagined. They went up a flight of stone stairs and along another corridor and then the man stopped before a door and knocked. Upon being instructed to enter he did so, announcing the new arrivals in a respectful tone.

'You're to go in,' he muttered, holding the door open.

On entering the room Ellen was pleasantly surprised to find that it was bright and well furnished and that the woman who sat behind the large old-fashioned desk didn't look as condescending or as intimidating as she'd feared. She was dressed in a plain dark blue dress and wore a white starched cap over hair severely pulled back from her face, but the brown eyes that regarded her and her children were kind.

'Mrs Shaw, good morning. You are very punctual. These are your children, I take it?'

Ellen nodded, relaxing a little at the warmth in the tone of the woman's voice. 'This is Jane, ma'am, she's ten and this is Alfred . . . Alfie . . . he's eight.'

Matron nodded and glanced down at the paperwork before her. 'You must address me as "Matron", Mrs Shaw. The Board of Guardians has approved your application for residence here. I understand that your husband is dead?'

Ellen nodded again. 'He was killed in an accident on the docks, Matron, nine months ago now, and I . . . I . . . just can't manage any more.'

'I understand,' Florence Stanley replied sympathetically. She dealt daily with the misfortunes of the poor souls who came here and though this woman was no different in her shabby and neglected appearance to so many others, the assessment officer's report had stated that she was a woman of good character who had been overtaken by unfortunate circumstances. 'Well, let me explain what happens now and how things are done here. Whatever you might have heard to the contrary, these days conditions have improved considerably. We're no longer living in the Victorian era. Firstly, you will all be . . . checked for lice, then bathed. You will then be provided with your uniform clothes and you will stay in the reception wing until you have been passed by the medical officer, just to ensure that you are not suffering from anything contagious. That usually takes twenty-four hours. But if you do have the misfortune to become ill while you are here, we have an infirmary and a doctor and fully trained nursing staff.' She smiled reassuringly. 'After that you will be allocated a bed in a dormitory, shown where you are to take your meals and where your work will be done. We are virtually self-sufficient here.' She paused. 'I think perhaps that work in the kitchens would be suitable for you, Mrs Shaw. I take it, having managed a household, you are used to preparing food and washing dishes and pans?'

'I am, Matron,' Ellen replied, trying not to feel too shocked by the fact that they were all to be deloused, although she knew it would be an unnecessary procedure. She had always striven to keep them free of vermin.

Matron then turned her attention to Jane. Although pale and undernourished the child was attractive with that mass of rich dark auburn hair and eyes, fringed with thick dark lashes, like amber. 'And, Jane, you will attend lessons until dinnertime and then in the afternoons you will help in the laundry, but nothing too heavy yet.'

Jane could only nod apprehensively for the matron and the large, bright, comfortable room had overawed her completely. She wanted to ask if she would sleep in the same room as her mother but she couldn't pluck up the courage.

'Now, Alfred,' Matron said briskly, having quickly appraised the lad and noted his sullen, resentful expression. He had the same colour eyes as his sister but his hair was much lighter, more of a gingery shade, and with his sharp features and the wary look in his eyes he reminded her of a young fox. One to watch, if she was not mistaken, she thought, but thankfully he wouldn't be her problem. 'You will be housed in the men and boys' quarters under the authority of the master – Mr Ribchester. You will attend lessons all day until you are ten; then, like your sister, you will work in the afternoons, very probably picking oakum. But that will be the master's decision.'

Ellen uttered a startled cry as she realised that Alfie was to be separated from her. 'Oh, ma'am – Matron – I didn't realise we would be split up!'

'I'm sorry, Mrs Shaw, but it's the rule, I'm afraid,' Matron said gently but firmly. 'The sexes are segregated in all workhouses and for quite obvious reasons, except for elderly married couples. And it's usual for children of both sexes, once they reach the age of five, to be cared for in separate areas. That way any "laxness" they may have developed in their behaviour can be remedied and of course they start their education.'

'But . . . but he's so young,' Ellen protested, wondering how he would cope without her.

'We have boys here much younger than Alfred, I can assure you, but you will be able to spend half an hour each afternoon with him, which should reassure you of his wellbeing.'

She rose and Ellen, although still upset, realised that the interview was almost over.

'I'll have the porter show you to the reception wing where Superintendent Willis will take charge of you.'

Alfie looked down at his scuffed boots with their broken laces and holes in the soles. He wasn't at all happy about being separated from his mam and Jane and being put in with a crowd of other boys, and he wondered what this 'Master' Ribchester would be like. It wasn't fair and it wasn't what he had expected. And why hadn't Mam made more of a fuss about it? Demanded that he be allowed to stay with her? Maybe if she had Matron might have changed her mind, he thought resentfully. Still, he'd at least have a bed and hopefully clothes that weren't too small for him and proper food. You never knew, it might not all be as grim as it appeared.

The rooms they were shown were small and furnished sparsely with three narrow beds, each with a flock mattress, a pillow and, folded at the end of each bed, sheets and blankets. Against one wall was a chest of drawers, on top of which was a jug and basin set, and woven rush matting covered the floor. In the other room there was a fireplace in which a fire had been lit, a small brightly coloured rag rug in front of it. A scrubbed deal table and four rustic chairs stood by the wall in which a window was set high up near the ceiling but which gave ample light. In the centre of the table sat a Bible.

As the porter left Ellen looked around. 'This isn't too bad, is it?' she said, thinking it was far better than she had hoped for and infinitely warmer and more comfortable than the home she'd been forced to leave. 'We've got a bed each, sheets and blankets and our own table and chairs, we must have to eat here . . . for now.'

Before either of the children had time to comment a tall, thin, angular woman entered. She was dressed in a similar style to the matron but with her dress covered by a white apron. 'You're the new arrivals, I take it? I'm Superintendent Willis. Right, I assume Matron has instructed you on the procedure?'

Ellen nodded, once again feeling her stomach churn with apprehension, for this woman's attitude was very brisk and offhand.

'Then follow me,' came the curt instruction.

They were all taken to a tiled anteroom from where a corridor led off to the bathrooms. The superintendent extracted from her pocket a large key, which she passed to a young woman who was obviously her assistant with the instruction to make sure she gave it back immediately she'd finished with it. Ellen and Jane were then ushered into a cubicle by the girl while Alfie was put in a separate cubicle by the older woman.

'You've to take everything off, missus, and put it all in those baskets to be stored and washed and packed away until you leave,' the girl informed them.

Ellen felt waves of humiliation creep over her; they were obviously to be subjected to an inspection for lice before being taken for a bath. Although Matron had previously mentioned it she had not realised that she would have to strip and stand naked in front of her daughter and worse still before complete strangers. As she slowly placed her shabby garments in the basket she felt the colour rising in her cheeks at the sheer indignity of it all.

Jane had never seen her mother naked before and she studiously kept her gaze averted, sensing Ellen's acute embarrassment. She felt so sorry for her mam and upset and humiliated at this treatment.

Superintendent Willis was quick and businesslike, seemingly oblivious to their discomfort and embarrassment. She checked them for body and head lice and on finding nothing she gave a brief nod of approval. They were then ushered into separate tiled cubicles each of which contained a large cast iron bath on claw feet. From the brass taps on the wall cold water was already gushing. Ellen's mood lightened a little; it was such a long time since she'd had the luxury of a proper bath that she now looked forward to this unexpected pleasure.

Jane stood shivering on the slatted wooden platform beside the bath, her arms crossed over her thin chest, watching the water splash against the sides. She'd never seen a bath like this before; they'd only ever had a small tin bath that used to hang on a nail on the wall in the yard. The girl appeared and handed her a coarse but clean towel and a small piece of lye soap. She then inserted the key into an aperture under the brass fitment, turned it and hot water gushed forth, sending clouds of steam upwards. Despite her discomfort Jane was fascinated when, after testing the bath water, the girl turned the key, removed it and pocketed it.

'Get in and give yourself a good scrub all over and wash your hair,' she instructed. 'I'll come back when Superintendent Willis tells me to, then you have to get out and dry yourself.'

She disappeared and slowly Jane lowered herself into the water. As she felt the warmth seep through her body for the first time in days she felt the knot of anxiety in her stomach loosen its grip. This was sheer bliss, she thought as she sank lower until she was almost entirely submerged. After a few minutes she remembered she was supposed to be scrubbing herself and set about the task with more enthusiasm than she'd shown for anything of late.

Before she was reunited with her mother and brother the girl brought a pile of clean clothes for her to put on. Underclothes, then a blue and white striped shapeless cotton dress which came down to her ankles, a similar but sleeveless smock to go over it and thick black woollen stocking and black boots. She dried her hair as best she could but it was so thick it was still very wet.

'Here, tie it back with this or you'll not get it all under your cap,' the girl instructed her, handing her a piece of tape and the white cotton, old-fashioned mob cap.

'Thanks. It takes ages to dry,' Jane confided shyly.

The girl glanced quickly towards the corridor and lowered her voice. 'You're lucky she didn't make you have it cut. She would have done if you'd had nits. I'm Maisie Mellor, by the way, and she's not too bad. Her bark is worse than her bite.'

Jane smiled at her. 'I'm Jane Shaw. I . . . It's just everything is all so . . . strange.'

'You'll soon get used to things,' Maisie said confidently. 'No one really wants to come here but it's better than being out there, especially in winter.'

'Have you been here long, Maisie?' Jane asked, encouraged by this first friendly overture.

'Oh, years! I'm fifteen and I was six when me mam died. Me da had been long gone by then so . . . so they brought me here. If you do as you're told, stick at your lessons and don't shirk any work you'll be all right. You can even get a position of "trust" like me. You know, jobs with some responsibility to them. I help her with the new inmates, but I sleep in the girls' dormitory with the others so I'll probably see you – once you've been moved across.'

There wasn't time for further conversation as the super-intendent ushered them back into the anteroom where the medical officer was waiting.

Ellen took both Jane and Alfie's hands and tried to prepare herself for the next ordeal. They all looked so different, she thought. None of them had ever had to wear such clothes before. Jane looked like a smaller version of herself in an identical outfit. The shapeless, striped garments made her feel as if she were indeed an "inmate", even though she knew she should be grateful for clean, warm clothing and boots. Alfie wore heavy corduroy, knee-length trousers with long thick socks, a grey flannel shirt, a corduroy jacket, serviceable new boots and a cap and in fact looked far cleaner and tidier than she had seen him look for a long time. She had to admit it was an improvement, although judging by the look on his face he wasn't happy about being separated from them. But there was nothing she could do about that.

They were given a very cursory medical examination, asked a few questions regarding their general health and past illnesses and then passed once more into the care of Superintendent Willis, who conducted them back to their rooms, informing them that a breakfast of porridge with bread and butter and tea would be brought to them. After that they were to spend the time until dinner 'settling in quietly'. Tomorrow they would be moved across to the main wings.

Ellen pulled one of the chairs over to the fire and sat down. She realised for the first time that she was shaking. The morning's events had been an ordeal that had exhausted her. She felt confused and anxious and wished she had Ada to confide in. What would the days, weeks and months ahead be like? she wondered. There seemed to be so many rules and regulations; they'd given her a list of them. There was to be no talking in dormitories at night, no smoking, no swearing or uttering of oaths, no quarrelling or fighting, no consumption of alcohol, all members of staff were to be addressed respectfully at all times, prayers were to be said twice a day, attendance at Church on a Sunday was obligatory – the list went on. Their days were to be strictly regulated, a set time for everything. Rising in the morning, taking meals, periods of work, and bed by eight o'clock at night, each activity announced by the ringing of a bell. She had begun to realise with despair that she would see very little of either of her children. She would only see Alfie for a bare half-hour each day. Jane would spend her mornings at lessons, her afternoons working in the laundry. She wouldn't eat in the same room as her daughter or sleep in the same dormitory: she was beginning to wonder if she had done the right thing.

Alfie, having ignored the Bible, was half-heartedly reading the list of rules; they seemed endless and it was beginning to dawn on him that he would be closely watched. He wondered what this 'Master Ribchester' would be like? Probably even stricter than old Mr Beddows, his headmaster, and he'd been bad enough. The adventurous, carefree days he'd spent with his mates when he should have been in school were definitely over now. Judging by all these rules he'd have no free time at all and there would be no adventures either. The more he thought about it the more mutinous and rebellious he felt. It wasn't fair! His mates' parents were just as hard up as his mam but Jimmy and Richie hadn't been dragged in here to live. Why should he have such a dull, miserable existence forced on him? Why had Mam brought him and Jane here? They'd been managing, hadn't they? But glancing across at his sister he realised that she didn't feel the same way.

Jane, taking off the bonnet that covered her head, had knelt beside her mother. 'Mam, if you'll brush my hair out, the heat from the fire will dry it more quickly,' she said quietly, sensing her mother's unhappiness. She held out the hairbrush, the only thing she'd had left to bring with her.

Ellen nodded and began to brush out the tangles in the thick auburn locks.

'Mam, like Aunty Ada said . . . we'll cope. I'll still have some lessons and I won't mind working, our Alfie will be kept busy all day and that girl, Maisie, was really nice. She said it's not so bad here when you get used to it. We'll all make new friends.'

Ellen managed a weak smile for Jane was trying so hard. How could she confide in her that all she felt was a terrible sense of foreboding, guilt and hopelessness? They no longer seemed to be people with their own personalities, hopes and dreams, or even possessions. They'd lost their identities. They were just *inmates*, little more than numbers.

When Alfie first met Master Ribchester all his suspicions were confirmed. He disliked the master on sight. The man was very tall, well built and in his dark suit reminded him of a policeman.

'So, you are Alfred Shaw and you are eight years old,' the master said, fixing him with a calculating stare.

He looked very old to Alfie and the fact that he had a short, neatly clipped grey beard and moustache added to the illusion. Alfie nodded his assent.

'When I ask a question, boy, you answer me! You don't just nod.'

'I'm Alfie Shaw and I'm eight,' Alfie muttered.

'"Sir"! You call me either "Sir" or "Master",' the man instructed curtly.

'Sir,' Alfie added.

Charles Ribchester's manner relaxed a fraction. 'I take it you've had time to study the regulations. If you abide by them, work hard at your lessons and are punctual and obedient, you'll find me a fair man.'

Alfie stared at the floor and didn't reply. He wanted to say he didn't want to be in this place at all. He didn't want to be separated from his mam and Jane and be away from his old mates. He didn't want to work at lessons or anything else.

The master clasped his hands behind his back. 'You'll polish your boots every evening, make your bed in the morning before breakfast, make sure your appearance is clean and tidy at all times and of course there will be prayers each morning and evening and church on Sundays.'

A look of horror followed by a scowl of defiance crept over Alfie's features. This was all far worse than he'd expected. 'Will I get any time at all to meself, sir? For . . . er . . . play?' he asked.

'You'll be allowed time each afternoon to see your mother, lad. Now, I'll pass you over to Superintendent Green, who'll show you where you'll sleep and eat and introduce you to the other boys. You'll soon settle in,' the master replied. The boy was obviously finding things difficult to take in but would soon become accustomed to life here, he thought, although he'd noted the disgruntled expression. Something to watch out for, he noted.

As Alfie followed the superintendent out of the room he thought he'd never, never 'settle in' here. Already he hated it.

Chapter Three

———◆———

FOR WEEKS ADA HAD worried over Ellen and her family. She'd heard nothing since that awful day when they'd gone into the workhouse, and she had hoped that Ellen might have got a message to her.

'. . . even if it was only a bit of a scribbled note. I know Ellen's not great at the writing, even though she can read well enough,' she confided to Joe one afternoon in early December.

'Maybe they're not allowed to have writing stuff,' he replied, more interested in an old copy of a comic he'd found on the floor of the school yard. It was a bit tattered and missing a few pages but still fairly readable. He was an avid reader but there was never much opportunity outside school.

'They must be. Jane and Alfie will have lessons – they have school in those places – so what do you suppose they use to write with?' she persisted.

Joe laid aside the magazine; he was a quiet, thoughtful, wiry boy with dark eyes and dark curly hair. 'Look, Mam, if you're that worried about them why don't you go up there and ask if you can see them?' He hated to see her so anxious and the long silence was unsettling him too. He often wondered how they were managing. Was Jane making friends? Was Alfie settling in? And with Christmas approaching how they would spend it?

'Do you think they'd let me visit?' Ada asked doubtfully.

'All you can do is ask, Mam. They can only say no,' he urged before returning to his reading.

Ada made up her mind there and then. 'Right, I'll go now. Strike while the iron's hot . . . or before I lose my nerve,' she added as she reached for her heavy shawl from its place on the hook at the back of the door. 'Tell our Emily to keep her eye on Sonny for me,' she instructed as she let herself out.

She bent her head against the bitterly cold wind that was sweeping the dark, narrow streets. She had to try to find out if her friend was all right, whether she was being treated well; if she could just see Ellen for a few minutes it would put her mind at ease.

When she reached the gates they were of course closed, so she rang the bell set into one of the pillars and waited, her shawl clutched tightly to her.

At length a porter came out and very reluctantly came across to her. 'What do you want, missus?' he asked bluntly, not at all pleased that he'd had to leave his fireside.

'Could I see a friend of mine who's been here since October? I'm worried about her – and her kids. I haven't heard a single word about her since the day she left. I won't take up much of anyone's time, I promise. It would put my mind at rest.'

'You'll have to make an appointment,' he stated flatly and made to turn away.

'How do I do that?' Ada demanded, annoyed by his attitude.

'You write to the matron and if you're lucky she'll agree and give you a day and a time to come, but it's up to her – it's nothing to do with me. Now, I'd get off home, Ma. It looks like snow.'

Ada glared at him. Typical, she thought, he just wasn't interested. 'I'll thank you to show a bit of respect. I'm not your "Ma", thank God! And if I were I'd have taught you better manners!' she snapped before turning away. She *would* write to this matron person, she thought determinedly. Well, at least Joe or Emily would write for her for, like Ellen, she wasn't very proficient at writing, and then she'd hand the letter in at the gates. No, on second thoughts she didn't trust that feller to see it was delivered; she'd post it, which meant she'd have to find the money for a stamp.

After their meagre supper was over she told Fred of her conversation with the porter and Emily duly produced a sheet of paper, neatly removed from the back of one of her school books. 'Shall I write it, Mam?' she asked.

'Thanks, luv, but our Joe's writing is a bit better than yours. Mind you, I don't know what we're going to do for an envelope.'

'I'll go and see if I can cadge one from Tommy Larkin at the pub. His missus writes to her family back in Ireland so they're bound to have paper and envelopes,' Fred offered.

Emily wished she'd known that earlier, before she'd defaced a school book for which she would be punished if the crime was discovered.

Slowly Ada dictated to Joe: '*Dear Matron, I have been a friend and neighbour of Ellen Shaw's for fourteen years and I am worried about her.*' She paused, frowning as she wondered what to say next.

'How about: *I would appreciate it if I could come and visit her as it is getting near to Christmas*?' Joe suggested.

'. . . *and if it wouldn't be too much trouble,*' Emily added. She missed Jane and hoped she was settling in in that place. Perhaps her mam could find that out.

Ada nodded. 'Yes, that's good, write all that down, Joe,' she instructed and as she watched him carefully put the words down on the paper she felt relieved. She'd get it posted in the morning and then all she could do was wait and hope that the woman would agree.

Jane folded the last pillowcase and placed it on the top of the pile. The laundry was as usual a hive of activity and she was surrounded by women and girls who pushed the piles of dirty washing into the huge copper boilers with long wooden tongs. The room was filled with steam and the smell of soap and boiling linen. Others were rinsing the clean washing in the big shallow troughs filled with cold water before heaving it out and passing it through the rollers of the big hand-operated mangles. After that it was folded before being taken to the drying rooms. It was hot, heavy, back-breaking work for them but her task was to fold the small items, such as pillowcases, towels, aprons and underclothes, for they took in laundry for other people as well as that used on the premises.

She was used to the work now but that first day when they'd been transferred from the reception wing had been confusing and unsettling. Mam had hugged Alfie tightly before he'd been taken to his new quarters.

'I'll see you this afternoon, Alfie, luv. Now you be good and do as the master tells you, and you can tell me what everything is like later on,' Ellen had urged.

'You'll be fine, Alfie,' Jane had told her brother confidently as she'd hugged him too, but she'd suspected he didn't believe her for he hadn't said a word. Then it had been her turn to leave her mam. She'd been shown where she would eat and sleep and then been brought here to the laundry.

She pushed back a damp strand of hair which had escaped from her cap, thinking it wouldn't be long now before the bell would sound and the afternoon's work would be over for her.

'Jane Shaw, stop daydreaming and fold these and add them to the pile!' came the curt instruction as another dozen pillowcases were deposited on the table.

'I wasn't daydreaming, I was just wondering if I'd get time to see my mam before supper. I didn't see her yesterday at all, Lucy,' she replied. She'd soon got to know some of the other girls; Lucy Mitchell was a year older than her.

Lucy relented a little. 'I don't suppose the mistress will mind as long as you're not late,' she said, using the formal term of address for the superintendent in charge of them. 'You're lucky you've got a mam, Jane,' she added quietly before turning away to return to her tasks.

Jane resumed folding. She supposed Lucy was right. There were a lot of girls here who had no parents at all. In a way she knew she was lucky. Oh, it had all been very strange at first for she hadn't ever been so strictly regulated. She couldn't please herself at all and nothing was ever done spontaneously. It had taken her a while, too, to get used to the fact that she saw little of her mother and virtually nothing of her brother, although she knew he had already been in trouble a couple of times – the instances had been imparted to her mother by Matron. But as the weeks had progressed she had become accustomed to eating and sleeping in the same room as many other girls and had become friendly with a couple of them. The food wasn't too bad either, she admitted, thinking back to the bread spread with dripping which had been their mainstay when things had become desperate at home. Now breakfast was usually thick porridge, sometimes with a slice of bread and butter. Dinner was often gruel or pea soup, also with bread, and for supper there was meat or a meat pie with potatoes. On Sundays dinner was always meat and vegetables and usually there was a steamed pudding to follow and either tea or milk accompanied the meals. She'd gained weight and so had her mam for the cook had taken pity on Ellen, declaring she'd never seen such a bag of bones and that if she were to work satisfactorily in her kitchen she'd have to fatten her up a bit or she'd be dropping with exhaustion.

The last of the pillowcases had been folded when the bell rang and gradually the activity around Jane slowed down. If she hurried she might catch her mam as she left the kitchens and have the chance of a few words before her mother's afternoon visit with Alfie. Before supper she had a bit of home-work to do for there was never enough time after the meal when it was prayers and then bed. What little time they all had to themselves was spent in sewing or learning to knit and crochet but sometimes magazines, books and pamphlets were donated by well-off people from outside and avidly read by those who could read until they virtually fell to bits.

On her way along the corridor she was joined by Maisie. 'Where are you off to now, Jane?' the older girl asked amiably.

'I'm hoping to see Mam,' she replied. Since that first day Maisie had been kind and open and she hoped in time she and the older girl might become friends.

'Wonder what we'll get for supper tonight? If you see your mam, find out,' Maisie urged.

Jane smiled for Maisie loved her food. 'I'll ask her what they've been making this afternoon, although sometimes she's just been scrubbing pans.'

Maisie grinned. 'I'm looking forward to Christmas dinner. We get a slap-up meal with roast beef, roast spuds, parsnips and plum pudding and custard to follow. They decorate the place up too with holly and stuff and we have a tree. It'll be your first Christmas here, won't it?'

Jane nodded; she hadn't really wanted to think much about Christmas for it would be the first one without her da.

'Don't expect lots of presents though,' Maisie added.

'I won't. We . . . we never got very much anyway; we never had enough money even before . . . Da was killed. I always got a card for my birthday though,' she added sadly.

'When's your birthday then?' Maisie enquired. No one ever remembered hers, sometimes not even herself.

'It's tomorrow. I'll be eleven,' Jane replied flatly.

'I'll wish you "Many Happy Returns" then – tomorrow,' Maisie promised before she turned off down the corridor that led to the refectory.

Jane smiled as she caught sight of her mother hurrying from the cavernous kitchens, straightening her cap. 'Mam! I hoped I'd catch you,' she cried.

Ellen looked perplexed. 'Oh, Jane, luv, I've to go to see Matron. She sent word down to Cook. I just hope it's not our Alfie again!'

Jane frowned. Wasn't it bad enough that they were stuck in here without him causing trouble and upsetting Mam? she thought crossly. She'd heard that Mr Ribchester was very strict and when her brother misbehaved it made Mam look as if she hadn't brought him up properly. Alfie just never seemed to learn, even though as punishment he had to miss certain meals. 'Shall I walk there with you? I know I won't be able to go in with you but . . .'

Ellen smiled at her gratefully; they got so little time together and she hadn't forgotten that it was Jane's birthday tomorrow. She'd even asked Cook if she could have a piece of fruit to give her as a treat. 'Have you homework? I don't want you being late for supper, luv.'

'Oh, I'll manage to get it done in time,' Jane replied firmly, wondering if she actually could. But if Alfie was in trouble again she could at least try to give Mam a bit of support.

She waited at the far end of the corridor for she didn't want Matron to see her and ask if she had nothing to occupy her, a circumstance that would be reported to the mistress. She leaned against the wall and wondered just what her brother had been up to now. Last time he had been caught acting as a lookout for some older boys who had been smoking – something that was strictly forbidden – and there had been an interrogation as to just where they had got the cigarettes from. Of course Alfie, being Alfie, had said he knew nothing about any cigarettes and that they had threatened and bullied him into being a lookout – which the other boys had denied. Alfie hadn't escaped retribution though for an illicit cigarette had been found in his pocket, payment for his co-operation. They'd all been punished.

She hadn't long to wait before the door opened and her mother appeared. To her relief Ellen didn't look upset, worried or guilty.

'What did she want, Mam?' she asked as they descended the stairs to the ground floor. 'Was it about Alfie?'

Ellen shook her head. 'No, luv, not this time, thank goodness. I'm still trying to take it in. She . . . she said she'd had a letter from Ada saying she was worried about me and that she's given permission for her to visit me. She's coming tomorrow morning, just for half an hour. Oh, I'm so pleased, Jane! Isn't it great? I've missed her so much.'

Jane nodded happily. Ada must really have been concerned to have gone to the trouble of getting either Joe or Emily to write. 'You'll be able to catch up with all the gossip from Gill Street, Mam. Will you make sure and ask how Emily is? And Joe and Danny and Sonny,' she added.

'Of course I will, luv. Now, I've to go and inform Cook that I'm having a visitor and will need half an hour's leave of absence.'

'She won't say no, will she?' Jane asked, praying the woman wouldn't be annoyed.

'Of course not, not after Matron has given permission for Ada to come. Mrs Burrows is a decent woman; she wouldn't be so petty-minded.'

Jane smiled and took her mother's hand. 'So, tomorrow is going to be a good day after all.'

Ellen squeezed Jane's hand. 'It is and I haven't forgotten it's your birthday either. There might even be a little something as a treat.'

'Aunty Ada coming is a treat enough, Mam. Give her my love,' Jane said as she took her leave of her mother. She hadn't seen her mam looking so cheerful since they'd been here, she thought. Tomorrow would really give Mam's spirits a lift.

Chapter Four

———◆———

A DA SHIVERED AS she stood in the corridor where the porter had instructed she wait while he went in search of the matron. She glanced around. It was as grim on the inside as it appeared from outside, she thought, what little she had seen of it so far. At least that porter feller had minded his manners today, which gave her some satisfaction. She wondered how long she would have to wait and just where she'd see Ellen. Probably in some large, dismal communal hall, she surmised. Oh, how she wished she could take her friend home, but that was impossible. There were new neighbours now in Ellen's old house and a rowdy, slovenly lot they were too. She drew her shawl more tightly to her; this place was very probably cold even in summer.

Her deliberations were interrupted as a woman she judged to be slightly older than herself appeared, dressed plainly but smartly, with a small white cap covering her hair. Ada wished she possessed a hat. Every respectable woman wore some kind of head covering when out, but she'd always had to make do with her shawl and when she'd been shown inside the building she'd rearranged it around her shoulders.

'Mrs Ellis?' Matron queried.

'It is, ma'am, and thank you for letting me come to visit,' Ada replied hesitantly.

'It is occasionally permitted for inmates to have visitors and I agreed because you were concerned about Mrs Shaw, and of course the festive season is drawing near. Would you follow me, please?'

She was a pleasant enough woman if a little formal, Ada thought as she followed her along the corridor, and Ellen must be all right for otherwise surely the matron would have made some comment to that effect. That fact relieved a little of her anxiety. She was surprised to be shown into a small room furnished with two chairs and a cheery rag rug, in which a fire had been lit.

'If you'd like to wait here, Mrs Shaw will, I'm certain, be on her way up. I'll send someone to inform you when visiting time is over,' she advised.

'Thank you, ma'am, this is very . . . comfortable. It was thoughtful of you,' Ada said sincerely. She certainly hadn't expected something as welcoming as a fire.

Matron smiled. 'We try to be amenable, Mrs Ellis.'

Ada didn't have long to wait before the door opened and Ellen stood there looking a little hesitant.

'Ellen, luv! I've been that worried about you!' Ada cried before hugging her old friend. 'I'd hoped you might have got word out to me. Let me have a good look at you. How have they been treating you? Do you get enough to eat?

Is it . . .' The questions tumbled over each other.

'Oh, Ada! It's . . . it's . . . so wonderful to see you!' Ellen let herself be led to the fire and sat down facing her friend. 'It's not too bad, once you get used to . . . things, and yes I get enough to eat.'

'You certainly look better – there's more flesh on your bones – but . . . but do you have to wear that thing all the time?' Ada asked, thinking the long shapeless dress and smock seemed to swamp her friend.

Ellen nodded. 'I know it looks awful, but it's warm enough. Everyone wears them, it's the uniform, so you forget what normal clothes are like. But I'm all right, Ada. I work in the kitchens and Mrs Burrows – the cook – is a decent soul and most of the women are friendly enough and I chat to a few in the dormitory. Jane has lessons in the morning then does light work in the laundry in the afternoon. We . . . we're all coping. But it did take a bit of getting used to at first; everything is so regimented.'

Ada nodded. Ellen did seem to be coping well enough and she was glad to hear that Jane wasn't expected to work a full day.

'What about meladdo? Your Alfie. Are they keeping his nose to the grindstone?'

Ellen sighed. 'He was separated from us, Ada, the very first day; he's in another wing with the men and boys. I found that hard to get used to but I do get to see him for half an hour most days. He doesn't have to work yet, he has lessons all day.' She bit her lip. 'But I do wish I could see more of him for he doesn't tell me much about what he's thinking or . . . feeling.'

'That's hard, Ellen, but is he behaving himself?' She had a

strong suspicion that discipline would be strict here.

Ellen shrugged. 'He's been in trouble a few times, I have to admit, but I suppose that's just lads. And he's with some boys who are much older and who I think encourage him.' She smiled, pushing her son's predicament from her mind. 'Jane asked me to give you her love and I'm to find out how Emily and your boys are doing. I know she misses your Emily even though she seems to have made a few friends.'

Ada didn't comment on the fact that she thought Alfie Shaw didn't need much encouragement; he was quite capable of causing trouble on his own. Since he'd been in here her Danny's behaviour had improved considerably. 'They're all doing well. Our Danny seems to have calmed down a bit but now it's Sonny who's starting to get into mischief. It's our Joe's last year at school, can you believe it? I don't know where the time has gone. Still, hopefully he'll get some kind of a job, which will help me out. Now, tell me everything. What you do all day, what's the food like, what are the other women like . . .?' she urged, settling back in the chair.

All too soon a woman whom Ellen informed her was called the mistress appeared to say that time was up and with hugs and promises to try to keep in touch Ada was shown out. Despite being very relieved that Ellen and her children appeared to be well enough Ada couldn't help but feel a little depressed. Life in here must be desperate, she thought, governed as it was by other people's rules. Still, from what she'd heard from Ellen, Christmas for them wouldn't be a gloomy time. The food would be good, the place decorated, they wouldn't have to work and apparently sometimes they were given small gifts by the members of the Board of Guardians. It was one of the few times when alcohol – in the form of ale – was served, not that either she or Ellen were very partial to that.

Maybe she could persuade Emily and Joe to write notes wishing Ellen and the kids a happy Christmas, just so they would know they were being thought of, for their first year without Eddie would be hard on them all, she reflected as she walked home.

When she reached the top of Gill Street she caught sight of two lads hanging around on the corner. Her eyes narrowed as she recognised them. Jimmy Cobham and Richie Corrin, and it was no surprise that they were not in school. 'Both your mams will have the truant officer banging on the door before long!' she addressed them curtly.

'We was waiting ter see if we could catch yer, Mrs Ellis,' Jimmy Cobham replied, totally ignoring her comment.

'Oh, were you. What for?' she demanded. She disliked them both. They were always in trouble or causing it, not that their parents seemed to care much.

'Your Danny said yer were goin' ter the workhouse ter see Mrs Shaw,' Richie informed her.

'Did he indeed,' Ada snapped, thinking she'd have a few words to say to her son about informing the likes of these two of things that she preferred to keep to herself.

'Well, did yer? See 'er?' Richie demanded cockily.

Ada glared at the taller of the two lads. 'Don't you use that tone with me, Richie Corrin. And what if I did? It's no concern of yours.'

'We was just wonderin' 'ow Alfie was, that's all. 'E's our mate and 'e didn't want ter go inter that place.'

'I remember, but he didn't have much choice, did he? Well,

for your information, his mam told me he's fine, that they're all fed and clothed but that they're very strict in there, they don't stand any nonsense. He has lessons all day and you can be sure that they keep his nose to the grindstone so he'll end up a damned sight cleverer than the pair of you, seeing as you're never at school. And he has to clean his boots every day, make his bed, say prayers, and when he's a bit older he'll have to work as well.'

They exchanged horrified glances at the mention of prayers, bed-making and lessons all day. 'Do yer think 'e'll ever get out of there?' Jimmy asked.

'One day I suppose he will, when he's old enough to get a job that'll pay enough to let him to support himself.'

Richie looked thoughtful. 'Do yer think they'd let us go in ter see 'im, Mrs Ellis? I mean seeing as it'll be Christmas soon, like?' His tone was far more respectful now.

Ada looked at him blankly. The nerve of him, she thought, the brass-necked cheek! 'No I do not, Richie Corrin. What do you think that place is – a rest home, or some sort of hotel? And the less Alfie Shaw has to do with the likes of you the better! Now, stop wasting my time, I've plenty to do even if you two haven't!' she snapped and walked away determinedly, leaving them muttering together.

She related the day's events to Fred that evening over supper. She felt much more cheerful now for he'd been lucky and for the past three days he'd had work. She would at least have a bit of money towards Christmas, for which she was very grateful, and now she'd ascertained that Ellen was all right her anxieties seemed to be receding.

'So, you feel happier now that you've actually seen her,' Fred remarked as he mopped up the last of the gravy from his plate.

'I do. She looked quite well, less strained and . . . gaunt. I suppose it's having all that worry taken off her shoulders. Oh, it doesn't sound exactly the greatest place to be but at least it's better than trying to struggle along on her own. And the kids both appear to have settled down.' She broke off to remonstrate with Sonny about kicking his heels against the stretcher of the bench, asking him did he not think it was battered enough already without him making it worse?

'And they'll have a decent Christmas?' Fred probed.

Ada nodded. 'Sounds like it. I have to say, Fred, luv, that I won't worry half as much about them now. Alfie's been in trouble a few times but Ellen says he's been punished. They're strict in there, which might be the making of him. Mind you, those two young hooligan mates of his were hanging around waiting for me; *someone* had taken it on themselves to tell them I was going' – she shot a sharp glance at Danny – 'and they only wanted to know did I think they would be let in to see him? I sent them off with a flea in their ears, I can tell you.' She turned again to her errant son. 'And I'll thank you, Danny Ellis, to keep your mouth shut in future and not go blabbing to those two about *anything*!'

Joe frowned. 'Bunking off school as usual,' he muttered.

'I heard that those two were nearly carted off by the scuffers the other night,' Emily informed them all.

'That doesn't surprise me one bit,' Ada retorted.

'What's surprising is that they let them go,' Joe added. 'Apparently they were caught trying to break into Cooper's newsagent's. They were in the jigger at the back, trying to force open the yard door, when the copper nabbed them. It was the talk of the school yard.'

'So, what happened?' Fred demanded. Obviously his son knew more of this than he did but then he didn't frequent the local pubs so he didn't hear much of the gossip.

'They said they were looking for Jimmy's dog that had run off, and thought they'd heard it barking in the yard—' Joe answered.

'Jimmy Cobham hasn't got a dog,' Danny interrupted.

Joe raised his eyes to the ceiling. 'Everyone in the street knows that, but the copper didn't, so he just gave him a belt around the ear and told him he'd be watching him in future.'

Ada shook her head. 'That lad will end his days on the gallows, you mark my words. All I can say is thank God Alfie Shaw will be in that place for a good few years yet and might come out a damned sight better behaved and wiser than when he went in.'

Fred nodded his agreement but Joe and Emily exchanged glances. Would the workhouse prove to be the making of Alfie Shaw? Only time would tell.

Chapter Five

1926

ELLEN QUICKLY PUT the heavy pot back down on the stove before gripping the edge of the wooden draining board to steady herself. She'd gone faint, her head swimming; she was flushing hot and cold and then shaking until she was afraid she'd let the pot slip, spilling the boiling-hot broth.

'Mrs Shaw, are you all right? You've gone very pale,' Edith Burrows asked, her sharp eyes having noticed the incident – there was little in her kitchen that she missed. In the four years since Ellen Shaw had been here she'd discovered that she was a good worker and a quiet, pleasant, obliging woman and she'd grown to like and trust her.

'Just a bit dizzy, Cook. I'll be fine in a couple of minutes,' Ellen replied, feeling her strength slowly return. But doubt was nagging at her for this wasn't the first time this had happened. She hadn't been feeling well at all lately but she'd

43

put it down to middle age and its attendant problems. Sometimes she felt as if she'd been tired all her life.

'Get a cup of water and go and sit down for five minutes,' Cook instructed.

Before Ellen could reply she was overtaken by a bout of coughing which racked her whole body.

'How long have you had that cough?' Cook demanded.

'Only . . . a few . . . weeks and it usually doesn't bother me during the day . . . just at night,' Ellen replied breathlessly when the bout had subsided.

'Then, before dinner, go up to the infirmary and ask if you can see the doctor. I don't like the sound of that at all.' Cook looked closely at Ellen who remained pale and a little drawn, something she hadn't really noticed before now, although two bright pink spots of colour stood out on her cheeks. 'And I think you've lost weight,' she added.

Ellen shook her head. 'No, I'm fine, really, Cook.'

Edith Burrows pursed her lips and nodded curtly but she had already decided that she would take the matter up with Matron, who she was certain would insist Ellen see the doctor. Ellen couldn't refuse Matron.

After breakfast next morning when she reported for work, and a night when she hadn't slept well at all, Ellen was dismayed to learn that Matron had agreed with Cook and she was to go up to the infirmary to see Dr Gates immediately. She had never been to this part of the workhouse before and so it was with great trepidation that she pushed open the door. She was greeted by a nurse in her crisply starched uniform and cap. They were called 'Nightingale Nurses', she'd been told by

Cook, having been trained at one of the schools set up by that illustrious but now long-dead lady, and Liverpool had been the first city in the country to employ them in the workhouse infirmaries. So she would be in good hands indeed, Cook had assured her.

'I'm Mrs Shaw, I was told by Matron to come to see Dr Gates,' she informed the nurse.

She was asked to wait and as she sat down she again began to cough. She hoped there was nothing seriously wrong with her. Maybe she was just run down with a bit of bronchitis and the doctor could give her some sort of tonic or cough medicine, but she felt very uneasy at the concerned look the nurse had cast in her direction.

Florence Stanley too was very concerned by Dr Gates's report, which lay on the desk in front of her. In the years Ellen Shaw had been here she had proved honest, diligent, quiet and well mannered and Matron was certain that had she not suffered the tragic loss of her husband she would have continued to be a good wife, mother and housekeeper in her own home. To add to her concern was the fact that it had been decided that young Jane, who was now fourteen, was to go out to work and a place had been found for her in the Empire Laundry, an establishment within the immediate neighbourhood, the proprietor of which – Mr James Davenport – was an acquaintance of one of the guardians. Jane would be paid the appropriate rate for her work there and therefore able to contribute to her upkeep here. In fact she had sent for the girl to inform her of the fact. She sighed. Now it appeared that she must break some bad news too.

She was standing staring out of the window contemplating the task that lay ahead when Jane was shown in. Turning she smiled and indicated that the girl should sit down.

Jane sat nervously on the edge of the chair, wondering why she had been summoned. Mistress Casey, the superintendent of the laundry, had told her she was pleased with her work; as far as she knew she hadn't broken any of the rules, and she always tried to keep herself neat and tidy, even though that wasn't easy when working in such a damp atmosphere. As Jane twisted her hands together she hoped it wasn't something to do with Alfie. But then her mam would have been sent for, not her, and of late her brother seemed to have managed to stay out of trouble – or at least he hadn't been caught. She took some hope from the fact that the matron was smiling.

'I have some news for you, Jane,' Matron said, sitting down behind her desk.

Jane looked at her expectantly while Matron drew what looked like a letter towards her.

Florence Stanley had decided to impart the good news first, thinking that despite the drab, shapeless uniform Jane Shaw was growing into a very attractive girl and, what was more important, quiet, well behaved, biddable and hard-working. 'The guardians have decided that you are now old enough to have a job outside of here, and one has been obtained for you in Mr Davenport's Empire Laundry in Mount Vernon Street.'

Jane's eyes widened in surprise. She'd never dreamed she'd be offered a job outside. 'Thank you, Matron,' she said automatically. After all this time she would be able to go out of the gates every single day! She tried to concentrate on what Matron was telling her about the hours of work, the wage she would be paid and the fact that she would be allowed to keep a little of it but that the rest she would have to give up to cover her bed and board here. Oh, it would be great to be able to go out again, she thought as excitement began to bubble up inside her. There wouldn't be so many rules and her life wouldn't be totally governed by the bell. She would mix with people whose world wasn't entirely encompassed by these walls, who would be lively and interesting, *and* she would even have money of her own – something she'd never had before. She knew where the Empire Laundry was – Mount Vernon Street wasn't far away – and she remembered the laundry as a big brick building, a busy thriving establishment; she would have to pass shops on her way there and back and with money of her own . . .

'So, Jane, you will start there next week, and it goes without saying that I expect you to work well, be diligent and obedient and to return here promptly at the end of each day.'

'Oh, yes, Matron, I will, and thank you, thank you so much!' she replied readily, her thoughts still in a whirl as she realised she could buy little treats for her mam, herself and maybe Alfie too.

'Now, I'm afraid I have some news which you won't find as . . . pleasing.'

Some of Jane's excitement drained away for Matron's tone had changed, as had her expression, and she felt a frisson of apprehension run through her. 'Is it . . . is it our Alfie, Matron?' she asked.

Matron shook her head, wishing it was just a misdemeanour on the boy's part. 'No. It concerns your mother, Jane. I insisted she see Dr Gates yesterday as she hasn't been feeling well and Cook was concerned about her, and rightly so as it happens.'

Jane's apprehension turned to a feeling of dread. 'She's had a cough for a few weeks, Matron, but she said . . . it was nothing for me to worry about. It would soon go.'

Matron sighed; sometimes she found her job very difficult. 'I'm so very sorry to have to tell you, Jane, that Dr Gates has confirmed that she has contracted tuberculosis. Of course we will do everything we can for her, and will pray for her recovery, but . . .'

Jane looked at her in horror as the impact of Matron's words began to dawn on her. 'She . . . she's got . . . *consumption*!'

Matron nodded. 'I'm afraid so. She won't be able to continue working; in fact she's been moved to the infirmary where she will be more . . . comfortable and will of course receive excellent care.'

The colour had drained completely from Jane's face, even her lips were pale and bloodless and she had begun to tremble. There was no cure for consumption, there was never a recovery, you . . . you *died*! Mam was going to die! All the feelings of shock, panic, despair and grief that she'd experienced when her da had been killed came flooding back and she fought down the sobs. Mam was too young to die and she . . . she was too young to be left an orphan.

Matron rose quickly and went to her side, putting an arm around her shoulders. 'I'm so very, very sorry, Jane. We'll do everything we can and of course you can visit her every day. The master will inform your brother and he, too, will be able to visit her. You must try to be strong for both your mother and Alfred.'

Jane nodded mutely, her vision blurred by tears, wondering how she was going to face the days and weeks that lay ahead, watching her poor mam grow weaker, fighting for every breath and coughing up her life's blood. How could she be 'strong' as Matron had urged? Her mam was going to die!

Matron herself took her up to the infirmary and after a few quiet words with the sister in charge left Jane in their office.

Sister Kelly gave her some water but Jane's hands were shaking so much that Sister Kelly had to hold the glass to her lips. She was vaguely aware that before she'd gone Sister had said she could see her mam in about fifteen minutes but everything seemed so *unreal*. She didn't even remember the fact that next week her days would be spent outside the workhouse. As she waited she dashed away the tears from her cheeks with the back of her hand. She would have to *try* to be strong but it was going to be the hardest thing she had ever done, harder even than facing her first day in the workhouse.

Sister reappeared and she got to her feet.

'Can I see her now, please?'

'Of course. She's upset, which is only natural, but try not to upset her further. I know it will be hard for you but I don't want her to experience another bout of coughing. She's had two already this morning. Chin up, lass. I always say the Lord never gives us a burden too heavy for our shoulders to bear,' she said kindly.

Jane managed to nod although she couldn't agree with those sentiments; a terrible weight seemed to be bowing her down and yet she was going to have to try hard not to upset her mam or let her see how utterly dejected and afraid she was.

Ellen smiled as Jane approached the bed. 'Hello, luv.'

Jane bent and kissed her cheek. 'How are you feeling, Mam?'

'Tired but don't you be worrying about me. I'm getting the

best of care.' Ellen too was trying hard to be optimistic. When they'd told her that she had contracted tuberculosis she'd closed her eyes and nodded slowly. In her darkest moments she'd suspected that this was what was really wrong with her and, like Jane, she knew that it was almost always fatal. There was no cure and they'd told her that as she had been diagnosed so late there was little they could do. She was still trying to come to terms with the shock.

Jane managed a smile. 'I know you are, Mam. Just make sure you do everything they ask,' she urged. 'And I have some good news. I'm going to work outside at the Empire Laundry in Mount Vernon Street. I'll be earning a wage.'

Ellen grasped her hand and squeezed it. 'Oh, Jane, that's great,' she replied.

When Jane was in the infirmary she had controlled her feelings for her mam's sake, and had left Ellen in reasonable spirits. But once outside in the corridor Jane broke down, unable to hold back the tears. Stumbling along she didn't see Maisie until she almost collided with the girl.

'Jane, what's wrong? What are you doing up here? Who's upset you?' Maisie demanded, putting an arm around Jane's shoulder.

'Oh, Maisie! I . . . I've been to see my mam. They brought her up here; she's . . .' Jane sobbed.

'What's wrong with her, Jane? Why's she in the infirmary?' Maisie probed but Jane could only shake her head and then the reason for Ellen being brought to the hospital suddenly occurred to the older girl. 'Is it . . . has she got . . . consumption?' Maisie whispered the name of the dreaded illness.

Jane nodded, wiping her eyes with a corner of her smock.

'Oh, Jane, I'm so very sorry, really I am. I hate to see you so upset,' Maisie said sincerely. She paused. 'I understand what it's like, what you're going through,' she added, tears in her eyes. She had only vague memories of her mother as a well woman but she had a vivid recollection of her last, awful days when diphtheria, that scourge of the Liverpool slums, had finally won its battle. She knew how much Jane loved Ellen and what a blow her mother's fatal illness was for her.

Jane had calmed down a little and she nodded her thanks. 'I'm so glad I have a friend like you, Maisie. It helps a bit.'

'And you must come and talk to me when you're feeling really miserable, promise?' Maisie urged.

Again Jane nodded as they walked along the corridor, Maisie's arm still around her shoulder. She would need a friend in the days and weeks ahead for she and Alfie were still so young.

Joe Ellis walked down Gill Street deep in thought, his hands thrust deeply into the pockets of his jacket. He was weary and looking forward to his supper. His fingers curled around the small brown envelope that contained his wages which he knew would be increased by one shilling and sixpence next month, a fact he knew his mam would be delighted with. He realised he was fortunate to have a job at all; not many of the lads who'd left school with him had something as steady and regular. He'd worked as a delivery boy for the Empire Laundry for two years now and it wasn't bad. He quite enjoyed riding his bike with the big basket on the front through the city streets, collecting and delivering items required more urgently than the weekly collection and delivery service the company provided. It was great in the spring and summer months not being stuck indoors but not so great in winter. It was just that lately he'd begun to want something more, something better, something more . . . *interesting*.

As he cut down the back entry he ignored the glances cast in his direction by Jimmy Cobham, Richie Corrin and two other lads playing pitch and toss. The game was illegal, and he wondered briefly where they managed to get the money from to gamble with in the first place. Probably thieved it, he mused. Still, it was nothing to do with him.

'Wash your hands in the scullery sink and leave your boots in there too; I've scrubbed this place out today!' Ada called from the kitchen.

Joe smiled as he bent to unlace his boots. Mam fought a constant battle with the dirt and dust but an appetising smell was wafting in from the kitchen. 'What's to eat, Mam? I'm starving,' he enquired, hanging his jacket and cap behind the door.

'Cottage pie. I got a nice bit of minced shin beef this morning in the market,' Ada informed him, thinking that with what Fred managed to earn, Joe's money and now Emily's bit of a wage from the factory, meals had improved lately. When Danny finally left school things would be looking up indeed.

'Did you have much to deliver today?' she asked him for she loved to hear his descriptions of some of the big houses he called at, fascinated by how sumptuously some people in their city lived.

'A fair bit, but at least it's pay day, Mam, and only half a day tomorrow. Is Da not in yet?'

Ada shook her head. 'No, but he won't be long now and he's had almost four days this week. A miracle!'

'It's a fine evening and I was thinking of asking him if he'd come down to the Pier Head with me later on, just for a bit of air and to have a look at what ships are in,' Joe confided. He'd decided to ask his father's advice on a matter that had occupied his mind lately.

'If you do go you can take our Sonny with you to give me an hour's peace and quiet,' Ada asked. Her youngest son was very much a live wire; being at school didn't seem to damp his energies.

Joe frowned. 'Won't he want to play in the street with the other kids?' He couldn't envisage having a serious conversation with his da with his little brother in tow.

He was thankful therefore when Sonny flatly refused to accompany them, insisting he'd sooner play cherrywobs with his mates than go for a boring walk with his older brother and his da for he wasn't really very interested in ships – they were just like trams and buses. Trains were a different matter but they weren't going near Lime Street Station. He was happy to leave his father and Joe to their wanderings.

'Even though I've spent most of my life working down here on the docks, I never get tired of watching all the traffic on the river,' Fred commented as they walked down the floating roadway to the Landing Stage. The sun was sinking lower in the sky and the usually grey, turgid waters of the Mersey had turned a reddish bronze. The wake of the *Manx Maid* as she pulled out into mid river was like a ribbon of liquid gold.

'I wanted to ask you something, Da,' Joe ventured as they

both leaned on the parapet watching the steam packet ferry boat heading towards the estuary, the Irish Sea beyond and eventually the port of Douglas.

'I thought there was something more to it than just "getting a breath of air" – something we both get plenty of every day,' Fred stated. 'So, lad, out with it?'

'It's . . . it's . . . my job, Da,' Joe began tentatively.

'You've got one, lad, and a steady one too. You haven't gone and lost it, have you?' his father demanded.

'No! And I know I'm lucky but . . . but I'd like to do something a bit more . . . interesting.'

'Like what?' Fred asked, thinking he'd count himself very fortunate indeed if he had a steady job with a regular wage even if it wasn't in the least bit interesting. But, he told himself, the lad was young.

Joe pointed to where a Union Castle Line ship was being guided towards the entrance to the Princes Half Tide Dock by two tugs. 'Like getting a job on something like that. The *Windsor Castle*, I mean, not the tugs, and see a bit more of the world than Liverpool.'

His father didn't reply for a few minutes as they both watched the manoeuvring.

'You want to give up your job to go away to sea?' Fred at last said quietly. 'And what do you think they'd take you on as? You've no training or experience so all you could do is shovel coal in a stokehold and believe me, you'd hate that.'

'I thought I could start out as a deck hand or a porter in the kitchens, something like that,' Joe informed him.

Fred thought about it: this didn't appear to be just a whim; the lad had quite obviously given the matter some consideration.

'So, what do you think, Da?' Joe probed.

'I'll make a deal with you, Joe. Stick with the Empire Laundry for another year, try to save a bit of money, and then we'll talk about it again.'

'That long, Da?' Joe pleaded. Another year seemed an interminably long time, he thought.

Fred nodded. 'Twelve months, that's all, and if you're still determined then I'll come with you to the Pool and see what they can give you. And we'll say nothing about this to your mam for the time being, Joe – she'll only get herself into a state.'

Joe nodded and grinned. He wouldn't mind sticking the delivery job for twelve more months if his da would come with him to the employment office known as the 'Pool' where ships' crews were signed on. He didn't want to deliver laundry all his life, he wanted to gain experience in another type of work and see something of the world too. It was something to look forward to.

'Thanks, Da,' he replied happily. 'Shall we have a trip across to Birkenhead and back on the ferry, to sort of celebrate?'

Fred grinned at him. 'Only if you're going to pay the tuppence each.'

'It's pay day, don't forget, and it'll be a bit of experience in getting my sea legs.'

Fred looked askance at him as they walked towards the *Egremont*, which was tied up awaiting the last passengers. 'You'll need more than a few trips across the Mersey, lad, to set you up for the Atlantic Ocean, or even the Irish Sea come to that, but lead on and dig deep in your pocket for the brass for the fare.'

Chapter Six

———

As SHE HAD WALKED through the gates of the Empire Laundry that first morning Jane had felt very apprehensive, even though she had found the feeling of freedom quite exciting.

'I've to report to a Miss Roberts. I'm Jane Shaw,' she timidly informed the man on the gate.

'Ah, she's expecting you,' he said, smiling. 'I expect you're a bit nervous?'

She nodded. 'It's my first paid job, you see.'

He winked. 'Don't you worry, you'll be fine. By the end of the week you'll feel as if you've worked here for months.'

She smiled back and walked in the direction he'd indicated. She found Miss Roberts to be pleasant and amiable too and even though everything seemed different and everyone was a stranger to her, her confidence began to grow. It felt so good to be back in the outside world again. Yes, she'd soon get used to working here, she thought.

Now her first week at the Empire Laundry was coming to an end and despite the weight of desolate unhappiness that was always with her she found that she could almost separate her life into two halves and enjoy the freedom of being able to leave the confines of Brownlow Hill behind and walk to her new place of employment. She was also relieved that she didn't have to wear the awful shapeless uniform outside, which would have made it so obvious to all that she belonged in the work-house. Of course the clothes she'd worn when she'd arrived wouldn't fit her now so she'd been given the ones her mother had worn then. They'd been washed, pressed and stored for all this time; they were a bit big but she didn't mind. At least she felt she looked more 'normal' now as she walked the short distance to Mount Vernon Street.

She had quickly noticed that skirts nowadays were very much shorter, ending just below the knee, often pleated or gathered into a loose, dropped waistband and fabrics were softer, the colours lighter. Hats were small and framed the face and astonishingly hairstyles had changed drastically too. Girls and the younger women wore their hair cut short just covering their ears, either heavily waved or with a full fringe. She felt dowdy and old-fashioned in her ankle-length skirt and with her long, thick auburn hair piled on top of her head. It seemed as if only women of her mam's age and older still clung to the long skirts and long hair fashionable not so long ago. But the area had hardly changed, she'd realised, and she had found the work very similar to that in the workhouse laundry, though not quite as heavy. When Miss Roberts, her supervisor, had instructed her on her duties she had informed her that Mr Davenport was a gentleman with very progressive ideas and had invested heavily in the latest machinery, which made the various processes more efficient and speedy and work for them less back-breaking. She had instantly liked Miss Roberts, whom she judged to be in her thirties. She was a little brisk but she hadn't been at all dismissive or patronising.

All week Jane had worked diligently but silently, pre-occupied by her mother's predicament and her own sense of impending loss, but she had felt grateful for the fact that most of the other girls and women seemed friendly, chatting amiably as they worked. However, there were a couple whom she noticed were not, who openly viewed her with suspicion and scorn, and she'd heard herself referred to by Maggie Rosbottom, a big-boned, loud and coarsely spoken girl, as 'the workhouse girl'. Her silence and preoccupation hadn't served to endear her to them either but she ignored them.

Late on the Friday afternoon they were all paid, although they worked on Saturday mornings too, and she was the last one to be called into Miss Roberts's tiny office in the corner of the cavernous room.

'Your first week's wage, Jane. I always think it is something of a milestone in life,' Cynthia Roberts said pleasantly as she passed over the small brown envelope.

'It . . . it's something I never thought I'd have, Miss Roberts. Wages – money of my own. Of course,' she confided, 'it's not *all* mine, I have to give most of it to Matron to help pay for my keep.'

The older woman nodded, thinking the girl must find it a bit disappointing to be working for so little reward. 'You are settling in well, here, Jane?' she enquired.

Jane nodded her agreement. 'I am, miss, thank you.'

'You're a good worker, I observed that the first day, but you seem a little . . . quiet. Do you find it hard to mix?' She wondered whether what spirit or vivacity the girl might have possessed had been quashed by the conditions she must have endured in that place. She couldn't begin to imagine what life for her was like there.

'I suppose I am quiet, miss, but usually I do make friends. I have a good friend in the workhouse, Maisie, and she and I get on well but . . . but you see I'm very worried and . . . upset about my mam just now and so I suppose I'm not as talkative as I might be.'

'Why are you worried about your mother, Jane?' the supervisor asked kindly.

Haltingly Jane told her about Ellen and the shock and grief of learning her mother had consumption. Of how she visited her in the infirmary every day, of how sometimes she was sitting in a chair and seemed cheerful but at other times she was in bed, pale and depressed, and that her cough had become worse and she knew that it was only a matter of time before Ellen's condition would deteriorate and she would . . . die. She couldn't bear the thought of a future without her mother in it; the idea of never being able to see her again was unthinkable.

Cynthia Roberts, whose own elderly mother had passed away the previous year, nodded sympathetically as she listened. It was no wonder the poor girl was preoccupied and disinclined to chat and gossip with the others when she had this terrible weight of sadness to bear. And she was so young. She determined then that she would keep a close eye on her for the likes of Maggie Rosbottom, Bertha Higgins and some of the others were loud and insensitive. 'I am really very sorry to hear that, Jane. Do you have any sisters and brothers? Any other relatives?'

Jane shook her head. 'There is no one else, miss, just our Alfie, my brother. He's twelve and I haven't really seen much of him in the four years we've been in Brownlow Hill. The men and boys are separated from the women and girls, you see.'

Cynthia Roberts shook her head in disbelief. Lord, but they were so old-fashioned in those places, she mused. They seemed stuck firmly in the eighteen hundreds. You'd think they would try to move with the times, be a bit more modern in outlook. 'What does he do? I mean do they make him work?'

'He still has lessons in the mornings but he works in the afternoons. At the moment he's just picking oakum to be made into rope but Mam is hoping that when he's older they'll apprentice him to a tradesman. With a good trade he'll never be without work.'

Cynthia Roberts nodded. It must be terrible for the poor woman, knowing she was dying and being unable to help her children or even envisage what the future would hold for them. 'Well, I'd better go over these dockets and see what's being brought in for tomorrow,' she announced, gathering together a sheaf of papers. Jane pocketed her wage packet and headed for the door.

To her dismay when she walked out into the yard she saw that Maggie, Bertha and their friends were still hanging around by the gates. She ducked her head as she walked towards them.

'Look, it's the workhouse girl!' Maggie shouted, pointing at Jane. 'Yer been tryin' ter suck up ter Miss Roberts then?'

The others laughed but although she felt her cheeks begin to burn Jane kept her head down.

'Perhaps she's 'oping ter get a few bob more in 'er pay packet cos she's got no proper 'ome, although she's too stuck up ter talk to us,' Bertha jeered, encouraged by the sniggers of the other girls.

'Just looking fer sympathy, so she don't 'ave ter work as hard! Crafty little slummy! We've met 'er sort before, 'aven't we?' Maggie laughed cuttingly.

They had surrounded Jane but she tried to push past. 'I . . . I've got to get back so would you let me through, please?' she said quietly but firmly, although she was smarting at their taunts, aware of distress and anxiety building up inside her.

'And what iffen we don't want ter let yer out? What yer goin' ter do about it?' Maggie said threateningly.

Jane felt the tears prick her eyes but she was determined not to cry. She wasn't going to let them see how they were upsetting her. 'I have to get back. It's . . . it's one of the rules,' she said, trying not to think of her mother who would be anxiously waiting to see her.

Bertha let out a hoot of coarse laughter. ''Ark at 'er! "It's one of the rules,"' she mimicked. 'She thinks we was —'

Before she could finish a male voice interrupted harshly. 'Who are you lot picking on now? Haven't you got homes to go to?'

Maggie and Bertha held their ground but the others fell back and as Jane looked up she gasped. 'Joe! Joe Ellis!' she cried.

Joe stared at her in disbelief. 'Jane Shaw? Is that you?'

'Yes! Yes, it is. Oh, I'm so glad to see you, Joe! I . . . I have to get back but . . .'

Joe turned on her little group of tormentors. He was a good

head and shoulders taller than all of them. 'Leave her alone and clear off, the lot of you! Go on before I report you all to Mr Turner. You're a loud-mouthed bully, Maggie Rosbottom, and you know how the manager hates bullies – *and* I know you've been called into his office before so I shouldn't wonder if you got the push this time. Clear off!'

Bertha and the others had already edged away but Maggie, her cheeks red, glared up at Joe. 'Just mind who yer're calling a bully, lad!' she snapped but at last she turned away and followed the others.

'What are you doing here, Jane?' Joe asked, thinking how much she'd grown and that despite her old-fashioned clothes she was far more attractive than any of those other girls, which was probably why they had been trying to bully her.

'I . . . I work here, Joe. This is my first week. But I don't know why they . . . don't like me.' The tears that had been threatening now began to fall. 'They call me "the workhouse girl"!'

'Jane, take no notice of them,' Joe urged. He was surprised to hear they had let her out to work.

To her consternation Jane started to cry in earnest, the uncalled-for hostility and mockery of Maggie and her friends, her mother's illness and the fact she would now be late all suddenly seemed too much to bear.

Joe became concerned. 'Look, why don't you come home with me? Mam would love to see you and so would our Emily,' he suggested.

Jane sobbed harder and shook her head. 'I . . . I can't! I can't, Joe!'

Joe didn't know what to do, he felt helpless and wondered

if he should put his arm around her or try to find her supervisor. 'Jane, what's wrong? Why are you so upset? It's not just that lot calling you names, is it?'

'It . . . it's Mam, Joe. She . . . she's . . . dying.'

Joe was both confused and horrified. 'But she can't be, Jane! She was fine last time Mam went to see her.'

'She is, Joe! She is!' Jane sobbed.

Joe could see she was becoming hysterical at his doubt – it must be true, he thought. Although profoundly shocked, he came to a decision. He'd always liked Jane and now his heart went out to her. Putting his arm firmly around her shoulders he guided her towards the gates. 'I'm not letting you go back in this state. You're coming home with me, Jane.'

Jane let him lead her out of the yard, her only thought one of relief at the prospect of unburdening herself of her grief to people she had known all her life.

Ada let out a cry of disbelief as Joe ushered a calmer but still pale and tearful Jane into the kitchen in Gill Street. 'Lord above! Jane! Come on in, luv,' she instructed. 'Where did you find her? Has she run off from that place?' she asked her son.

'No, she's not run off, she works in the Empire Laundry, Mam, and I found that Maggie Rosbottom from Hart Street and her mates tormenting her, but . . . but . . .'

'But what? Surely she hasn't let that loud-mouthed slattern upset her? What's wrong? What's got her in this state?' Ada demanded, a sickening feeling of unease creeping over her.

'It's her mam. She says her mam's . . . dying,' Joe replied bluntly.

Ada's hand went to her throat and her eyes widened in

horror at his words but she quickly pulled herself together. Matron had allowed her to visit Ellen twice a year ever since that first visit but she hadn't seen Ellen since before Christmas and it was now the end of June. In fact she'd been planning on going within the next few weeks. Easing Jane down into a chair by the range Ada knelt down beside her, taking her hands. 'Jane, luv, what's wrong with your mam? She seemed all right last time I saw her. What's gone wrong?'

She listened with growing sorrow as Jane told her of Ellen's illness and her own despair and grief; of her first week at work outside the workhouse and her first wage, both of which she should have enjoyed; and the fact that she really should be back in Brownlow Hill by now. Her mam would be worried and Matron would very probably be furious and maybe not allow her to keep the job.

When Jane had at last fallen silent Ada, with some difficulty, got to her feet. 'Emily, love, make a pot of strong tea,' she instructed her daughter, who had stood silently listening with tears in her eyes. 'Jane, luv, when we've had a cup of tea I'm going back with you to explain to that matron why you're late and to see your poor mam,' she announced firmly. 'Emily, I'm leaving you in charge of getting supper ready and keeping your eye on our Danny and Sonny. Joe, you'll come with me. I'll need you to back Jane up, to tell the matron about that brassy trollop Maggie Rosbottom and her cronies.'

Joe nodded, feeling relieved that his mam had taken charge.

Emily handed Jane a mug of tea. 'I'm glad to see you, Jane, I really am, I just wish I could do something to . . . help,' she said quietly.

Jane nodded her thanks and as she sipped the tea she felt relief seeping through her. She was once more amongst friends and she knew they would help her to cope.

Chapter Seven

'WHAT'S THIS, SOME sort of *deputation*?' the porter demanded as the little group walked through the gates.

'I've brought her back because she's late and I don't want her to get into trouble for it because it's not her fault,' Ada stated bluntly. She still had little time for the man.

'So, what's he doing here then?' he asked, pointing at Joe. He was familiar with Ada now for she visited more than most and of course young Jane Shaw went back and forth each day, though he never took much notice of the girl.

'That's between me, Matron and him and I'll thank you not to delay us any longer,' Ada replied firmly, ushering Jane and Joe towards the door to the corridor.

Joe shivered involuntarily as his mother led them upstairs and towards Matron's office. There was something very depressing about the atmosphere in here, added to by the stone floors and dark-painted walls, that had nothing to do with Ellen's plight.

Matron was taken aback to observe the little group when she opened the door in response to Ada's knock. 'Jane! I'd been informed that you were not back yet. And . . . Mrs Ellis! Has something happened?'

'Ma'am, I'm sorry to descend on you like this, with no warning but—' Ada began.

'Please, come in,' Matron interrupted, sensing that there was something amiss.

'Jane's late back, Matron, because our Joe here, my son – who works at the Empire Laundry – found her in a terrible state in the yard and brought her to our house and she told me then that Ellen, her mam—'

'I think you had better begin at the beginning, Mrs Ellis,' Matron said firmly, indicating that Ada should sit.

Ada told her of the bullying by Maggie and her friends and insisted that Joe describe the incident to Matron, something he did quite calmly and articulately, Matron thought. Ada then described how upset Jane had been by it all and of her own shock at hearing the dreadful news concerning Ellen. 'And, if possible, ma'am, I'd very much like to see Mrs Shaw,' she finished.

Matron nodded. There was no need for her to reprimand Jane; she had been badly treated by those unpleasant girls and she could well understand how upset she'd become: she was a quiet, sensitive girl who was trying to come to terms with her mother's illness and what the future would hold. 'I'm certain Mrs Shaw will be very pleased to see you, Mrs Ellis. Jane will take you to the infirmary.' She smiled at Joe. 'Thank you for escorting her back and for assisting her, young man.'

'She isn't in trouble for being late, is she?' Ada pressed.

'Of course not, under the circumstances. I think it would be wise of me to send a note to Miss Roberts at the laundry to ensure that something like this doesn't occur again,' Matron said grimly as she stood up, thinking the woman was remiss in her duties if she couldn't keep her staff in order. Then she smiled as Jane passed over her wage packet. 'Thank you, Jane. I'll make sure your little allowance is passed on to you.' She frowned and looked perturbed as she glanced at Joe again. 'I'm afraid your son will have to wait in the corridor for you, Mrs Ellis. I can't allow him to accompany you, but perhaps he would like to see young Alfred while he's waiting?' She couldn't bend the rules but it did seem a little churlish to leave the boy standing in a corridor after he had assisted Jane.

Joe shot a quick glance at his mother; he really didn't have any desire to see Alfie Shaw.

'I'm sure he would like to see him, thank you, Matron,' Ada replied firmly, ignoring Joe's look and thinking that if Joe had any gumption he'd take the opportunity to find out just how Alfie was getting on.

Jane was very relieved to see that it was one of her mam's better days; she was sitting in a chair, a light shawl over her knees.

Ellen's face lit up as she caught sight of her daughter and her friend. 'Oh, Jane, I was getting worried about you, luv. And Ada! What a surprise!'

Jane bent and kissed her mother on the cheek. 'I was . . . delayed, Mam, I'm sorry, but—'

'She bumped into our Joe, Ellen, at work, and he insisted she come to see me. Fancy them working at the same place,'

Ada said quite cheerfully, determined not to worry Ellen by informing her of Jane's ordeal at the hands of Maggie Rosbottom. Her heart had sunk as she'd caught sight of Ellen. She'd lost a lot of weight; she looked pale, gaunt and anxious. 'I was going to come and visit you next week but I thought I'd come along with Jane.'

Ellen nodded and her eyes filled with tears. 'I'm so glad you did Ada. Did . . . did she tell you?'

Ada nodded sadly. 'She did, luv. And I . . . I'm so . . . Oh, Ellen, if you hadn't come into this place you wouldn't have caught . . . it!' she cried, feeling so helpless, confronted now by the stark reality of Ellen's condition.

Ellen managed a smile as she nodded. 'But, Ada, if I hadn't come here I'd have been in a worse state by now, and Jane and Alfie too.'

Ada sighed heavily as she realised Ellen was right.

'Come and sit down and we'll have a long talk. You too, Jane, luv. Did you get paid today?'

Jane nodded, wondering if next week she would be able to afford to buy her mam some sweets as a treat. 'I gave it to Matron and she'll make sure I get my bit of pocket money,' she informed her mother.

'How are you feeling, Ellen?' Ada asked.

'Today I don't feel too bad, luv. They take good care of me and they give me something to try to ease the cough but . . . there's nothing much more they can do.'

'You must get plenty of rest, Ellen, and try not to worry too much about things,' Ada urged.

'I do rest. In fact it's the first time in my life I don't have to do . . . *anything*, but with nothing to occupy me all I seem able to do is dwell on . . . what's going to happen to me and to . . . Jane and Alfie.'

Jane reached and took her thin hand. 'Mam, we'll be fine. You know that. I'm working now and when he's old enough Alfie will get work too and you know Matron is very . . . considerate. We're lucky in that.'

'And you know, Ellen, that I'll always do whatever I can for them both,' Ada promised.

'I . . . I didn't want to have to ask you that, Ada,' Ellen replied thankfully. In the hours of darkness when sleep wouldn't come and the cough racked her she had worried so much about her children and their futures.

'You know I'll keep an eye on them, Ellen, and they know they can always come to me if anything is troubling them. I don't want you to worry about anything. It won't help you, luv.'

Ellen nodded but then her thin shoulders hunched as a spasm of coughing overtook her and she clutched the piece of linen she held to her mouth. The cough seemed to take hold of her entire being, racking her body mercilessly.

Ada stood up, concerned by the sheer intensity of the attack. 'Jane, I think you'd better go and find a nurse, luv,' she urged as Ellen fought for her breath.

Jane nodded and went hastily down the ward although she'd witnessed these attacks before and knew a nurse couldn't do much to help her mam.

Ada stood looking helplessly at her old friend and feeling a terrible sadness overwhelm her. Finally, to Ada's relief, Jane appeared, accompanied by a woman in uniform.

'Is there anything I can do for her, nurse, please?' Ada

pleaded, twisting her hands together as Ellen's coughing continued.

'You can help me get her on to the bed, then we'll prop her up with pillows: that seems to help a little. And then I think it best if you leave her to rest – both of you,' she instructed, not unkindly.

Between them they got Ellen on to the bed and supported by pillows but the linen cloth was now bright scarlet. The nurse replaced it with a fresh one, which to Ada's dismay quickly became stained, but at least the spasm seemed to be passing.

'You rest, Ellen, and I'll ask Matron if I can come and see you more often,' she promised as she put her arm around Jane's shoulders and they left Ellen to the ministrations of the nurse.

'It's no use me saying she'll be all right, Jane, luv, because she won't. There's no cure and she's getting worse, isn't she?'

Miserably Jane nodded. 'I . . . I . . . wish there was something I could do for her, Aunty Ada!'

'So do I, luv,' Ada replied sincerely. It was clearly what people termed 'galloping consumption' and she doubted poor Ellen would see Christmas.

Joe shoved his hands deeper into the pockets of his jacket and frowned as he stood waiting for Alfie to appear for he wasn't looking forward to seeing his former neighbour. He'd been shown into a small, rather bare room containing a single wooden bench, which he'd ignored, choosing instead to stand staring out of the window down into a dismal yard below, wondering just what he would say to Jane's brother.

He turned as the door opened and was surprised to see how much taller Alfie was; somehow he'd expected him to look exactly the same as when he'd last seen him nearly four years ago.

'You've grown!' he commented, staring at the lad who was just a head shorter than himself now. He still had the same sharp features and gingery hair but there was now a speculative, calculating look in his eyes that hadn't been there when he was younger. Then his expression had been just mischievous, now he seemed . . . watchful and mutinous.

'So've you,' Alfie replied, eyeing Joe up and down, noting the adult and more modern clothes Joe was wearing and feeling resentful of his still childish corduroy jacket and trousers.

'I came with my mam and your Jane. I . . . I'm sorry about your mam,' Joe added.

Alfie shrugged and sat down on the bench. 'They give me time to go and see her every day, I suppose that's something,' he replied sullenly. At least it was half an hour's break in his grindingly dull routine that his superintendent couldn't object to since it had been Master Ribchester's decision to allow him to make the visits. As time had passed his attitude to his situation in life had hardened. He'd become more and more resentful and rebellious and deliberately sought ways of causing trouble but taking care to make sure he was never caught. He'd grown to loathe the master, who was a strict disciplinarian, and had sworn to himself that he'd get out of this place at the first opportunity and then no one would ever tell him what to do again. From the first day they'd arrived he'd seen little of his mam and he'd got used to it but he blamed her for inflicting this life on him. Jane didn't really seem to care much about him either; she was only interested in Mam and the job she now had outside.

'What do you do all day?' Joe asked, sitting down beside him. He was finding conversation difficult and wasn't even sure if the lad was upset about his mother's illness or not. Joe hadn't detected any note of regret or sorrow in his voice.

'Still have flaming stupid lessons each morning and work in the afternoons,' Alfie replied flatly. 'It's dead boring – as usual.'

'What kind of work?' Joe probed, although he wasn't really interested.

'Picking oakum, which has got to be the worst kind of work in the world. They bring in loads of "junk" – that's pieces of old rope that've been cut up – and we have to sit and pick it apart until it's in little shreds, then they send that away to be made into new rope. It's all a waste of time as far as I can see. Like I said – dead boring.'

'Do you get paid?' Joe asked, thinking it certainly didn't sound like much of a job.

'Fat chance of that! Even our Jane doesn't get to keep all her wages; they give her a few pence back, Mam says. What's the point in that? Slaving away in that laundry all day for a couple of coppers a week – it's a mug's game.' Alfie was scornful. He hated picking oakum, it was dirty, dusty and mind-numbingly dull and it was hard on his hands too. Sometimes at the end of the afternoon his fingers were cut and bleeding. Still, he supposed it was better than breaking stones all day to be used for road repairs, which was what some of the older boys and the men did.

Joe digested this, thinking that although he turned up his 'keep' to his mam he still had half of his wages in his pocket each week. 'Will you have to do that full-time, like, when you're fourteen or will they let you go out to work too?'

Again Alfie shrugged. He had plans for when he was older but he wasn't going to say anything about them to Joe Ellis. 'Might get an apprenticeship, who knows?'

'That won't be bad. At least you'll finish up with a proper trade.'

'But I'll still be stuck in here for years until I come out of my time,' Alfie replied grimly. 'Do you see anything of Tommy or Richie?' he asked.

'Not if I can help it,' Joe answered cautiously, wondering why Alfie was still interested in them. 'If I do ever see those two they're always up to no good so I stay well clear.'

Alfie's eyes narrowed but he looked thoughtful. 'Next time you see them will you tell them . . . tell them they're still my mates.'

Joe nodded, although he had no intention of informing those two that he'd seen Alfie. 'You'd be better off forgetting about them, Alfie, and concentrating on getting that apprenticeship. At least if you're learning a trade your mam'll be happy.'

'Mam won't be around by then so it won't matter,' Alfie stated flatly. He'd never really forgiven her for bringing them here in the first place. He was sure they could have managed somehow if she'd got some kind of a job but she hadn't even tried, she'd just given up. He'd quickly grown to hate all the restrictions, the enforced learning and tedious work; he was utterly bored with the life she'd inflicted on him. He couldn't wait to get out. He stood up. 'Well, just tell Richie and Tommy that I won't be stuck in here forever. I'll have to go now.'

Joe got to his feet, quite thankful that Alfie was departing. 'If I see them I'll tell them,' he replied, thinking Alfie certainly didn't seem very upset about his mother. 'My mam will be coming in to see your mam more often now, I suppose, and I work in the same place as Jane, so I'll hear how . . . how . . .' He left the rest unsaid but for the first time Alfie showed a spark of interest.

'I didn't know you worked in that laundry.'

'I don't work *in* it, I'm on the . . . delivery side of it,' Joe stated. He wasn't going to tell Alfie Shaw that he was just a delivery boy, not when Alfie was turning his nose up at the chance of getting an apprenticeship, something a lot of lads would give their right arm for. 'And I've got plans.'

Alfie stared at him, his gaze speculative. 'So've I. I'll see you around sometime – when I get out.'

Joe stared after him as he left and then shrugged. It would be at least another two years before Alfie Shaw would be old enough to go out to work full time and by then . . . well, he hoped by then he'd have a job at sea.

Chapter Eight

⊹

As summer turned to autumn and the weather grew colder Ellen deteriorated quickly. When Ada visited in late November she realised that her old friend didn't have long left on this earth and so it was with a very heavy heart that she bade goodbye to Jane at the door of the infirmary at the end of the visit. Alfie had already left after spending the bare minimum of time with his mother, Ada mused grimly. He didn't seem to have any feelings at all for his poor mam, the selfish, hard-hearted little sod.

'I'll be in to see her again at the end of the week, Jane, luv,' she promised. 'Now, off you go and get your supper and have a chat to that Maisie. She's a nice girl.'

'I don't feel much like eating, Aunty Ada,' Jane confided. Although she hadn't let on to anyone else, not even Maisie, in her heart she too knew her mam was now dangerously ill.

'You've got to keep your strength up, girl, it's not an easy job you've got in that laundry and it's a job you want to keep.'

Jane nodded; she knew what Ada said made sense. 'Will you thank Emily for the hat and scarf?' she added. Although Emily had far more money than Jane did, Jane knew it didn't amount to very much and yet from time to time her old friend sent in some small item of clothing, the latest a bright green felt cloche hat and matching scarf. They weren't new of course but Emily had told her mam to tell Jane that the colour would suit her. At any other time Jane would have been delighted with such a bright and fashionable gift but now all she could think of was her poor mam, coughing up her lungs as she fought to breathe.

'Course I will, luv. She thought it might help to cheer you up a bit.'

Jane nodded as she turned away. At least she had Ada and Emily and Maisie to help her through this dark and fearful time.

Ada wasn't going straight home to Gill Street; she had determined that she would see Matron to enquire about the funeral arrangements for there was little she could do now for poor Ellen.

'And how did you find Mrs Shaw today?' Matron asked as she ushered her in. She had grown to respect Ada Ellis for she had shown loyalty and compassion for her friend and Florence Stanley knew that she had quite a large family of her own to care for.

'Worse if anything, ma'am, I'm afraid. I . . . I don't think it will be long now and . . . and I wanted to ask you about the arrangements for when . . . after . . .'

'I understand, Mrs Ellis. I'm afraid I have to tell you it will be a very, very brief and quiet affair, unless perhaps you and your husband . . .?'

77

Ada shook her head. She knew what Matron was saying. That Ellen would have a pauper's burial: the final humiliation inflicted upon the destitute. Oh, there had been times when she had struggled to pay the penny a week into the Burial Club but somehow she'd managed it to avoid that terrible fate befalling her family. But she couldn't afford to contribute anything towards Ellen's burial and that fact broke her heart. 'I'm sorry, ma'am, you don't know how much it . . . hurts me, but we can't afford . . .'

Matron nodded slowly; she'd thought as much. She was aware of how people dreaded this final indignity. A brief prayer followed by the interment – that was all in the way of a service – and a cheap base wood coffin with no adornments, no flowers, no mourners, no headstone; nothing at all to mark the fact of that person's very existence on this earth. 'I understand,' she said quietly.

'But I'd like to be there please, ma'am, if you'll agree. It's the very least I can do, and perhaps if I have a bit of a whip round in the street, then we could manage a few flowers or a small wreath.'

'Of course, Mrs Ellis, and Jane and Alfred will be present.'

Ada surreptitiously wiped away a tear. 'Those poor kids, first their da and now . . .'

'I'll get word to you, Mrs Ellis, when . . . when the sad event occurs,' Matron promised.

Ada rose and nodded her thanks as she left, too overcome to trust herself to speak.

All the way home as she walked along the cold, dark narrow streets of soot-blackened houses she thought how cruel, how utterly unfair life had been to Ellen and her children. Oh, she didn't have much herself but she was so grateful that she had her health and strength, a good husband and that her children were all growing up within a stable, happy, if very humble home. She pulled her shawl more closely around her, for frost was already beginning to settle on the cobbles and the circle of light around the streetlamp had a whitish tinge. From the distant river on the clear night air she could hear the three blasts of a ship's steam whistle as it left Liverpool. It was a mournful sound, she thought sadly, a sound of farewell, and soon, so soon she would have to bid farewell to her dear friend. But what hurt her dreadfully was the thought of Ellen being laid to rest a pauper.

After supper Jane begged permission from Mistress Hayes, the superintendent in charge of the refectory, to go to say good-night to her mother.

At first she shook her head uncertainly. 'It's almost a quarter to eight and you know that it's lights out for everyone at eight,' the woman reminded her. Then, looking at the crestfallen girl, she went on. 'But, under the circumstances, I suppose it will be all right, just as long as you're in the dormitory by eight. I'm not risking a reprimand from Matron because of your tardiness, Jane Shaw.'

Jane nodded, too preoccupied to be upset by the woman's sharpness, and hurried up to the infirmary. The lights had already been turned down and the ward was in semi-darkness. A fire burned brightly in the large fireplace at the far end giving out a soft apricot glow which washed the white-tiled walls and made them appear far less austere than in the cold harsh light of day. She walked quietly towards the sister's desk in the centre.

'Can I see my mother, please, Sister?' she asked in a whisper.

The woman looked up and then nodded, aware how ill Ellen Shaw was for she'd been reading the doctor's notes. 'Just for a few minutes.'

Jane crept towards the narrow iron-framed bed with its spotless white cotton counterpane and was relieved to see that her mother seemed to be breathing without too much trouble. Ellen's eyes were closed but Jane bent over her. 'Mam! Mam, I've come to say goodnight,' she said softly.

Ellen slowly opened her eyes and smiled tiredly. 'You shouldn't be here, luv. It must be almost eight o'clock; we've all been settled for the night.'

'I got permission, Mam, it's all right. I just wanted to see you, to make sure you are . . . comfortable.' She took one of Ellen's thin hands, wishing she could sit on the bed beside her mother but she knew that was strictly forbidden.

'I . . . think I might sleep quite well tonight,' Ellen murmured.

'Good. That's good, Mam,'

'There's something . . . I want to ask you, Jane, luv. I know . . . I know I haven't got . . . long now.'

'Oh, Mam, don't say that!' Jane urged gently, feeling the tears beginning to sting her eyes.

'I'm not afraid now, Jane. I . . . I'm happier that I know Ada will look out for you, but, Jane, will you promise to take care of our Alfie? He's still only young and . . . he . . . he doesn't say much but I'm worried about him. I think he's sort of . . . bottling it all up inside.'

'I'll take care of him, Mam, as best I can in here. You know I hardly see anything of him because of the rules,' Jane reminded her mother.

Ellen's grip on her hand tightened. 'I know that, luv, but I mean when . . . when you both leave here. One day you'll both have a life . . . outside, when you're old enough. Promise you'll make sure Alfie is all right.'

'I promise, Mam,' Jane replied, but she didn't want to think about the years that lay ahead; these few precious moments were far more important.

'And, Jane, one day I hope you'll marry, but make sure you . . . choose . . . wisely.'

Through her tears Jane managed a smile. 'The way you chose Da? You were happy, Mam, weren't you?'

Ellen nodded but Jane could see she was rapidly tiring. 'I'll remember that, Mam. I . . . I hope I find a man like Da.'

'Make sure, Jane, that he's a man of some means. Means enough that if . . . if anything terrible happens, like it did to your poor da, you won't end up . . . like me: ending my days in poverty, in . . . *here*, and my children with me.'

Jane felt the tears sliding down her cheeks and grief filled her heart. 'Please, Mam, don't think about things like that. We've been well cared for and Alfie and me, we'll . . . manage. Please, just try to sleep now,' she begged.

Ellen nodded and closed her eyes. Jane kissed her again and tucked her thin hand under the coverlet before walking quietly away but she was almost sure she heard Ellen whisper something. It sounded like 'Choose wisely, Jane. Choose . . . wisely.'

She wore the green hat and scarf for work the following day. It seemed churlish not to after Emily had been so generous and thoughtful but it did little to lift her spirits. Neither could the cheery wave Joe gave her as he cycled out through the gates, his basket full of small parcels neatly wrapped in brown paper. She'd gone to see her mam before she'd left but as Ellen had been asleep she hadn't disturbed her and Nurse O'Connor had promised she would tell Ellen of her visit when she woke.

Thankfully since that first incident she'd had little real trouble with Maggie and her friends. Oh, they still made cruel comments and jibes when they thought Miss Roberts wasn't around but they'd never been as openly hostile or threatening. She'd been aware that the supervisor had had them all in the office and had given them a strict warning that any further such behaviour would result in the extreme penalty of dismissal for neither Mr Davenport, Mr Turner nor herself would tolerate bullying.

This morning she tried to ignore the nudges and smirks of Maggie and Bertha as she passed.

'Oh, get 'er in a new 'at and scarf!' Bertha commented in a loud whisper to Maggie.

'Must 'ave found 'erself a feller cos she 'as ter give *them* all 'er wages, so I 'eard,' Maggie replied.

Bertha sniggered. 'Perhaps that Joe Ellis bought them for 'er.'

Maggie couldn't help but guffaw and jabbed her friend in the ribs. 'But what did she 'ave ter do fer 'em, that's what I want ter know?'

Jane had taken off her coat, hat and scarf and had hung them on the peg allocated to her. Suddenly she hated them both with their coarse laughter, crude remarks and constant innuendo.

'I didn't have to do *anything* for them because Joe didn't

buy them, I did!' she snapped, her cheeks flushed with anger.

Maggie's eyes narrowed. 'Yer can't 'ave! Yer don't 'ave any money. Yer're lyin'! Unless yer thieved 'em? But we always knew yer were a lyin', thievin' workhouse girl, Jane Shaw!' Her voice had risen but Jane faced her squarely.

'I'd be very careful of what you say, Maggie.'

'Are yer threatenin' me?' Maggie demanded, placing her hands on her broad hips. 'Are yer goin' ter slope off and snitch ter Miss Roberts then?'

'I'm not going to stand here arguing with the likes of you, Maggie. You can think what you like about me, I don't care. Why should I? At least *I* haven't got a reputation for being an ignorant, loud-mouthed bully.'

Maggie's face turned puce. 'Yer 'ard-faced little slummy!' she shouted.

Bertha had become wary and tugged at her friend's arm. 'Shurrup, Maggie! Leave 'er alone. *We'll* be the ones who come off worse. Remember what Miss Roberts said?'

Jane turned away, her anger fading. Her mam wouldn't want her to engage in a slanging match with the likes of Maggie Rosbottom.

'Come away! Leave 'er, Maggie, she's not worth us gettin' the push for,' Bertha urged, pulling at Maggie's arm, for a couple of other girls had drawn closer and were staring at them and she was afraid that might draw the attention of the supervisor; she knew her mam and da would kill her if she lost this job.

'You'll always be the "workhouse girl", Jane Shaw!' Maggie hissed venomously before walking away, demanding to know what everyone was gaping at.

Jane got started on a pile of dirty sheets, poking them vigorously into a large steaming copper boiler with the long tongs. Oh, why couldn't Maggie just leave her alone? Why did she always try to make her life more of a misery than it already was? What had she ever done to Maggie? She wished she could leave here but she knew that was impossible, she'd never get another job – and why *should* she let them drive her away? She was feeling so low at the moment because of her mam, she told herself. She'd just keep on trying to ignore Maggie and hope that one day she would indeed find another job, a better job, or that maybe Maggie might leave.

She worked in silence all morning, concentrating hard on her work and wishing it were time to go back to Brownlow Hill, but when she heard the bell sound for dinner she vowed that despite the cold, she'd go out into the yard for some air and stay out of Maggie's way.

She'd put on her coat when she saw Miss Roberts approaching. She hoped that this morning's incident hadn't been reported to her although judging by the supervisor's grave expression it seemed more than likely.

'Jane, could I have a word with you in the office, please?' Cynthia Roberts said.

Jane nodded and followed her, her heart sinking.

The supervisor closed the door behind her. 'Jane, I . . . I'm sorry but I have some bad news I'm afraid. Mrs Stanley – Matron – has sent word that . . . that your poor mother has . . . passed away.'

Jane stared at her in shocked silence for a few seconds. 'But . . . but I saw her before I left . . . She was . . . asleep, she . . .' And then grief claimed her and she broke down.

Cynthia Roberts sat her down in her own chair and tried as best she could to comfort her. The least Florence Stanley could have done was to have waited until the girl had returned and broken the terrible news to her herself or just sent word that Jane was required urgently at the workhouse! But no, she'd forced her to undertake this difficult task. It was typical of the way they did things in these institutions, she silently fumed; they had no consideration at all.

'Jane, you must of course go back now, is there . . . anyone, *anyone* at all you want to go with you?' she asked, flustered by the girl's distress.

Jane couldn't think straight. Oh, she'd known her mam was dying but . . . but she had expected to be with her, at her bedside, holding her hand and with . . . 'Aunty Ada! Please, can you find Aunty Ada?' she sobbed.

Miss Roberts looked mystified. 'Who is she, Jane?'

'Joe . . . Joe Ellis, it . . . it's his mam. She's . . . was Mam's friend.'

The supervisor handed Jane her handkerchief, still mystified. 'And this Joe Ellis?'

Jane dabbed at her swollen eyes and fought down a sob. 'He's a delivery boy . . . here,' she managed to get out.

The older woman inwardly breathed a sigh of relief. 'Sit there, Jane. We'll find him, don't worry. We'll find them both,' she promised.

The dinner break was over but Jane still sat in the little office, tears sliding down her cheeks and trembling with shock, despite Cynthia Roberts having wrapped a blanket around her and urged her to try to sip the strong sweet tea that had been brought. They hadn't been able to locate Joe Ellis, he was out on his rounds, but they'd gone through the records in the main office and found his address and the junior had been sent with a note to Mrs Ellis. All she could do was wait until the woman arrived. She'd instructed Mrs Lafferty, her most senior operative, to make sure that work progressed as normal and she was very relieved when Ada, signs of shock and grief evident on her face, at last appeared.

'Oh, Mrs Ellis, thank goodness! Poor Jane, she's terribly upset. They sent word . . . and she's to go back.'

Ada nodded wordlessly. She too had had a note from Matron herself and, like Jane, felt stunned by the shock: she'd not expected Ellen to go so soon. Gently removing the blanket she drew Jane to her feet and put her arm around her. 'Come on, Jane, luv, we'll go back together.'

'She will of course be allowed time off, Mrs Ellis, and not only for the . . . funeral. I myself will speak to Mr Davenport and explain the situation and hopefully he will agree to let Jane have the remaining two days of this week off. Without pay of course.'

'Thank you, miss,' Ada replied.

'I'll see if she had a hat or anything else . . .' Miss Roberts said a little distractedly. Of course there had been bereavements amongst her staff before but nothing quite as distressing as this for she'd never been as personally involved and Jane was very young.

'There's no need, miss, but thank you. If there is anything, our Joe can bring it home to me. I think it best if I get her back now. Her brother's up there in Brownlow Hill, you see, and he's younger than her.'

Cynthia Roberts watched them leave, wondering how both

Jane and her brother would cope in the days to come. But at least Mrs Ellis seemed to care for the girl, she thought. She wasn't entirely alone in the world.

Ellen was buried two days later in a deserted and rather overgrown corner of a nearby graveyard. Ada, accompanied by Emily who had begged an hour off work, had brought the small wreath she'd managed to buy with the halfpennies, farthings and occasional penny she'd collected from the neighbours and she'd been gratified that so many had given freely of what they had for poor Ellen. A black dress and shawl had been provided for Jane and a black armband for Alfie. Jane had been very pale, her eyes red and swollen, and as the coffin had been lowered into the ground she had clutched Ada's hand tightly and sobbed. Alfie too had been pale but tight-lipped although Emily later swore to her mother that she'd seen tears in his eyes.

When the brief service was over Ada had turned to Matron, determination in her eyes although her heart was heavy. 'Ma'am, can I take these two home with me, please, for a few hours? I . . . I can't bear to think of them being . . . left to themselves.' There would be no traditional 'funeral tea', she knew that, and she also knew that the brother and sister would be separated once back in the workhouse.

Matron had frowned. 'This is very irregular, Mrs Ellis.'

'I'm aware of that, ma'am, but for pity's sake can't the rules be bent – just this once? They have no one else now and they're just children!' she'd pleaded.

Very reluctantly Matron had agreed but stipulated that they must both be back by six o'clock and so the little group had returned to Gill Street, Alfie for the first time in four years.

He'd looked eagerly down the street hoping to see Richie and Jimmy but there was no sign of them and he was sorely disappointed. It had been a terrible day so far. He'd known his mam was dying but she'd seemed a bit better the last time he'd visited her. He'd hated that bare, white-tiled ward that smelled of sickness and disinfectant and the visiting had been a chore, something he hadn't looked forward to despite the break from work. He'd never been able to find anything to say to his mam, except to ask her how she was feeling and answer any questions she'd asked. Deep down he was more angry with her than ever for how they'd ended up, because she'd allowed the workhouse to hasten her own death and left him an orphan. Still, he'd be glad to be back in Gill Street for a few hours and Aunty Ada's cooking was better than what he was usually served.

Jane had returned to work on the Monday morning, still wearing the black dress and shawl, and she received sympathetic glances from all her fellow workers, even Bertha Higgins, although Maggie had studiously ignored her. Miss Roberts greeted her cordially and asked how she was feeling.

'Sort of . . . numb and dazed, miss,' Jane answered truthfully. 'It's so hard to realise that she's really . . . gone. Twice I've got to the door of the infirmary before I've remembered.'

'It takes time, Jane, I know, but it does get less painful, believe me. After my mother died I thought I would never get used to living in the house alone, but I have. Now, before you start work would you take these dockets to the office for a final check, please?'

Jane took the paperwork from her and made her way to the much larger general office where she handed them in to the clerk. She was on her way back down the staircase when she encountered Mr Davenport. She'd only ever caught a glimpse of the proprietor before this and she stood respectfully to one side to let him pass. He looked quite forbidding in his expensive dark suit, heavy overcoat and dark grey trilby hat but she remembered her manners and managed to murmur, 'Good morning, sir,' as he drew level with her. To her astonishment he stopped.

'And you are?' he asked.

She was surprised that his tone wasn't sharp or stern but more . . . curious. 'Jane Shaw, sir. I . . . I work in the laundry room. Miss Roberts is my supervisor,' she replied timidly, not daring to look up at him.

Her plain black dress made her skin look almost ethereal, he thought, and for the first time he noticed that she was a very attractive young girl with an abundance of dark auburn hair and unusual, amber-coloured eyes. 'Ah, yes. Miss Roberts spoke to me about you. You have recently been bereaved, I understand,' he said kindly.

She nodded, not knowing whether to speak or not. 'My . . . my mother, sir.'

He nodded gravely. 'You have my deepest condolences.'

'Thank you, sir,' she managed but tears had filled her eyes.

'I mustn't detain you any longer. Good morning, Miss Shaw,' he said quietly before moving past. He'd noted her tears and thought how vulnerable she looked. She was indeed very young to have suffered such a loss. He knew he would miss his own indomitable mother greatly when her time came.

But, he thought wryly, since he was still in his thirties that wouldn't be for a very long time, for she was remarkably fit for her age and ran the household with rigid discipline, his father having died many years ago.

Jane hurried on, dismissing the meeting from her mind as thoughts of the long weary days ahead filled her head.

Chapter Nine

1927

It Hardly Seemed possible that Mam had been dead a year, Jane thought as she made her way to Ada's house after work that December evening. She still missed her mother but her feelings of loss and grief were not as acute as they'd been in the first months after Ellen's death. She smiled sadly to herself as she walked down Gill Street, for she had some good news to tell Ada and Emily tonight.

In January Ada had sought an interview with Matron and had requested that on three evenings a week Jane be allowed to come for supper for she had turned fifteen; Ada hadn't included Alfie knowing that would be a request too far. Matron had been dubious at first but Ada had pressed the point that Jane was very trustworthy and would not abuse the concession. So Matron had taken the matter to the Board of Guardians and they had eventually agreed, which meant Jane spent three pleasant evenings a week with Ada and her family. She and Emily had had the kind of friendship that could be picked up easily and they had become much closer; Joe sometimes waited at the gates of the laundry for her so they could walk to Ada's together, although tonight there had been no sign of him. She'd noticed that over the last few months Joe didn't seem very happy at his work, not the way he once was, but she hadn't questioned him.

'Oh, it's really cold out there now, Aunty Ada,' she announced, holding her hands out to the warmth of the fire in the range.

'They're saying we'll have snow for Christmas this year and I wouldn't be a bit surprised,' Ada replied, frowning as she stirred the pan of thick oxtail soup.

'Isn't Joe home yet?' Jane asked, for both Emily and Danny – who had a job after school selling small bundles of kindling known as 'chips' – were in and Sonny was engrossed in sorting his very small collection of marbles, most of which he'd won from his mates and so were highly prized.

'No, nor is his da. Our Joe was going off to meet Fred, said they had an "appointment", would you believe? They're up to something, you mark my words. I wasn't born yesterday.'

Jane looked enquiringly at Emily, who just shrugged and raised her eyes to the ceiling. Emily was growing into a pretty girl; she'd had her hair cut into a bob with a heavy fringe, which suited her and drew attention to her large dark eyes. She still had on the overall she wore for work but out of it she looked very different, Jane knew. Both girls were developing a keen interest in fashion although neither had much money to spend on themselves – Jane almost nothing at all.

'Well, I told them we weren't going to wait for them, so get up to the table all of you,' Ada instructed.

'I hope they're back before I have to go; I've got some good news,' Jane remarked. 'Lights out' was still eight o'clock for everyone in the workhouse.

'What's that, luv?' Ada queried as she ladled the soup into the bowls, thinking it was high time the girl had something good in her life.

'Miss Roberts called me into the office before I left and told me I've been promoted,' Jane announced, smiling at Emily.

'Oh, that's great, Jane! Promoted to what?' Emily asked, her eyes full of delight for her friend.

'To the despatch room. I'm to start to learn to be a "checker" on Monday. From what she said you have to check each item against the dockets and lists to make sure everyone gets their own laundry back and that nothing is missing.'

'That will be much better than heaving all that wet linen around all day,' Emily agreed.

Jane nodded. 'She said that she put me forward when she heard there was a vacancy because I work hard and my reading and maths are better than anyone else's.'

'And you deserve it, Jane. I know for a fact that that Maggie Rosbottom is as thick as a plank; you'll be well away from that lot,' Emily remarked cuttingly.

'Will you get paid more? It seems to be a more responsible job,' Ada enquired.

Jane nodded. 'Quite a few shillings more but . . .'

'Oh, you won't have to give *them* more, will you?' Emily demanded, thinking it very unfair if Jane were forced to contribute more for her keep.

'I don't know. I'll ask Matron tomorrow evening but I hope not. I . . . I'd really like to have a bit more money to buy some decent clothes,' Jane confided.

'And seeing as they don't have to give you supper on the evenings you come here I should think they'd have a flaming cheek asking you to cough up more. You just remind her of that, Jane,' Ada said grimly before glaring at her youngest son. 'Sonny Ellis, will you stop messing about with those marbles and eat your meal before it goes stone cold or I'll confiscate the damned things!'

'What's "confiscate" mean, Mam?' Sonny asked.

'I'll take them off you and keep them myself,' his mother warned.

The marbles were quickly pocketed and the lad concentrated on his meal.

Emily and Jane cleared the dishes and washed them while discussing if Jane would be able to save enough to buy something to wear for Christmas – providing she were allowed to keep more of her wages – and if Emily would have saved up enough to buy a nice jacket for the spring. Danny had gone out to see one of his mates and Sonny was again engrossed in his marbles while Ada dozed in the chair.

It was after seven when Joe and his father at last appeared, cold and hungry. Joe, however, was looking very pleased with himself, Jane thought.

'Where've you been until this hour?' Ada demanded, getting to her feet. 'The pair of you look frozen stiff and half-starved.'

'It *is* freezing and I'm certainly starving, luv,' Fred replied, taking off his cap and unwinding the muffler from around his neck. Neither of them possessed an overcoat and their jackets provided little protection against the bitter cold.

'We've been down to the Pier Head, Mam. I waited at the dock gate for Da and we . . . we went together to the Pool,' Joe announced.

Ada turned and stared hard at her eldest son. 'You've been *where*?' she demanded.

'You heard, luv. Now, just give us time to eat and then we'll explain everything,' Fred promised, sitting down and warming his hands on the sides of the bowl. He wasn't looking forward to telling his wife their news.

'I knew you were up to something, Joe Ellis! I just *knew* it!' Ada cried, glaring at her son as she put their dinner on the table.

Jane looked curiously at Joe, who shrugged, although he couldn't hide the excitement in his eyes. 'I've got something to tell you, too, Joe. I'm being promoted to a checker in the despatch room starting on Monday. It's a much better job than the one I've got now.'

'That's great, Jane. I'm really glad for you,' Joe replied, smiling. She deserved a bit of good luck and he was sorry that he wouldn't be here to wait for her after work next Monday to find out how she'd got on in the new job.

Emily frowned at her brother. 'Hurry up and eat or Jane will have to leave before you've had time to tell us whatever it is you've been up to,' she instructed.

'Well, are you going to tell me why the pair of you have been down to the Pool?' Ada demanded when they'd finished.

Joe looked at his father, who nodded his encouragement. 'Mam, I've been wanting to get a better job for ages – haven't I, Da?' Joe started.

'Aye, he has,' Fred agreed.

'And what's wrong with the job you've got? It's steady and the pay isn't too bad,' Ada interrupted.

'But it's not very interesting, Mam, and the way things are I expect I'll always have to just collect and deliver parcels,' Joe replied firmly.

'They might promote you too, like they've done Jane. You might get to drive the van one day.' Ada couldn't see why Joe wanted to leave the Empire Laundry.

Joe shook his head, becoming frustrated. 'But I'll still be *here*, Mam, and I want more out of life, to see a bit of the world. For months now I've been trying to get a job at sea but with no luck. But tonight it was different . . . I've signed on with Canadian Pacific.'

Both Jane and Emily were so surprised that they just stared at Joe.

'As what?' Ada demanded. She wasn't at all happy about this.

'A porter in the kitchens but I hope that in time I might get to be a waiter or a steward, then I'll get tips as well as a wage.' Joe looked a little abashed at explaining his ambitions.

'A skivvy! That's what you'll be, lad. Fetching and carrying all day and for how much?' Ada demanded.

Joe shrugged. 'A bit more than I earn now but I'll get to see Halifax, Montreal and Quebec and lots of other places, Mam.'

Ada shook her head as she glared at Fred. 'What you'll get to see, Joe Ellis, is the dockside, that's if you get any time off at all. And why didn't you tell me, Fred, that he wanted to go to sea?'

'Because I knew this was how you'd carry on, Ada. He's

96

waited for over a year; this isn't just a whim. I can't say I'm too delighted either but he's young so he might as well get it out of his system now. And you never know, he could end up with a good job.'

Ada shook her head, thinking Joe wasn't old enough for what was often a hard and hazardous life. And what if he hated it? He couldn't expect to get his old job back; it would quickly be filled.

'So, what ship is it and when do you go?' Emily asked, thinking it sounded exciting to visit these foreign places.

'It's the *Empress of Scotland* and we sail on Monday morning. There're loads of things I've got to do before that,' Joe replied, relieved that at least his sister seemed pleased for him.

Ada was perturbed. 'That soon! When will you tell them at the laundry?'

'Tomorrow, then I've got to get my Discharge Book and some sort of uniform jackets from Greenberg's. Don't worry, Mam, I've been saving up so I've got the money to pay for them,' Joe informed her. He couldn't stop a broad grin spreading over his face. Now that he'd finally got a ship he felt that life was definitely taking a turn for the better.

Ada shook her head. 'They don't even provide them for you? What kind of a company is that?'

'It's a big one, Ada. They carry a lot of passengers, nearly all emigrants, and some cargo. And as far as I know none of the shipping lines provide uniforms,' Fred informed her.

She didn't reply, still trying to digest the news that on Monday her eldest son would be setting sail across thousands of miles of ocean in winter. Oh, she'd seen those ships – 'the White Empresses' as they were known – at the Landing Stage and they *were* big. There were at least five of them, she thought, and they were all painted white except for the funnels, which were a sort of mustard-yellow colour.

'How long will you be away for, Joe?' Jane asked. She was pleased for him because it was obviously something he really wanted to do but she would miss him.

'Just over two weeks, Jane, so it's not *that* long,' he informed them all.

'Joe, I've heard they have great comics over there, will you bring me some?' Sonny pleaded. 'My mates will be dead envious,' he added.

'Oh, trust you, Sonny Ellis, to think of something like that!' Ada admonished him.

Joe laughed. 'I'll try, Sonny, promise.'

Ada sighed heavily. 'Well, lad, you've signed on now so you'd better make the most of it but I can't say I'm happy about it.'

Reluctantly Jane got up. She wanted to stay and ask Joe more about his new job but time was getting short. 'I'll have to be getting back now or I'll be late, but good luck, Joe.'

Joe too got to his feet. 'Seeing as I won't be here next time you come for supper, I'll walk back with you, Jane,' he offered.

Ada nodded her approval: she was never happy about Jane walking back alone in the dark for this was a rough neighbourhood and usually either Joe or Fred walked her back.

'I'll see you all next week,' Jane promised as she left.

They both shivered as they went out into the street for a heavy frost had settled, turning the pavement white. Where shafts of moonlight penetrated between the houses the roadway glittered icily.

'You'd better hang on to me, Jane, in case you slip,' Joe instructed, turning the collar of his jacket up.

'Do you think you'll really like it, Joe? Being at sea?' Jane asked as she clung tightly to his arm.

'I think it will be great. I mean I know I'll have to work hard but I'm prepared for that and I really do want to see places other than Liverpool,' Joe replied firmly.

Jane could understand that, although travelling was something she had never thought about for herself. 'Will the weather be bad, do you think? On the way across, I mean?'

'I suppose there's a good chance it will be, it's winter after all, but I'll be all right,' he replied confidently. 'And I'll be back before Christmas, although I might have to sail again and be at sea for the holiday,' he added.

'Oh, that will be a shame, Joe. I'll . . . We'll all miss you.' She knew Ada had already obtained permission for herself and Alfie to spend Christmas afternoon with them in Gill Street.

He looked down at her and smiled. The moonlight and the glow from the street lamp illuminated her face and she really did look disappointed, he thought, and . . . and pretty too. He felt an unfamiliar stirring of regret. 'I'll miss you, Jane, I really will. I'd have liked to have waited for you on Monday to see how you've got on.'

She smiled at him. 'I'll be able to tell you all about it when you get back.'

He nodded. 'I'll try and bring you something. A sort of souvenir.'

'Oh, Joe, that's really kind of you but you won't have much money. They might not pay you until the end of the trip and you promised to bring comics for Sonny, don't forget.'

'As I told Mam, Jane, I've managed to save up a bit and even after I've paid for the uniforms I'm sure to have *something* over and surely I'll be able to get a sub on my wages.'

Again Jane smiled at his generosity. 'Buy something for your mam then, Joe. I know she'll worry about you.'

Joe sighed. 'She's always worrying about us all – you included.'

'I don't know what I'd have done without her this past year, and that's the truth.'

Joe nodded and tentatively patted her cold hand. She'd had so much to contend with and he was glad his mam had sort of taken her under her wing and that she now had a better job. She deserved it.

They'd reached the gates of the workhouse and Joe rang the bell for the porter.

Jane smiled up at him. 'Good luck, Joe. I wish I could go down to the Pier Head to see you off on Monday but . . . but I'll be thinking of you. Come home safely.'

Impulsively he bent and kissed her on the cheek. 'I will, Jane. Goodbye.' Feeling a little embarrassed he turned away as the porter appeared with his bunch of keys.

Jane stared after him fondly. She hoped he'd like the job and she prayed he would have cold but calm weather like this for the whole trip. And she *would* miss him, she thought as she touched her cheek. That was the first time a boy had kissed her, and she was, she thought, more than happy it had been Joe Ellis.

Chapter Ten

1929

JANE'S FACE LIT UP as she caught sight of Joe waiting across the road for her when she'd finished work. It was a beautiful warm sunny September evening and she'd known his ship was due to dock early that morning but she hadn't expected him to come to meet her – she'd thought to see him for supper. 'Joe, what a lovely surprise! Was it a good trip?' she greeted him, her face one big smile.

He grinned at her. 'It wasn't bad. Busy of course but easier on the return trip and we docked earlier than expected owing to the tide, so I thought I'd come and walk you back. You're looking well, Jane,' Joe replied as he tucked her hand through his arm.

'So are you.' He seemed to have grown taller, Jane thought, and he looked very healthy.

'Mam told me not to dawdle as she's got something she

wants to discuss after we've eaten,' he informed her. She *did* look well, he thought, in her light blue cotton jacket over the plain navy dress she wore for work with a small navy hat covering her hair, which she now wore short like Emily's. He noted that on the lapel of her jacket she wore the little brooch shaped as a maple leaf that he'd bought her on his very first trip. She'd done well for herself at the Empire Laundry for in the two years since she'd been promoted she had worked her way up to the position of a deputy supervisor in the despatch office. His mam reckoned she was probably well liked for her quiet efficiency and the fact that she would never be overbearing or pushy to those she managed. Jane herself had told him she seldom came into contact with Maggie and Bertha and their cronies now. He just wished his career had progressed as well, he thought, but at least he was now a waiter: in third class of course, which ruled out tips since the passengers he served were all emigrants with no money to spare. But his aim also was to work his way up, hopefully to first class. He worked hard and the hours were long but he didn't mind that; the food was good and plentiful and he enjoyed the life at sea and the great camaraderie amongst the crew. Of course, despite his optimism, on his first trip three days out the weather had changed and he'd been so seasick he'd thought he was dying. But he'd eventually found his sea legs and now the often rough conditions didn't bother him too much, except to cause difficulties in serving meals. Even that had its compensations – fewer passengers actually made it to the dining room – but he didn't envy the poor stewards and stewardesses who had to clean up after them in rough weather. His mam had been right, though, he mused: in the two years he'd been away he hadn't seen much of the great cities of Montreal and Quebec apart from the docksides. He had seen more of Halifax, Nova Scotia, where they docked during the winter months when it was so cold that the St Lawrence River froze solid and became impassable to shipping. Until he'd experienced the Canadian winter he'd never realised what *real* cold was like.

Jane's voice broke into his reverie. 'Did you know that Emily's got an "admirer"?'

He looked at her quizzically for this was news to him. 'Anyone I know? And more to the point, does Mam know?' he asked, thinking this new admirer might be what his mam wanted to discuss. Emily was seventeen and his mother might think she was a bit young for a romance. Then again Jane was the same age and he was very fond of her but somehow that seemed . . . different. He'd known Jane all his life.

'Of course your mam knows and she quite likes him – she knows the family too,' she informed him. 'It's Georgie Taverner from Clarence Street.'

Joe grinned ruefully. 'I remember him from school; he was always a bit of a swot. We all used to torment the life out of him about it.'

'Well, being a swot paid off. He's a clerk with an insurance company in the Liver Buildings now. He goes to work in a suit and wears a hat – not a cap – and Emily's so proud of him. He's taking her to see *Bulldog Drummond* on Saturday evening. Ronald Colman's in it, you know.'

Joe looked thoughtful. He'd been paid off and so had money in his pocket but it was no use him asking Jane to go anywhere, they still had that damned stupid rule in that place of sending everyone to bed at eight o'clock. 'I have to say he's done all right for himself then. How's your Alfie?' he asked to change the subject.

Jane frowned. 'I really don't know, Joe, and it worries and upsets me. You see, I promised Mam I'd look after him. I've tried time and again to see him regularly but when I go and ask they either can't find him or he just doesn't appear. He . . . he seems to have grown away from me, but I still care about him and want what's best for him.' She paused, wondering if she should confide more in Joe. 'I . . . I did see him a few weeks ago and then it really hit me how . . . how much he's changed. I know he's growing up but it's . . . it's as though he blames Mam for us being forced to go into Brownlow Hill and he *hates* it. He even hinted that one day he might just up and leave but I tried to persuade him not to. He just laughed and told me to mind my own business.'

'That wasn't a very kind thing to say!' Joe retorted. 'You're his sister, he must realise you care about him.'

Jane bit her lip. 'I don't think he really meant it and he's been working with Mr Phillips now for nearly a year so I suppose he's doing all right – he'll have a trade eventually – but I wish I could see more of him, try to help him. I do worry about him and his future.' Alfie had been apprenticed to a cobbler when he'd turned fourteen and went out each day to work, as she did. She sighed heavily. 'He's probably too tired when he gets back after work to be bothered with me.' Her brother's indifference towards her troubled her for she often thought about the promise she'd made to her mother.

Joe shook his head; he couldn't see that Alfie Shaw would be so exhausted every night he couldn't spare a few minutes for his sister. 'I suppose he is. Well, we'd best get a move on.

You know what Mam's like when she's got something on her mind,' he added.

From his office window on the third floor, which looked out over Mount Vernon Street, James Davenport watched his workers leave. His gaze settled on Jane Shaw and the young man walking with her. He knew she was still sometimes referred to by some as 'the workhouse girl' even though she was now a deputy supervisor, but he'd come to know her better since she'd worked in despatch. She seemed to have grown more attractive in that time, blossoming, he thought, into a quiet beauty: she had something about her of one of those pre-Raphaelite paintings he rather liked. Of course she was years younger than he was, he being thirty-seven and a bachelor, but he did admire her. He assumed, from his limited knowledge of the poor working classes, that she'd had a very hard life having ended up in Brownlow Hill and having later lost her mother. But she'd turned into an unassuming, intelligent and pleasantly mannered girl who had worked hard to attain her position. He wondered who the lad was. She knew him well enough to be seen walking arm in arm with him so he was obviously a close friend; perhaps they were even walking out. He sighed as he turned away, checking the time on his heavy gold watch before returning it to his waistcoat pocket. He'd never found the time to socialise even when he'd been younger for improving, expanding and modernising the business he had inherited on his father's sudden demise had always been paramount in his life. He gathered the few papers that lay on his desk and placed them in a drawer, locking it and leaving the desk top clear and tidy for he was meticulous in everything he did. He'd better leave now himself, he thought, for his mother had instructed him to be home at six thirty prompt as she had invited the archdeacon, his wife and daughter for dinner at seven and he would need to change. He shook his head ruefully, aware that she was trying her hand at matchmaking – again – but he found Cecily Breaton insipid and her parents pleasant but a little boring. But duty called, he told himself, and as ever he would endeavour to be polite and please his mother.

'So, what's on your mind, Mam? What's to be "discussed"?' Joe asked when they'd finished supper.

Ada nodded in Emily's direction and Joe turned to her expectantly. 'For ages now she's been on at me to ask Jane to come and live with us, haven't you, Emily?'

'I have. It just seems the *right* thing to do. She can't stay in that place forever and you're away so much now, Joe, that with a bit of moving the furniture around Jane and me could share a room,' Emily announced.

Ada nodded her agreement. Because there were only two bedrooms, when they'd all been at home, she, Emily and Sonny had shared one and Fred had shared the other with his two older sons. It had been a far from ideal situation and now Sonny was really too old to be sharing with herself and his sister and Joe was away most of the time so she'd decided very reluctantly that she would turn her precious little parlour into a bedroom for herself and Fred. Emily could share with Jane, and the boys would share the other room. After all, as Emily had pointed out, the boys would only be a bit cramped for the couple of days Joe was home. 'I've also heard a rumour that in a couple of years they're going to close down all the workhouses, so it does make sense for you to come here, Jane, luv,' Ada stated.

'It's about time they did away with them. I mean we're not living in the dark ages now and people resent all the rules and regulations they lay down,' Fred added, although he'd not heard this rumour.

'But what'll happen to the likes of Alfie and all the other kids who are even younger?' Joe asked.

Ada shrugged. 'They've thought of that. They'll provide something better for them, something less like an institution. "Cottage Homes" they're going to call them, so I heard.' Ada sniffed. 'Still an orphanage but with a fancy name and I suppose they'll have to make some kind of provision to help the adults but as to what that will be is anyone's guess.'

'It's really very good of you, Aunty Ada, to let me come to live here,' Jane cut in, surprised by Ada's decision and thoroughly delighted at the thought of leaving Brownlow Hill at last, although she wondered what would happen to her brother. Would he be moved into one of these Cottage Homes until he could provide for himself? She hoped so for there just wasn't room for him in Ada's house too. 'And of course I'll pay my own way, like I do now,' she added.

Ada smiled at her. 'But I won't take as much off you, luv, as they do. You can give me the same as our Emily does and clothe yourself. I think that's fair. And I'll feel easier in my mind knowing you've got a proper home again. I'd take Alfie too if I had the room,' she added, although she hadn't given the matter of his welfare a great deal of thought. In her opinion that Master Ribchester seemed far better able to keep Alfie Shaw out of trouble, and maybe it *was* just a rumour about the workhouses being closed down, for there was still plenty of poverty in the city. 'So, I suppose I'll have to go and see Matron again but I can't see her objecting,' she continued. 'You'll be eighteen in a couple of months, Jane, and she knows you'll be coming to a decent home and that we'll be responsible for you until you come of age.'

Jane smiled at her. 'I'll tell her you will be coming to see her yourself but that you want me to come to live here.'

'So, when will you move in?' Emily asked, feeling delighted that she would have Jane to chat with every night now. It would be like having a sister but better because she and Jane were the same age and had always been friends and quite often sisters didn't get on well at all.

'As soon as I can but I think I'd better leave it until Joe goes back,' Jane replied.

Joe looked thoughtful. 'I don't mind sharing with the other two for a couple of nights, Jane. Perhaps . . . perhaps we could go to see *Bulldog Drummond* as well on Saturday? If you'd already moved in you wouldn't have to get back to that place by eight.'

'You could come with Georgie and me, make it a foursome,' Emily enthused happily. 'He won't mind and it will be such a treat for you, Jane, won't it?'

Jane's cheeks flushed and her eyes were bright with excitement as she thought of her life without the restrictions she'd become so used to. She'd never seen a moving picture before – and there were so many other things girls of her age did that she'd be able to do too. 'Oh, Joe, it would be really great!'

Emily too beamed at him, already planning what both she and Jane would wear for such a special occasion – she'd be more than happy to lend her friend something if needs be.

'You'd better make sure Matron will give her consent for you to leave so soon, Jane,' Ada advised. 'There might be formalities – paperwork and the like.'

'Oh, Mam! Don't go putting the damper on things. I'm sure she won't object,' Emily cried, not wanting anything to spoil what was looking to be a great night out. 'After all it's one less she'll have to worry about – if she does worry, that is.'

'I'm just pointing it out, Emily, that's all,' Ada replied, though she too was pleased at the prospect of Joe taking Jane on her first 'proper' evening out. She'd be quite content too if this was the start of a closer relationship between them, she reflected, feeling quietly satisfied at the way things seemed to be turning out. After all, she already viewed Jane as another daughter. It would be perfect if she and Joe could find a way to make each other happy in the future.

Jane was so buoyed up by excitement that she felt as if she was walking on air as she made her way to Matron's office. She'd left Ada's early to give herself time for this important interview and Joe had walked back with her. She could hardly believe that after seven years she was finally to leave here and live a 'normal' life again, and after years of sharing a dormitory with dozens of girls she'd love sharing a room with just Emily. She didn't want to get her hopes of being able to leave and be installed in Gill Street by Saturday up too high, after all that was only four days away, but she really did want to go to the cinema with Joe and Emily and Emily's young man. And the film sounded so exciting.

Matron could see she was happy about something as she

ushered her in. 'Ah, Jane, I was going to send for you when you arrived back.' Then she frowned. 'Mr Ribchester has just returned to his office.'

Jane's heart sank at the mention of the master. 'Oh, Matron, is Alfie in trouble?'

'I'm afraid so, Jane. It appears that he has absconded. Mr Phillips came to see the master this evening to report that Alfred has not turned up for work for the past two days but it also appears that he has not returned here this evening.'

Jane looked perturbed. 'But, Matron, surely . . . surely Alfie was here last night?'

Matron nodded. 'The Master assures me he was here but this morning he must have taken his few clothes and . . . gone.'

'What will happen now, Matron? Will the police be told? Will they look for him?' Jane asked, wondering frantically where Alfie could be. What would he do for food and shelter? He'd only have a few pence from his meagre wage, which wouldn't last long. Oh, she'd known he'd never accepted life here the way she had and he had hinted he would run away. She'd promised her mam she'd look out for him and now she had no idea where he was.

'Of course they'll be notified, Jane, but in the meantime we can only hope he comes to his senses and returns. Now, was there something else you wished to see me about?'

All the elation she'd felt when she entered this room had drained away. She shook her head. 'Only to say that Mrs Ellis will be coming to see you in the morning, Matron, if that's convenient.'

Matron nodded. 'Under the circumstances I think it most

fortuitous, Jane. Perhaps she will have heard something concerning his whereabouts.'

Jane left the office with a heavy heart. She wondered if Ada *would* have heard anything. Probably not. She told herself Alfie would be all right but he was still so young. She should have been able to look after him like she'd promised – she couldn't help feeling she'd let her mam down badly. All she could do was pray he'd be brought back safe and sound, with no real harm done. Was that too much to hope for?

Chapter Eleven

———◆———

I T WAS SUCH A shame for poor Jane, Ada thought as she returned home after her visit to Matron next morning. The girl had been thrilled that she would at last be leaving the workhouse and was so excited about going out on Saturday night. Trust that little hooligan Alfie to run off and ruin everything for now she knew Jane would be taken over by worry about her wayward brother.

After Matron had informed her of his latest escapade she had confided to the woman that he'd always been difficult but they'd put it down to pure mischief which they'd hoped he'd grow out of. Even when poor Ellen was desperately trying to keep the home and family together despite her grief, Alfie had frequently missed school and spent his time running the streets with two of the local reprobates whom he called his mates. Well, she'd answered Matron truthfully that she couldn't throw any light on his whereabouts but now she knew exactly who to ask about him; the lad was predictable, if nothing else.

At least Matron had agreed that it would be perfectly acceptable for Jane to come and live with them; in fact she'd seemed quite relieved Ada had thought, and such formalities as there were could easily be completed before Saturday. It had been agreed that Jane would leave Brownlow Hill on Friday after supper so they'd start to move the beds and things around this evening when Fred and Danny would be in to give Joe a hand.

Before going home she would go down the street and see either Mrs Corrin or Mrs Cobham. She decided to approach Maud Cobham first for she at least had had the decency to contribute something towards the flowers for Ellen's funeral.

As she drew nearer the end of the street she could see that there would be no need to knock for Maud Cobham was standing on her front step gossiping with another neighbour.

'Could I have a bit of a private word, Maud?' she asked, looking pointedly at the other woman, who shrugged and disappeared into her own house.

'What's the big occasion then, Ada?' Maud demanded tartly, folding her arms over her ample bosom. Ada Ellis seldom made an effort to speak to her and she had a feeling her visit wasn't good news.

'Have you seen or heard anything of Alfie Shaw lately?' Ada asked bluntly. There was no point beating about the bush with the likes of Maud.

'Can't say I 'ave. Why?' Maud was equally blunt.

'Because he's run off from Brownlow Hill and he hasn't turned up for work for the past two days.'

'So? What's that got ter do with me?' Maud demanded.

Ada thought she detected something furtive about the other

woman's manner, the way that, despite her tough words, she wouldn't quite meet her eyes. 'I thought, seeing as how your Jimmy used to be good mates with him, that he might have said something about Alfie or know where he is.'

The woman shrugged. 'Our Jimmy 'asn't seen Alfie Shaw fer years an' neither 'ave I.'

'Well, the coppers are looking for Alfie, the matron up there told me, so if—'

Maud suddenly thrust her face towards Ada's, her expression quite altered. 'Don't you go sendin' the scuffers ter my door, Ada Ellis! Whatever Alfie Shaw's been up to 'as got nothin' ter do with me nor our Jimmy! And I can't see what it's got ter do with you either cum ter that!'

Ada glared back at her. 'I promised his poor mam, God rest her, that I'd do my best to keep an eye on both her kids. Jane is coming to live with us now and she's worried sick about her brother – as any decent soul would be. As I am myself. He's only fifteen,' she snapped.

'Old enough ter take care of hisself then! Now clear off, I've things ter do.' Maud turned abruptly and went inside, closing the door firmly.

'Well, housework's not one of them judging by the state of your steps and windows!' Ada said in a loud voice, knowing Maud would be listening behind the door. She hadn't really expected to get much information out of the woman and she hadn't been disappointed.

Alfie shrank back against the wall as he heard the faint scuffling sound. He'd been grateful when Jimmy and Richie had found this place for him even though it didn't amount to much. It was a hayloft above the small backstreet stable where the horse that pulled the milk cart was kept. A room to live in was very hard come by in this area, families were crowded in on top of each other and, even if he'd had the money to pay rent, questions would have been asked about him. At least it was fairly dry and clean here and although he'd heard the sounds of the milkman coming and going in the stable beneath no one had ventured up here until now. He could hear someone below and though he kept quiet, the scuffling persisted. It sounded like someone was coming up into the hayloft but he didn't dare light the bit of a candle he had in case it attracted attention. He held his breath, praying he wouldn't be discovered.

'Alfie! Alfie, are yer still there?' someone hissed in a loud whisper.

Alfie breathed a sigh of relief. 'God, Jimmy, you gave me a fright! I thought it was the milk feller or the scuffers.'

Jimmy grinned at him as he hauled himself into the loft and then Richie's head appeared at the top of the ladder. 'We've brought yer a few bits ter eat,' he announced, placing half a loaf, a lump of cheese and a couple of apples, wrapped in a piece of cloth, down on the straw beside Alfie.

'Thanks, I'm starving,' Alfie muttered, tearing off a piece of the bread. They'd planned all this between them for months for he'd been able to meet them for a few minutes most days after he'd finished at the cobbler's shop. He'd been determined that he wasn't staying in the workhouse for much longer and his mates' horror at the rigid, disciplined routine of his life had only reinforced his determination to escape it. He'd felt so humiliated by their appalled disbelief that he had to be in bed by eight o'clock each night!

'Yer're fifteen, lad, not a bloody baby!' Richie had exclaimed.

'And I've no intention of spending my life mending sweaty old boots and shoes for a pittance either,' Alfie had informed them and so they'd started to look around for somewhere for him to stay and when they'd at last found this place the final plans had been made.

'Me mam said that Ada Ellis was asking 'ad I seen yer terday,' Jimmy informed Alfie, picking his teeth with a piece of straw.

'She didn't say anything, did she?' Alfie asked, looking alarmed.

'Course not. Sent 'er off with a flea in 'er ear, but she said your Jane is goin' ter live with them. Oh, and the scuffers are lookin' for yer,' he added as an afterthought.

Alfie nodded. He'd known the master would have alerted the police by now.

'But they'll not find yer 'ere,' Richie added.

'I'll have to just lie low until they get fed up looking, which probably won't be long because they really don't care about anyone from the workhouse. Then I can start to go out.'

'What'll yer do then?' Jimmy enquired. Neither he nor Richie worked if they could help it but spent their time indulging in various illegal activities that usually provided them with a bit of cash to spend on cigarettes and the cinema.

'Same as you two,' Alfie replied, taking a bite of an apple, but then he grinned. 'There're plenty of rich pickings down on the Landing Stage. There're always crowds of people waiting to board ferries or liners.'

Richie looked doubtful. 'Aye, and there're always plenty of porters, clerks and scuffers around those who've got a few bob.

All them comin' over from Ireland or goin' off ter live in America 'aven't got much.'

Alfie nodded his agreement. 'We'll leave them alone – unless we happen to see a bag or bundle left unattended. We'll concentrate on the posh ones coming off the trains at the Riverside Station.' Over the years he'd heard from other workhouse inmates how emigration from Liverpool to America and Canada and even Australia had increased and of all the docking arrangements, trains, hotels and boarding-house facilities the city now provided for the people who had travelled from all over Europe. 'I've got a plan of how we can work it; I've been thinking it out all day. Jimmy, you'll be the lookout, watching out for coppers, porters and the like, while Richie will go and pester the feller or woman we've picked out. You can beg for a penny or offer to carry a bag – something like that, just keep on mithering them and I'll nip in quick, like, and pinch something. A bag or purse, gloves, stole or anything we can sell for a few bob. And just so as we don't get noticed too much, we'll swop around. One day I'll do the pestering and, Richie, you can be lookout. We'll work it like that, all right?'

Jimmy and Richie considered this and then nodded. 'That could work, Alfie,' Jimmy conceded.

'Better than tryin' ter pinch bits of stuff offen carts and lorries,' Richie added eagerly.

Alfie grinned as he finished the apple. 'The Gill Street Gang will be back in business, lads!' It felt good to be able to say that, he thought. It was great just to be away from that bloody workhouse and cobbler's shop and if they were careful they wouldn't get caught and they'd always have a few bob in their pockets. And what's more in time they could move on to shops and houses. That would take more planning and nerve, Alfie knew, but that wouldn't be a problem. He hadn't survived all those years in the workhouse without learning a trick or two.

Some of the pleasure Jane felt as she bade farewell to Matron on Friday evening was tempered by her anxiety for her brother for there was no news of him. Her few belongings had been packed into the old carpet bag Ada had lent her and Joe was waiting for her at the gates.

'I bet you're not in the least bit sorry to shake the dust of that place off your feet, are you?' Joe greeted her, smiling as he took the bag from her.

'No, but . . . but my last memories of Mam will always be bound up here,' she answered a little sadly. 'And I will miss Maisie; she was always so cheerful. Not that I really saw much of her after she got work and left,' she added.

'Your mam would be really proud of what you've achieved, Jane. A good job and a better future to look forward to now,' he reminded her. 'And your first real night out tomorrow,' he added as they walked towards Gill Street.

'I'm really looking forward to that, Joe!' she replied more happily.

'Oh, come and see your room, Jane . . . well, our room!' Emily enthused as soon as she arrived. 'Mam got two bedspreads that match and a nice little rug – cheap from Lawson's,' she added, mentioning the local pawnbroker's.

'For heaven's sake, Emily, let the girl get her hat and coat off!' Ada admonished although she was smiling. The new furnishings had only cost a few shillings but she'd wanted to brighten the room up a bit for the girls.

Jane looked around the tiny room with pleasure. There were two single beds each with a yellow and white cotton counterpane and the bright rag rug had been set on the floor between them. There was a chest of drawers and a rail for them to hang their clothes on. 'Oh, Emily, it's really great to have a room like this and not have to share a big dormitory with everyone coughing or snoring or muttering all night.'

'Well, when you've unpacked come down and we'll have a cup of tea,' Ada instructed, thinking it was well worth every penny just to see the look on the girl's face.

As they drank their tea Ada informed Jane that she'd asked Maud Cobham about Alfie but that the woman swore she knew nothing and neither did Jimmy.

'She wouldn't tell you if she had, Ada,' Fred remarked grimly.

'I know that and I'm certain that lad of hers knows something.'

'I just hope the police find him and take him back, Aunty Ada. He'll have no money by now, no food and nowhere to sleep,' Jane said, biting her lip.

Ada nodded. 'But if he doesn't want to be found, Jane, luv, there're hundreds of places in this city he can hide and as those two lads he calls mates live by their wits, then I expect Alfie will too.' She shook her head; it wasn't what poor Ellen would have wanted for the lad at all but if he was determined not to go back to the workhouse or his job then she was sure that, aided and abetted by Richie Corrin and Jimmy Cobham, he wouldn't starve, though she doubted the three of them would stay out of borstal for very long. But she didn't say that to Jane. 'Now, let's not dwell on Alfie any longer. He's made his own choices, and if he doesn't want to be found he won't be and us worrying won't help,' she said firmly.

Joe smiled at Jane. 'He'll be all right, and if he isn't, he'll go crawling back to them up there on the hill.'

Jane smiled back at him wistfully. She just wished she *knew* where Alfie was.

She managed to put her brother out of her mind on Saturday for she was caught up in the novelty and excitement of being able to go straight to Ada's after work and then spend time up in the bedroom with Emily getting ready to go out.

'I feel so . . . *different*, Em,' she confided as she sat on her bed and brushed her thick auburn hair. 'I can do more or less whatever I want now, go wherever I please. I feel as if I'm . . . *free*!'

Emily laughed as she slipped the long link of green glass beads she'd bought from Woolworth's last week over her head; they matched her blouse perfectly. 'You can, Jane, and we're going to have a great time tonight. Georgie is meeting us outside the cinema – I've told our Joe that he only ever takes me in the decent seats – and we'll all sit together. Georgie usually buys me a quarter of sweets too,' she added.

Jane digested this while wishing she had some beads like Emily's. They were so fashionable and would brighten up her rather plain royal-blue dress, but then she thought that maybe next Saturday afternoon she would go to shop at Woolworth's in Church Street herself. She would have more money in her purse then and even more time to herself, not having to return to Brownlow Hill. She shivered with excitement once more – there was suddenly so much to look forward to.

Jane liked George Taverner on sight for he was a quiet, unassuming but rather earnest-looking lad of Joe's age who obviously thought he was very fortunate to be walking out with a girl as pretty as Emily. He'd pressed a bag of Everton Mints into Emily's hand rather bashfully as they made their way inside, and Emily had rewarded him with a beaming smile.

The inside of the cinema completely overwhelmed Jane. 'It . . . it's like a palace!' she exclaimed to Joe, taking in all the polished wood, the sweeping staircase and the plush carpet. She'd never seen anything like this before, never imagined a mere cinema could be so opulent.

Joe laughed good-naturedly. 'If you think this is grand you should see the first-class dining room and the first-class lounge on my ship.' He delved into his pocket and brought out a small round tin decorated with flowers. 'I bought these for you, seeing as it's your first real night out.'

Jane took the tin. On the lid in gold lettering were the words 'Barker & Dobson's Fruit Pastilles'; they were obviously expensive. She smiled up at him. 'Oh, Joe, thank you! No one has ever bought me sweets before.'

He shrugged. They had been more expensive than other sweets but he wanted her to feel special tonight. 'I just thought you'd like them.'

'You certainly pushed the boat out, our Joe!' Emily remarked, catching sight of the sweets and winking at her brother before Joe and Georgie went off to purchase the tickets.

Jane examined her gift. She'd never owned such a pretty object before and the knowledge that Joe'd bought it especially for her made her feel even happier. 'It's such a lovely tin, I'll keep it to put . . . things in when it's empty!' she decided.

Chapter Twelve

⟡

AS CHRISTMAS APPROACHED the excitement in Ada's house grew, particularly for Jane as it would be the first Christmas in years that she would spend entirely away from the workhouse. Both she and Emily had been trying to save as much as they could to buy little gifts for the family and Saturday afternoons were spent browsing in Woolworth's and speculating what they could afford. Ada had confided to Fred that as she had far more money in her purse these days with Joe and Emily working and with what Jane contributed, she could buy some treats and they could all look forward to decorations, a tree and a slap-up meal – except Joe of course; he'd be away.

'But I bet he'll have a great time just the same, Ada. They make a big thing of it,' Fred had remarked when she'd bemoaned the fact that her eldest son had announced he would be spending Christmas on the high seas.

'They make a big thing of it for the passengers but I

wouldn't bank on it with regards to the crew,' she'd sniffed, sure that no ship's kitchen could compete with her home-cooked Christmas dinner.

When Joe had returned home a few days ago Jane had begged him to go and see Jimmy or Richie for there was still no news of Alfie and it was three months now since he'd disappeared, and although Ada kept abreast of all the news and gossip in the neighbourhood she'd heard nothing concerning him either. Reluctantly Joe had promised he would to try to set her mind at ease. After deliberating on the matter he decided he would try to follow one or other of them for he was certain if confronted they would deny all knowledge of Alfie or his whereabouts.

It had taken him a couple of days but eventually he had followed Richie one evening and got lucky. Richie had been carrying a bag of some kind but Joe couldn't make out what it was. Joe had taken great care not to be seen, dodging into doorways and jiggers whenever Richie turned around to look over his shoulder. When Richie had eventually gone around the back of Bates's stable Joe had waited a few minutes in the shadows and then crept forward. There was a lamp attached to the wall in the tiny yard at the back of the building so he'd been able to see Richie go in through a rickety door. He'd waited, shivering in the cold night air, until Richie had emerged, minus the bag. He'd smiled grimly to himself. So, this was where Alfie Shaw was holed up; no wonder no one had spotted him. At least the lad had a roof of sorts over his head and obviously Richie and Jimmy brought him food and other things. He'd waited until Richie had gone; pressing himself close to the yard wall which was deep in shadow as the lad passed; then he'd made his way home.

Jane and Ada had been eagerly awaiting his return in the kitchen. 'Did you find him? Do you know where Alfie is?' Jane asked as soon as he walked in.

Joe had nodded as he sat down. 'I followed Richie and I presume Alfie is holed up in the loft above Bates's stable. It looked as if Richie was taking him food; he had a bag with him which he didn't have when he left. So, Alfie's certainly not starving in a gutter, Jane,' he'd informed her.

'But it must be freezing in that place!' she'd replied, relieved that Joe had found her brother though still anxious about Alfie's welfare.

'But not as cold as if he were on the streets and don't forget, Jane, that it's his choice. And those two are obviously getting money from somewhere to feed him,' Ada had remarked. She'd heard the gossip in the street about both Maud Cobham and Lizzie Corrin spending far more time in the pub these days, which meant they had money to spend on drink and she, like everyone else, wondered where it was coming from. She was certain those lads were up to no good.

Jane had nodded but she wished Alfie would return to Brownlow Hill and to Mr Phillips's shop. Living rough and consorting with Jimmy and Richie meant trouble, she was certain of that. 'Do you think that if I went to see our Alfie . . . tried to talk to him . . .?'

Ada had shaken her head. 'Jane, luv, I don't think it would make any difference what you said. That lad will do as he pleases.'

'And it might make Alfie take fright and leave that place,' Fred had pointed out.

'Then you'd have no idea where he was or how he was

faring. We know where he is, Jane, and that he's not starving, so unless he comes to his senses and goes back, you'll have to stop worrying,' Ada had urged.

She had tried but at times, particularly as the weather became even colder, she couldn't help but think of him shivering alone in that cold dark stable loft.

Joe was sailing the week before Christmas and as he'd walked her home the evening before he left she felt the happy glow of the approaching festivities fade. 'Oh, I wish you could be home, Joe. I'm looking forward to Christmas so much but . . . it would have been just perfect if . . .' She fell silent, wishing that Joe didn't have to go and that some way could be found for Alfie to spend the holiday with them, but neither was possible.

'I know but it can't be helped, it's all part and parcel of the job. You'll have a great time, Jane. I know our Emily's planning to get Sonny to make crêpe paper decorations for the kitchen and Mam's already making shopping lists for food and she's even taking about getting a tree this year.'

Jane smiled. 'I know. Sonny's delighted about that. Will you have to work on Christmas Day?'

Joe nodded. 'Of course. There'll be a big Christmas dinner to serve to all the passengers but we get some too – later on.'

Jane sighed. 'It doesn't sound half as good as sitting down with your family.'

'It's not but you have to make some sacrifices, Jane, if you want to get on in life,' he replied – and he did want to get on. He didn't want to spend his life like his da, living in a slum, never knowing from one day to the next if he had work, always short of money, always living just on the edge of poverty.

When – sometime in the future – he had a family of his own he was determined that the shadow of the workhouse would never fall on them as it had on Ellen Shaw's.

'Well, we'll all miss you,' she replied disconsolately.

He stopped and they stood in the faint light of the street-lamp. 'I'll miss you too, Jane, you know that. You know I'm . . . very fond of you.'

She nodded, looking up at him as he gazed seriously down at her. As she searched his familiar features she felt a stirring of joy in her heart. The feeling spread but she did not know why. Was it . . . could it be . . . did she *love* him? she wondered.

Joe took her in his arms and gently kissed her. It was true, he cared deeply about her but he wasn't sure if it was *love* he felt. For so long she'd been a part of his life and now she was a part of his family, but he was only twenty and she was just eighteen and there was so much more he wanted to see and do before he could even think of settling down.

As he kissed her Jane felt a wave of happiness engulf her. The kiss was wonderful – tender and soft. She had never experienced anything like it. She *did* love him, she was suddenly sure, and she wished with all her heart he wasn't going away in the morning.

At length he drew away from her. 'We'd best get home before the whole street starts gossiping about us,' he said, smiling as he tucked her hand through his arm.

Jane did enjoy the festive season for Ada had kept both herself and Emily so busy that she hadn't had time to think much about either Joe or Alfie. Emily had supervised her younger brothers who were making chains of red and green crêpe paper and Jane had put up the holly and when Fred had brought home the tree she, Emily and the boys had spent hours decorating it with homemade decorations and tinsel they'd bought in Woolworth's. They'd gone with Ada to the market for the Christmas fare which included a capon, vegetables, fruit and nuts and they'd carefully wrapped the small gifts they'd purchased and placed them under the tree with strict instructions to the boys not to go poking at the wrapping paper.

When Christmas morning dawned Jane hugged Ada, Fred, Emily and the boys in turn, wishing them 'Happy Christmas', her eyes shining and happiness radiating from her face as she remembered years past when there had been little to celebrate. Now she had a home with dear friends and . . . Joe, and even though he was absent she knew he'd be thinking of her.

'This is going to be the best Christmas we've ever had,' Emily announced and everyone agreed although as Jane helped Emily set the table she couldn't help wonder what Joe would be doing at this precise moment.

Before they ushered in the New Year of 1930 the *Empress of Scotland* returned to the Mersey and when Jane and Emily arrived home from work it was to find Joe happily settled before the range in the kitchen, toasting his feet on the fender. He hadn't been expected until tomorrow morning but they'd made good time and had just managed to catch the tide at the Mersey bar, he informed them cheerfully.

'Welcome home, Joe. Isn't it great that you're here in time to celebrate New Year?' Jane greeted him.

'And the new decade,' Emily added, taking off her coat and

hat. 'We can all go down to the Pier Head together before midnight – there'll be hundreds of people there – and we'll hear the church bells all over the city ring out and all the ships sound off their whistles. Georgie's already asked me to go with him.'

'You'll have to walk home then because there won't be any public transport running at that hour,' Ada commented, busying herself with the pie for supper.

'Oh, we won't mind that, Mam; will we, Jane?' Emily responded, smiling at her friend and thinking she would be quite happy to walk back in the cold, frosty air with Georgie for she hoped that perhaps later on, as the new decade opened, he might 'pop the question'. He'd be twenty-one in March and in May she'd be eighteen and that she felt was definitely old enough to get engaged. And he'd confided to her that, having reached his majority, he'd get a substantial increase in his pay, so that boded well for the future.

Jane smiled back. Of course she'd heard the cacophony of bells, sirens, steam whistles and motor horns that always ushered in a New Year in Liverpool but she'd never actually been *part* of it and it was yet another exciting experience to look forward to and to share with Joe.

Joe glanced around the cosy kitchen and smiled, thinking no matter how far he travelled, and no matter how cramped and cluttered the room was, this was how he would always remember 'home'. 'Then that's settled. It'll be a great way to spend the evening. And it'll be something special for me to remember as well, especially since it was announced that on our next trip we won't be coming directly back to Liverpool.'

This news was greeted with astonishment by everyone but

Ada gathered her wits first. 'Why? Where are you going?' she demanded.

'The company have decided that it will be more profitable for us to spend the time cruising around the islands of the West Indies instead of coming back here. So, next trip we won't be going to Halifax, we'll be sailing in and out of New York. There won't be any second or third class, the whole ship will be first class and we're all being promoted – just for the cruises – which is great for everyone as we'll all get tips as well as our wages! We'll be quids in! They're being advertised to Americans as "Sunshine Cruises". They'll charge from three dollars a day which' – he explained knowingly – 'is about one pound. Of course the bigger the cabin the more it costs. The company think it's great value for money and I suppose it is, if you can afford to pay at least fourteen or fifteen pounds for a holiday.' Joe couldn't keep his enthusiasm for this venture out of his voice. Everyone had been stunned at first when this 'New Policy for the New Decade' had been announced by the captain. They had all been summoned to the first-class lounge for the announcement and as the news had sunk in a ripple of excitement had run through the room as they realised they were off to the calm, warm waters of the Caribbean instead of ploughing the cold, stormy waters of the North Atlantic for the next three months. And there were tips from wealthy Americans to look forward to as well!

'They're *sure* there *are* people in America who can afford to pay that, even after the stock market collapsed?' Fred asked, frowning with concern. It would cost twenty-eight pounds for a couple and that was a huge sum of money to squander on a holiday – the company's strategy sounded risky to him. Men had thrown themselves from office windows to their deaths on Black Monday, so he'd read in the newspapers, and people had lost vast fortunes overnight and not only in America.

Joe shrugged. 'There must be, Da, or they wouldn't have made such a big decision.' Then he grinned. 'Just think though, I'll get to see New York and the Statue of Liberty, the Empire State—' he enthused.

'They say that place is full of gangsters with guns so you just be careful!' Ada interrupted for she wasn't as enthusiastic as her son.

'Oh, Mam, you take too much notice of what they say on the wireless,' Joe laughed.

'So, how long will you be doing this "cruising" around the West Indies for?' his mother demanded.

'For three months. We'll be coming back to Liverpool in April. The St Lawrence will have thawed by then and we'll go back to doing the trips to Canada, but if it's a success we'll be cruising every year,' Joe replied.

Ada sighed heavily. She wasn't happy at all about him being away for so long and she hoped that the company hadn't made a decision which would put Joe out of a job and hundreds of others with him.

As soon as the words 'New York' had passed Joe's lips, Jane's heart had sunk and now dismay and disappointment replaced the excitement she'd felt earlier. It was bad enough him being away for a few weeks but when he sailed in four days' time she wouldn't see him again for *three whole months*. Oh, New Year's Eve wouldn't be the entirely happy occasion she'd been looking forward to; it would be the beginning of a heartache she would suffer for weeks on end. But he was obviously so looking forward to these new trips that she tried desperately not to let her feelings show. She knew he wanted to get on in life, he'd told her that, and that you sometimes had to make sacrifices, but she realised sadly that it was she who was going to have to make the sacrifice this time. He couldn't wait to embark on what he was obviously viewing as new experiences and adventures – ones that could never include her.

She tried to put aside her disappointment when on New Year's Eve, together with Emily and Georgie, she and Joe got the tram to the Pier Head. Already there were crowds of people milling about on the cobbled expanse in front of the buildings known as the 'Three Graces' of the Liverpool water-front, as well as congregating beneath the supports of the overhead railway.

'Let's try and get as near to the Landing Stage as we can. We'll be able to see more,' Emily urged, linking Georgie's arm, her eyes dancing with excited anticipation.

'Not too close. If there's a sudden surge in the crowd we could end up in the river,' Joe cautioned.

Jane noticed that there were many in the crowd who seemed to have begun their celebrations early but she wasn't worried, Joe would look after her.

Georgie had noticed too. 'The pubs are doing a roaring trade tonight,' he remarked as they decided to settle for a spot near the top of the floating roadway. 'This should suit us fine,' he added.

It was a clear cold night and the dark sky seemed filled with twinkling stars and the reflection of the moon danced on the dark waters of the Mersey. Both Jane and Emily pulled the collars of their coats up higher around their ears, glad they'd heeded Ada's advice to 'wrap up warm' with scarves, hats and gloves. Despite that fact, as they stood stamping their feet and waiting for the minutes to tick by, Jane began to shiver with the cold. 'We must be mad, all of us, it's freezing!' she laughed.

Joe put his arm around her. 'Not long to wait now,' he said, pointing up at the large illuminated clock face on the tower of the Royal Liver Building that faced towards the river. It was matched by an identical one facing the city centre.

Georgie laughed. 'You can tell too by the way this crowd is getting bigger.'

Jane looked up at Joe as the crush of people hemmed them in and she was glad of his protective arm. She'd never experienced anything like this before and was feeling apprehensive as well with excited at the mêlée. But as people began to chant, counting down the last seconds of the old year and the old decade she found herself laughingly joining in, watching expectantly as the big hand on the clock finally reached midnight and the first stroke of the New Year chimed out. Instantly it was drowned out by the spontaneous cacophony of noise that erupted and she was clasped tightly in Joe's arms and suddenly he was kissing her. She forgot that he was going away; she forgot everything except his warm mouth on hers, his strong arms holding her close and the feeling of sheer joy that was coursing through her as she kissed him back. She loved him and he loved her! It was impossible to ignore it now! All around them people were hugging and kissing lovers, friends and perfect strangers. 'Happy New Year' was being yelled to compete against the background of noise. And, against the backdrop of the river ablaze with lights from the rigging of the ships at anchor, the bells of all the city's churches pealed out, motor horns sounded, ships' steam whistles blasted across the expanse of water accompanied by the 'whoop, whoop, whoop' of naval vessels and tugs.

'Happy New Year, Jane!' Joe cried as he at last drew his lips from hers.

'Oh, Joe! Happy New Year! Isn't this just . . . fantastic! I never realised . . . I never knew it was as *wonderful* as this! I'll never forget this night!' she cried, her cheeks flushed, her eyes dancing with pure delight.

Joe gently smoothed back a stray auburn curl from her forehead, thinking she'd never looked so animated, so beautiful or so happy. 'Neither will I, Jane! It's always a bit of a special night but tonight – this first night of nineteen thirty – I'll always remember because I'm with you. I'll never forget how . . . beautiful you look tonight, Jane, or how . . . how much I care for you. Tonight is very, very special. You are very, very special.'

'Oh, Joe!' she cried, seeking his lips again, her love shining from her eyes.

'Come on, you two, break it up! We can hardly wish you "Happy New Year" with you welded together like that!' Emily interrupted, laughing, as she pulled Jane gently away and hugged her before turning to her brother.

Georgie kissed Jane on the cheek and shook Joe's hand vigorously, Joe kissed his sister and then everyone was holding hands and singing 'Auld Lang Syne' and they were all caught up in the euphoria of the moment and Jane had never felt so happy or elated in her life.

'Let's hope nineteen thirty is a really *great* year for us all!'

Emily cried, looking archly at Georgie when they at last managed to break away from the crowd and head towards the road that led home.

'I *know* it will be, Emily!' Joe laughed good-naturedly, thinking of the new places, sights and sounds that awaited him on the other side of the ocean.

Some of Jane's happiness faded away as she remembered that he would soon be leaving but then she cheered herself up with the knowledge that she would have her memories of tonight and the certainty that she and Joe were in love.

Chapter Thirteen

———◆———

THE WINTER MONTHS seemed to have dragged on and on, the days short, dark, cold and dismal. Of course there had been postcards from Joe; he wasn't much of a letter-writer, Ada complained, but at least by the postcards they knew he was well. The cards had pictures of famous New York landmarks, then exotic islands with misty mountains and white sandy beaches fringed with palm trees: the colours of the sky and sea had to be seen to be believed, Emily had exclaimed. Jane missed him dreadfully and Ada had been most upset when she'd realised that he would be celebrating his twenty-first birthday so far away from home. He'd left them a list of shipping agents where letters could be sent to be delivered to the ship and, thinking they might arrive more quickly than letters, Jane had sent him postcards depicting familiar city scenes below the caption 'From Liverpool with Love' and on the back of which she'd written 'Missing you'. Now, however, she bought a birthday card and went to the Central Post Office in Whitechapel to post it, hoping that he would receive it at a date as near to his birthday as was possible.

As March ushered in the first days of spring, traditional gale-force winds whipped up white-topped waves on the Mersey and shook the still-bare branches of the trees in the parks and Emily was getting excited about Georgie's big birthday.

'I've got a secret, Jane, but if you swear not to say anything I'll tell you it,' she announced as they were getting ready for bed one blustery night. She was so happy and excited that she could barely suppress her feelings.

'Of course I won't tell anyone,' Jane promised eagerly for she could see her friend was bursting to tell her.

'Georgie has asked me to marry him and I said yes and we're getting engaged on his birthday. We're going for the ring on Saturday afternoon; he's been saving *so* hard for ages,' she burst out, struggling to keep her voice low so her brothers in the adjoining room didn't hear through the paper-thin walls.

Jane hugged her. 'Oh, Em, I'm so pleased for you! He's such a nice lad.'

'Of course he really should have asked Da for his permission and he wanted to but I said it would just spoil the surprise because you know his mam and da are having a bit of a do in their house for him, and asking permission is so old-fashioned.'

Jane nodded. They had all been invited around to Clarence Street on Saturday evening. Ada had commented that Lily Taverner must have come into money to be pushing the boat out like this. Oh, she knew it was a 'special' birthday but still not many people in this neighbourhood could afford to go throwing do's at the drop of a hat. 'Will you announce it at the party?' Jane asked.

Emily nodded, her dark eyes shining as she thought of the impending trip into Liverpool city centre on Saturday and the party to follow.

'Then I'll act as surprised and delighted as everyone else,' Jane promised. She wished Joe were home to accompany them for she'd never been to a party in her life and this was to be a very significant one for both Georgie and Emily and their families. He seemed to be missing out on so much lately, she thought sadly, but then she brightened up. Only a couple more weeks now and the *Empress of Scotland* would return from the tropical waters of the West Indies, bringing Joe with her. Maybe then they could have a belated celebration for his birthday, Georgie's and the engagement. Perhaps they could go out somewhere and Joe could tell them all about the places he'd been. It was something else for her to look forward to.

On the following Saturday evening Emily could hardly contain her excitement as they all got ready to go to Clarence Street. She had persuaded her mother to splash out on a new dress, something she hadn't had for years, and although it wasn't strictly brand new, having been purchased from a second-hand shop, Ada thought the plum-coloured wool with its bit of matching lace on the collar looked very smart.

'It's just a pity you've got to wear your shawl over it,' Emily said as she fastened up her own red and black checked wool jacket which she'd bought from T. J. Hughes in London Road, having saved for it since Christmas.

'Well, you can't have everything and although we're better off than we were, there isn't money to be wasting on coats or jackets that I'll get no wear out of. The shawl is more serviceable,' Ada replied firmly. She'd brushed and pressed Fred's jacket, his shirt was clean and the collar starched and the lads looked tidy for, as she remarked, she was certain that the Taverner family would all be smartly turned out, and she wasn't having her own menfolk showing her up.

'But a shawl is so old-fashioned, Mam,' Emily protested.

'I *am* old-fashioned, miss! Not like all you young ones, wanting fashionable clothes all the time,' Ada replied firmly, thinking both Emily and Jane were fortunate to have money to spend on themselves.

As they walked behind Ada and Fred on the short journey to Clarence Street the two girls linked arms, Emily looking smart in her bright jacket and red skirt and matching hat and Jane in a blue and green checked dress with a blue jacket and hat.

'Are you feeling nervous?' Jane whispered, keeping her eyes fixed on Ada's back in case she turned around and wanted to know what was being said.

Emily nodded. 'A bit, but the ring is gorgeous. Wait until you see it,' she hissed.

Jane smiled at her. If it were she who was about to become engaged to Joe then she'd be nervous too, though happy and excited of course. But he'd soon be home, she thought, and she was really looking forward to the evening.

Both Ada and Lily Taverner were stunned into silence when, after the initial greetings and 'Happy Birthdays', Georgie, looking proud but a little bashful, announced to everyone that he and Emily were going to get married, with Mr Ellis's permission of course. It wouldn't be for a good while yet, he went on nervously, as they were determined to save hard, but they had been for the ring that afternoon. He then produced the small velvet-covered box and took Emily's hand while she beamed joyously up at him as he slipped the ring with the tiny diamond on to her finger.

'Well, that's a turn-up for the book, Lily! I take it you were just as much in the dark as us?' Ada pronounced when she got over the initial shock. She and Lily had been engaged in discussing the merits of Pegram's Grocers for cold ham over those of the Home and Colonial Stores.

'He never uttered a single word about it, Ada! Not that I've any objections mind, she's a nice girl and I'm fond of her,' Georgie's mother replied, still looking taken aback. 'I think this calls for a drink. I'll get us a small port and brandy each – for medicinal purposes,' she added, for neither of them usually drank anything stronger than sherry or port and lemonade and rarely at that.

As Jane kissed the happy couple, wishing them all the happiness in the world, Ada slowly sipped her drink. 'I thought our Joe would be the first to get wed,' she remarked to Fred, thinking she'd be delighted to welcome Jane as a daughter-in-law the way Lily was now welcoming Emily. 'And I'd be quite content if he settled on Jane,' she added.

'So would I, luv, but the lad will make his own choice when the time comes. Still, I don't think we'll have anything to worry about with Emily; he's a decent, hard-working lad, even if he is a bit on the quiet side.' He was happy that Emily seemed to have a secure future ahead of her with Georgie for the lad had a good steady job and few – if any – vices, but he wasn't at all sure that Joe had got the wanderlust out of his system yet.

'Come on, luv, we'd better go and wish them luck,' he urged, not in the least put out that Georgie hadn't adhered to tradition and come to ask his permission first. He supposed that sort of thing was getting a bit old-fashioned now – a new decade would bring in so many new ways of doing things, he mused, and there was no point in being dog-in-the-mangerish about what was always inevitable – change, for better or worse.

Alfie looked speculatively around at the crowds milling about on the platform at the Riverside Station. The evenings were staying lighter longer now, he thought grimly. All during the dark winter it had been relatively easy to melt away quickly into the shadows after rapidly lifting a purse or wallet or bag. The gang only came down here two or three times a week, sometimes not even that often if what they got proved to be valuable – and it often did. He'd become very good at picking out someone who was both rich and vulnerable – women or girls, usually – and they'd all become experts at pulling off what he called 'a strike'. After Christmas Richie had found him a room above an alehouse in Dale Street where questions were not asked; all his landlord was interested in was the bit of money for the rent each week. It was a damned sight better than that stable loft.

He grinned slyly as he watched Jimmy pestering a well-dressed woman who was trying to supervise three children while her husband went off looking for a porter for the luggage. Jimmy was very convincing in his torn, dirty jacket and ragged trousers, his cap pulled down low as he begged for a penny, 'or just a ha'penny or even a farthin', missus! I'm starvin'! He'd already noted the leather Gladstone bag she'd put down on the

141

floor beside her while she fastened the girl's bonnet ribbons, which had come undone. Quick as a flash he darted forward, snatched up the bag and was now pushing his way determinedly through the crowd in the opposite direction, not running or even hurrying for that would draw unwelcome attention to him. He'd made sure he was clean and fairly tidy and if approached would say he was on an errand, taking the bag to the stationmaster's office. He'd only ever had to use the excuse once before but it had worked. Judging by the weight of the bag there would be plenty of stuff to sell to the old miser of a pawnbroker who fenced the stuff for them. They never got its true value but couldn't complain too much because old Sarsfield kept his mouth shut. He'd meet the other two back at his lodgings; he wouldn't even open the bag until he was safely off the streets. With what they made he was managing to live fairly well. But risks were going to become greater in the months to come, especially during the summer when it stayed light until after ten at night. He had no desire at all to get caught and sent to borstal. He would need to be on his guard, and he'd have to start thinking of some other way of getting enough money – without resorting to finding work.

It was the last day of the month when the letter arrived and Jane vowed she would always remember that day. When she got home from work she'd found Ada sitting at the kitchen table with the single page of thin blue paper spread out before her. There was no sign of Sonny or Danny or anyone else and Ada unusually hadn't made a start on the evening meal. In fact there were still unwashed mugs on the table.

'Aunty Ada, what's wrong? What's happened?' Jane asked,

sitting down beside her, not even bothering to take off her hat or jacket. Ada's face was white.

'I just can't believe he'd . . . he'd do such a thing, Jane! And why didn't he write before this?' Ada shook her head, frowning.

Jane's heart began to beat in an odd jerky sort of way. The letter must be from Joe. 'Is it Joe? What . . . what's he done, Aunty Ada?' she asked hesitantly.

Ada pushed the letter towards her. 'He's not coming home, Jane. I've managed to grasp that much. Read it for yourself.'

Jane's hands began to shake as she scanned the lines. It was from Joe and it was true. He wasn't coming home – not yet anyway. One of the passengers had taken a shine to him and asked him to go and work for his family in the big house they owned in upper New York State. It was just too good an opportunity to turn down, Joe wrote. The man was very wealthy and he would be taught to drive a car and be paid far more than he earned now, and as this Mr Ibsen travelled a lot he would get to see places all over America and Canada. Tears of bitter disappointment pricked her eyes; she'd been so looking forward to his return but now . . . now . . .

'He doesn't seem to have thought how much we've all missed him and worry about him; he just seems totally taken up with this offer. Who is this "Mr Ibsen"? What are the family like? Will they treat him well?' Ada was worried. It was one thing being employed by a big shipping company as he travelled to and from foreign parts, but quite another to work for a private individual whom none of them knew and in a country so far away. 'And he doesn't say when or even if he's coming home. I don't know how he could be so . . . selfish, Jane! Oh, I know what Fred will say, that he's turned twenty-one, he's a man now and old enough to make his own decisions, but this is just such a huge step for him to take!'

Jane couldn't speak; she felt as though her throat had closed over. He obviously hadn't given her a moment's thought. He hadn't meant all the things he'd said on New Year's Eve. It didn't seem to have crossed his mind that she loved him and wanted him home and would be bitterly disappointed. He obviously didn't love her, she thought miserably, otherwise he wouldn't have decided to take this job in America – and there had been no mention at all of his coming back. She pushed the letter away and covered her face with her hands. This must be how it felt when your heart broke, she thought.

Chapter Fourteen

FOR THE PAST MONTH she'd felt as though there wasn't anything in life to look forward to, she thought as she tidied the dockets into a neat pile ready for tomorrow. She got up each morning, came to work, went home and it was all such an effort. Emily had been very sympathetic and tried each day to bolster her spirits but nothing seemed to help.

Ada's disappointment had turned to fury at what she termed Joe's 'crass ingratitude' and even Fred had voiced the opinion that his eldest son should have come home and discussed it with them. He could then have gone back to take up the job and if this family were halfway decent they wouldn't have objected to that. Ada had asked Jane if she would write to him – he had at least enclosed an address – but she'd shaken her head. She couldn't, she'd said. She just couldn't bring herself to tell him how upset and disappointed she was. Nor could she bring herself to tell Ada that she loved him and she'd thought he loved her, although she'd cried out her heartbreak to Emily.

Ada said she quite understood but that she'd get Emily to write and inform him of just how angry she herself was.

The bell had already gone to mark the end of the working day but she lingered on, not wanting to have to try to join in with the conversations of her fellow workers as they walked to their various tram and bus stops. Finally she left, closing the door to the office behind her, and walked along the deserted corridor and out into the yard. She nodded politely to Bert Hedges, who always locked up, as he remarked that she was late leaving tonight. The April evening held the first real warmth of spring and as she walked on she thought that she should have been feeling happy, looking forward to him arriving home in two days' time. The weight of heartache and despair settled even deeper. What was the point of *anything* now? What use was there in trying to look forward when he'd probably forgotten all about her?

Tears misted her eyes and blurred her vision as she stepped off the kerb and into the road and then everything happened so fast that afterwards she really didn't recall the event clearly. One minute she was stepping off the kerb; the next she was half lying, half sitting in the roadway at the side of a big black car and a man was bending over her. She looked up at him in confusion. 'What . . . what . . . happened?'

'Miss Shaw! Are you hurt? There was nothing I could do; you stepped right out in front of me!' James Davenport's face was white with shock. He'd just driven out of the gates and so fortunately had been travelling slowly otherwise . . .

'Mr Davenport, sir! I . . . I'm sorry . . .' Jane stammered, feeling very shaky.

He helped her to her feet. 'Are you hurt? Do you think I

should take you to the hospital?' She looked ashen and was trembling.

'No! No, I'm not hurt . . . just a bit . . . bruised, I think.'

'Then at least you must let me drive you home. You've had a very nasty shock,' he urged, thinking it hadn't been a pleasant experience for himself either.

Jane tried to pull herself together. 'No, sir, that won't be necessary, I'm all right, honestly. I . . . I'm just a bit shaken up, that's all.' She couldn't put him to the inconvenience of driving her home, nor did she want to have to endure the stir it would cause in Gill Street where cars were seldom seen. It was her fault that he'd knocked her down, after all.

She still looked terrible, he thought, and in all decency he couldn't just get back in the car and drive off and leave her here. 'Miss Shaw, I insist that you at least sit in the car with me until you are feeling stronger. Strong enough to take the tram home,' he said firmly as he opened the door on the passenger side and helped her in.

She was aware of the faint odour of good leather as she leaned back in the comfortable seat. Her shoulder was beginning to throb and she'd grazed her knee but all she wanted to do was get home to Ada's.

'Now, sit back and rest for a little while,' he urged, wondering what had possessed her to just walk into the road like that. She'd always seemed such a sensible girl.

'I am so sorry, Mr Davenport. I just wasn't . . . thinking,' she started to explain and then to her horror she began to sob.

He became alarmed. 'Miss Shaw, whatever is the matter? Who or what has upset you to this degree?'

Jane could only shake her head; she couldn't possibly tell

him that she'd been so miserable, so overcome by thoughts of Joe that she hadn't been aware of what she was doing.

He was at a loss; he'd never been confronted by a weeping girl before and prayed she wasn't going to have hysterics. He delved into a pocket and withdrew a clean, folded white handkerchief and handed it to her, noticing now that she'd badly grazed her knee. 'Now, I insist I drive you home for you've hurt your knee and are very . . . upset,' he said firmly.

Jane calmed down enough to give him Ada's address and then sat wiping her eyes as he drove the short distance to Gill Street.

She was unaware of the openly curious stares as the car drew up outside Ada's house and he helped her out before knocking on the front door. By now, not only were her shoulder and knee throbbing but also her head.

'Oh, my God! Jane! Whatever happened?' Ada cried when she opened the door.

'I'm afraid she's been involved in a bit of an accident, madam. She walked out into the road in front of me – I couldn't avoid her. She assures me she's not hurt but she's very upset and shaken,' James Davenport informed the stout, poorly dressed woman who had gently put her arm around the girl.

'Thank you, sir, for bringing her home. I'll see to her now,' Ada replied, having taken in his expensive, well-cut clothes, the cultured accent and the car.

'She's not to come in to work tomorrow; she must rest and get over the experience. She won't be penalised for it, you have my word,' he informed Ada, thinking it was the least he could do.

Ada looked at him, completely puzzled. 'Work? Who are you?'

'I'm James Davenport, madam. I'm Miss Shaw's employer. I was just leaving the premises myself.'

She nodded. 'Thank you, sir. I know she'll appreciate it when she's calmed down a bit. Now, if I were you I'd see to the car before one of those little hooligans damages it. They're not used to seeing fancy cars like that around here,' she urged, looking pointedly at the group of small boys who had clustered excitedly around the car.

He smiled at her before tipping his hat and turning away, relieved that Jane Shaw would now be in safe hands, hands far more capable than his own at calming down distraught young girls.

As he drove home, thinking he would have a very stiff whisky when he arrived, he wondered what on earth had upset her to the extent that she'd been so distracted she hadn't seen or heard his car approaching. Maybe when she returned to work he would try to find out for the whole incident had disturbed him greatly.

As Ada bathed her knee, tutting sympathetically, and Emily made her a cup of very strong sweet tea, Jane was able to inform them of what little she could remember about the accident.

'Well, it was decent enough of him to make sure you weren't badly hurt and bring you home,' Ada remarked. 'It must have given him a bit of a turn too. I thought he looked a bit sort of . . . pale and drawn.'

'I just don't know how it happened. I know my mind was . . . miles away—'

149

'Somewhere in upper New York State, where it's been since meladdo decided he wasn't coming home,' Ada interrupted grimly. 'Jane, luv, you're going to have to put all thoughts of our Joe out of your mind. I know it won't be easy, I still can't help but worry about the young fool myself, but if it's causing you to walk out into the traffic then it's got to stop. You could have been killed!' she admonished.

Jane nodded, knowing Ada was right. She just wished she *could* stop thinking about him, stop feeling so bereft and bitterly hurt.

'Still, that Mr Davenport said you were to take tomorrow off and rest and you won't lose any pay either,' Ada reminded her. 'He's a real gentleman, Jane. Very considerate indeed, which is rare for the likes of his class,' she added, nodding approvingly. Yes, very considerate, unlike some people she knew, she thought bitterly, for she was aware how fond Jane was of her errant son.

The following day Jane ached all over and was very grateful that she didn't have to go into work. She still felt upset and rather foolish for letting herself get into such a state that she'd walked blindly out into the road. Wearily she admitted to herself that she would just have to try very hard to get over the feelings she had for Joe, for they were obviously not reciprocated. She had spent the day dozing but felt well enough to come down for her supper for which Ada was thankful. It was probably one of the few times in her life that she wished she could write more than her name, Ada had thought, for she'd certainly like to write and give Joe a piece of her mind for his treatment of them all but especially Jane, for hadn't the poor girl had enough to contend with in her short life? As she scrubbed the kitchen table after their evening meal she wished it was her Joe she had hold of; she couldn't believe he'd been so inconsiderate, and she was only sorry he was too far away for her to let him know what she thought of his behaviour.

When Jane returned to work the following day to her surprise she was informed that Mr Davenport had asked to see her at two o'clock.

'Don't worry, Jane, it's probably just to see that you are all right after your . . . experience,' Mr Edwards, her supervisor, informed her, having been told of the reason for Jane's absence.

She'd felt nervous all day but as she approached his office she felt even more apprehensive; after all, the whole thing had been her fault.

He got up from behind the desk as she was shown in and indicated that she should sit down. 'And how are you today, Miss Shaw?' he asked, thinking she looked composed but still lacked colour.

She twisted her hands nervously in her lap. 'Much better, sir, thank you. I . . . I'd like to say how really sorry I am. I should have been looking where I was going.'

'The important thing is that you were not seriously hurt,' he said kindly, looking closely at her. Even though pale and with a slight bluish bruise beginning to appear on one cheek she was a very attractive girl and after having experienced Gill Street he felt a stirring of pity for her. 'What had upset you so much, Miss Shaw? Was it something that had happened here?' he asked.

Jane shook her head. 'No, sir, nothing like that. It . . . it was something at home.'

He was reluctant to pry but relieved it was nothing appertaining to her work here. 'You live with that . . . lady, I take it?' he asked, knowing of her background.

'With Mrs Ellis, yes. She very kindly took me in a couple of years ago. We . . . we used to live next door to her and she was a good friend of my . . . my mam's.'

He nodded, remembering her mother was dead and he presumed her father also.

'And you are happy living there?'

She smiled. 'I am, sir. You see I grew up with Mrs Ellis's children. Emily in particular is my close friend.'

He leaned back slightly in his chair. When she'd smiled it had completely transformed her face; her amber-coloured eyes had lit up and her lips parted slightly. He felt a stirring of something he'd long forgotten: a strong liking for a young woman. 'And you are quite . . . content with your position here?'

Again she smiled, thinking he didn't seem to look quite as old or severe as she'd always thought him to be. 'I'm very content, sir. I enjoy both my work and the company of the people I work with.'

He smiled back at her. 'I'm very glad to hear that, Miss Shaw.' He got to his feet. 'And I mustn't detain you any longer, but I'm glad you are feeling better.'

Jane rose and prepared to take her leave, smoothing down the skirt of her dress.

'Miss Shaw, would you think it very forward of me if I asked you to have tea with me this Saturday afternoon?' he asked. As soon as the words were out he felt a sense of complete astonishment, wondering why he had just done that?

Jane was very taken aback and felt the colour flooding her cheeks. 'Tea . . . sir? Me?'

He nodded; well, he had no intention of retracting the invitation now. 'Yes, at Brown's Tea Rooms – you know them?'

She did and they were much, much smarter and more expensive than a Lyons' Corner House. 'Yes, I know of them.'

'Good, then shall we say half past three? I'll meet you there and I'll reserve a table too as they are usually busy on Saturdays.'

'That will be . . . very . . . nice,' she replied, flustered and not knowing quite what to say. Somehow 'nice' just didn't seem an appropriate word at all.

'Then I'll look forward to it,' he said truthfully as he ushered her courteously to the door.

She smiled back shyly wondering if she should reply but decided against it.

He stared at the back of the door and shook his head in a bemused sort of way. Was he embarrassing her, he wondered? He hadn't intended to. He just wanted to get to know her better in a place that wasn't as . . . formal as here. He doubted she would immediately rush back and inform the whole department that he'd asked her to have tea with him; he instinctively knew she wasn't that type of girl. And now he *was* indeed looking forward to seeing her again and perhaps finding out a little more about her.

She didn't say a word to anyone about it at the laundry but when she got back home she poured out her astonished excitement at the invitation to both Ada and Emily, finishing with the words thousands of girls and women before had uttered. 'And I just don't know what I'll wear!'

'It's a very posh place, Jane,' Emily agreed, thinking she herself just wouldn't know what to do or say in a place like that. It was one of those establishments that had a uniformed commissionaire on the door. 'But don't worry, we'll sort out between us something that will look smart and suitable.'

Ada too was very surprised although she didn't show it. 'Now, the pair of you, just don't go getting over-excited,' she advised. 'It will probably only be the once, Jane, and more than likely he feels it's a sort of . . . compensation for it being his car that hit you. After all, he is much older than you are.' It couldn't possibly be anything more than that for gentlemen like him seldom – if ever – mixed voluntarily with the poorer classes. He had seemed very . . . honourable so she doubted very much if there was anything improper on his mind and of course as she'd stated he was so much older than Jane. But deep down she felt unsettled by this unexpected turn of events.

Chapter Fifteen

———

JANE HAD TRIED on everything they both owned and had finally settled for her own dark blue skirt, Emily's green and white blouse and her own blue jacket and hat which Emily had said they could smarten up with a band of green ribbon. Her best shoes and bag had been polished up but the problem had come with the gloves.

'You'll have to wear gloves or at least carry a pair going to a posh place like that,' Emily had insisted.

'But I haven't got any,' she'd protested. 'And when am I going to get the time to go and buy a pair? Anyway, I don't know if I can afford them.'

'Will you have time when you finish work on Saturday to nip down to London Road?' Emily had enquired.

Jane had bitten her lip. 'I'd really wanted to take my time getting ready so I'd be sure everything was just *right*.' She hadn't planned on rushing into town to look for gloves but it seemed as though she might have to now.

Ada had settled the matter, stating she would go to T. J. Hughes on Friday afternoon. She kept the thought to herself that buying a pair of gloves was an unnecessary expense for just one occasion.

'You won't go and get anything . . . tacky-looking, Mam, will you?' Emily had asked apprehensively, for neither of them had ever owned a pair of dressy gloves.

'She wants a decent pair of navy gloves and I think I can be trusted to come back with a pair, miss!' had been the tart reply.

She'd brought back a pair of navy cotton gloves that had a cut-work pattern around the cuffs which were approved of by both girls for they looked smart but hadn't cost the earth, for as Ada had said Jane would probably never go anywhere as posh to wear them again.

Both Emily and Ada had pronounced that she looked very smart in an understated sort of way before she'd left but now, as she approached the tea rooms, which were adjacent to one of the city's more prominent and expensive hotels, the butterflies in her stomach began a wild dance and she clutched her bag tightly. Would she look dowdy? Would her outfit look cheap beside those of the other women? Would Mr Davenport feel ashamed of her and regret he'd asked her? But then she suspected that Ada was right in assuming that it was a way of making amends for the accident, so what he thought of her appearance should be irrelevant, she told herself firmly.

The commissionaire greeted her cordially. 'Good afternoon, miss.'

She smiled at him nervously. 'I'm to meet Mr Davenport inside,' she informed him and the door was duly opened and she was ushered in.

Beyond another set of frosted glass doors there was a small ornate desk behind which sat a very smart-looking woman in a black silk dress with two ropes of jet beads around her neck and jet and silver earrings.

'Good afternoon, Miss . . .?' she enquired, glancing down at a large book on the desk in front of her.

'Miss Shaw, Jane Shaw, and I'm to meet Mr James Davenport,' she replied, trying to keep her voice steady while watching the elegant hand that moved across the page.

The woman smiled. 'Of course. One of the waitresses will escort you to his table.'

As she followed the girl in the neat black and white uniform she dared not gaze around, much as she wanted to, feeling it wasn't the right thing to do. She was aware however that nearly every woman and girl in the room was far better dressed than herself and her confidence began to wane rapidly.

He stood up and smiled and extended his hand as she arrived at the table, which was covered with a pristine white damask cloth. 'Miss Shaw, you are very punctual. Please, do sit down,' he greeted her. She looked very smart, he thought, although her clothes were obviously not expensive. But then she wasn't a wealthy woman: she worked to support herself. Yet she was far more attractive than many of the women in the room and the blue and green suited her colouring.

Jane sat and took off the new gloves and tucked them into the strap across the back of her bag designed for the purpose, although up to now it had never been used. The table was set with beautiful gold-rimmed, delicate bone china decorated with deep red roses and cutlery she was certain was solid silver. Her nervousness grew as she eyed the silver cake forks; she'd never used one before. Thankfully he ordered for them both but when he asked if she preferred Indian or China tea she looked up at the waitress in mild panic.

'Most people prefer Indian, miss,' the girl advised kindly.

Jane nodded, beginning to wonder why she had ever agreed to come here.

As the girl moved away he leaned across towards her, sensing her nervousness. 'Try to relax a little. No one is going to bite and they really do serve an excellent afternoon tea. I just want you to enjoy it,' he urged, smiling encouragingly.

She smiled back. 'Thank you, sir, I'll try.'

He shook his head, still smiling. 'No more "sirs". We are not on business premises now and I'd like to get to know you better.'

'What should I call you?' she asked.

'Will you be happy with "Mr Davenport"?'

She nodded, relieved he hadn't asked her to address him by his Christian name. She just *couldn't* have done that.

'So, Miss Shaw, you have no lasting effects from your accident?' he enquired, taking the thick white napkin and unfolding it.

Jane copied him and placed her napkin across her lap. 'No, just a few bruises. I'm fine now.'

'And Mrs Ellis was quite happy for you to come out this afternoon? I take it she is your guardian?'

Jane frowned as she pondered this. 'I'm not quite sure about that but I know she promised Matron she would be responsible for me and, yes, she was quite happy for me to come today,' she replied and then wished she hadn't mentioned Matron at all.

He nodded his understanding. As the waitress arrived with a large tray on which reposed a heavy silver teapot, hot water jug and a three-tiered china cake standbearing tiny sandwiches, cakes and scones, he decided he would have to draw her out slowly about the details of her personal life. He had no intention of making her even more uneasy than she already was.

She had never seen sandwiches or cakes like those now set before her and she was very grateful that the waitress poured the tea – she knew she was just so nervous that she would have spilled it. But despite their size and the fact that the crusts had been cut off the sandwiches were delicious and after a few minutes she began to relax and chat more easily as she told him about her working day and then Ada's family.

'And do you have a young man, Miss Shaw?' he asked, dropping two cubes of sugar into his cup using the silver tongs and feeling slightly embarrassed that he'd asked. It really was none of his business.

Slowly she shook her head. 'No, not really, Mr Davenport. At least not . . . any more.' She pushed the thought of Joe from her mind.

'That does surprise me. You are a very attractive young lady – if I may say so,' he continued, surprising himself yet again with a personal remark.

She blushed as she smiled at him – he really was rather nice.

'Of course I've always been so busy with the business that I've not really had time to socialise – much to my mother's annoyance and I suspect disappointment. You see I am an only child and my father died quite suddenly when I was twenty-two, leaving the business in a rather unsatisfactory state.'

She nodded. 'My father died when I was ten. In an accident

on the docks. He fell down into the hold of a ship.'

'How tragic. It must have been a terrible shock. I know it was very hard for both my mother and myself when Father had that fatal seizure, and it does take time to get over something like that,' he said sympathetically as he offered her a choice of cakes.

She carefully selected a pink macaroon. She'd never tasted anything quite like this before, she thought, it just melted in your mouth. She found that it wasn't hard to use the small silver fork. She forgot about everyone else in the room and as her nervousness slowly disappeared she answered his questions easily and even asked some herself.

To her surprise the time flew by and all too soon the food had been eaten, the tea drunk and as he signalled to the waitress to bring the bill she felt a little disappointed that the occasion was over.

'Thank you so much, Mr Davenport. I have enjoyed myself and . . . and you were right, everything was delicious,' she thanked him.

'Then perhaps you would like to join me again next Saturday afternoon, if you haven't any prior engagements of course,' he enquired. It was a spur-of-the-moment invitation but he'd found her quite delightful to talk to. She had spoken plainly and sincerely without any false modesty or contrived coyness or that arch, affected way some young women had these days. It suddenly occurred to him: was he starting to develop feelings for her beyond courtesy and concern?

Jane was surprised but pleased. 'I'd like that very much.' She paused nervously. 'And . . . and you can rely on me not to be gossiping at work,' she added.

As he held the back of her chair he smiled and leaned a little closer. 'I knew I could, Miss Shaw. I'll meet you here at the same time then.'

As he escorted her towards the door she did glance around her, determined to note everything to tell Emily and Ada when she got home. She also noticed a few envious glances being cast in her direction and she realised with a little start that Mr Davenport was a handsome man.

Emily was all agog at the detailed account Jane gave of the décor, the clientele, the china and cutlery and most of all the food. 'Oh, Jane, I'd have been so nervous I wouldn't have been able to eat a thing!'

'Of course you would, Em, and he has a way of putting you at ease,' Jane replied smiling.

'And you didn't feel . . . awkward or anything? Emily pressed.

Jane shook her head. 'The time went by really quickly and . . . and he's asked me to meet him again next Saturday at the same place.'

Emily's eyes widened in surprise; he was so much older than Jane 'And did you agree?'

'Yes. I enjoyed myself and he's honestly very . . . kind and thoughtful too,' Jane replied shyly.

'How old is he?' Emily queried.

Jane shrugged. 'I think he's in his thirties.'

'I'd say thirty-six or -seven,' Ada commented but before she had time to add that in her opinion he was far too old for Jane young Sonny burst into the kitchen, his face flushed with excitement, his hair standing up in untidy spikes and his socks

– as usual – in a crumpled heap around the tops of his boots. 'Mam! Mam! Guess what I've just heard? It's all around the street! Jimmy Cobham and Richie Corrin have been arrested and taken down the main Bridewell in Dale Street and put in the cells! They were caught pinching a handbag from a posh woman at the Riverside Station. Those coppers that don't wear uniforms have been watching them; they think they've been nicking stuff for ages and there was a third feller too but he gave them the slip and ran off! Everyone's saying they'll go to jail for sure now!' All this information was delivered in one breath and now Sonny stood watching them for their reactions to the news that had the whole street buzzing.

Jane and Emily exchanged glances.

'Well, I can't say I'm surprised, Sonny. It was only a matter of time before those two got caught and went to jail; I've been saying that for years. Did anyone say who they thought the other lad was – the one who ran off?' Ada asked. She couldn't help but suspect it was Alfie Shaw and if she were right then yet again he'd be upsetting his sister. Judging by the look on Jane's face, he already was.

Sonny shrugged; it wasn't quite the reaction he'd hoped for. 'Tommy Jones said his mam thought he used to live in this street but she couldn't remember his name, and then someone else said it wasn't him, that he didn't live in this neighbourhood at all.'

Ada nodded. 'Well, just let that be a lesson to you, Sonny Ellis. Be very careful who you choose as your mates and stay out of trouble. Now, go into the scullery and take off those filthy boots and wash your hands and face,' she instructed. 'You look as though you've been playing on a midden heap.'

When the lad had left the room Jane turned to Ada. 'Aunty Ada, do you think Alfie was mixed up in all this? Do you think he was the one who ran off?'

Ada nodded. 'Very probably. We knew he was hanging around with those two. And if you're going to meet that Mr Davenport again, Jane, I'd say nothing at all about you even *having* a brother,' she urged. Now that those two had been caught she wouldn't be a bit surprised if the plain-clothes coppers didn't go looking for Alfie and no doubt they'd find him too. Everyone knew they had their own ways and means; they were a law unto themselves were that lot – even their uniformed colleagues were wary of them. She was also a little perturbed by the fact that Mr Davenport had asked to see Jane again and that the girl had agreed for she was concerned by the age difference. Of course Joe had treated Jane very badly so she didn't blame the girl but she still felt disappointed; she'd had hopes for her son and Jane. She sighed. No one had any idea when or if Joe would return and she acknowledged to herself, with a pang of sadness, that Jane had to think of her own future.

Jane bit her lip. She knew Ada's advice was well meant but Alfie was still her brother and it might not have been him with Richie and Jimmy. If it was, she hoped that his mates getting caught might bring him to his senses. He was still young enough to mend his ways and turn over a new leaf. But her poor mam would have been so disappointed and humiliated by his behaviour. And she knew Ada was right: James Davenport would look on her differently if he knew she had a potential jailbird for a brother.

Chapter Sixteen

1931

JANE HAD TAKEN Ada's advice and not mentioned Alfie to James Davenport. By some stroke of luck Alfie hadn't been caught but nothing more had been heard of him in the year that had elapsed so she'd assumed he'd moved away from Liverpool. Richie and Jimmy were now serving a lengthy sentence in Walton Jail.

She was still seeing James Davenport regularly at the weekends – they were on first name terms now. She always felt relaxed and content in his company; the differences in their ages seemed unimportant. She'd found out that he did indeed have a very limited social life, for she appeared to be his only female companion. He was humorous and kind, generous to a fault, worked hard and was progressive in his ideas where his business was concerned, and she was sure he was fond of her. She had slowly come to realise that she was attracted to him, despite the fact that he was so much older than her, for he was a handsome man. While her heart did not race at the thought of kissing him – only one boy had made that happen – she could not help wondering what it would be like, and had a strong suspicion that she would enjoy it.

After a year of meeting regularly in Liverpool they had begun to take trips together outside the city. Quite often when the weather had been fine they'd driven out to the North Wales resorts of Llandudno and Colwyn Bay or along the coast to Southport and even up to Morecambe, often stopping to have lunch or tea at some of the most fashionable hotels. Secretly she preferred the tea rooms in smaller towns en route – she still felt a little overawed at the formality of some of the larger establishments – but he was unfailingly interesting and thoughtful, and she always enjoyed her excursions with him. Gradually she had told him of her childhood and her time in Brownlow Hill but she never mentioned Alfie – she told herself there was really no need, since Alfie seemed to have disappeared from her life. As time passed she acknowledged that her feelings for James had certainly grown deeper but she was aware, despite her growing attraction to him, that she didn't think of him in the same way as she'd thought of Joe. She was sure she would never feel that way again for someone – it was as if a fragment of love for Joe always remain in her heart, freezing it for anyone else. But, she told herself, Joe hadn't come back, nor was he likely to any time soon. Oh, Ada had had the occasional note from him from places as far apart as California, Texas, Indiana and Toronto, for Mr Ibsen, his employer, travelled a great deal, but there had never been a letter addressed solely to her. His notes to Ada described in brief his new life and, as Ada had remarked tersely, he seemed to be seeing places and enjoying himself into the bargain. She'd told herself that she had to forget all about Joe, that he'd clearly forgotten her. In time he would probably meet someone else and settle down.

She had to think of her future now, she knew; she would be twenty soon and she had grown fond of James Davenport. It had been on their first trip to Llandudno when it had become apparent that he was indeed fond of her too. It had been a beautiful summer day when they had arrived at the smart seaside town and James had parked the car on the promenade.

'Oh, this is lovely, James! Why didn't we come here last summer?' she exclaimed, gazing around at the ornate Victorian buildings and then out across the wide sweep of the sandy bay to the towering outcrop of rock called the Great Orme. 'Shall we walk along the pier?' she urged.

He laughed, thinking how delightful she looked in her pale lemon and white cotton dress and the wide-brimmed hat which shaded her face from the strong rays of the sun. 'You do realise that it's over a mile long? Are you sure you want to walk that far?'

'Oh, I don't mind, James, it's such a lovely day,' she replied and so he took her hand. She blushed but felt quietly happy as they strolled the full length of the pier.

'I feel as though I'm on a ship, we seem to be so far out,' she said as they reached the end and stood, surrounded by the sea, gazing out over the calm blue water.

'I don't think I'd relish the experience very much in winter,' he replied, 'but today it's beautifully tranquil.' He sighed happily, gazing out to the horizon.

She nodded. 'It is peaceful, with just the gentle sound of the waves and the cries of the gulls. We could be entirely alone,' she mused, relishing the warmth of the sun on her back.

He turned to her. 'We *are* almost entirely alone, Jane.'

She glanced around; very few people did seem to have ventured this far.

He reached out and gently stroked her cheek. 'Do you have any idea how beautiful you are, Jane, or how much . . . joy I find in your company?'

She blushed slightly. 'I . . . I never think of myself as being beautiful, James, but I'm happy when I'm with you, you are so . . . thoughtful and generous.'

'I hope you'll always feel like that, Jane,' he replied and took her in his arms and kissed her gently.

She didn't experience that dizzy surge of emotions she'd felt on New Year's Eve but she felt a sort of warm glow, a feeling of security, happiness and . . . contentment. A feeling that continued to grow as she stood within the circle of his arms.

'I have become very fond of you, Jane, and that special . . . affection is something that has been lacking in my life for a long time,' he confessed.

'I . . . I don't know what to say, James,' she whispered.

'I don't want to rush you into saying something you might regret, Jane, but . . . but do you think there might be a chance . . . ?'

She nodded. 'I am fond of you, James. We get on well together . . . I enjoy being with you . . .' For an instant she wondered if she was making a mistake in not telling him about Alfie for he was obviously serious about his feelings for her and she really didn't want to hide this side of her life from him, but was now the right time? She decided it wasn't.

He smiled down at her delightedly. 'That's all I wanted to hear, Jane, dearest. Now, I think we should walk back and find somewhere for lunch.'

They were shown to a table in one of the large windows of the Imperial Hotel that overlooked the promenade and he promised that on their next visit they would take a trip on the Great Orme Tramway. The view from the summit was quite breathtaking, he told her, and she listened happily as he made plans for future outings. When the waitress arrived to take their order Jane was astonished to see that it was Maisie.

'Maisie! What on earth are you doing here?' she gasped.

'Jane! Goodness, haven't you grown up! I work here now and I live in. It's great, I love being by the sea,' Maisie informed her, delighted to see Jane again.

'James, this is Maisie Mellor, a friend from Liverpool. She was very kind to me when my mother was dying,' she informed James, who nodded and smiled at the girl.

'We were in Brownlow Hill together,' Maisie replied, lowering her voice and then becoming a little embarrassed, wondering if she should even have mentioned that fact. 'I take it you've left there and are working,' she continued, turning to Jane.

Jane nodded. 'I live with Aunty Ada and I work for . . . James. He owns the Empire Laundry in Mount Vernon Street.'

Maisie looked a little puzzled but, noticing the looks of disapproval being cast in her direction by the head waiter, said hastily, 'I'm pleased to meet you, sir. Now, can I take your order?'

As she left their table Jane suddenly felt a frisson of fear. What if Maisie asked about Alfie? What should she say? What could she say? She couldn't try to pass it off; she'd just have to admit that she had a brother. She was on tenterhooks for the rest of the meal but to her great relief Maisie, when she came over to clear their plates and take their dessert order, didn't mention Alfie. Her usual cheerful self, she just brought Jane up to date with the series of jobs which had culminated in her being employed here in the hotel.

'It's been great to see you . . . both. I hope I'll see you again,' she said when they were leaving.

'I'm sure you will, Miss Mellor,' James replied affably.

Jane just nodded and smiled, thinking she couldn't take that chance. She couldn't risk Maisie mentioning Alfie and she would do all she could to make sure they didn't return to the Imperial again.

They paid two more visits to the seaside resort. To Jane's relief, on both occasions James suggested they try different hotels for lunch, unless of course she wished to see her friend again. She had smiled and shaken her head for as yet she still hadn't mentioned her brother. There just didn't seem to be a 'right' time to do it.

'Maisie's got a new life and new friends now, James and so . . . so have I,' she'd replied and when he'd nodded his agreement she felt the anxiety that had been dogging her seep away.

By their last visit the weather had turned cold and grey, with a thick mist rolling in silently from the sea, and James remarked that summer was over.

'That's such a pity, James,' she replied sadly. 'I don't think I've ever spent such a happy summer, thanks to you.'

He'd reached across the table and had taken her hand. 'And neither have I. We'll come back next spring, Jane.'

She'd smiled at him. 'I'd like that, I really would.'

'But in the meantime there are still plenty of places in Liverpool I'd like to show you,' he'd promised.

And so the weeks had slipped past and her birthday was approaching and James had hinted that he was going to take her somewhere special. She didn't think of him now as being so much older than herself for she felt she had grown up in the last year and she realised that her feelings for him were growing deeper all the time.

Emily and Georgie were planning on getting married next summer and Emily was becoming increasingly excited about the wedding: inevitably Jane's own thoughts were turning to settling down.

'So, has he told you yet where he's taking you?' Emily asked as Jane got ready to go out the evening before her birthday. Emily had become used to her friend 'walking out'. Like her mother, she had been outraged by her brother's treatment of her friend for she'd been aware of Jane's feelings for Joe. Now she was pleased that she had found someone else. She seemed happy with James Davenport and Joe only had himself to blame when all was said and done, but sometimes Emily wondered was James Davenport too old for Jane? Would Jane miss out on the joy of being in love with someone her own age? She had tentatively broached the subject a couple of times but Jane had just laughed and said she never even thought about James being much older, it seemed so unimportant, so Emily had let it drop

'No, and I wish he had because I don't know if this outfit will be suitable,' Jane replied as she placed a small dark brown hat with a veil over her hair. Now December was under way and the nights cold and dark, James was coming to pick her up. They didn't usually go out during the week but her birthday was on Wednesday and he'd said he didn't want her to have to wait until Saturday to celebrate the occasion. She'd saved up hard and bought a nice wool dress in a shade of creamy beige with a matching jacket edged with brown velvet ribbon. She'd wanted it primarily to wear at Christmas and it was only because she would be travelling to wherever he had in mind by car that she had decided to wear it tonight.

'That outfit will take you anywhere, Jane, so Mam says. It's smart and very . . . versatile,' Emily added. She herself hadn't bought anything new for ages but she didn't mind, she was saving hard for her wedding outfit. She wasn't going to splash out on a long white dress and veil; that would be a waste, she'd informed her mam, she'd get something she could wear again, even though secretly she would have loved a traditional gown.

Jane was very glad she had decided to wear the wool dress, she thought as James escorted her into the Washington Hotel on Lime Street. She'd never been here before but it was a very elegant place.

'I've reserved one of the private booths they have off the main dining room,' James informed her as they followed the uniformed bellboy along the thickly carpeted corridor. He hadn't wanted to eat in the large ornate dining room for this was to be a very special and important occasion and he wanted their table to be as intimate as possible. Jane looked lovely, he thought, in the simple dress and jacket; the creamy tones enhanced her pale skin and set off her rich auburn hair. He reflected how in the year and a half he had known her she'd grown so much more self-confident and poised. She no longer glanced nervously around as they entered a hotel or restaurant; she no longer plucked nervously at her gloves or cuffs, or fiddled with her hair. She was relaxed now in his company and he had become very fond of her, very fond indeed.

'This really is lovely, James,' she said as they were seated in the small booth containing a dining table and two chairs upholstered in maroon and gold cut velvet and lit by an alabaster table lamp with a silk fringed shade. The maroon and gold material lined the sides of the partition walls, which were topped with a stained-glass panel: it felt as if they were in a totally private space. There was a bottle of champagne in an ice bucket and two tall crystal flutes on the table.

'I thought this would be perfect for your birthday celebration,' he informed her as he held the chair out for her.

She smiled. 'Everywhere you take me, James, is perfect. You really do spoil me.'

They perused the menu while the maître d' opened and poured the champagne. Menus certainly didn't cause her the anxiety they once had, she thought with some amusement. In the early weeks and months when she'd accompanied him she had become used to asking him if the menu contained something she wasn't quite sure of but now she could negotiate the dishes with some ease, even those listed in French.

When they had given their order James raised his glass to her. 'A very happy birthday for tomorrow, Jane, my dear.'

She sipped it tentatively and then laughed. 'Thank you. I've never had champagne before. The bubbles get up your nose!'

He laughed too. 'You are delightful, Jane! If you like it then you shall have champagne every time we go out.' He set the glass down and became serious. 'Now, before the waiter returns there is something important I would like to . . . ask.'

She didn't reply but her heart had begun to beat a little faster so she took another sip of her drink.

'I think you know that I've become very fond of you over the months. I've never met anyone quite like you and I both admire and respect you and your achievements. I know life hasn't been easy for you, Jane, in fact it's been very hard at times but you've overcome . . . everything without becoming bitter, defeated or downhearted.' He'd practised this speech over and over but he was still nervous. He paused. 'Could you . . . do you think you could . . .' He shook his head at his own ineptness. 'Jane, what I am trying to say – and making such a mess of it – is: will you marry me? I do love you, Jane, and I will give you the best of everything in life,' he blurted out, feeling like a gauche sixteen-year-old instead of a mature businessman of thirty-nine.

Jane took a much deeper drink this time as she felt the colour rush to her cheeks. She was fond of him but did she love him? Her feelings were confused but she knew that she didn't want to hurt him and it was obvious that it had taken a good deal of courage for him to propose. 'James, I . . . I don't know what to say. You know that I'm very fond of you too . . .'

'Will you think about it, Jane? I don't want to rush you into making such an important decision,' he asked, thinking at least she hadn't screamed or fainted or turned him down flat.

She nodded slowly. 'Yes, yes, I will, James, and . . . and I promise I won't keep you waiting forever for an answer. That wouldn't be fair.'

He relaxed a little and reached across, took her hand and squeezed it gently. 'You see, that's one of the reasons I love you, Jane. You are so thoughtful and sincere.'

Their first course arrived and Jane finished her drink. She was feeling slightly light-headed, wondering if it was the wine or the decision she would now have to make. For it would be one that would change the course of the rest of her life.

It had been a very pleasant evening, she thought later as he drove her home. The food and wine had been excellent and they had enjoyed them, although his proposal was very much on both their minds. As they drew up outside Ada's house he leaned across and kissed her gently. 'Take as much time as you need, Jane, and happy birthday for tomorrow. You don't have to come into work if you don't want to, you know that.'

She touched his cheek gently. 'We've discussed this already, James, and you know my feelings about it. I'll see you tomorrow. Birthday or not, it's still a working day.'

He watched her as she let herself into the house, wishing she'd already said 'Yes' and hoping that they'd spend all her future birthdays together. Of course he doubted his mother would approve even though she was aware that he was courting Jane and intended to ask her to marry him. She'd made her feelings quite clear, that she considered Jane to be totally unsuitable owing to both her age and background, but he'd informed her that he was a grown man, not a child, and quite capable of choosing his life partner. So far Jane hadn't met his mother and that was his doing for he didn't want to create any tension between them. There would be time enough for that if Jane accepted him.

Jane lay awake for what seemed like hours, listening to the wind howling around the house and rattling the window panes. She had promised she wouldn't keep him waiting for an answer but was she really ready for marriage? she wondered. Could she promise to live with him as his wife forever? He was kind, thoughtful, generous and honest; he'd declared he loved her and she had no reason to doubt him, but could she come to really love him? Would she be happy or would she become increasingly *un*happy and make him miserable too? She would want for nothing, she knew that. Her life would be far more comfortable – luxurious even. She would never have to work again, never have to count her pennies, she would be secure, but still her doubts persisted. Would she be happy giving up a job she enjoyed, her little bit of independence? And how would her departure be received by those she worked with? Would she always love Joe Ellis? Would she carry that love in her heart forever and would it make her unable to love anyone else? She tossed restlessly. Oh, she *had* to forget about Joe. His future was quite obviously in America. He wasn't coming home again. He couldn't have really loved her at all in the first place; if he had he wouldn't have just gone out of her life like that. She wondered should she ask Ada's advice? After all she was like a mother to her now, though at the end of the day she was also his mother, and that might affect how she looked at things, but she'd always thought that Ada had approved of her relationship with James. She'd never told her directly that she didn't. And then her mother's words came back to her forcefully; it was almost as if she heard Ellen's voice. 'Choose wisely, Jane.'

Before she'd died Ellen had begged her to think carefully about the man she married. To think about her security, about what would happen if the kind of misfortune that had ruined her mother's life struck her. Ellen had begged her to think about her future, about not having to end her days in despair and poverty in a workhouse because of a malign stroke of fate. What if she and James had children and something awful happened to him? She would be well provided for, she would never know the despair and humiliation her poor mother had suffered on top of her grief and shock and her children would never go without; they would still have a secure future. Could she turn her back on all that and live on in the vain hope that someday maybe, just *maybe*, Joe would return and *maybe* still want her? She sighed deeply and buried her face in the pillow. No, she couldn't do that. She couldn't let this opportunity slip away. She'd been much younger when she'd thought Joe loved her; now she felt she had grown up and must take control of her life, of her decisions. She would heed her mother's advice, the last she'd ever given her. She would marry James and hope that she would grow to love him. She would put Joe Ellis out of her mind and out of her heart forever.

She said nothing about her decision to Ada and her family next morning, just accepted their birthday greetings with a smile and went to work as usual. But upon arrival she went straight to James's office.

He was surprised to see her, concerned to see that she

looked pale and tired. 'Jane, I can see that you didn't have a very restful night, please sit down,' he urged.

She shook her head. 'No, James, but thank you. I . . . I came straight to tell you that I've made my decision, I promised I wouldn't keep you waiting.' She took a deep breath; she had rehearsed this. She wouldn't lie and say she loved him. 'I . . . I would very much like to marry you and I will try to be a good and affectionate wife.'

The tension that had built up inside him at her unexpected appearance melted away and his delight was plain to see as he took her in his arms. 'Oh, Jane, my dearest, you won't regret it, I promise!'

She felt a huge sense of relief wash over her as she buried her head against his shoulder. She *was* doing the right thing. It was what Ellen had wanted her to do.

'I know I won't, James. You do know that I am very, very fond of you?'

He looked down into her amber eyes and thought she'd never looked so beautiful and he'd never loved her so much. 'I love you, Jane, and I'll care for you forever, I promise. Now, I have to admit that I was hoping against hope that you would agree so . . .' He released her and opened a drawer in his desk. 'In anticipation, I bought you this.'

She almost gasped aloud at the sight of the ring nestling on its velvet cushion inside the box he held out. She'd never seen diamonds as big or as brilliant. 'James! It's . . . it's . . . stunning!'

'Just as you are, Jane Shaw – soon to be Jane Davenport,' he replied quietly as he slipped it on to her finger. 'You have made me a very happy man, my dear, and happy birthday!'

She smiled up at him. 'I've never had such a gorgeous

birthday present, James, and I . . . I'm very happy too,' she added sincerely. And she was, she thought. It was a birthday she'd always remember.

'Now, as you are officially my fiancée, you can no longer work here – or anywhere else for that matter. It's just not acceptable.'

'What . . . what shall I do then?' she asked. She hadn't considered that.

'Firstly go home and wait until I come to collect you later on. Leave it to me to inform Mr Edwards of the situation and the reason for your sudden departure. Then I will take you to meet my mother and we can make all the arrangements,' he instructed. He knew it wouldn't be an easy meeting for either himself, his mother or Jane. But he was determined that his mother should accept his choice of wife. She had voiced her views on the matter when he'd started courting Jane and in fact she'd been tight-lipped whenever he'd mentioned Jane since but now he hoped with all his heart that after she'd met his fiancée that would change.

She nodded. 'I hadn't thought about the . . . arrangements. All I'd thought about was making a decision and telling you. But I . . . I don't want a long engagement, James, and I don't want a big, fancy wedding. I don't think that would be . . . acceptable to anyone.' She knew Mrs Davenport was aware of her son's liaison for James had informed her of the fact months ago, but she wondered how she would feel on learning that he had proposed and she had accepted.

He nodded his agreement. 'Then we'll have a quiet ceremony as soon as it can be arranged. Shall I drive you home?'

'No. You have a business to run and I'd like to walk. It's fine and sunny outside,' she answered, thinking she would now have to start thinking about her immediate future.

'Then I'll call for you at about five o'clock,' he said, kissing her on the forehead before she left.

As she was crossing the yard to the gates she was suddenly confronted by Maggie Rosbottom, who was staggering beneath the weight of a huge basket of dirty laundry. She'd rarely seen the woman since she'd gone to work in the despatch office and that had suited her but she noted that she hadn't changed – in fact she looked harder than ever and very disgruntled.

Maggie dumped the basket at Jane's feet, her brow creasing in a frown. 'Well, if it isn't Miss High an' bloody Mighty from the office! I notice yer keep clear of the likes of us from the wash 'ouse now days.'

'Hello, Maggie,' Jane greeted her quietly.

'An' didn't yer do well for yerself an' all, Jane Shaw! For a "workhouse girl", that is.' Maggie was openly derisive.

'I worked hard to get that promotion, Maggie. I've always worked hard.'

'So 'ave I but I don't see the likes of me nor Bertha getting "promoted", nor gettin' more brass in our pockets either, like! Yer're a bloody creep, that's what yer are! That's what yer've always been!' Maggie didn't bother to hide the jealousy she felt.

Jane had had enough. She wasn't going to let Maggie take the shine off her day. 'I don't know why you dislike me so much, Maggie. I've never done anything underhand. I've always been honest and open and I've never said a bad word about you or your friends and I could have . . .'

'That's a lie, Jane Shaw! Yer were always sneakin' in ter

Miss Roberts an' talkin' about us,' Maggie shot back.

Jane stared straight at the girl and squared her shoulders. 'I was not but I'm not going to stand here arguing with you about it. And in a matter of weeks you will address me not as "Jane Shaw" but as "Mrs Davenport" for I've just become engaged.' She held up her hand and the sunlight caught the diamonds in her ring and they seemed to blaze with a myriad of colours. 'Now, I have things to attend to and you, Miss Rosbottom, have your work to get on with.'

As she turned away she did feel a little sorry she had spoken to the woman like that for Maggie's mouth had dropped open, her eyes wide with pure astonishment, but surely she'd asked for it? She had tormented her for so long and without any justification. All that was at an end now, Jane thought, and in any case her engagement would soon have become public knowledge.

As she walked the short distance in the cold, sharp air she realised that she would now have to tell Ada. At least when she got home everyone else would be out and Ada would have the time to sit and talk to her without interruptions.

'In the name of heaven, what are you doing back so soon?' Ada demanded as she walked into the kitchen where the older woman was clearing away the breakfast dishes.

She didn't reply, instead just stretched out her hand on which the cluster of diamonds twinkled dazzlingly.

Ada stared at the ring in amazement, then at Jane, and then she sat down at the table placing the pile of plates down heavily. 'You . . . you never said *anything*! I take it it's James Davenport? Jane, luv, are you doing the right thing?'

Jane sat opposite her. 'I . . . I hope so, Aunty Ada.

He . . . James asked me last night and I was awake half the night making up my mind and so I went straight to him this morning to give him my answer.'

Ada had regained some of her composure. 'Jane, you're a good girl and you know how fond I am of you and I'd like nothing more than to see you settled in a home of your own and with a good husband at your side. I'm not saying he won't make you a good husband but . . . but his background . . . his life is so . . . different to ours and then he . . . he's so much older. Will you be able to cope with it all?'

'I think so. His age doesn't matter to me, you know that,' Jane replied seriously.

'And do you love him, Jane?' Ada asked, thinking of Joe with a pang.

'I'm very fond of him. I know that I'm happy when I'm with him and that he loves me. I . . . I do realise that my life will have to change but I've sort of got used to fitting in with his lifestyle,' she added, thinking of how terribly nervous she'd been when he'd first taken her to Brown's Tea Rooms and how much she'd altered since then.

Ada was concerned. Yes, it was true Jane had become used to accompanying him to these places but she would now be moving totally into his world. A very different world that had its own rules and prejudices. And Jane hadn't said she loved him. Would affection be enough to make her content with him in that world? 'And where will you live, luv?' she asked quietly.

'With him in the house in Upper Huskisson Street, I suppose. I hadn't thought about it,' Jane replied truthfully.

'With his mother?' Ada persisted.

Jane nodded. 'He's picking me up at five and taking me to be introduced. I've not met her yet,' she informed Ada.

Ada looked grim. It was a far from ideal situation, she thought. She wondered if Mrs Davenport even knew he had been courting Jane, never mind that he'd asked her to become his wife. Just how would she take it? She herself wouldn't be very happy in Mrs Davenport's place if suddenly confronted with a future daughter-in-law, one who was not only an employee but an orphan who had spent years in a workhouse. She was sure that wasn't what Mrs Davenport had planned for her only son.

'I don't want to upset you, Jane, but I'd be prepared for her to be a bit shocked to say the least. But don't let that put you off; just be yourself. He's asked you and you've agreed.'

Jane looked thoughtful. 'Do you think I should have turned him down? That I . . . I'm not good enough for him, Aunty Ada? Be honest,' she urged.

'Of course you're good enough for him, luv, and he obviously loves you. He's not a young lad who doesn't know his own mind and . . . and no, I don't think you should have refused. It's just that you might find it hard to fit in at first and his mother might also find it hard to accept you. But,' she went on optimistically, 'I'm sure you'll cope very well.'

Jane smiled. 'I'll do my best. Last night when I was trying to make up my mind I thought about what Mam said to me just before she died. She begged me to choose wisely, to think about my future.'

Ada nodded slowly. 'She was right, luv, and I . . . I think she'd be proud of you now. You'll have a very good life, Jane, a secure and comfortable one. A far better life than either she or I have had. But remember, luv, wealth and status aren't everything.'

'I know, Aunty Ada,' Jane replied.

Ada smiled. 'But it certainly helps to have plenty in the bank. Now, let's have a cup of tea and you can show me that ring properly. I've never seen stones as big as that!' she added, shaking her head in wonder at the expense. What it had cost would have kept her whole family in comfort for years, she thought, and it would certainly completely eclipse Emily's little diamond, but this was the life that Jane had agreed to embrace and she was glad for her. She'd had so little in life so far. It was certainly a better life than Joe could have offered her but she still regretted that her eldest son had dismissed the love of a girl like Jane. Mrs Davenport might not welcome Jane as a daughter-in-law but she certainly would have.

Chapter Seventeen

———◆———

Edith Davenport looked out of the window of the comfortable drawing room on the first floor of the large, elegant house that had been her home for more years than she cared to remember. The December afternoon was deepening into the heavy dusk of evening and the skeletal branches of the trees that lined the wide thoroughfare were only faintly visible now; soon the street would be illuminated by the lamps. She shivered and turned away; walking back to the large ornate fireplace she pushed the button of the bell set into the wall beside it. She would have the curtains drawn and the fire made up before James arrived home with this Miss Shaw, the girl he'd announced last night he intended to marry and had telephoned this morning to say he was bringing home.

As she sat down in the brocade-upholstered armchair she drew the soft lilac cashmere shawl closer around her shoulders. She had tried to discourage him, she mused, when he'd informed her of his outings with her, and he'd reminded her quite forcefully that he was no longer an impressionable young man. But she'd hoped it would come to nothing, that perhaps the girl would become bored with a man of his age or he would tire of her – neither of which had happened. She'd been surprised and shocked when he'd hinted he intended to ask her to marry him. She had gone to great pains over the years to introduce him to eminently suitable young ladies but no, he had chosen this girl who was employed in the despatch office at the laundry. She sighed heavily, wondering just what Edmund would have said to his son about his choice of wife. A great deal, she surmised, but after a good deal of thought she had decided not to voice her opposition. She would reserve judgement until she had actually met Jane Shaw. She was getting old and tired and her bones often ached and, though at one time she would have launched into battle with her son, she felt reluctant now to face a confrontation of such proportions. However, if the girl proved to be a total social disaster she would be quite prepared to do so.

Her deliberations were interrupted by the young maid who had answered her summons.

'See to the fire and the curtains, please, Renshaw, and when Mr James arrives please bring up some tea,' she instructed and watched in silence as the girl carried out the tasks. At least the room looked warm and welcoming, she thought, glancing around and wondering what kind of a home the girl was used to.

She didn't have long to wait for within minutes she heard voices and then the door opened and she was faced with her son and – she presumed – his fiancée.

'Mother, this is Jane, and I am delighted to tell you that she has agreed to become my wife,' James announced, looking proud and apprehensive at the same time.

Edith stood up using the aid of a silver-topped ebony cane. The girl wasn't at all what she had expected, though she was careful to hide her surprise. She was young, but Edith had been aware of that; she was also very attractive with that auburn and alabaster colouring. Smartly if plainly dressed, she showed no sign of arrogance or impertinence, nor any indication of servility or nervousness. In fact she looked quietly confident and rather pleasant. She nodded as Jane stepped towards her, her hand outstretched.

'I am very pleased to meet you, Mrs Davenport,' Jane said quietly, having rehearsed this.

Edith winced slightly at the accent but shook Jane's hand and indicated that she should sit. 'I've asked that tea be brought up,' she announced.

Jane sat down tentatively on the edge of a sofa and James sat beside her and took her hand. 'I bought the ring a few days ago, Mother, in anticipation.'

Edith nodded as she took in the engagement ring. It was substantial enough without being ostentatious or vulgar. 'And so, Miss Shaw, you are quite happy to become part of this family?'

Jane nodded. The old lady was very formal and a little intimidating but she had half expected it. 'I am, Mrs Davenport, and hope that I will prove to be a good wife although . . .' She paused, glancing quickly around. '. . . although I am sure you are aware that I come from a much . . . humbler home and background than this.'

Again Edith nodded. James had told her that the girl lived

with a Mrs Ellis and her family in a very poor and dilapidated part of the city, and that she was an orphan. Apparently this Mrs Ellis had been a friend of her deceased mother.

'Jane has said that she doesn't want a long engagement or a big wedding and I agree, Mother,' James put in, trying to judge his mother's mood. She had said very little so far but he was thankful that she hadn't been openly hostile.

'That sounds very sensible – in the circumstances, James.'

'We thought perhaps after Christmas, early in the New Year,' James informed her.

'It will give me time to spend my last Christmas with Aunty Ada and her family, who have been very good to me, and to buy an outfit and . . . other things that I think I'll need,' Jane added. They'd discussed this in the car en route to his home and James had said he would give her an allowance each month, which she should spend entirely on herself. She had been staggered by the amount he had suggested but realised that her wardrobe would have to be increased and its quality greatly improved.

'And you will then live here?' Edith enquired, thinking that so far Jane Shaw hadn't put a foot wrong though she would like to meet the girl without her son being present. She wanted to find out for herself just what the girl expected from her future life and, most importantly, if she genuinely cared for her son.

James nodded but before he had time to say anything more Renshaw arrived bearing the tea tray.

Jane was thankful that she was now used to delicate china, sugar cubes and silver tongs and the like, but she hadn't expected the Davenports to have a maid. On reflection, she realised it was something she should have anticipated.

'And I take it you will stop working now, Miss Shaw?' Edith enquired as she poured the tea, observing that the girl seemed quite unfazed by her Royal Crown Derby.

'Yes. I left this morning, immediately after I told James I would marry him,' Jane replied, stirring her tea slowly with the small silver spoon.

'Then you must come and take tea with me tomorrow and we can become better acquainted and discuss the formal arrangements, announcements in the press and so on,' Edith urged. It would be easier to get the girl to talk more about herself when James wasn't present; she was sure of that. She could then assess her and her motives – if indeed she had any. And then she would decide if she herself wished to continue to live here or move and set up a small establishment of her own. She had no wish to do so but she would if she felt she couldn't endure living with James's wife.

'Thank you, Mrs Davenport, I'd like that,' Jane replied, wondering if she would ever call the woman anything less formal.

The next half-hour seemed to drag on interminably, Jane thought as they made polite small talk, and she felt far from comfortable in her future mother-in-law's presence. The room, although comfortable, was very grandly furnished compared to Ada's kitchen and she hoped that perhaps tomorrow a smaller room would be used. She was quite relieved when James stood up and announced that he would drive her home.

'Then I shall expect you at four thirty, Miss Shaw,' Edith replied when Jane thanked her for both the tea and the invitation and gathered up her bag and gloves. Jane left, feeling as though she'd just endured a school test. She really wasn't sure if she had passed or not.

'So, how did it go? What's she like? What kind of reception did you get?' Ada questioned when she arrived home. She'd confided to Emily that she hoped the old lady hadn't forbidden Jane to darken her door again and Emily had replied that in Jane's position she would be absolutely terrified. She'd added that Jane must love him to be prepared to endure such a trial.

'She didn't actually say much,' Jane replied, taking off her jacket and hat. 'And if she disapproved of me she certainly didn't show it. She's very formal though. She kept calling me "Miss Shaw".'

Ada nodded, relieved that at least there hadn't been any harsh words or hysterics. 'Women of her age and background usually are sticklers for such things.'

'She's asked me to go for tea tomorrow, without James,' Jane informed them.

'Has she indeed?' Ada remarked succinctly.

'So we can discuss the formal arrangements and I suppose so she can try to get to know more about me, which is only natural. Maybe she'll be a bit more talkative too.'

'What's the place like?' Ada enquired curiously. 'I know the houses are big, I've passed along there on the tram sometimes.'

'It is big and elegant and very nicely furnished. All rather . . . grand,' Jane supplied.

'Oh, Mam, never mind the house. Jane, let me see your ring!' Emily demanded for her mam had said it was quite amazing.

Jane smiled as she held out her left hand.

'Oh, heavens above! It's . . . it's . . . gorgeous! It makes mine look . . . tiny!' Emily cried; she didn't dare to think how much it had cost.

'But James chose it for me, Em,' Jane replied, reminding her friend that she had had the pleasure of choosing her own engagement ring.

Ada stood up. 'Well, I'll have the lads in any minute now starving hungry and the table's not even set. Emily, get the knives and forks out while I drain these potatoes.'

'I'll do that, Aunty Ada,' Jane offered, thinking that she would miss the happy informality of meals with Ada's family.

'Then you'd better take that ring off first. We don't want it getting dirty or, worse, ending up down the plughole,' Ada instructed. 'And don't go getting into a state about tomorrow, just be yourself and tell her the truth,' she added. But she was relieved that so far Jane seemed to have been accepted without a huge amount of upset.

Jane *was* nervous when she walked up the steps of the house that was to be her new home and rang the bell. The same girl who had served the tea yesterday answered the door and ushered her into the hall.

'Mrs Davenport is expecting you, miss.'

Jane smiled and nodded. 'Is she in the drawing room?'

Renshaw shook her head. 'No, miss, the breakfast room.'

Jane followed her up the stairs and into a much smaller room, which overlooked the garden at the back of the house. The December sun filtered through the window, adding its feeble warmth to that of the fire burning brightly in the hearth.

'Miss Shaw, ma'am,' the girl announced. 'Shall I bring up the tea now?'

Mrs Davenport nodded and indicated that Jane should sit down in an armchair opposite her. The room was decorated in shades of green, beige and cream and it felt far cosier and more restful than the one she'd been in yesterday, Jane thought with some relief.

The old lady looked intently at her, noting the same neat appearance, the same quiet, unassuming manner. 'There are some questions I would like to ask you, Miss Shaw.'

'Of course, I expected there would be,' Jane replied, feeling her stomach tense.

'Do you love my son?' Edith asked bluntly.

'I am very fond of James and he has been exceptionally kind to me,' Jane replied. She had decided to be completely frank with his mother about her feelings for James. 'I have to admit that no one was more . . . astonished than me when he asked me out. I'm not of his . . . your class and I was very nervous about embarrassing him.'

'You haven't answered my question, Miss Shaw,' Edith persisted.

Jane's forehead creased in a frown. 'I'm not entirely certain that I know exactly what *love* is, Mrs Davenport. Is being happy and content in someone's company and wanting to care for that person, live with them and make them happy too? That's what I consider to be meant by *love*. I know it is what my mother felt for my father, while he lived,' Jane answered.

Edith nodded; she'd answered that well enough. Hers had been more or less an arranged marriage and her mother had said that love would grow with time and indeed it had.

'So, there have been no other . . . relationships?'

For a second Jane looked away before shaking her head. 'When I was growing up I was quite . . . close to Mrs Ellis's eldest son, but it was really nothing more than friendship and I don't think he even remembers me now. He went to live and work in America.'

'And your parents are both dead?' Edith continued, watching Jane closely.

Jane nodded and informed her of her father's accident.

'Very tragic. How did your mother manage . . . afterwards?'

Jane didn't answer at first. She'd assumed James had told his mother that when she'd first gone to the Empire Laundry she'd been called 'the workhouse girl', but obviously he hadn't. She decided it would do no good to try to evade the question. 'She didn't – manage. She tried desperately hard but . . . but for people like us there are never any savings to fall back on when times are hard. Every penny earned is needed just to live. In the end she was forced to take us into the work-house – herself and myself,' she added, deliberately omitting Alfie as she saw the dawning horror in the old lady's eyes.

'Good God!' Edith exclaimed, unable to suppress her shock. They must really have been paupers.

Jane pressed on, determined now not to discredit her mother's memory. 'She was at her wits' end and when I think of her . . . desperation and her shame I . . . I could cry. She was a good wife and mother. She managed on what my father could earn although it wasn't very much nor was it even a regular amount – she never knew from day to day how much money there would be, if anything at all – and what little we had in the way of furnishings and clothes she made sure were kept clean and cared for. She brought me up to be honest, respectful and thrifty. It broke her heart to end her days in Brownlow Hill, for she died there. It was through no fault of her own, Mrs Davenport, that she was left destitute and had to suffer such awful humiliation. Believe me, it is a very humiliating experience.' There were tears now on Jane's cheeks but she brushed them quickly away. 'I . . . I promised myself I would be honest with you but I make no apologies for my family, my background or my upbringing. My parents were good people, our circumstances were not of our making, and I really do believe that I will make James as good a wife as my poor mother was.'

Edith Davenport leaned back in her chair. At first she'd been shocked and horrified but as Jane had quietly yet obviously sincerely explained, that shock had been tempered by both pity and admiration. 'And so you spent most of your early years in *that* place.'

Jane nodded. 'I did but when I was seventeen Mrs Ellis, whom I call Aunty Ada, offered me a home. Before we had to go into Brownlow Hill she did what she could to help us but she had no room to take us in, nor could she afford to, but her circumstances changed when her eldest son went to sea and her daughter got a job and started to earn a wage and so . . . I had a home again and I've been grateful for it. But I've worked. I've worked hard ever since I was fourteen, Mrs Davenport, to support myself.'

The old lady nodded in her turn. She now felt there was no need for her to move to a smaller establishment, she could get on quite well with this girl. 'I understand and . . . and I respect you for it.'

'Thank you, Mrs Davenport.'

Edith leaned forward. 'For heaven's sake, will you stop calling me "Mrs Davenport"! If you are going to marry my son you must learn to call me "Mother-in-law" and I shall call you "Jane". You will get used to my ways in time as no doubt I shall get used to yours. Now, if you would be so kind as to ring that bell. Heaven knows where that girl has got to with the tea! And then you can tell me what plans you have made.'

As she got to her feet Jane smiled. She probably would get used to the old lady's rather abrupt manner but it would take time. At least they'd got off to a better start today – although she didn't know how long that would last if she ever found out about Alfie.

Chapter Eighteen

'ARE YOU VERY NERVOUS?' Emily asked as she adjusted her own sage-green and cream satin hat in the mirror. Her outfit was the most fashionable and expensive she'd ever owned for Jane had insisted on paying for it; she fully intended to wear it for her own wedding in June. She could never have afforded to pay what this dress and matching coat had cost, to say nothing of the hat. They'd both gone to the Bon Marché in Church Street no less, a shop neither of them had ever set foot in before, and the two outfits had been chosen and purchased. Jane's dress and matching coat was of vibrant cobalt-blue wool crêpe and her hat of a similar shade trimmed with a paler blue. The rather sniffy assistant who had served them had thawed enough to say the colours really suited her and that she looked very chic and elegant.

Jane slowly pulled on her soft black leather gloves and nodded. 'Of course I'm nervous, Em. It's the beginning of a totally new and . . . different life.'

Emily sat down on the bed beside her. 'You are *sure* about it all, Jane? You know how fond I am of you and I'd hate you to end up miserable. Marriage is forever.'

'I'm sure, Em. I promised Mam I'd choose wisely and I know I have. James is . . . Oh, I couldn't have wished for a kinder, more generous man and I *think* I do love him.'

'You thought you loved our Joe,' Emily reminded her quietly, remembering how heart-broken Jane had been when Joe hadn't come home. She was very sure that she loved Georgie.

'Maybe I did, but maybe we were both too young to know exactly what we felt and . . . and he decided not to come back, so I realised that it couldn't have been love on his part. No, I'm certain James and I will be very happy.'

'And you're not nervous about . . . well, you know . . . *tonight*,' Emily pressed.

Jane smiled and shook her head. 'Not really, I know he'll be . . . considerate, but well, I have to admit that it's . . .'

'It's all a bit of a mystery how we'll feel about *it*. I think I'm looking forward to it; there have been times when I wished we didn't have to wait. And', Emily confided, 'Georgie has hinted that seeing as it's not long now we could . . . but Mam would murder me!'

Jane smiled. Ada wouldn't have gone quite that far but she would have been bitterly disappointed in Emily. 'Oh, we'll both be fine, Em. Now, come on or we'll be late. I know it's quite traditional but I don't want to upset either James or my mother-in-law by keeping them waiting in a draughty church!' Old Mrs Davenport had insisted her only son be married in the church in which he'd been christened and which she attended regularly, and Jane had felt she had no choice but to agree.

Emily picked up her bag and gloves, ready to go.

'You both look very elegant,' Ada complimented them when they came downstairs, 'and your poor mam would have been so proud of you, Jane,' she added, kissing her on the cheek. Poor Ellen would have hardly recognised Jane now for she looked every inch a lady, Ada reflected, swallowing hard to keep the tears from coming into her eyes.

'And so do you, Aunty Ada,' Jane replied, smiling. She'd miss living here but she would visit Ada frequently. She'd begged her to come and see her in her new home but Ada had been evasive, saying she just wouldn't feel comfortable in a big posh house like that, being waited on and having to fiddle about with sugar tongs and fine china that would break if you so much as looked at it. No, Jane must come back here to visit, she made that much clear.

'Well, I have to say I'll give the neighbours something to jangle about when they see me in this good coat *and* a hat,' Ada replied, reaching for her new charcoal wool coat with its velvet trimmed collar and her silver-grey and black velvet hat. Jane had been very generous but Ada had flatly refused to go to shops such as the Bon Marché or Hendersons and had opted instead for Blackler's – usually well out of her price range – where things were still smart but a fraction of the cost.

Emily was standing for Jane and Fred was giving her away; neither Danny nor Sonny was going and both had seemed relieved at the fact. On James's side there would only be his mother and an old school friend as best man. After the ceremony James had arranged for them all to have a meal in a small hotel. After that he and his wife and mother would return to Upper Huskisson Street and Ada, Fred and Emily would come back here. Even though she would be delighted to see Jane happy and settled the whole occasion was going to be quite an ordeal, Ada had confided to Fred. She'd also wondered about the wisdom of Emily choosing to wear green for, she'd said ominously, she'd heard it was bad luck. He'd replied scathingly that she should keep that piece of information to herself as it was just an old wives' tale anyway. As she followed the two girls out of the door, Ada just hoped the future brought them everything they wanted, for as she and poor Jane's mother had found, life didn't always turn out just the way you'd planned.

Edith Davenport looked around the church and sniffed a little disparagingly. Of course Christmas was over and it was the depths of winter but the place seemed entirely without cheer. The only floral decorations were the evergreens and waxy hellebores and the candle flames provided little in the way of illumination. It was also very chilly and she was grateful for her sable coat and the violet wool dress she wore beneath it. James didn't seem to have noticed the rather dismal atmosphere, she thought. He looked happy and confident.

In the weeks since she'd first met Jane she had become used to the girl, who had visited most afternoons. She had been quietly relieved and pleased when Jane had asked her for advice, saying she knew nothing of the running of a house such as this or of dealing with staff, although she realised that she, his mother, would continue to supervise everything. It boded well for the future that the girl was willing to learn, Edith had thought, for when the time came for her to cast off 'this mortal coil' her daughter-in-law would be more than accustomed to providing James with a correctly managed and comfortable household.

As the notes of the organ died away and the vicar commenced the marriage service, she glanced across at the little group who had accompanied Jane. They looked respectable enough, she thought, but a little uncomfortable, and Mr Ellis had quite obviously stuffed his cap into his pocket when he'd arrived for part of it was protruding. The girl – Emily – who was Jane's bridesmaid was a very pretty young thing with huge dark eyes; her outfit must have been bought at the same time as the bride's. Jane did look very smart, though, she thought approvingly, and very attractive. She'd known that her future daughter-in-law had no intention of wearing a traditional gown and veil for she'd told her so, and she thought the well-cut coat and dress not only suited Jane but was also far more practical for January. She shivered as she concentrated on the service. The girl would have caught pneumonia in this glacial atmosphere in lace or satin.

Jane looked up at James and smiled as she made her vows, her voice quite steady. The nerves that had plagued her as she'd arrived at the church had disappeared as soon as she'd taken her place beside him and he'd smiled reassuringly at her. She was certain she was doing the right thing, and she would 'love, honour and obey' him until death did them part. Joe Ellis no longer had a part of her, she was sure; she was setting out to share a new life with James and when he placed the ring on her finger and bent and kissed her, she suddenly realised that she was now Mrs James Davenport. Things had changed utterly.

There was no wind but it was freezing cold, Alfie thought as he sat huddled on a seat in the saloon of the ferry as it crossed slowly from Birkenhead to Liverpool. Beyond the windows the Mersey was flat calm and the night sky was studded with stars and the brilliant light of the full moon caught the foamy wake, turning it to silver, but he was oblivious to everything except the fact that when the ferry docked he had nowhere to go. Jimmy and Richie were in jail; Ada wouldn't have him over her doorstep and he knew Jane was living with the Ellises for Jimmy had told him ages ago; there was no way on earth he would go back to Brownlow Hill; and the Birkenhead Police were looking for him. He didn't know if they swopped information with their mates in the Liverpool City force so he'd again have to lie low.

He shifted his position on the uncomfortable wooden slatted seat. He'd been dead lucky the day his mates had been caught. He'd been the one on lookout and had managed to scarper when the plain-clothes police had nabbed Jimmy and then Richie almost before any of them knew what was happening. He'd realised immediately he'd have to get out of the city for a while so he'd crossed to Birkenhead and with the few shillings he'd had left had found lodgings in one of the crowded, narrow streets by the shipyards. He'd had to familiarise himself with the roads and streets for he didn't know the place very well but he'd soon found out that there was a regular market and he'd managed to earn a few shillings fetching and carrying and running errands for any of the stallholders who needed such help. He'd soon tired of that though and gone back to his old ways of earning money, and he hadn't done too badly, especially at Christmastime, until yesterday when he'd almost been caught.

The noxious smell of oil wafting up from the engine room was making him feel sick for he hadn't eaten since early morning and it was now nearly nine o'clock, so reluctantly he got up and left the dubious warmth of the saloon and went up on deck.

At least the sharp frosty air made him feel a bit better although he shivered in the freezing temperature as he stood watching the lights of the Pier Head drawing closer. He wondered if he should go and find Jane. She might take pity on him and give him a couple of shillings since she had a job in that laundry, but he couldn't go there until morning. He'd already dismissed the idea of seeking her out at Ada's – and maybe she was no longer living there anyway. Had she moved, he wondered? Should he go to Jimmy or Richie's house and see if there was a chance of him staying there tonight? Mentally he shrugged. Better not: it was too close to Ada's and someone might recognise him and he doubted either of their mams would be very pleased to see him knowing he'd managed to escape while their lads were banged up in Walton. Then he remembered the loft above the stable where he'd stayed when he'd run off from the workhouse. He'd go there; it had been safe enough and it was a roof over his head with straw to sleep on. He'd be reasonably comfortable and tomorrow he'd try and work out just what he was going to do next. What money he possessed he had in a little bag slung around his neck and he decided he'd spend a few pence on a chip supper. In his pocket he had two Woodbines and a few matches. Suddenly, despite the cold, he began to feel much better.

The ferry drew alongside and he felt the gentle bump as it

nudged the Landing Stage and he watched the deck hands secure the hawsers.

'Right, lad, move yerself! We've all got 'omes ter go to,' one instructed as the gate was slid back and the gangway came down with a thump.

Alfie nodded and walked quickly, head bent and cap pulled down, across the wooden platform and up the floating roadway, steep tonight due to the outgoing tide. At least he was back home, he thought. At least he knew the streets and alleys of this city like the back of his hand and he was sure he'd be all right. He had been fine so far; he'd learned how to look after himself and something was bound to come up. He'd manage. He'd not starve. He'd been away long enough for the scuffers not to recognise him and there were still good pickings to be had – and this time he'd be far more careful, for he wouldn't have the help of his mates. He grinned to himself as he reached the top of the roadway and headed for the tram terminus. A penny would get him as far as London Road and he'd walk from there; he knew where there was a chippy and he'd eat his supper as he walked. It felt good to be home.

Chapter Nineteen

———◆———

'MOTHER-IN-LAW, I can't make up my mind which outfit to wear, so I'd like your advice. I want to look smart but I don't want to eclipse the bride,' Jane informed Edith as she entered the drawing room and laid the two dresses across a sofa. Emily's wedding was in two days' time.

The old lady laid aside her book and smiled. Despite her initial misgivings she got on very well with James's wife. Jane's vocabulary had improved greatly she thought – noting the word 'eclipse' – which she put down to the fact that the girl was an avid reader. Jane had confided that now she didn't have to spend her days working to earn a living she loved nothing more than sitting in the breakfast room engrossed in a book and indeed she seemed to be working her way slowly through the library that Edith and Edmund had built up over the years.

'I really prefer the pale green and white floral crêpe-de-Chine dress and the white sugar-spun straw hat with the wide brim and pale green ribbons, but do you think I should perhaps settle for the plain lilac with the matching hat? It's not quite as showy,' Jane pondered. She didn't want to draw any attention away from Emily on her big day.

'What is the bride wearing?' Edith asked.

'She wanted to wear the outfit she wore for my wedding but I persuaded her it would be too warm for this time of year. So we went into town and she chose a lovely dress of silk taffeta overlaid with chiffon in a shade of pale peach, and a cream picture hat trimmed with big peach roses. It's the very latest fashion,' Jane replied, remembering the pleasant afternoon she and Emily had spent.

'And I suppose you insisted on paying for it?' Edith surmised aloud. Jane was very generous where her friend was concerned. But Emily appeared to be her only friend and Jane was to be her bridesmaid, so she didn't question it.

'Of course. I told her it was my wedding gift to her otherwise she wouldn't have agreed.'

Edith nodded. 'Then if I were you I'd settle for the lilac. It's bad luck for a close member of the family or a bridesmaid to wear green.'

Jane looked puzzled. 'Why? I've not heard that before.'

'It brings tragedy to the bride, so they say. And apart from that, the green and white looks more suitable for a garden party at Knowsley Hall or a day at Royal Ascot.'

'Then I'll definitely wear the lilac,' Jane agreed.

'I suppose she has her poor mother's nerves shredded with all the fuss. I know I drove my mother to distraction,' Edith confided happily.

Jane smiled. She couldn't imagine Mrs Davenport as a nervous young bride. 'She has. Aunty Ada said she'll be glad when she's finally married and taken herself off to live with Georgie's mother. "Let her go and drive Lily Taverner mad with all her nonsense," were her exact words. And she added she was very glad that she only had the one daughter.'

Edith nodded amiably. 'I know. There were three of us and our weddings must have cost my poor father a small fortune. How long does she intend to live with Mrs Taverner?' she enquired. She enjoyed hearing the gossip from Gill Street for these days, apart from church, she didn't socialise a great deal.

'Not long. Georgie is earning more now but they haven't been able to find anywhere decent they can afford. When they do they'll move. They'll be a bit cramped in Clarence Street but Aunty Ada told her she'd like her parlour back. When I went to live there she turned it into a bedroom for herself and Uncle Fred as they only have two bedrooms,' Jane informed her.

Edith shook her head, thinking it was deplorable that some families had to make do with so little space.

Jane gathered up the dresses. 'I'll take these and hang them up.' She smiled. 'Thank you for your advice. The lilac will be perfect.'

'When you've done that I'll ask Renshaw to bring up some tea and then you can tell me what plans my son has for when his workers have their annual week's holiday. I do hope he doesn't intend to still go into work each day.'

Jane shrugged. 'So do I, but you know James.'

As she hung up the dresses she pondered the old lady's words about the green and white dress. She'd never heard that saying before about the colour green but her mother-in-law surely wasn't the sort who would believe in old wives' tales so perhaps there was something to it? She frowned; she was glad she'd asked her advice but she also recalled that when Emily had been her bridesmaid Emily's coat and dress had been green. Oh, it was just superstitious nonsense. Mentally she shook herself, and smiled when she remembered talking to Emily as her friend adjusted her green and cream hat, the morning she was getting married: how Emily had asked her if she was nervous about the wedding – and about the wedding night. Well, she had reassured Emily then, and she had been right. James was always considerate, and just as he had charmed her into sharing his life, so he charmed her in his bed, and the physical side of their marriage was enjoyable and fulfilling. She smiled again. Her life was secure and comfortable now. What possible 'tragedy' could befall her?

The morning of Emily's big day dawned bright and sunny; in fact it promised to be a perfect June day, Jane thought as she and James had breakfast. His mother took hers in her room for her arthritis was getting worse and she found she needed time in the mornings to 'get moving', as she put it.

She loved this room, Jane thought, glancing around. It always seemed to be sunny – even in winter – and today was no exception, though the brilliant sunlight was diffused a little by the canopy of green leaves on the trees outside in the garden. 'Emily's certainly got a lovely day,' she said, smiling at James.

He laid down his newspaper and smiled back at her. He still couldn't quite believe that he'd been so fortunate to find love so late in his life. 'It could get rather hot later on.'

Jane nodded as she poured herself a cup of tea. 'Well, as we're coming back here after tea with Aunty Ada it won't be too bad. These rooms have such high ceilings that they don't get unbearably hot and stuffy and we can open the windows, unlike in the rooms on the ground floor.'

'Don't forget Mother will want to know every detail of Emily's day,' he reminded her.

'I know. I do wish Aunty Ada would come here to visit. Your mother would enjoy her company even though their lives are so different. They both like to gossip,' she laughed.

'She's still refusing?' James asked, knowing the answer.

Jane nodded. 'I've stopped asking her now. I know she wouldn't feel comfortable.'

James rose and kissed her on the cheek. 'I'd better be going but I promise I'll be back in plenty of time.'

She smiled up at him. He wasn't even taking the whole day off – just a few hours. He still worked very hard and when she commented on the fact he always replied that a successful business didn't run itself. While he was very confident of his manager Mr Turner's abilities he felt that greater efficiency and high staff morale was better achieved if he were present.

James was as good as his word and as he drew up in the car at three o'clock sharp she was ready and waiting, looking cool and smart in the pale lilac dress and the matching light straw hat banded with violet ribbon. They were going straight to the church for Ada had said Emily's outfit was going to cause quite enough of a stir in Gill Street without herself, James and the car adding to it. She knew it wasn't 'traditional' but she also knew her nerves wouldn't stand more strain than they were already being subjected to. Emily was constantly fussing, Ada was having a hard time convincing Sonny that his presence at his sister's wedding was absolutely necessary and Danny, who at nearly nineteen was very self-conscious, hadn't helped by saying gloomily that they'd be better off leaving him at home because he was bound to make a show of them all.

The church felt pleasantly cool after the midday heat, Jane thought as she and James entered. She would wait here for Emily's arrival whilst James went to take his place with such relatives of Ada and Fred that had been invited. There weren't nearly as many as those on the Taverners' side, she thought, and Georgie looked rather nervous and uncomfortable in his new suit and stiff collar.

At last Ada and her family arrived, having walked the short distance so Emily's outfit could be admired by everyone they passed en route.

'You look very smart, Aunty Ada, but is everything all right?' Jane greeted Ada, who was looking rather flushed and harassed.

Ada adjusted her hat, which was already giving her a headache, thinking that of all days for that damned letter to arrive it had to be today when Emily had almost reduced her to a nervous wreck with her antics.

'It's just the heat, Jane, and Madam here getting into a state and our Danny complaining about having to walk with us, saying it's awful having everyone staring at him. Young fool! No one was even giving him a second glance, not with our Emily looking as if she's going to Ascot in that frock and hat,' Ada replied in a loud whisper.

'She does look gorgeous though, Aunty Ada, the colour really suits her,' Jane enthused as she handed Emily the small bouquet of cream roses she'd brought with her.

'She's certainly given the residents of Gill Street something to jangle about,' Ada agreed while Fred muttered that it wasn't just the residents of their street but all those they'd passed through that had been gobstruck by Emily's finery.

'Well, you'd better go and take your seat, James has already gone up to the front,' Jane urged her.

Ada peered intently down the aisle to make sure the bridegroom had arrived.

'Their lot have certainly turned out in force,' she remarked to Jane. 'I hope Lily doesn't intend to bring them all back to our house. "Immediate family" I told her; we're not made of money,' she added tartly before taking her leave of them, her attention diverted by the imminent event from the letter she had received that morning, now lodged safely in her handbag.

Jane smiled at her friend as the first notes of the organ sounded. 'Go on, Em, he'll be delighted with you and I hope you'll be as happy as I am with James.'

Emily nodded and swallowed. She had looked forward so much to this day and now she felt nervous, happy, excited and full of trepidation all at the same time.

Alfie wandered slowly along the street, his gaze going over the façades and gardens of the big, four-storeyed houses. There was plenty of money in this neighbourhood, he surmised, but just how easy would it be to get into them? Obviously not from the front, he'd have to try to find a way to get around the back; there must be an entry at the back of them for they'd been built at a time when people had carriages and horses. Nowadays they had cars and they must keep them somewhere because they weren't parked outside on the road.

The sun was beating down on his head and the sweat was trickling down the back of his neck. The summer months weren't the best of times for him; people were glad to be out and about, the evenings were long and dawn came very early. There was just too much damned daylight. He didn't know which was worse: winter spent shivering in that freezing stable loft or summer when he sweltered in the tiny attic room of the alehouse. He'd gone back there when his finances had improved at the end of January and again no questions had been asked as long as he paid his rent. The landlord's daughter, Sylvie, seemed to have taken a shine to him and often brought him up something to eat and a glass of ale and stayed to chat. He didn't give much away about how he spent his time, but she was a pretty enough girl and easy to get on with.

He'd found it harder 'working' the Landing Stage and the Riverside Station without Jimmy and Richie but he'd managed well enough. But now he'd decided it was time he gave both places a wide berth until the evenings got darker and the complaints to the coppers about thieves and pickpockets got fewer: he had no intention of joining his mates in Walton Jail. That was why he was now idling along the street in this affluent part of the city.

He'd finally come to a gap between two houses which looked promising, and as he meandered down the narrow entry which led into a much wider one he noted that it ran directly behind the houses and that some shade was provided by the high stone walls and overhanging tree branches. So, they had gardens, he mused, that was a bonus. It would be easier to hide in a garden where there would be shrubs and other plants, but not now. He'd have to wait until either very late tonight or very early in the morning. He'd have to select one house and then climb over the wall and locate the back door or a window that would give him entry.

He stopped and looked around quickly and then tried a small door which was set into much larger double doors. It opened but he didn't go inside; instead he peered in. It appeared to be some kind of old coach house but it was obviously in use for it was clean and the floor had been swept, although it was empty. Cautiously he ventured in, pulling the door behind him but not shutting it completely in case he needed to get out in a hurry. Through a gap in the wall where there had once been a small window he peered out into the garden beyond. This looked very promising, plenty of trees and shrubs and he could just see a back door into the house. There didn't seem to be any sign of activity. Although he'd broken into a few shops he'd never attempted a house of this size, but he had to find a way of getting money to tide him over these next few months. He'd come back after midnight, he decided, although he felt decidedly nervous, wishing he had his mates with him for support.

As he turned to slip back out into the entry he heard the sound of a car approaching. He looked around in panic for somewhere to hide but there didn't appear to be anywhere. A car door slammed and there came the sound of approaching footsteps. Then he spotted the ladder resting against the wall and quickly shinned up it to the top. It didn't go any further, he realised in horror as he stared up at the dark, dusty wooden rafters. He froze as the big doors were opened wide, huddling as close as he could to the wall. If he didn't move he stood a chance of not being detected for surely no one would look up there?

The sound of the engine grew louder as the car was driven slowly into the space below and he held his breath and closed his eyes. A man spoke as he closed the doors: 'Go on in, Jane, I'll lock up. Mother will be waiting.'

'I'll be glad to take this hat off and have a cup of tea while I embark on the saga of Emily's big day. You know, I think I'll go and see Aunty Ada tomorrow. I think something has upset her, she seemed a bit preoccupied though I suppose it could just be losing Emily,' came the reply.

Alfie slowly opened his eyes, unable to believe his ears, but as he glanced down his heart turned over with shock. It *was* Jane! What was she doing here and who was the feller? He'd told her to go in, so she obviously lived here. And she wasn't in service, not in an outfit like that and being driven around in a car. As he heard the doors being closed he breathed out. They hadn't noticed him but he might well be locked in. But then if she was living here it didn't matter. He was in luck.

Chapter Twenty

———◆———

H E'D HAD TO WAIT for what seemed like hours because the doors to the entry were indeed locked and there was no sign of a key. But he'd found that the door leading into the garden had been left open and so when the sun had finally sunk below the rooftop he'd crept outside and sat in the deep shade cast by a large hydrangea bush. He'd planned to go around to the front door but he had no idea if there was any way he could get back out into the entry, except by climbing the wall, but if he did that he risked being seen. At length he decided he couldn't stay here all night. He'd knock on the back door and hopefully his sister would be the one to answer. If not, well, he'd just ask to see her.

He left it another half an hour and then made his way across the rapidly darkening lawn to the back door and knocked.

A girl opened the door dressed in the uniform of a maid. 'Yes, what do you want?'

'Does a woman named Jane live here?' he asked bluntly. He hadn't expected a servant.

Renshaw nodded. 'You mean Mrs Davenport, I suppose. What do you want with her at this time of night?' she asked.

'I'd just like to see her, never mind what for. Could you just go and tell her that Alfie is here. She'll see me,' he stated boldly.

'Alfie who?' Renshaw demanded.

'That doesn't matter, just go and tell her. I'll wait.'

With a very bad grace the girl disappeared and he leaned against the door jamb, peering inside. The door led into a long, badly lit corridor with doors leading off it, and he deduced that these were the kitchens and pantries or store-rooms.

James was working in his study and his mother had gone to bed but Jane was reading in the drawing room where it was cooler than the breakfast room, which seemed to retain the heat of the day. She looked up in surprise as Renshaw appeared.

'I'm sorry to disturb you, Mrs Davenport, but there's someone at the back door wanting to see you. '

Jane frowned. 'At this time? Ask him what it's concerning and tell him to come back in the morning.'

'He said to tell you that "Alfie" would like to see you. He was quite insistent, ma'am,' Renshaw informed her.

Jane's heart dropped like a stone at the mention of her brother's name. After all this time he'd suddenly reappeared. How had he found her? What did he want? What was Renshaw thinking? She laid aside the book and got to her feet slowly, her heart still thumping as she desperately tried not to show her feelings. 'I'll come down, Renshaw. It . . . I think it's . . . someone I used to know.'

'Shall I show him up then, ma'am?' the girl enquired.

'No! No, that won't be necessary. I doubt he'll be staying . . . long,' she replied as she followed the girl out of the room and down the stairs. She'd find out what he wanted and then get rid of him for she certainly didn't want James to learn of her brother's visit.

Renshaw went into the kitchen, leaving Jane to continue along the passageway. When she reached the back door she nodded to the shadowy figure. It was indeed her brother, she registered numbly. He'd certainly grown. His clothes were poor quality and rather grubby, his hair needed trimming and he was thinner but she'd have recognised him anywhere.

Abruptly she indicated for him to follow her, leading him into a large pantry and then closing the door. She wanted to make sure Renshaw heard nothing of this conversation and that she didn't mention anything to the old lady either. She'd speak to the girl later. 'Alfie! What are you doing here? Where've you been all this time?' she asked, scrutinising him closely.

'I've been living over the water in Birkenhead but . . . but I'm back in Liverpool now. You've done well for yourself, Jane, or "Mrs Davenport" it is now, I believe. Your husband must be a wealthy feller to be living in this big posh house.'

Jane clenched her hands tightly together. There was no proper explanation about his absence, no sign of concern at all the anxiety he'd caused, no affectionate greeting, only the fact that she appeared to have found herself a rich husband. 'What do you want? Why have you come here?'

'I'm skint, and I'm starving hungry. I haven't had a crust all day,' he stated, his gaze roving over all the pots of preserves and chutneys, the tinned food and bags of flour and sugar.

So that was it, she thought frantically. He wanted money but she'd have to go back upstairs for that and she didn't want to leave him down here alone. She pretended to have misunderstood. 'I'm . . . I'm sure there is something in here we can find for you to eat—'

'Is that it? Aren't you going to invite me upstairs to meet my brother-in-law?' he interrupted. He could see she was very wary of him.

Jane swallowed hard, feeling fear rising in her but she fought it down. 'No, James is . . . busy working in his study and it is really very late, Alfie. Now, let's see what we can find and then . . . then tomorrow . . . I presume you've got somewhere to stay?' she asked, turning away and beginning to search the shelves. She just wanted him to leave and as quickly as possible but she wouldn't see him going hungry.

So, he thought bitterly, she wasn't going to let him stay or give him any money or introduce him to her husband. She obviously had a very good life now and was ashamed of him. But she was very uneasy; in fact he thought she was afraid of something.

'Yes, I've got a room but I need the money for the rent or I'll be out on the streets and you wouldn't want that, would you? Shall I come back tomorrow, Jane?' he asked slyly.

'No! No, why don't I meet you . . . somewhere, and I'll bring some money. You're right, I don't want to see you without somewhere to live,' she replied quickly, handing him a collection of items she'd picked out which would make a scratch meal.

'Where?' he demanded.

Jane thought frantically. 'Lyons' Corner House in Hanover Street, say at eleven o'clock?'

'I just told you I'm skint, Jane. I've no money for cups of tea.'

'Then I'll meet you outside,' she replied quickly. She just wished he would leave.

Alfie nodded. 'All right, I'll go now and thanks for this stuff. But don't be late and don't forget to bring your purse, Jane.'

She closed the door behind him and leaned against it, relief washing over her that he'd finally gone. But she would have to meet him tomorrow and her relief swiftly turned to guilt that she'd not told James about him and, worse, that she'd turned her brother away from her door after she'd promised Ellen she'd look out for him.

Thankfully Renshaw said nothing about the visit. After a sleepless night and restless morning she arrived in Hanover Street at eleven to find Alfie waiting. He looked a bit tidier than when she'd seen him last night and they went into the café and she ordered tea, sandwiches, hot buttered crumpets and toasted teacakes. He quickly ate the food while she just sipped her tea and then she silently passed him two guineas.

'Thanks, Jane. That should keep the wolf from the door for a bit,' he said as he pocketed the money, thinking it was a start. From now on he knew where he could come if he was hard up: she clearly had access to funds since she didn't appear to consider two guineas a huge amount and she was paying the bill for all this without blinking.

'You'll be all right, Alfie, now? You're not in any . . . trouble?'

she asked, watching him closely and thinking how much he'd changed since the last time she'd seen him. It seemed so long ago now. He'd been just a boy then but now he was an adult. She'd noticed the way he'd looked around at the other customers, almost as if he was assessing how much money they had in their purses and wallets. There was a hardness about him that hadn't been there before and she was certain now he'd been involved with Jimmy and Richie.

He laughed. 'You know me, Janie, I've always been in "trouble" with someone. But I can look after meself, don't you worry. I take it your husband knows all about me?'

'Of course he does!' Jane lied, feeling panic rising as she thought of James and his mother. 'But . . . but I do worry about you, Alfie! I . . . I promised Mam I'd try to look out for you but you just . . . disappeared and no one knew anything about you. Were you with Richie Corrin and Jimmy Cobham when they were . . . caught?' She lowered her voice. 'Alfie, were you part of that gang of thieves?' she asked with concern.

He shrugged. 'Maybe I was, maybe I wasn't; it's water under the bridge now. How long have you been married?' he asked abruptly to change the subject. He wasn't going to admit to anything and he was certain now that she hadn't told her husband about him. Jane had never been a convincing liar, she was just too honest and transparent.

'Six months. James is a good man and we're . . . happy.'

Alfie didn't reply; he wasn't really interested in whether she was happy or not, he was just wondering how wealthy James Davenport was. 'Where did you meet him, Jane? I mean you didn't exactly mix with the toffs, did you, living with Ada Ellis and her lot?'

'I worked for him at the Empire Laundry and we . . . we became . . . friendly.'

Alfie's gaze narrowed. This was a very interesting bit of information indeed. 'He *owns* the Empire Laundry?'

Jane nodded but before she could expand on the subject Alfie got to his feet.

'Well, I can't stay here all day drinking tea. I'd better go and pay the rent. Thanks, Jane, for the tea and stuff. I've enjoyed seeing you so why don't we do this again, in another few weeks? After all, you are my sister.'

She gazed up at him but couldn't hide the consternation in her eyes. 'Yes . . . yes, in a couple of weeks, Alfie.'

'Right. I'll be in touch.' He grinned and nodded and then to her relief he left. Feeling dazed, she asked for the bill. She just wanted to get out of the place for she felt as though she were trapped. She'd intended to go to see Ada today and she knew now she really needed to: she had to talk to someone, to confide in Ada the fear, guilt and confusion that were threatening to overwhelm her.

She found Ada alone in her kitchen peeling potatoes for the evening meal.

'Jane, I'm glad to see you, luv, sit down. I was going to make a cup of tea when I'd finished this lot. I'm doing it now because this afternoon I'm going to try to have a bit of a rest. I'm worn out after yesterday. But it all went off well enough, thank goodness.'

Jane took off her hat and gloves. 'You finish that and I'll make the tea.' She went to fill up the kettle, put it on the stove and then took a deep breath. 'I called to see you for two reasons, first because I thought you were a bit . . . preoccupied and worried yesterday. Is everything all right?'

Ada nodded as she wrapped the potato peelings in a sheet of old newspaper. She'd spent hours wondering how she was going to tell Jane that she'd had a letter from Joe saying he intended to come home, hours wondering what the girl's reaction would be. She'd barely got used to the news herself.

'It was just the heat and all the fuss and I suppose I was worried about things going well,' Ada replied, thinking she would leave it a bit longer before she broke the news of her son's impending return, for Jane looked anxious about something herself. 'You said two reasons: is everything all right up there at your house?' she queried.

'Everything is fine, except . . . I had a visitor last night, Aunty Ada. Alfie turned up at the back door asking for me. Thankfully Edith had gone to bed and James was in his study.'

'Oh, my God!' Ada exclaimed, sitting down suddenly. 'Where the hell has he been all this time? What did he want?'

'I told Renshaw he was someone I used to know but that his visit wasn't important and . . . and he wouldn't be calling again. Oh, Aunty Ada, I'm so worried. He said he'd been living over the water in Birkenhead but that he was back now, and he had no money for his rent, that he hadn't eaten . . .'

'We hear nothing from him for ages, don't even know if he's alive, dead or in jail and then he turns up like a bad penny with a hard-luck story! How did he find you?' Ada demanded.

'I don't know and I didn't think to ask I was so . . . taken aback. I think he was expecting me to invite him to stay but I couldn't do that; I gave him some food and I met him this morning at Lyons' in Hanover Street. I just couldn't risk him coming to the house. He asked me if I'd told James about him and I said of course I had but I'm sure he knew I was lying.'

'Why would he think that?' Ada asked, thinking Jane was right not to have encouraged him to go back to the house.

'It was just the impression I got. And I'm certain he was involved with Jimmy and Richie – although he wouldn't admit it, he didn't deny it either. I . . . I gave him a couple of pounds and bought the tea and sandwiches but he . . . he said he wants to see me again in a few weeks and his parting words were to remind me that I am his sister. What am I going to do, Aunty Ada? I . . . I don't want to see Alfie again and I can't let James find out. I can't admit that I've blatantly deceived him. I just *can't*! It would hurt him so much, he's so honest and open and—'

'He'd be mortified if he knew about your Alfie and his criminal mates and I don't even want to think what old Mrs Davenport would have to say about it all,' Ada interrupted, her anger mounting. Oh, she had a good idea of what Alfie Shaw intended, wanting to see Jane again. If he thought Jane was hiding his existence from her husband it would serve his purposes very well indeed. He wouldn't be averse to using that fact as an excuse to extort money from her. She was sure he was capable of blackmailing his own sister to serve his own ends. 'No, luv,' she said decisively. 'The next time you meet Alfie tell him it's positively the last. Tell him that you've spoken to James about it all and that you've both agreed it would be best all round for you and Alfie to go your separate ways. After all, it's what your Alfie has been doing for years and you can't say you're . . . close. You were separated when you were growing up.'

Jane was still unsure. 'Will he believe me?'

'He will if you seem confident enough. Tell him firmly that James has agreed to give him . . . Oh, I don't know . . . say ten pounds to get him on his feet until he finds work, but that there will be no more money after that. Can you afford that much?' Ada queried. It was a lot of money but it would be worth it; it just might keep Alfie from pestering Jane.

Jane nodded; she never spent her entire allowance and had money saved. 'But what if he does think he can come back for more money?'

'Then tell him that James was quite firm about that. If he keeps pestering you then James will go to the police and your Alfie definitely won't want that. He's not a fool; he'll realise that the police would take the complaint of a gentleman like James seriously and they might still be looking for Alfie. Jane, luv, your brother is trouble and always has been but he needs to be made to understand that he can't ruin your life.'

Jane bit her lip. It seemed as if she were sinking deeper and deeper into a quagmire of lies. But it was too late now to tell James about her brother; she couldn't bear to hurt him and – if she were honest – she was desperately ashamed that she had a brother like Alfie. She hated to admit it to herself but it was true.

'Now, let's have that tea and then you get off home and stop worrying about Alfie because you can be certain he won't be back until he's spent what you gave him today and by then you'll have got it firmly fixed in your mind what you're going to say to him next time,' Ada urged. She'd wait until Jane had sorted out all this unpleasantness with Alfie before she told her about Joe. After all, he wouldn't be back until the beginning of September and that was weeks away.

Chapter Twenty-One

A DA PAUSED ON THE front step of Jane's home and looked upwards at the fancy glass fanlight above the front door. All the windows were clean, the curtains pristine, the paintwork fresh and unchipped and the brasses highly polished. It was a far cry from her own home in Gill Street, she thought as she pressed the bell and waited. She fervently wished now that she'd made time to tell Jane about Joe's return but somehow the weeks had slipped by with Emily always calling round and Danny's new – and painfully shy – young lady to contend with. And then James had announced that he was taking his wife and mother to a big fancy hotel in Morecambe for the annual holiday when the laundry closed which meant another seven days had gone by before she could call, and now Joe would be home at the end of this week.

She fiddled nervously with the brim of her hat wondering how long it took to get to the front door but finally it was opened and the maid Jane had spoken of stood looking enquiringly at her.

She plucked up her courage. 'Good morning, Renshaw, I'd like to see Mrs Davenport – Jane Davenport. I'm Mrs Ada Ellis.'

The girl nodded and held the door wide. She'd never seen this Mrs Ellis but she'd certainly heard about her. 'Come in, ma'am. If you'll wait in the hall I'll tell the mistress you're here.'

'Thank you and I'd prefer "Mrs Ellis" if you don't mind, luv,' Ada said frankly. '"Ma'am" is far too grand for me.'

Lizzie Renshaw smiled. '"Mrs Ellis" it is then.'

As she disappeared up the wide sweeping staircase Ada looked around. You'd fit the whole ground floor of her house into this hall, she thought, noting the black and white tiled floor, the fine paintings in their heavy gilded frames that adorned the walls, the highly polished console table upon which sat a large arrangement of flowers and leaves. There was an ornately carved grandfather clock standing in one corner and two chairs upholstered in gold brocade stood against the opposite wall and she thought of all the dusting and polishing that would be required – and this was just an entrance hall.

'Aunty Ada! Oh, I'm so pleased to see you!' Jane greeted her, hurrying down the carpeted stairs. 'But there's nothing wrong is there?' Jane had been astonished when Renshaw had informed her that Ada was here in the hall but had immediately wondered what had prompted this visit since she'd always said she'd never come here.

'No, there's nothing wrong, luv. I just wanted to talk to you so I thought I'd come over,' Ada replied as Jane ushered her towards the staircase. 'Where are we going?'

Jane smiled. 'Oh, I forgot to say, the drawing room is on the first floor but perhaps you'd prefer the breakfast room – it's smaller and cosier.'

Ada nodded, wondering just how many rooms there were in this house. It seemed enormous but as Jane showed her into the room she began to relax a little for it was quite small and comfortably furnished and warmed by a good fire in the hearth.

'Oh, this is nice, Jane, luv,' she commented, taking off her hat and unbuttoning her coat, the charcoal wool she'd worn for Jane's wedding and which she kept for special occasions.

'Renshaw really should have taken those for you. I'll ring for her,' Jane remarked, crossing to the bell beside the fireplace.

'No need to bother the girl, luv, I'm sure she has enough to do,' Ada replied, placing them down on the sofa beside her.

Jane smiled, delighted Ada had come. She hoped it would be the first of many visits. 'It's no bother and anyway now that you're here we'll have some tea.'

'And there's no need to get the best china out for me either, Jane. Now, did you enjoy your holiday?' Ada asked, settling herself more comfortably on the chintz-covered sofa.

'Oh, we did and the weather was wonderful: it didn't rain once. The hotel was beautiful, very modern and light and spacious and the rooms James had booked had wonderful views; you could see right across the bay. We even managed to persuade Edith to come for a couple of walks with us and I think the sea air did her good – and James was far more relaxed being away from work. We all enjoyed it so much that he said we'll go again next year. Now, tell me all your news. Has Emily found a house yet?'

'She thinks she has but Georgie's dithering so she's going to get Lily to have a serious talk to him. Lily's to tell him that she's been to see it and even though it's a bit small, it's in a respectable neighbourhood and there're only the two of them anyway. When they start a family they can find somewhere a bit bigger *and* Lily's getting a bit fed up being overcrowded, which I can understand.'

Jane nodded. 'I'm glad she's found somewhere. Georgie always was a bit cautious, which I suppose is no bad thing.'

Ada took a deep breath. It was now or never, she thought. 'I've got a bit of news I've been meaning to tell you about for quite a while, Jane. But what with our Emily's wedding, then all that business with your Alfie and you going off to Morecambe—'

'What is it?' Jane interrupted.

'Our Joe's coming home. I had a letter from him . . .'

Jane just stared at her not knowing what to say but her heart had begun to beat more rapidly.

Ada hurried on. 'That Mr Ibsen he works for, he's all into mining apparently – not coal but things like iron and something called zinc – well, he's taken it into his head to take them all off to Australia as apparently they have tons of stuff like that there and there's a fortune to be made from it, and he wanted Joe to go with him but our Joe said he thanked him but that he felt it was just too far away and that he thought it was about time he came home. Myself, it sounds as though he's finally missing us all, but I'm glad he's coming home and not even considering going to the other end of the earth.'

Jane nodded slowly, trying to take this all in. Of course Ada would be glad he was coming home but was she? She didn't know. She'd often wondered if he would one day return. To her immense relief before she had time to try to find the words to respond to Ada the door opened and Edith entered followed by Renshaw bearing a tea tray.

'Oh, Jane, I didn't know you had company,' Edith apologised. 'It's Mrs Ellis, isn't it?' she added, recognising Ada.

'It is indeed, Mother-in-law, she's finally come to visit,' Jane replied, trying to sound bright and cheerful. 'And will you join us for tea?' she asked, thinking it would at least divert Ada from asking her how she felt about Joe's impending return.

'If Mrs Ellis doesn't object,' Edith replied, curious about what had brought the woman here, for she knew she had resolutely refused in the past.

'Lord, no! It is your house, after all, aren't you entitled to have a cup of tea in your own home?'

Edith seated herself and presided over the tea tray, as she almost always did.

Ada felt rather uncomfortable as she handled the delicate china cup and saucer, carefully taking her lead from Jane in the matter of the sugar cubes and tongs. But she began to relax as Edith enquired about all the members of her family in turn.

Jane sipped her tea slowly, letting Ada and her mother-in-law chat on. She would have to face Joe at some stage, she realised. Had he changed? Did he still have feelings for her? she wondered. He might not even know she was married for he seldom wrote and Ada couldn't so it was left to Emily and she'd been totally preoccupied with her wedding and finding a house. She'd never thought he'd return, she'd put him out of her mind and chosen James and truly she was happy with him. Oh, she'd never felt for James the way she had for Joe but all that was in the past now. She was a married woman and her future was here with James. But she couldn't help a tiny dart of regret creeping into her mind.

She suddenly realised that Edith had spoken to her. Firmly she pushed all thoughts of Joe away. 'I'm sorry, I was miles away, forgive me for being so rude.'

'I was saying to Mrs Ellis that we're delighted she called and that she really must come again,' Edith informed her. Ada Ellis was a pleasant enough woman, Edith had decided, and she'd been entertained both by her news and the odd turns of phrase she used when speaking of her children. Overall, she'd enjoyed her company.

'Of course you must come again, Aunty Ada,' Jane added enthusiastically.

Ada nodded. Sitting here in such comfort, having a cup of tea and a chat had been a treat, and she wondered why she'd been so foolish and stubborn in the past. 'Well, it won't be for a few weeks yet, Mrs Davenport. You see my eldest lad – our Joe – will be home at the weekend from America. Of course we'll go down to meet him – he's coming in on the *Aquitania*. So, what with our Emily moving and him home I'll have plenty to do to keep me occupied for a while.'

'Well, when you have some time to spare to do come again,' Edith pressed, thinking Ada Ellis seemed to have a rather hectic life.

'Yes, do,' Jane urged. 'I'd like to know how Emily's settling in and of course . . . Joe,' she added, thinking that in other circumstances she would have helped Emily move and have gone to welcome Joe home.

Ada stood up, preparing to leave. 'And don't forget that

you're always welcome in our house,' she reminded Jane. But even as she spoke the words she wondered if Jane would visit her again once Joe was home. Only time would tell.

Things were certainly improving, Alfie thought optimistically as he stared up at the damp patches on the ceiling of his attic room. The warm darkness of the early September night was heavy and through the dirty, cracked glass of the skylight above him he could faintly see a few stars. Tomorrow his mates were being released from Walton Jail and he was looking forward to seeing them again. Two nights ago he'd broken into a newsagent's and got away with cigarettes, tobacco, chocolate and ten shillings in cash. He'd easily sold the tobacco, chocolate and what cigarettes he hadn't kept back for himself and the money was very useful for he'd spent most of what Jane had given him. He'd treat Jimmy and Richie to a drink downstairs in the bar to celebrate their release: the barman, who was also his landlord, wouldn't ask stupid questions about their ages providing they didn't get roaring drunk and start fighting.

The girl lying on the bed beside him stirred and uttered a little sigh of contentment and he grinned to himself. Oh, he'd found Sylvie more than willing to give in to his demands and she crept up here whenever she could, usually when her parents were busy downstairs in the alehouse. She was a pretty little thing if none too bright and was childish in her delight whenever he gave her some small gift that he'd usually stolen especially for her. And she believed everything he told her, which wasn't a great deal.

He stretched his cramped limbs for the bed was very

narrow. He'd have to wake her for she couldn't stay here much longer and besides he had plans to work out. He shook her. 'Sylvie? Sylvie, you'd better get dressed and get back downstairs before you're missed.

She slowly opened her eyes and pushed her tangled tawny-blond hair back from her face. 'I wish I didn't 'ave to, Alfie.'

'Well, you do or your da will belt the living daylights out of the pair of us,' he reminded her bluntly. And if that happened he'd find himself out on the street as well. Though she was pretty and compliant and satisfied his needs, he wasn't going to risk a severe beating and becoming homeless as well. He didn't care *that* much for her. 'Come on, shift yourself, girl. It'll be chucking-out time soon and you know your da's strict about that. He won't risk having the coppers taking his licence away.'

Reluctantly she sat up and reached for her clothes, beginning to pull them on. 'I'll slip up here tomorrow night, Alfie, and I'll bring some ale,' she promised.

'Not tomorrow, Sylvie. I've got plans,' he replied, watching her as she fumbled with the buttons on her blouse.

'What plans?' she demanded, obviously disappointed.

'Nothing that concerns you.'

'You never tell me anything, Alfie and I . . . I thought you loved me?' she replied, pouting sulkily.

'Course I do, Sylvie, but I'm meeting a couple of mates that I haven't seen for a while. It's a bit of a celebration, like. In fact I'm thinking of meeting them in the bar downstairs.'

She brightened up. 'Then I'll still see you, Alfie. I'll give me mam and da a hand; Saturdays are always mad busy.' She bent and kissed him and, tiptoeing to the door, quietly left.

He sat up and took a cigarette from the packet of Senior Service that lay on top of the battered washstand. All he could usually afford were a couple of Woodbines so a decent smoke was an improvement. He'd get the tram tomorrow morning to Walton and wait on the opposite side of the road to the jail until his mates appeared. He supposed they would want to go home first, which was only natural, so he'd travel with them but make sure to stay away from Gill Street. He'd tell them to meet him later in the day here in the Chandler's Arms – and that he was buying the drinks.

He lay back and drew deeply on the cigarette and then watched the bluish-white smoke drift up towards the ceiling, frowning as he remembered his last meeting with his sister. She'd been bloody insistent that the ten guineas she'd passed him was the last money he'd get from her. She'd said her husband had given it to her to help him get on his feet but that they should now go their separate ways and if he continued to pester her then James Davenport would go to the police. He wasn't sure he believed her but he doubted that she had so much money of her own. Anyway, he couldn't gamble on the fact that she might be not be telling the truth because if she had indeed told her husband the scuffers would be bound to take him seriously because he was a man of some standing. So, there would be nothing more to be got from Jane. However, he'd made some enquiries and found out that Davenport was indeed a wealthy man. He was determined to take advantage of the hand he'd been dealt with Jane's marriage. Now his mates were out, he was sure he could persuade them to help him plan and carry out the biggest job they'd ever attempted. If Jane and her husband wouldn't give him any more money then he'd just take it. There must be a safe in that house, he'd surmised, and no doubt silver and jewellery as well. They would all be well set up for the future with what they could get from Davenport, he was sure of it. After all, why should Jane live a life of luxury and not him, just because she'd had the good fortune to catch a rich feller? Davenport wouldn't miss it; he must have made thousands from that laundry over the years – it was a big place and had belonged to his father, maybe even his grandfather. But he'd have to make his plans carefully and they'd have to be foolproof because if they were caught then they'd all go down for God knew how long – they might never even be free to walk the city streets ever again.

He stubbed out the cigarette on the cracked marble top of the washstand and pulled the stained and crumpled sheet up over him. The noise from downstairs and the street outside had abated, apart from the odd drunken curse. He'd sleep on it all and tomorrow he'd broach the matter with his old mates. The nights were starting to draw in now and for his purposes darkness had always proved a welcome asset. It would be one last job for the Gill Street Gang but a big one and if it went well then he might even think about marrying Sylvie and settling down. He might even become respectable, like his ma would have wanted, he thought as he nodded off into oblivion.

Chapter Twenty-Two

———◦◦◦———

ADA AND HER FAMILY were amongst the crowd on the Landing Stage that fine sunny September day when the *Aquitania* docked. Ada eagerly scanned the faces of the passengers waiting to disembark but it was Sonny who spotted his elder brother first.

'There he is, Mam! There's our Joe! Look, he's standing waiting just behind that feller in uniform at the top of the gangway,' he cried, pointing, and then began to wave madly. He couldn't wait to hear of all Joe's adventures and about the places he'd been to. He wondered if he'd brought back any souvenirs with which he could impress his mates.

Ada too began to wave. He looked older, she thought affectionately, more grown up, but then he was a young man of twenty-three now. His skin was tanned and he was far more smartly dressed than she remembered him ever being before. His clothes were very modern and he was even wearing a hat.

'Oh, look at the style of him! He looks more American than

English,' Emily remarked to her mother as Joe made his way down the gangway carrying a heavy suitcase.

'Welcome home, lad! We've missed you!' Ada greeted him, hugging him with tears of joy in her eyes. There had been times when she'd seriously wondered whether she would ever see him again.

He was then engulfed by a hug from his sister, had his hand shaken by his father and brothers and then they were all pushing their way through the crowds towards the tram terminus.

'Nothing seems to have changed very much, Mam,' Joe remarked, taking in the familiar buildings of the waterfront and the overhead railway. 'Except that our Danny and Sonny have certainly grown up a lot.'

'Danny's got a young lady now and Emily's married. Oh, you've missed so much, Joe, we all wish you'd come home sooner,' Ada replied, settling herself down on the wooden slatted seat as the driver pulled the overhead trolley to the front of the vehicle and climbed aboard.

'Well, he's back now so let's not go dwelling on the past,' Fred said firmly, although he wondered just what plans Joe had for the future. Times were still hard and jobs not easily come by and his son was now used to a steady job with a decent wage. Even before the new decade had dawned a tunnel had been started under the Mersey to Birkenhead, providing desperately needed jobs. It was now nearing completion and was to be officially opened by the King, so he'd heard, so there wouldn't be much more work coming from that front. But he wondered if his eldest son would even want to settle here in Liverpool, or would he find it dull and uninteresting after America? It was a bittersweet thing, Fred reflected, seeing your children grow up and away, but he should just be thankful Joe was back, even if just for a short time.

It felt strange to be walking down Gill Street again, Joe thought. The streets appeared narrower, the houses smaller and the whole area looked cramped, crowded, dilapidated and grimy – or was it just that he'd become used to bigger houses, broad thoroughfares, wide-open spaces and modern buildings? He'd enjoyed living in America, relished all the experiences of travelling, but when Mr Ibsen had decided to increase his fortune by mining in Australia, he'd been very reluctant to accompany him quite so far. He'd realised that he missed his family and he missed Liverpool. As neighbours called out or waved to him, he grinned happily; with all its failings this city was 'home'. He wondered, as he walked along, why Jane was not with the family. Maybe she was working or had something else of importance to do.

When they'd all eaten he'd unpacked and distributed the gifts he'd brought them: souvenirs of the cities he'd visited, small items of clothing, even gramophone records of the latest songs, even though they didn't have anything to play them on. His mother chided him for not saving his money, but Sonny and Danny were delighted when Joe promised they'd now get a gramophone.

At length Emily decided it was time she returned to her own home. 'Come and see us, Joe. I'm made up we've got a little house of our own at last and Georgie will be glad to see you again,' she urged before she left.

He promised he would and then his brothers disappeared to pursue their own activities, leaving him with his parents.

'Where's Jane, Mam?' he asked Ada for there was still no

sign of her and he'd been looking forward to seeing her again.

Ada glanced quickly at Fred, who raised his eyebrows. 'Jane doesn't live here now, Joe. In fact she hasn't lived here for eight months. She has a home of her own in Upper Huskisson Street and she's . . . she got . . . married. She's Mrs Davenport now. She married James Davenport, the owner of the laundry,' she informed him.

Joe stared at her, trying to take it in. He'd been looking forward to seeing Jane. He hadn't forgotten her, in fact he'd thought a great deal about her on the way home, remembering the New Year's Eve they'd spent together before he'd sailed. She would be twenty-one soon, a young woman. He'd wondered if she had changed but he'd not expected this. 'She . . . she's married!'

Ada nodded. 'We were all upset, lad, when we got that letter telling us you weren't coming home but I think it hit Jane very hard. I know she was fond of you . . . then.'

'But . . . but she was so young,' Joe interrupted.

'Yes she was, and so was our Emily, but she knew that Georgie Taverner was the only lad for her. Jane was really cut up and you couldn't expect her to wait for you.' Ada paused and, placing her hands on her hips, ruefully shook her head. 'None of us knew when you'd come back or even *if* you'd come back. Jane couldn't just put her life on hold. James Davenport asked her out and she agreed and . . .' Ada shrugged. 'She got married in January and she seems happy enough. He's a lot older than her of course but he's a real gentleman, she gets on well with his mother and she has a life of luxury now. She'll never have to work again, no expense is spared – they've just had a week's holiday in a big fancy hotel – they employ staff and after the life she'd had, she deserves it all, Joe.'

Joe nodded slowly. He felt a pang of guilt for he'd not treated her very well, thinking only of himself and his own ambitions. She would indeed now have a life of luxury, marrying a man like James Davenport, but he couldn't help feeling disappointed and strangely hurt. Somehow he'd thought she would be waiting for him, but, as his mother had pointed out, they'd not known if he was ever coming home. 'Does she know I'm back?' he asked quietly.

Ada nodded. 'I went to see her a few days ago and no doubt she'll come to see us . . . in time.'

'So, lad, what do you intend to do now?' Fred asked, thinking a change of subject was needed for obviously the lad was upset by the news that Jane was married.

Joe shrugged. 'See if I can get a driving job. I've plenty of experience.'

'There're not many jobs like the one you had in this city. It's mainly driving lorries or vans or buses and I doubt you'll earn anything like what you're used to being paid,' Fred informed him.

Joe shook his head. 'I don't fancy driving a delivery van or a bus. Maybe I'll go back to sea. I don't know. I've a bit of money saved,' he replied. On the crossing he'd given some thought to his future, wondering if he should look for another job as a chauffeur with someone like his former employer. But he'd realised he'd more than likely have to move away from Liverpool for that. He'd pondered a few other options but not come to a firm decision. He'd just wanted to get home.

'Let him get settled in here, Fred, before he decides what to do in the future,' Ada interrupted, not liking the sound of him returning to a life at sea. 'At least he's got prospects, which is more than can be said for some lads in this street,' she added. 'Jimmy Cobham and Richie Corrin got released from Walton this morning – so I heard.'

Joe frowned. 'So, they finally got caught. What were they up to?'

'Thieving from passengers at the Pier Head and the Riverside Station – they'd been at it for months,' she stated. 'But Alfie Shaw got away, he managed to give the coppers the slip.'

'So he hasn't changed then,' Joe said grimly, thinking of Jane.

'No, and while I think on about it, Jane hasn't told her husband about Alfie, just so you know. I advised her against it. The Davenports don't know she's got a brother. She's already had to give Alfie money to keep his mouth shut and stay away. But it's all sorted out now and he won't be pestering Jane again.'

Joe nodded slowly, wondering if it *had* been 'sorted out'. He'd never liked or trusted Alfie Shaw and he could understand why Jane hadn't told the Davenports but he also wondered was she just storing up trouble for herself?

Alfie watched as the small entrance set into the big iron-studded double doors of the jail was opened and Jimmy stepped out clutching a brown paper parcel and blinking in the bright morning light. Richie followed him and they both stood looking around as though confused by the wide expanse of sunlit road in front of them and uncertain what to do next. Taking his hands out of his pockets and pushing his cap to the back of his head Alfie crossed the road towards them.

'They finally let you out then?' he greeted them, grinning, though thinking they looked thinner and paler than the last time he'd seen them.

'Alfie, lad! It's great to see yer!' Jimmy cried with delight.

Richie was more cautious. 'I didn't expect yer ter come and meet us. I'd 'ave thought yer'd 'ave been nicked yerself by now.'

'Not me, mate,' Alfie said jauntily. 'Now, let's get out of here, that place gives me the creeps!' He glanced back over his shoulder at the grim walls of the prison, which had been built almost a century before. 'There's a tram stop over there on the corner.'

'Yer want ter try bein' banged up in there, that'd give yer more than the bloody "creeps",' Richie muttered sullenly. He never wanted to see the inside of that jail ever again. For much of his time he'd been in 'I' block in the cell next to number 216 where condemned men were held before they were hanged and taken via an underground tunnel to the mortuary. The sounds of the obvious distress of some of his brief neighbours still haunted his dreams.

'Well, you're out now, mate, and to celebrate I'm standing you both drinks tonight in the Chandler's Arms, ' Alfie responded cheerily.

'Are yer back livin' there?' Jimmy asked as they approached the tram stop and Alfie handed them each a full pack of Senior Service cigarettes.

Alfie nodded as he lit his own and then their cigarettes. 'I had to scarper, like, after you two got nicked. I went over to Birkenhead but came back in January. I've been doing all right but I've got great plans for us now.'

Richie eyed him suspiciously. 'Not sure iffen I want ter 'ear them. I'm not goin' back in *there*!'

'You won't be. I'm still working them out and there're a few things I've got to do. But the thing is, our Jane's married now to the feller who owns the Empire Laundry and he must be worth thousands! They live in a big posh house and have servants and a car. You'd hardly recognise our Jane: got up like a proper lady she is.'

Jimmy's eyes had widened in amazement. 'Your Jane married *that* feller?'

'I've just told you she did and my plan is to do with him and his money. Here's a tram so I'm not saying another word about it now but meet me tonight in the bar. I take it you're goin' home?'

Richie nodded. 'I'm lookin' forward to me mam's cookin' after all them years eatin' pig swill.'

Alfie slapped him on the shoulder. 'If everything works out you'll be eating steak and roast beef every day of your life, Richie, lad!'

Jimmy grinned, drawing deeply on his cigarette, but Richie still didn't look very convinced. Those pitch-dark, terrifying nights he'd spent in the cell next to 216 had taken their toll.

When his mates got off the tram Alfie stayed on, glancing out of the window as it trundled up Brownlow Hill and past the workhouse. The sight of the building deepened his resolve. He had a lot of watching and waiting to do to try to fathom out James Davenport's routine and that of his sister, the maid and anyone else who lived there, but there would be no mistakes this time; nothing would be left to chance. In a couple of weeks he intended to visit his sister again, during the day, and he was determined to get her to let him into the house proper. He had a sharp eye and a good memory so he'd remember the details of where doors and windows and stairs were located, and then he'd draw a plan. Of course he'd have to try to work out where Davenport would keep a safe, probably somewhere in what Jane had called his 'study'. He'd have Jimmy and Richie with him so they could search bedrooms for jewellery and other rooms for silver and valuables and he intended to give himself an alibi. He would tell Jane that he was leaving Liverpool for good; that he was going to London. He'd invent a job for himself down there and maybe she'd even give him a few more pounds, but it wouldn't matter if she didn't. The important thing was that she would have no idea that he'd been involved in the robbery.

It was going to be tedious, he thought as he got off the tram at the end of the road, spending hours and hours waiting and watching and trying not to attract too much attention, but it would be well worth it in the end.

Chapter Twenty-Three

'HAVE YOU HEARD how Mrs Ellis is coping now that her son is home?' Edith asked as she poured the tea. She and Jane were sitting in the drawing room. The end of September was approaching and Jane was overdue her regular fortnightly visit to Gill Street. Mrs Ellis had told them she would be too occupied to visit them for a while so she thought it odd that Jane hadn't been to visit Ada herself.

Jane frowned, realising her mother-in-law had noticed her lapse. 'No, I thought I'd leave it for a little while longer than usual to let him get settled in. But I intend to go and see her tomorrow afternoon.'

Edith nodded. 'I expect he will find it rather difficult at first, getting back into the routine of life here. America is such a . . . "fast" country, I always think. At least that's what you're led to believe from the newspapers and the wireless broadcasts. Everyone always seems to be in such a rush to do things.'

Jane smiled but inwardly she was dreading the visit, which

was why she had put it off for so long. But if she left it any longer Edith would be bound to comment and ask if anything was amiss. And she had missed Ada's chat and gossip, she thought fondly. 'I suppose I really should go and see Emily's new house too. I promised I would. But it would have to be in the evening. She's still working even though both Aunty Ada and Georgie's mother disapprove. I don't like leaving James to his own devices in the evening, though, not when he's worked so hard during the day.'

Edith nodded. 'I can see you'd want to visit Emily. But as for her job, a married woman's place is at home making sure her husband's comfort is well taken care of.'

'That's just what Aunty Ada says but Emily's insistent that she wants to have the place well furnished and a little money saved before she thinks about giving up her job or starts a family.' Emily had also said that her mother's was a very old-fashioned outlook and Jane agreed but they both acknowledged that would cut no ice with the older generation. 'Perhaps Aunty Ada can tell me if it would be more convenient for me to call on Emily on Saturday,' she added, her gaze straying briefly to the deep sash window which overlooked the street. She noticed that the leaves on the trees were beginning to turn orange and gold. The days were getting shorter and colder and soon the chill, damp mists of October would make her mother-in-law's arthritis even harder for her to bear. Edith tried to put on a brave face but Jane knew the old lady wasn't looking forward to the winter months. She sighed. Now that she'd told Edith of her intention to visit tomorrow she'd have to go.

*

244

Ada was pleased to see her for she'd been worried by Jane's absence and had been contemplating visiting the house in Upper Huskisson Street. 'Come on in, luv, I'll put the kettle on.'

'Is Joe out?' Jane asked, taking off her hat and coat and feeling a sense of relief as she realised he wasn't in the kitchen.

'He'll be back soon. He went to see if he could get one of those gramophone things cheap. Both Danny and Sonny have had us mithered to death about it. It's all our Joe's fault for bringing records in the first place, but I told him not to be going to the likes of Cranc's – they're far too expensive.'

'What does he intend to do . . . for work, I mean?' Jane asked, taking the dishes from the dresser. She'd bought Ada the china tea set for her birthday earlier in the year and she knew how Ada cherished it.

'I don't think he knows, luv, but he won't get a job as good as the one he had with that Mr Ibsen. Still, there's plenty of time for him to look around. Is Mrs Davenport well? How's her arthritis?' Ada asked as she poured the tea. 'This colder weather won't suit her, poor soul,' she added.

'I know. Both James and I think she should have the fire lit in her bedroom but she's insisting she couldn't sleep, that the room would get too stuffy,' Jane replied. When Ada had announced that Joe had gone into town she'd wondered if he would return before she left: despite her misgivings she *did* want to see him.

Ada was halfway through describing how Emily was furnishing her parlour when the kitchen door opened and Joe stood in the aperture carrying a large, awkward-looking parcel. 'You got one then? Thank the Lord for that; we might all get a bit of peace now,' Ada greeted him.

Joe set the gramophone down on the table. He'd not expected Jane to be here and he felt a frisson of surprise and delight run through him. 'Hello, Jane,' he said, smiling. She hadn't really changed, he thought, although she seemed to have an air of confidence about her now and of course her clothes were fashionable and obviously expensive.

'Put that thing in the parlour, Joe. I've decided that it can live in there and those lads can play it in there too,' Ada instructed. 'Your da and me don't want to be listening to this modern stuff, we prefer to listen to the wireless. Then come back here and have a cup of tea with us,' she finished.

'He . . . he seems to have grown up a lot,' Jane remarked when he'd left the room. He was a handsome young man now with far more self-assurance than he'd had previously

'He has. I actually think it's done him good being away. He's far more . . . mature – aye, that's the word – than he was. And his manners have certainly improved and he's lost some of his accent,' Ada replied.

Joe reappeared and sat down at the table opposite Jane. 'It was quite a surprise when Mam told me you were married,' he said, his gaze going to the gold band on her finger surmounted by an obviously very expensive diamond ring. He also noticed that she wore a neat gold wristwatch now.

Jane nodded. 'It must have been but . . . but James and I had been courting for a while—'

'And it was a very nice occasion, quiet but . . . happy,' Ada interrupted, sensing Jane's embarrassment. 'He's been telling us about all the places he's been to and the fancy hotels and buildings he's seen, Jane. Tell him about that hotel you stayed in in Morecambe,' she urged. She wanted to keep the conversation light for she was wondering how they were both feeling.

As Jane spoke Joe listened and realised that she had indeed changed. She was far more refined both in speech and manner now, clearly confident and at ease in her new life and quite obviously fond of her husband and his mother. He realised that it saddened him. She'd always been so much a part of his life when they were growing up, she'd been little Jane Shaw: his friend, confidante, soulmate, and he'd been very fond of her, even thought he loved her, but now . . . now he realised that she'd grown up and she'd grown away from him. He'd lost her and with a terrible feeling of regret and longing he suddenly realised that he still did love her, that he'd always loved her, and never more than at this moment – when it was too late. She was beyond his reach now and would always be and he knew in that instant that he couldn't remain at home, he couldn't stay permanently in the same city as her, he'd have to get away. He'd go back to sea.

Ada had been watching him closely. She detected the change in his mood and it grieved her. As for Jane, if she felt any regrets she wasn't letting them show.

'So, both you and our Emily are now happily married women and I missed both occasions,' Joe said when Jane had finished talking, unable to completely keep the note of sadness from his voice.

'Yes, and I really must go and visit Emily. Do you think Saturday afternoon would be convenient, Aunty Ada?' Jane asked quickly to fill the awkward silence, for she'd heard the change in his tone too.

'I don't see why not. I'll come with you, Jane. Lily Taverner seems to spend enough time popping in,' Ada replied as Jane got to her feet. 'Come about three and we'll get the tram up there.'

'Right. I'd better get back now, it's Renshaw's afternoon off and I don't want Mother-in-law summoning Cook to bring up her tea. *She's* not getting any younger either and shouldn't be running up and down stairs so I'll fetch it.' She turned to Joe, who had politely stood up, trying to keep firm control of her voice and emotions. 'I'll no doubt see you again, Joe, probably on Saturday. Enjoy the gramophone,' she added, smiling.

Joe nodded, unable to trust himself to speak. He'd make sure he was out on Saturday. He'd go down to the Pool to see if he could get a ship.

As she walked up Gill Street Jane rapidly blinked back the tears. She'd honestly not thought that seeing Joe again would have brought all the emotions flooding back, but it had. When she'd married James she'd truly believed that she was doing the right thing and she was very fond of him, she really *was*, and she'd been happy, but would she now continue to be so content? She bit her lip; she would try. She had no other choice. James deserved a happy wife, he cherished and cared for her, gave her security, comfort and companionship, he was a good husband and would always be so. She squared her shoulders as she boarded the tram. She'd put her feelings for Joe out of her mind when she'd made her choice and she'd taken her vows and that's the way things had to remain. There was no going back; she was no longer a girl of seventeen. She was nearly twenty-one, a grown, married woman, but she still couldn't entirely banish the memory of what they had shared that New Year's Eve and she wasn't even sure if she really wanted to.

When she got home she found Edith sitting by the fire in the drawing room, the elegance of its décor reminding her forcefully of how fortunate she was.

'How was Mrs Ellis?' Edith enquired, thinking Jane looked rather strained.

'She's fine. I'm going with her to visit Emily on Saturday afternoon,' Jane replied, sinking into an armchair opposite Edith. 'James is going to his club after work, but he'll be home in time for dinner and I'll be back before then,' she reminded her mother-in-law.

'You've had a visitor,' Edith stated bluntly.

'Who?' Jane asked, but even before the question was out she knew it had been Alfie.

'A young man – a boy really. He said he was a cousin from your father's side of the family. Alfred Shaw, he said his name was.'

Jane swallowed hard, feeling her blood turn to ice water. 'Yes, yes . . . I seem to remember him. Did he say what he'd come for?' At least he'd lied, she thought. He hadn't exposed her deception. But why? Why had he come and now when she was feeling so confused and vulnerable?

'Apparently he's leaving Liverpool very shortly. He has obtained work in London, so he said, and wished to see you before he left as he doesn't intend to return. I told him to call again tomorrow afternoon; you'd be here then. Did I do the right thing? I presumed you would wish to see him before he leaves?'

'Yes, of course. It would be very inconsiderate of me not to see him. I . . . I know his parents are dead,' Jane answered, feeling torn between relief that Alfie was leaving the city and a nagging anxiety that tomorrow he would again demand money or reveal that he was her brother. But she would have to see him. She pressed the tips of her fingers to her forehead. 'I have a slight headache but I'll go down and see Cook about tea.'

Edith nodded. 'Take an aspirin: I have some here. I find they help a little with the ache in my bones.'

Jane smiled and thanked her but on her way downstairs she thought that aspirin could do little to ease both her anxiety and the conflict of her emotions.

She was very apprehensive the following afternoon when Renshaw showed Alfie into the breakfast room but he looked far smarter than when she'd last seen him. He'd obviously got a new suit from somewhere, his boots were polished and he'd had his hair cut.

'I'm sorry I missed you yesterday, Alfie. I went to see Ada.'

He nodded. 'The old one told me that. How many rooms are there in this house, Jane?' he asked, looking around. Yesterday he'd ascertained that the living rooms and bedrooms were on the first and second floors. He knew the kitchens and storerooms were on the ground floor and presumed the servants, if they lived in, had the rooms in the attic.

'Too many. I sometimes think we'd be better off in a smaller place, but this has always been James's home,' she answered, sitting down and indicating he do the same.

'Does he sort of . . . work here too?' he asked, thinking of the study.

She nodded. 'He works too hard. He has a study at the end of the landing. Was what you told Mrs Davenport true, Alfie? Are you going to London?'

'I am. I'm fed up with this kip of a city *and* I've got a job to go to,' Alfie replied, having made a mental note of the location of Davenport's study.

'Doing what? You don't know anyone in London,' Jane demanded.

'There's a feller I sometimes talk to at Lime Street Station who told me there were jobs going at Euston Station in London for porters. He said they earn good money and that people often give tips too; he gave me the name and address of the feller to write to. Dead helpful, he was. So I wrote and I was lucky. I've always wanted to go to London; as I said I'm sick of Liverpool – there's nothing here for me. I'll soon get lodgings and get on my feet so I won't be bothering you again, Janie.'

She relaxed, thankful that for the first time in his life Alfie had got an honest job and seemed happy and optimistic about his future. 'Oh, Alfie, I'm so pleased for you and I know Mam would be too.' She'd expected he would be looking for money and had a small envelope with five guineas in it in her bag. 'I won't have you going off to start a new life without something to fall back on, so . . .' She took out the envelope and handed it to him.

'Thanks, Jane. I appreciate it but I didn't come looking for money. I just came to tell you I'm going so you won't worry and to say goodbye.' He stood up. 'So, I'll be off now, I've got . . . things to do.'

Jane hugged him. 'You take care of yourself, Alfie, and good luck! And try to keep in touch.'

'Thanks, I will,' he replied stiffly as he disentangled himself. She didn't mean it, he thought resentfully, she was just pleased to be rid of him. She didn't even care enough to admit he was her brother and not some distant imaginary cousin. But, he thought, thanks to her his luck was in – or it would be soon. He'd never need to come looking for a handout again. His plans could progress now he had a good idea of the layout of the house. All he had to do was chivvy Richie up a bit for he wasn't nearly as enthusiastic as Jimmy about the idea. Something had occurred in Walton Jail that had taken its toll on Richie, he thought.

Before he went downstairs he looked along the landing; he'd already noted three doors but now he realised the fourth door at the end was to the study. He smiled to himself; the whole place was carpeted too which would help deaden any noise and yesterday when he'd seen the old lady he'd noticed a large cabinet stuffed full of silver. He'd have everything worked out before Christmas when he planned to do this job, when the Davenports would think he was safely settled in London. Afterwards he might even go to the capital to live anyway and he'd have plenty of money in his pocket. Jane wasn't the only one who would be living the high life.

Chapter Twenty-Four

A DA WASN'T AT ALL happy as Christmas approached for yet again Joe would be away and she'd really hoped that this year he would spend it with the family. Emily and Georgie were coming for their dinner and then later they would go to Lily's for tea; she'd been looking forward to everyone sitting down together for the first time in what seemed like years.

She paused and stared hard at the dresser, which she'd been vigorously polishing in an attempt to make it look less worn. She pursed her lips; so far her efforts didn't seem to have made much difference. Her thoughts returned to Joe. He hadn't even attempted to find a driving job, he'd gone straight down to the Pool and signed on again with Canadian Pacific and on his old ship too, the *Empress of Scotland*. So he'd be off cruising again just after Christmas and she'd commented pointedly that she hoped this time he'd not go accepting jobs from rich Americans, and come back when the ship returned to its home port in the spring.

With a mother's intuition she'd guessed why he'd done it for she'd sensed the change in his mood after Jane's visit, although he'd made no mention of how he felt. She sighed heavily and gave up on the dresser. Well, it was too late now for him to realise that he loved Jane and as the girl's visits seemed to coincide with his absences at sea she wondered if Jane too was filled with regrets. Oh, it was all such a mess, she thought, flinging the duster down and replacing the lid on the tin of beeswax polish, which had been a complete waste of money where the dresser was concerned. 'If only'! Well, they were the two saddest words in the English language, she thought bitterly. She'd make herself a cup of tea and concentrate on trying to work out how she was going to fit everyone around the table for Christmas dinner.

She was surprised when half an hour later Jane arrived bearing a box, which she carefully placed on the table.

'When Cook was making the Christmas cake I asked her if she'd make one for you too. You'll have so much to do, Aunty Ada, that I thought it might help,' she said, unbuttoning her warm black and white tweed coat trimmed with black fur around the cuffs. Underneath she wore a skirt of the same material and a fine black wool twinset set off by a silver locket on a chain, a gift from James.

Ada smiled gratefully at her. 'That was good of you, luv. Sit down and I'll make a fresh pot of tea,' she instructed as she opened the box and nodded with approval at the festively decorated fruit cake. It was far bigger and no doubt much richer than anything she could have provided.

'You know I'm really looking forward my first Christmas with James and Edith,' Jane informed her. Ever since Joe had returned she'd concentrated all her efforts into making life as pleasant and comfortable for her husband and mother-in-law as she could by little acts of thoughtfulness, whilst trying to banish all thoughts of Joe from her mind. But it hadn't been easy. She'd been relieved and yet at the same time disappointed when Joe hadn't been at home that Saturday in September and then she'd learned that he'd gone back to sea. After that she'd been careful only to visit Ada when she knew he'd be away at sea for she didn't entirely trust her emotions or her self-control.

'Well, at least you won't have all the work and the worry that goes with Christmas in this house,' Ada reminded her as she poured the tea.

'No, apparently Edith discusses all the meals with Cook, who then does the ordering, preparing and cooking. But I'm going to take charge of the decorations. James told me they haven't had a tree for years, there just didn't seem much point, but we are this year. I'm going to order a big one for the hall and holly and mistletoe and I've already started shopping for presents for them both and of course Renshaw and Cook. Edith informed me that both Cook and Renshaw receive extra money as a gift but I thought something from me would be appreciated. They both work hard all year and I know Renshaw sends her mother money to help out at home. She's a thoughtful girl,' she added, thinking a little sadly that she'd barely had time to buy any little treats for Ellen when she'd started earning money just before her poor mother had died. She'd decided that rather than choose one large gift each for James and Edith she would look for smaller but still expensive gifts, wrap them nicely and put them under the tree so there was a real display – for she was determined that this Christmas would be really special for all of them. But it wouldn't be quite like the kind of Christmas she'd always dreamed of, she couldn't help thinking, for she hoped to have children and she knew James did too. As he'd remarked, he wasn't getting any younger. But perhaps by next Christmas she would be expecting a baby and then all her dreams would be fulfilled

'The only real family Christmases I had were here with you.' She smiled wistfully at Ada, remembering that in fact it hadn't seemed likely then that Joe would ever return and that last year she'd been engaged to James.

Ada nodded, thinking of years gone by. 'Aye, all those Christmases you spent in Brownlow Hill and before that, well, we none of us had any money to spend on toys, trees or decorations, we barely had enough for a decent meal. Still, things are much better now and I'm wondering how I'm going to get everyone around this table. Our Emily's insisting on coming with Georgie. I thought she'd want to spend it in her own house but—'

'I can understand why she wants to come, Aunty Ada. It's a time for families to be together,' Jane interrupted, smiling.

'Except that our Joe will be missing . . . but that's his choice and he hasn't been here for the past few years anyway. And talking of families, have you heard anything from your Alfie since he took himself off to London?' Ada asked to take her mind off Joe. Indeed, no one had been more astonished than herself when she'd heard that Alfie Shaw had got a proper job in the capital and she'd said as much to both Fred and Joe, who had still been home at the time.

Jane shook her head. 'No, but then I didn't expect to. Alfie never seemed to concern himself much with either Mam or me. But I hope I'll hear from him at some time in the future.'

'If you do, knowing him, it will mean he's in trouble again,' Ada commented grimly. Leopards don't change their spots, she thought, and she didn't believe for a minute that Alfie Shaw would continue to stick to the straight and narrow. She sighed. 'Well, those two so-called "mates" of his from down the street seem to be behaving themselves from what I hear, and our Danny said he thinks Richie has changed. Said he was talking to him last week and he seemed sort of quieter – more . . . subdued, so maybe the time in Walton did him some good. Danny said he swore he wasn't ever going back in there and he's actually looking for a job.'

'I hope he's learned his lesson. Maybe our Alfie getting a proper job and going to London had something to do with Richie's change of heart,' Jane said seriously; then she brightened up. 'Oh, and I forgot to tell you James is taking me to a concert – a Christmas concert – at the Philharmonic Hall. I've never been there but it does look very grand from the outside. I hope I'll enjoy it – I'm not really very musical, but James says it won't be heavy classical pieces but lighter, more Christmassy music.'

'It does look very grand. I expect that tickets will be expensive so you'd better *look* as if you're enjoying it at least,' Ada urged. It wouldn't be her cup of tea; she'd sooner have a night at the good old-fashioned music hall.

Jane laughed, getting to her feet. 'I will. Now, before I go, I'll wash these dishes and leave you to get on with your chores.'

Ada grimaced. 'I've given up. That dresser's never going to look halfway decent and neither is this table.'

Jane looked thoughtful. They seemed to have so many white damask and lace-edged tablecloths, she'd ask Edith if she could give Ada one to cover the table for Christmas. Ada would be so proud to have it and Jane wanted, if she could, to bring some happiness to the woman who had been so generous to her over the years.

Alfie hadn't given a great deal of thought to the approaching festivities even though Sylvie never seemed to stop talking about how busy her parents would be and hinting that she'd like to go out somewhere 'special'. For the most part he'd ignored her because her chatter distracted and annoyed him. His mind had been completely filled with his plans for the burglary and he'd realised that it was going to be harder than he had at first anticipated to pull it off successfully. He had to lie low and try to ensure that he wasn't seen – especially by Jane or the old lady or Ada Ellis – for he was supposed to be working in London. So he had to be very careful during the time he spent watching the house in Upper Huskisson Street. From his observations he had worked out that the staff lived in, surmising that they must sleep in rooms in the attic at the top of the house. The girl – Renshaw – appeared only to have one afternoon off in the week and every other Sunday but he'd not been able to ascertain what time the Cook had off – if any. The old lady went out very rarely and never at night and, apart from going off to the laundry each day, James Davenport didn't go out in the evenings a great deal either; nor did Jane. It all meant that they'd have to be very cautious and very, very quiet. He'd planned that they would climb over the garden wall at the back for he was sure the gates would be locked.

Force open the back door with as little noise as possible and make their way to the hall and then up to the floors above. Obviously they would have to do all this late at night and they'd need to carry torches – he'd never seen lights left burning anywhere in the house after eleven o'clock. He'd made a plan for each of them, marking the location of the rooms he'd seen and the position of windows and doors. He'd visualised how far down that landing from the breakfast room the study was and its position in relation to the drawing room with its cabinet of silver and had told Jimmy and Richie to study it until they knew the place like the back of their hands. If everything went to plan they would get out the back way and be down the jigger and away. The Davenports wouldn't realise until next morning that anything had gone.

He lit a cigarette and frowned. Richie was causing him a few worries. Both his mates had stayed out of trouble so far although he'd had to warn Jimmy a couple of times, threatening him not to do anything that would put the whole big job at risk, but with Richie it was quite the opposite. He still didn't seem to have much enthusiasm for the work at all: he just hoped he wouldn't lose his nerve and back out at the last minute.

He hadn't made up his mind either what to do when the job was over. They'd all have to lie low – the way he'd been trying to do for weeks now – and he was still contemplating heading off to London. If nothing else it would get him away from Sylvie for she was really beginning to irritate him and he was tiring of her, even wondering if he was the only one she bestowed her favours on. He got up and began to pace his tiny room. He was nervous – they were all nervous – but he and

Jimmy were both excited as well. There was just a week to go before Christmas now and he'd decided that tomorrow night was *the* night. Jimmy and Richie were coming here just in time for last orders; they'd have a drink to bolster their courage, then collect their equipment: the torches, the jemmy and the screwdriver for prising open doors and the canvas bags he'd obtained, already filled with pieces of rag to wrap the silver in to muffle any sound, as well as a small Gladstone bag to carry money and jewellery in. Then they'd go out through the back yard and head off separately and meet up in the entry behind Davenport's house.

As he paced he went over everything again in his mind; he didn't think he'd overlooked anything. Early tomorrow he'd go and see old Sarsfield and tell him he'd be calling late tomorrow night with some stuff he wanted to sell. He was suddenly jolted out of his deliberations by the appearance of Sylvie, who had brought with her a jug of ale, and he frowned.

'I thought you'd like some company, Alfie,' she announced, putting the jug down on the washstand. She shivered. 'It's freezing up here. I don't know how you stick it. Don't you ever get fed up? You don't go out very much,' she commented as she sat down on the bed and pulled the faded quilt around her shoulders.

Alfie shrugged. He was grateful for the ale but had no wish for her to linger, although that was quite obviously what she intended to do. 'I'm all right, Sylvie. Doesn't your mam need you to help collect and wash the glasses?' he asked pointedly.

She shook her head. 'She can manage – it's not all that busy down there – besides, I really wanted to . . . talk to you, Alfie.'

He grimaced. She was on to him again, he thought irritably. 'Not Christmas again, Sylvie?' he asked, sitting down beside her and noticing for the first time that the room was indeed cold. Still, when he had money he'd soon find a much more comfortable place.

She laid a hand on his arm. 'No, Alfie, it's sort of more . . .'

He looked at her, noting she looked rather sheepish. 'More what?'

'Serious,' she replied, biting her lip.

For a horrible instant he thought she'd discovered something or heard something of his plans and he instinctively drew away from her. 'Like what?' he demanded.

'Like . . . like, I . . . I . . . think I might be . . . expecting,' she blurted out. 'Oh, Alfie, if I am they'll *kill* me!' she cried, tears springing into her eyes.

He stared at her in horror. The stupid little bitch! She'd told him she knew about these things, knew ways . . . things her mam had told her about . . . and he'd believed her. 'They'll kill me too!' he snapped.

'They'll throw me out on the street, Alfie! What'll I do?' She sniffed, wiping her eyes with the corner of the quilt. She was terrified for she was sure she was pregnant but she loved him and he'd said he loved her so surely it would be all right? 'We . . . we'll have to get married!'

Alfie narrowed his eyes as anger and resentment filled him. So that was her game! She'd planned this all along to trap him into marrying her! And to spring this on him now, when he was so preoccupied and tense! Had she noticed that and thought he'd be more vulnerable? She'd asked quite a few times lately was there something wrong? Was he worried about anything? 'Are you sure, Sylvie?' he demanded, unable to hide the anger in his voice.

'Not absolutely certain but . . . but . . . I'll know definitely this week. I've missed my "curse" and if I miss again then . . .'

It certainly sounded as if she was pregnant, he thought, but he wasn't going to hang around to find out. He'd made up his mind. After tomorrow night he'd be away. Away from Liverpool and away from Sylvie whether she was pregnant or not. There was no place for her in his future. He had no intention of arousing her suspicions, however.

'Well, don't go upsetting yourself, Sylvie. We . . . we'll wait and if . . . if you are then we'll tell your mam and da that we're getting married.'

She flung her arms around him, relief washing over her for she hadn't been sure how he'd taken the news. At first he'd sounded annoyed. 'Oh, Alfie! I knew I could depend on you. I knew you really loved me! You won't regret it and we'll be so happy!'

He smiled at her as he disentangled himself from her embrace. 'Of course we will. Now, you'd better go and let me think . . . I've got plans to make.'

She smiled back happily. 'Plans for us?'

He nodded as she got to her feet but something nagged at him. 'You won't say anything to anyone about . . . this, will you, Sylvie? Not your mam?'

She shook her head. 'No! Didn't I just say they'll go mad? I'll say nothing until we tell them . . . together, Alfie.'

When she'd gone he poured himself a glass of ale, feeling as though he needed it. Didn't he have enough to think about without this? Well, he'd just put everything she'd said out of his mind. He'd be well rid of her. And if he ever did get married it wouldn't be to someone like her.

Chapter Twenty-Five

THERE WAS THICK cloud the following night and intermittent flurries of sleet as Jane and James set out in the car for the Philharmonic Hall.

'I'm really looking forward to this evening, James,' Jane confided.

He smiled at her. 'So am I. We don't go out often enough. Perhaps we can make it a regular monthly occasion to go to the theatre or a concert?'

Jane nodded eagerly. 'Yes, I'd like that, especially the theatre.'

'Then it's a promise. We'll treat ourselves and we'll have supper out either before or after the performance. Make it a special occasion, something we can look forward to.'

'And there will be a definite Christmas feel to the programme tonight?' Jane pressed.

James nodded his assent.

'Then I'll enjoy it even more: it will put us in the festive spirit.'

'Indeed it will. Both Mother and I are so looking forward to the holiday this year, Jane. You've gone to a lot of trouble.' James reached across and patted her hand.

She smiled at him happily. 'It's been a pleasure and a delight for me to do it, James. After all, it's going to be so different for me this year.'

'Different for us all,' he replied, thinking of all the Christmases ahead of them as they approached Liverpool's grand, ornate concert hall.

The thick cloud and flurries of sleet were things for which Alfie was thankful. At least there was no bright moonlight to contend with, he thought as he waited in the deep shadow of the garden wall for Jimmy and Richie to join him. It was bitterly cold and that too would deter people from staying out late; in fact he'd seen very few on his way here: the streets were deserted. Everything so far had gone to plan, even Richie hadn't seemed too nervous and the bar in the pub had been busy so no one had particularly noticed them. Sylvie had been in the back somewhere – washing glasses he'd assumed. He just hoped the rest of the night would also go to plan and then tomorrow or the day after at the latest he'd be on his way to London and a whole new life.

At last he heard the sound of footsteps coming down the entry and first Jimmy then Richie appeared, both keeping close to the wall.

'Right, this is it! You both ready?' he asked, to which they nodded their assent. 'We all know what we've got to do so give me a leg-up, Jimmy,' Alfie instructed.

Within minutes they were all over the wall and, moving

from shrub to shrub, quickly covered the distance to the back door of the house.

'It's not 'alf dark!' Richie muttered.

'Shurrup! The less bleedin' light there is the better,' Jimmy hissed back.

The splintering of wood as Alfie forced the lock on the back door sounded so loud that they all held their breath, ears straining for any possible reaction. Their nerves were strung out like piano wires, Alfie thought, but the silence of the winter night remained unbroken, and he breathed deeply again, gently pushing open the door.

Adhering faithfully to Alfie's instructions they crept along the corridor to the hall and with the aid of the torches made their way up the carpeted stairs. On the landing they paused, all listening for any sound which would indicate activity. There was none. Alfie pointed his torch towards the drawing room: he had marked on his plan the position of the silver cabinet so Richie shouldn't have any trouble locating it. He would go and tackle the study and Jimmy was to search the other rooms for valuables. He planned to obtain as much as possible in as short a period of time as he could; they couldn't hang about for too long, that would be pushing their luck.

He realised that his hands were shaking a little as he closed the study door quietly behind him. It looked to be quite a small room, he thought as the thin beam of light traversed it. There was a fireplace in which the embers of a fire still glowed, a bookcase and a desk with heavy curtains covering the window. He could see no obvious sign of a safe so he'd start on the desk, looking for keys and anything else of value, then move on to the bookcase. On the desk top there was a fine ornate silver writing set, which he stuffed into his canvas bag; in the drawers he found a couple of what he assumed were bank books and a small locked tin cash box, which he put into the Gladstone bag, but there didn't seem to be any keys. His heart was pounding as he directed the light beam over the walls, searching for evidence of a safe. There just *had* to be one here somewhere, he thought; where else would Davenport keep all the money from the laundry? He surely wouldn't leave it in the empty building overnight. He'd inspect the bookcase, and then start to look behind each of the pictures on the wall but, he fumed, it would use up precious time.

He'd gone over every inch of the bookcase and walls but to his increasing frustration there was no sign of a safe. Then, like a blinding flash of light, came the realisation that money from the laundry must be banked each week. Davenport didn't keep large sums here; that's what the bank books were for. What a bloody fool he'd been! Why hadn't he thought of that? It was so flaming obvious now. Money for day-to-day expenses was no doubt contained in that cash box; that's all the ready cash there was and he'd have to leave it at that. He'd relied so much on there being a safe stuffed with money! But now there was nothing for it but to search every single room for anything that could be sold and he'd wasted so much time.

As he cautiously let himself out on to the landing bitter disappointment mixed with mounting chagrin at his own stupidity and vexation at the added risk of being discovered. His nerves were being stretched further and further. But at least Richie had done well, he thought as his mate came stealthily along the landing carrying the two bags full of silverware.

'Put them down by the top of the stairs, Richie. There wasn't a bloody safe so we've got to search every room. We'll collect the bags on the way out,' he whispered.

Richie was horrified. 'Even the bedrooms? Christ! Alfie, what if they wake up?' he hissed back. It had been bad enough wrapping up all those pieces of silver and trying not to make a sound; it seemed to have taken him hours. He couldn't wait to get out of here. And he certainly hadn't bargained on having to search bedrooms with their occupants asleep in them. It was sheer madness. It increased the risk of being caught hugely and he was trying desperately not to think about that or cell 216 in 'I' block. He'd sworn he wasn't going back inside Walton and now he wished he'd never agreed to Alfie's plan, never set eyes on this house. He couldn't stop himself from shaking and that would make him clumsy. Oh, God! Why hadn't he just stayed at home? he thought with mounting panic. Why had he ever listened to Alfie Shaw and his plans to get rich quick?

'Get a grip of yourself!' Alfie growled, aware of Richie's abject fear. 'Just be careful and they won't hear a thing!' He gave Richie a gentle push towards the stairs, following closely behind to make sure he didn't turn and make a run for it. As they reached the next landing he caught a glimpse of a faint beam of light moving further down. Jimmy was already up here. He could always rely on Jimmy, he thought with some relief.

Richie had disappeared into a room on the left and, holding his breath, Alfie silently opened the door to the room nearest him. Women usually kept their jewellery in bedrooms, often in a fancy box on a dressing table or bedside cabinet. As he slowly shone the light around it he realised that this was a large room and very tidy. There were three big wardrobes, a tall chest of drawers, an armchair, a carved mahogany dressing table and stool. He let the beam wander over the dressing table, looking for a box . . . nothing but glass bottles, but silver-backed hairbrushes too: they'd be worth something. He moved the beam on and it fell on the bed and he steeled himself. His guts were churning, something he hadn't bargained on, then with a little gasp of relief he realised the bed was empty, the covers undisturbed. Was this some sort of spare bedroom? he thought frantically. It looked like it; it was too tidy. So there wouldn't be much of value here, another waste of time. He'd take the brushes, have a quick look through the drawers and move on. Up to now they'd got far less than he'd hoped for and time seemed to be racing by.

He'd put the brushes in the canvas bag, the first two drawers had revealed nothing of interest and he was opening the third when a high-pitched scream made him drop the bag. It was followed immediately by a crash, then shouting and in horrified panic he recognised Richie's voice. What the hell was he doing yelling like that? What had gone wrong? The screams continued and then a door slammed shut; the sounds seemed deafeningly loud and Alfie rushed to the door.

On the landing he collided with Richie, who was ashen and shaking like a leaf.

'Run! Alfie, for Christ's sake, run! The old woman . . .'

Alfie grabbed him by the shoulders and shook him. 'What the hell went wrong? Did you get anything?'

'I got nothing! She . . . she . . . saw me . . . screamed! I . . . dropped the box. . . ran!' He was almost gibbering in panic.

They'd all be caught now, they'd all go to jail and . . . the nameless dark terrors of that accursed cell claimed him and he started to sob nosily.

Jimmy appeared beside them. 'Jesus! What's up with 'im? What's 'e done? Alfie, we'd better scarper quick, like!'

The noises now coming from the attic above them made Alfie realise the severity of their predicament. Jimmy was right. 'Get back down the stairs. We'll grab the bags we left there and run. And then . . .'

Suddenly the landing was bathed in light and they heard sounds coming from below now as well as above. They all froze in horror as Edith Davenport appeared a few yards away on the landing, a wool shawl over her nightdress, her long grey hair straggling over her shoulders, her ebony walking cane clutched tightly in a gnarled hand raised as though to lash out at them. At the same time James, followed by Jane, appeared at the head of the stairs.

'What the hell is going on here?' James roared. They'd arrived home from the concert to hear Edith's screams and Richie's shouts from upstairs, and shock had turned to anger as he'd switched on all the lights, racing up the stairs.

'Oh, my God! It . . . it's . . . you . . . *Alfie!*' Jane screamed, her eyes wide with fright as she took in the scene before her. Then it seemed as if everything happened at once. She ran to help Edith, who had sunk to her knees, her face the colour of old parchment, her eyes closed and her lips blue. Richie, uttering a howl of almost animal terror, barged past James and disappeared down the stairs. James – angrier than she'd ever thought possible – grabbed Jimmy and appeared to be trying to throttle him. Alfie was standing behind James and had snatched up a bronze statuette from the console table while Jane was on her knees holding Edith, who was fighting for breath; she watched Alfie raise the figurine and, in horrified disbelief, realised what he intended to do.

'Alfie! No! No! For God's sake . . . *Alfie, no! Stop! Stop!*' Her screams seemed to fill the whole house but they had no effect on her brother, who carried on hitting James.

James staggered and fell forward, releasing Jimmy as he did so, blood covering the back of his head and rapidly staining his shirt and jacket collars. Jimmy, gasping for breath, his face puce, turned and staggered down the stairs and Alfie, his eyes wild as he stared down at James Davenport's inert form, finally dropped the statuette and then fled, following Jimmy downstairs, leaving his sister staring after him in horror.

Lizzie Renshaw, followed by Cook, at last reached the bottom of the attic stairs. 'Oh, Jesus help us! Mrs Davenport, ma'am! What's happened?' the maid cried.

Jane was almost hysterical. 'Get help! For the love of God, get help, Lizzie! James . . . Edith . . . Get the police! Run, Lizzie! Run!'

Lizzie Renshaw ran and an ashen-faced, shocked and disbelieving Cook bent and took Edith's frail form from Jane's arms. 'See to the master . . .' she urged.

Jane knelt beside James and tried to turn him over but her hands quickly became covered with blood and she could see he was no longer breathing. Alfie did this, she thought in horror. Alfie had lied to her, telling her he was going to London when all the time he'd planned to break in and rob them, and he'd *killed* James. Richie, Jimmy and Alfie had so terrified Edith that she too looked in a terrible state. Jane's shoulders began to heave as the full horror of the situation began to sink in and hysterical sobs overwhelmed her. James was dead and her own brother had killed him. But why, why had Alfie done this? Why had he wanted to steal from them and how . . . how could he have beaten James like that? Didn't he care about . . . *anything*?

She didn't know how much time had elapsed before Lizzie Renshaw arrived back with both the police and the doctor, she was too dazed and shocked. She'd sat beside James, wiping the blood from her hands on her skirt, shaking, crying, unable to take in what had happened. She let Lizzie draw her to her feet as Dr Treacy, the family doctor, bent and examined James, shook his head and then went to attend to Edith.

'Oh, come away, Mrs Davenport! You're in a terrible state. Come with me to the breakfast room,' Lizzie urged, still profoundly shocked herself.

Inspector Toner interrupted: 'Just a minute, madam, please. I'll need you to tell me just what happened here.'

'I don't think she's in any fit state to make any kind of a statement just yet, Inspector,' Dr Treacy said curtly. He'd already instructed one of the uniformed constables to call for an ambulance immediately to take the old lady to hospital. She was alive but in a very bad way.

'Well, Doctor, I'll need someone to tell me what happened if we're ever going to get to the bottom of who did this,' was the terse reply.

'Cook and me can tell you what we know,' Lizzie offered.

Inspector Toner took out his notebook. 'Which is what, miss?'

'We . . . we heard screams and shouts and someone running

down the stairs and then Mrs Davenport shouting at someone and we came down, sir, and found . . .'

'You didn't see anyone other than the family members?' the Inspector demanded a little impatiently. He needed descriptions and he needed them quickly.

Lizzie shook her head. 'No, sir, they'd . . . run off – gone.'

He turned to Jane. 'Then I'm sorry but I'm going to have to ask you again, Mrs Davenport.'

Jane nodded slowly. 'I . . . we . . . got home from the concert and heard . . . noises. Edith . . . screaming and someone yelling. James . . . James switched on the lights and ran upstairs shouting, then . . . then . . .' It was all too much and she began to sob, clinging to Lizzie tightly for support.

'I'm sorry, Inspector, but she is in far too distressed a state to continue. I insist that you leave any further questioning until she is . . . calmer and more composed or I fear for her state of mind. She has experienced events no woman should have to face. In fact I will administer a sedative now,' Dr Treacy informed him.

Reluctantly Inspector Toner had to agree. The poor woman was indeed too distressed to be of much use to him. 'Very well, but when do you expect she will be in a fit state to make a statement, Doctor? I don't have to remind you it's a matter of urgency.'

'I can't tell you that. It will depend entirely how well she gets over the shock, but it certainly won't be for at least a day or two. Now, if you'll excuse me, the ambulance is here and I'll accompany Mrs Davenport Senior to the hospital. Let's hope that she recovers.' He turned grimly to Lizzie and handed her a small bottle. 'Give your mistress six drops of this, preferably in a warm, sweet drink, and then try to get her to sleep,' he instructed.

'Sir, do you think Madam will . . . wake up?' Nellie Grimes, the cook, begged the doctor anxiously.

'We can only pray she does, but I fear that at her age the shock might have been too much for her.'

Lizzie led Jane towards the breakfast room while Cook stood watching as Edith was taken away on a stretcher and the uniformed police officers began to search for fingerprints and other evidence.

Inspector Toner put his notebook back in his pocket, looking looked very disgruntled. It was obviously a robbery, judging by the discarded bags of silver, but it had gone terribly wrong, resulting in the murder of James Davenport and if the old lady died, possible manslaughter too. And at the moment no one could shed any light on the perpetrators.

As the sedative took effect Jane finally slept while Lizzie and Cook waited until James's body had been removed to the city mortuary and the police had finished and at last left, with instructions that nothing was to be moved or touched and that they would return in the morning. A uniformed officer would remain in the highly unlikely event that one of the gang returned.

When she awoke at first Jane did not remember what had happened. Her head felt as though it was filled with cotton wool and her lids were so heavy it was difficult to keep her eyes open. She struggled to get up, wondering why she was not in her own room, and then as she remembered she uttered a cry of disbelief and grief. James was dead! Alfie and Richie and

Jimmy had broken in and . . . and Alfie had killed James! She dropped her head in her hands. Oh, what was she going to do? She remembered now that the police had been here, that sergeant or inspector or whatever rank he was, had asked her to describe what had happened but she hadn't been able to. But now she realised that he would come back and she would have to tell him.

She stumbled to the dressing table and sank on to the stool, staring at herself in the mirror. She looked terrible: her eyes were dull and dark-circled; she was ashen and her hair was tangled. What could she tell them? she thought frantically. That it was her own brother who had killed her husband? She would have to betray Alfie, which would send him to his death for certain. Oh, how could she do that when he was her own flesh and blood? She had promised Ellen she would look after him and she had failed miserably, but if she handed him over to the police wouldn't that compound her failure? Would Ellen have wanted that? Surely not – but neither would her mother want such a terrible crime to go unpunished.

She shook her head, trying to clear it of the clogging mist that seemed to have invaded it. But what of James? What of the loyalty and affection she owed him? He had been so good to her; he hadn't deserved to die and as violently, horribly as that. Alfie had committed a crime – a heinous crime – and James deserved justice. How could she deliberately conceal the identity of his murderer – wouldn't that be a crime too? If she did then Alfie would get off scot-free and that wouldn't be right. That would go against the morality and justice that she, James and Ellen too believed in.

She pressed her fingers to her aching temples. And there

was Edith. She didn't know if her mother-in-law was alive or dead, but if she lived she would be able to tell the police about Alfie. She'd seen him last night and she knew he was related to her for he'd called here the day he'd lied about going to London. But perhaps Edith would rather die than survive to learn that her only son had been murdered by his brother-in-law? Round and round the thoughts and questions swooped in her mind and her emotions were in turmoil. What on earth was she going to do? Oh, why had Alfie put her in this position? Why had he tried to ruin her life?

Renshaw entered with a tray and Jane turned away from the mirror.

'I've brought you some tea, Mrs Davenport. How . . . how are you feeling now?' the maid asked tentatively.

'Very confused – shocked and light-headed,' Jane replied heavily.

'That'll be the sedative,' Lizzie said sagely as she poured the tea. 'Cook and me stayed up until the police left but they said they'd be back this morning, which is why Cook said I should bring up some tea.' Neither of them had had much sleep and were still horrified and grief-stricken.

Jane sighed heavily. She would have to make that terrible decision and soon.

'But Cook said if you're not up to talking to them I should ring the doctor and ask him to come.'

Jane nodded thankfully. 'Oh, Lizzie, would you ring him? I . . . I really don't think I can . . . talk to them . . . yet.'

'Of course I will. Now, you drink that tea and then try to get a bit more rest,' she urged. Of course the poor lady wasn't yet feeling up to reliving the horrific events of last night, and then she remembered Ada Ellis. 'Should I get word to Mrs Ellis, to let her know?' Lizzie suggested.

Jane seized on her words. 'Oh, yes, please! Oh, I really would like to see her, Lizzie.'

The girl nodded and left to telephone the doctor and to get word to Ada.

By the time Ada arrived, in a state of shock and disbelief, Jane was dressed and feeling a little calmer.

'Oh, Jane, luv! Is it true? I couldn't believe it when I heard. It's beyond belief! I'm so very sorry!' she cried, putting her arms around Jane.

Jane nodded and there was a glimmer of relief in her eyes. The world that had so suddenly gone mad seemed to steady a little now that Ada was here. 'Oh, Aunty Ada, my poor James . . . and . . . Edith . . .!'

Ada nodded. 'Did you see what happened? Did you tell the police?'

'I tried but . . . but then Dr Treacy said I wasn't in a fit state and he gave me a sedative.'

'I should think you needed it, luv,' Ada agreed.

'I still feel that I'm living in a . . . nightmare! They are coming again this morning but the doctor is on his way and he'll tell them I'm still not . . .' Jane broke down. 'Oh, Aunty Ada, what am I going to do now?'

'You're going to try and get some rest, luv,' Ada soothed. 'And you can rely on me and the doctor not to let them . . . harass you.'

'I'll have to talk to them soon, I know that, but . . .'

'But not yet, luv. It's too soon,' Ada replied firmly. 'And I'll stay with you, Jane, for as long as you need me. I'll not let you face all this on your own.'

Jane clung to her, relief washing over her. 'Oh, thank you, Aunty Ada. I feel so . . . lost and confused.'

'You can rely on me, luv. Once we've got rid of the police I'll go back and let the family know what's happened and then, if you like, I'll go to the Royal to see how the poor old lady is. Then I'll be back, I promise, and for as long as you need me.'

Jane shook her head sadly. 'Oh, poor Edith! She . . . she looked so ill . . .'

'Well, luv, she's not a young woman and it must have been a terrible shock, but don't you dwell on it. Just try to rest and I'll be back later.'

When she'd gone Jane sank thankfully down on the sofa in the breakfast room; she felt a little unsteady on her feet. How could she 'rest', she thought distractedly, when she knew she would have to come to a decision as to what she would tell the police? Maybe when Ada returned she would confide in her but she already had a good idea what Ada would urge her to do. Oh, everything was so confusing.

True to her word Ada was back in the afternoon carrying a carpet bag into which she'd hastily packed a few things. 'How are you now, Jane? I see the police have gone. They didn't bother you?'

Jane shook her head. 'No, but . . . but I promised I'd be well enough to talk to them tomorrow.'

Ada shook her head, wondering at the wisdom of this. 'Well, I'm afraid there's little change in the old lady's condition and the doctor who was good enough to speak to me said she apparently had a stroke and that often it is followed by another one, and that at her age it could be . . . fatal. He said we should be prepared for it. I'm sorry, luv.'

'Poor Edith. She . . . she hasn't regained consciousness?'

'Well, when I was sitting with her she did open her eyes . . . once, and you know I think she recognised me because she managed a little lopsided smile before she . . . drifted off again. It gave me some hope, Jane. Now, all we can do is pray that she does recover. I suppose it will take time but . . . I feel there's some hope, luv. Now, have you had anything to eat at all yet?'

'I . . . I . . . can't eat, Aunty Ada,' Jane protested. 'Just the thought of food makes me feel ill.'

'But you'll have to try, luv. It's not good that you don't eat. I'll go down and have a word with Cook.'

Jane felt too tired, too heartsore, too confused to protest. She knew that despite the sedative drops she would get little rest tonight. She would have to come to a decision for she'd promised to speak to Inspector Toner tomorrow. But had that decision been made for her? Would Edith recover? Ada had said she was hopeful and if Edith had indeed recognised Ada then perhaps she was right to be. And if Edith recovered then she would be able to tell the police about Alfie. But what would the police think if Edith told them Alfie was involved? They might even believe that she herself had been helping him from the inside! They might think she was implicated . . .

She gazed in despair at the scrambled egg and toast Ada had brought up from the kitchen and begged her to try. She couldn't eat. She couldn't think. She felt paralysed by fear.

'You've got to eat to keep your strength up, Jane,' Ada reprimanded her gently. 'If, please God, Edith does recover and is able to come home it's going to be a very trying time for you both,' she mused, thinking that the old lady would need careful nursing and she would have to cope with the tragic death of her only son. The days and weeks ahead looked very grim to her.

Jane had barely slept at all, and when she awoke her head again felt as if it were filled with cotton wool and her eyes were heavy but she dressed and went down to find Ada already up and having breakfast.

'You look exhausted, Jane. I can see you've not had an easy night. Sit down, luv, and I'll pour you a cup of tea. See if you can manage a slice of toast and marmalade,' she urged.

Before Jane could protest Renshaw entered and both women could tell from her face that something was wrong.

'What is it, Lizzie?' Ada asked.

'It . . . it's Madam. She . . . she . . . died. She had another stroke during the night. The doctor called just now. He wanted to come up but Cook said it would be better if . . .' Lizzie Renshaw wiped away a tear with the corner of her apron.

'God rest the poor lady,' Ada said sadly. She had really hoped Edith would recover; she'd been certain that the old lady had recognised her but perhaps she hadn't? Well, they'd told her at the hospital that Edith might well have another stroke so at least they had been partly prepared.

Slowly Jane nodded her agreement. Poor Edith. She would confide now in Ada and it would be a relief, for in her heart of hearts she knew what she had to do.

'It's even more important now, Jane, that the police find who was responsible,' Ada remarked.

Again Jane nodded. 'I . . . know and I want to . . . tell you everything first.' She took a deep breath. 'When we got home we heard Edith . . . screaming. James . . . rushed upstairs and I followed him, and . . . and . . . they were there, the three of them. It was . . . horrible, Aunty Ada! It was like a nightmare! Edith . . . collapsed . . . Richie . . . just ran and James . . . James he grabbed hold of Jimmy . . .' she faltered, feeling she couldn't go on.

Ada's eyes widened in horror. 'Richie Corrin and Jimmy Cobham . . . were *here*? Did . . . did they do this?'

Jane's voice was a whisper. 'Yes.'

'And you didn't tell . . . anyone?'

Jane looked at her in confusion. 'No. I just didn't . . . couldn't . . .'

Ada got up, her eyes hardening. 'I'd better get Renshaw to phone that inspector and ask him to come now – that's if he isn't already on his way.' She paused. 'Do you feel up to telling him all this, Jane? I suppose the third one was Alfie?' she asked gravely.

Slowly Jane nodded. 'Yes. I know now what I've got to do, Aunty Ada. I . . . I can't protect Alfie, I have to think of James and Edith and . . . do what's right,' she replied.

Ada shook her head. Oh, thank God poor Ellen was not here to witness this.

Renshaw informed them that Inspector Toner was on his way and he arrived a few minutes later and was ushered upstairs. He was a tall, thin, dour man known for his efficiency and his ruthlessness as many criminals could confirm.

'I'm very sorry to hear that Mrs Edith Davenport has

passed away,' he said as Ada indicated that he sit down.

'God rest her, it was all too much for her at her age,' Ada replied. 'But Jane is feeling up to talking to you,' she added.

He was relieved that at last Mrs Davenport had decided to make a statement; now perhaps a manhunt could get under way.

'You're quite ready to make a statement, Mrs Davenport?' he asked briskly.

'And she knows who they were, Inspector,' Ada went on to inform him. She held Jane's hand tightly. 'She . . . she's just told me.'

'If she knows them then why didn't she say so before this?' he demanded.

'In the name of God you know the state she's in and on top of that we've only just heard that old Mrs Davenport has died!' Ada snapped, annoyed by his seeming lack of compassion. 'They're well known to you lot too. Jimmy Cobham, Richie Corrin and the third one was her own brother – Alfie Shaw. And you can be certain that this whole thing was his idea. He knew where she lived, he's been here before and the other two haven't got the brains of a rocking horse!'

At the mention of Alfie Jane broke down. 'I . . . I begged him to stop hitting James! I begged him . . . but he . . . didn't!' she sobbed.

Inspector Toner frowned. 'I'm sorry, Mrs Davenport, but . . . but who was it who . . . attacked your husband?'

Jane was utterly unable to speak. Alfie had killed James before her eyes and she'd never be able to forgive him for what he'd done to them all.

'All right, ma'am,' the Inspector said gently. 'Just nod if it was Alfie Shaw. We won't press you further but time is of the essence if we're to catch them,' he urged.

Jane nodded slowly.

'That's fine, ma'am. You can rest assured that we'll scour the city for them and we'll find them, I promise you that, even though they've had a bit of a head start,' he said grimly before he left the room.

Ada nodded, equally grimly. How had Alfie Shaw turned out like this? she thought. A heartless thief and a murderer. She wondered how Jane was going to find the strength and the courage to face the weeks and months ahead. Not only would she have to try to come to terms with the terrible events of that night and her grief and loss but she'd also have to face the ordeal of a trial – a very public trial too for her husband had been a man of some standing – and, God help her, James Davenport's murderer was her own brother.

Chapter Twenty-Six

<hr style="width:20%;text-align:center;margin:auto" />

JIMMY AND RICHIE were soon caught but of Alfie there was no sign: he appeared to have escaped, vanished from the face of the earth, or at least Liverpool. Richie had been so panic-stricken and traumatised by the ordeal that he had headed straight home to Gill Street without thinking or caring about the outcome of his actions, so he was the first to be apprehended. Jimmy had been picked up by the Dock Police trying to sneak on board a cargo ship. The deaths and the arrests made the headlines in first the local and then the national press and when Inspector Toner called to inform Jane and Ada he appeared grimly satisfied.

'But there's no sign of . . . the other one?' Ada pressed when she heard all the news, loath to even mention Jane's brother by name.

He shook his head. 'Not yet, but now his description is in all the papers I'm sure it won't be long, Mrs Ellis. And with that red hair he's not what you'd call "nondescript".'

'I told you those two didn't have the brains of a rocking horse. We might have known that idiot Richie Corrin would have run straight home to his mam,' Ada retorted scornfully.

'And it wasn't the brightest thing for Cobham to do either, to head for the docks. It's what nine out of ten of them do so the Dock Police are always on the lookout,' the Inspector added.

Ada nodded her agreement. 'But I still can't believe the barefaced lies that lad told us to try to give himself an alibi.'

'You mean Alfie Shaw? What lies? What did he say, Mrs Ellis?'

Ada turned to Jane, who so far had said nothing. 'He came here to this house to see Jane, didn't he luv? A good few weeks ago now, it was.'

'He . . . he told me he'd got a job as a porter or something at Euston Station and I . . . I was so pleased and relieved. He said he'd come to say goodbye. I just never dreamed he . . . he was . . .' Jane bit her lip.

'You're sure it was Euston?' the Inspector demanded.

Jane nodded.

Inspector Toner's expression changed. 'Then there's a chance that that's where he's scarpered to – London! I'll get straight on to Scotland Yard: we have to cover every eventuality. If he has headed there then those lads will find him. He can't hide forever. If you'll excuse me, ladies?'

Ada was a little taken aback. 'Of course, but you will let us know . . .?' she asked.

'Right away, that's a promise,' he replied as he turned to leave.

As Ada closed the door after him she couldn't help but feel

285

a little unnerved by what she might have unwittingly just done. Oh, of course she wanted Alfie to face justice – his actions were utterly unforgivable, and she had only to look at his poor, wrecked sister to witness their consequences – but she hadn't quite meant to help set the police on his trail so decisively. However, she told herself, he needed to be caught. The wayward little boy she had once known had turned into an evil man and who knew what harm he might do in the future? He had already destroyed poor Jane's life; he shouldn't be allowed to ruin anyone else's.

Sylvie couldn't believe her ears when she heard the big burly police sergeant demanding grimly to know from her father if Alfie Shaw lodged here and, if so, had they seen him in the last forty-eight hours? She stood frozen with fear and listened in total disbelief as her da demanded, equally curtly, what had Alfie done?

'Killed a man! We've picked his mates up and they gave us this address,' was the stark reply.

She gripped the edge of the bar counter to steady herself. 'He . . . he can't have . . . killed . . . anyone! Not . . . *Alfie*!' she cried.

'You keep your mouth shut, girl!' her da snapped, furious that the lad had admitted he'd lived here. Too late now to deny it. 'Yes, he lodged here but we never knew much about him or what he got up to. He never gave us no trouble. We can't be held responsible for anything he's done.'

'Well, he's in plenty of trouble now. Broke into a house in Upper Huskisson Street with his mates but the owner disturbed them. His mates legged it but meladdo battered the gentleman's head in, and he was a gentleman of some standing too. There was a reliable witness, his sister, so Alfie Shaw's for the gallows when we apprehend him!'

Both her mam and da looked deeply shocked and the sergeant demanded to see the room Alfie had lodged in and so her da took him upstairs.

'Mam! Oh, God, Mam!' Sylvie gasped and began to cry. She felt faint and sick, unable to believe what Alfie had done.

Her mother turned on her. 'Did you know what that feller was like? Did you know what he was up to? You're not mixed up in this, girl, are you? You seemed very friendly with him,' she demanded.

'No! No! I . . . I didn't know, Mam! Honest to God, I didn't know!' Sylvie sobbed.

'You'd better not! Your da'll beat you black and blue if he thinks you've got mixed up with a lad like that. Bye, he's a bad 'un! A real viper in our bosom is what he turned out to be. We're law-abidin', hard-workin' folk, and maybe this'll make your da more careful who he lets rent that room in future. Now, stop that snivelling and give me a hand, there's work to be done.'

Sylvie didn't reply but she continued to sniff quietly. She'd been disappointed and yet somewhat relieved when she'd got her curse that morning. She had been wondering if she should tell Alfie that it had all been a false alarm and if he would still marry her – she'd certainly hoped he would – but she hadn't seen hide nor hair of him and now she knew why. She'd heard him come in that night and go straight upstairs. She'd listened to him moving around but then she'd fallen asleep and it wasn't unusual for her not to see him in the mornings: he often slept late; sometimes she didn't see him all day. But she'd not realised that he'd . . . gone!

A wave of revulsion washed over her. She could have been carrying the child of a *killer*! She could have married a man capable of *murder*! It was . . . horrible! Oh, she could hardly believe it! He'd said he loved her and would marry her and take care of her and all the time he'd been planning to break into that house . . . yet he'd never seemed violent. But now that she thought more deeply about it all she realised that she'd never really known much about him at all. She didn't know where he came from or if he had any family. She didn't even know he had a sister. She didn't know how he got his money or where he went or whom he mixed with. And he'd had two mates here that night, she knew that. How could he have been so . . . hard-hearted and – there was no other word for it – wicked? They must all have gone off to burgle that house – his own sister's house – and then . . . Slowly it began to dawn on her that she had had a very lucky escape and she shivered. 'Mam, do you think they'll find . . . anything up there?' she asked hesitantly.

'I doubt it, girl. He'll not have left anything of value behind. I'd say he was all set to scarper after that robbery – his type always has some sort of plan to disappear and without paying what he owes.'

Sylvie nodded. Her mam was probably right. He hadn't cared about her at all. He'd gone off without a backward glance, leaving her to face the consequences had she indeed been in the family way. That hurt so much, and added to the hurt was humiliation and shame. Why had she been so foolish, so *stupid*? She should have heeded her mam's advice and valued herself more highly. Well, she wouldn't make the same mistake twice, she vowed as she carried the heavy tray of dirty glasses back to the scullery.

Christmas had effectively been forgotten, Ada thought sadly as she went down to the kitchen to speak to Nellie Grimes. True to her promise Ada had stayed with Jane and both Fred and Emily had proved to be towers of strength. Emily, after visiting Jane to offer what support and help she could, had quietly informed her mother that she would see to her father and brother's meals, do the shopping and whatever chores were necessary and she'd make sure they had some sort of Christmas meal but it would all be a very quiet affair now. Ada was to devote her time to Jane. 'She really needs you now, Mam, you're not to worry about anything else,' she had said firmly. Fred had been of great support to his shocked and subdued sons and had also taken upon himself the gruelling task of answering the questions of friends, neighbours, the police and even morbidly curious strangers.

As unobtrusively as possible Ada had got rid of the Christmas tree and all the decorations and had carefully packed away the gifts Jane had bought for James and his mother. Quietly she had replaced the festive decorations with the traditional trappings of mourning. She felt that the staff had been amazingly kind to Jane; they'd been loyal servants to James and Edith and in keeping her brother's very existence a secret Jane had brought sorrow and tragedy to them all. She had sent young Lizzie Renshaw off home for the holiday. She had asked Cook if she also wished to spend some time away from the house, stating that she was perfectly capable of managing the tragically depleted and stricken household.

'I've no one to go to, Mrs Ellis, and I feel it's the least I can do to stay. Perhaps I can tempt her to eat something,' Nellie Grimes had replied but Ada had not held out much hope of that.

'How is she this morning, Mrs Ellis?' Cook greeted her. She was rolling out pastry for a pie but she covered it with a clean muslin cloth and wiped her hands on her apron. She'd begun to realise that although Jane had made a terrible mistake in not telling poor Mr Davenport about her brother, she couldn't be held responsible for what had happened.

'About the same, I'd say. She wouldn't eat anything and I don't know if she slept at all. She hardly knows what day of the week it is and I don't wonder. I lost track myself until Fred reminded me earlier. He called in on his way to work.'

'Everything still seems so . . . unreal. I can't believe that Christmas is actually over,' the older woman answered as she made a pot of tea. 'Probably that medicine the doctor left makes her . . . vague, Mrs Ellis, and maybe in a way it's a blessing the funerals aren't going to be this week.'

Ada nodded. 'Maybe she'll be a bit stronger by then, but God knows how she's going to get through . . . everything,' she answered. Because of the post-mortem and the holiday the funerals of James and his mother were not going to take place until early in the New Year when hopefully some of the public furore would have abated.

'What will she do . . . afterwards? Do you think she'll stay here?'

Ada sipped her tea thoughtfully; it was a question she'd already asked Fred. 'I don't know, Nellie, I really don't. She might decide she wants to move, sell this house. The memories . . . And it's far too big for her anyway. She might decide she wants to get rid of the business too. Oh, I know she's got a good idea of how it all works and that Mr Turner is very efficient and trustworthy but . . . but she might feel as if it's just too much of a responsibility, and she's got the ordeal of the trials to get through first, don't forget.'

Cook nodded, frowning. 'Has there been any word about them?'

Ada shook her head. 'No. There's a police constable who seems to have been instructed to tell Fred what's happening and he said that the other two will be in the dock before long, he thinks,' she informed her companion grimly. Both Jimmy and Richie were in Walton Jail and the same constable had remarked to Fred that he'd heard that Richie was 'cutting up badly'. It served him right, had been her bitter reply. It was the constable's opinion, and the general consensus of those involved in the case, Fred had told her, that because Jimmy and Richie's offence had contributed to the death of Edith Davenport (even though it was less serious than Alfie's crime), it would be many long years before either of those two would be free to walk the streets of Liverpool again.

Nellie Grimes sighed heavily. 'Oh, the poor lass! I could weep when I think of everything she's still to get through.'

'So could I, Nellie, but she's coped with a lot of hardship and heartache in her life so far, has Jane, and she's got us all to help her get through what's ahead; she knows that. Now, I came down to ask you if you will sit with her for a couple of hours tomorrow morning. I have to go out. There's something I have to do and I can't put it off.'

'Of course, Mrs Ellis. Despite everything, life has to go on,' Cook replied.

Ada was relieved. One of the reasons Fred had called was to remind her that the *Empress of Scotland* was docking tomorrow morning and she'd resolved to go down and meet Joe to inform him of the tragic events before he either heard it as gossip or read about it in the newspapers.

Jane thought detachedly that she had never noticed just how loudly the clock ticked before. The room was so still, the air seemed heavy and dust motes, caught in the rays of weak sunlight that filtered between the partly closed curtains, drifted slowly downwards. Each tick of the mantel clock seemed to reverberate in her head and even though she could make out the hands of the clock she wasn't aware of what time it was. James had wound that clock each night; in fact he'd wound all the clocks in the house each night, he'd been such a stickler for punctuality. But now time had no meaning for her; it was as if it had been suspended for there was nothing she had to do or find time to do and James was no longer here, nor was Edith.

Slowly she got up and walked aimlessly towards the fireplace. How long ago was it now since that awful night? She had no clear idea at all; the days had merged together. People had called: the doctor, the vicar and the archdeacon, Emily and Georgie and Danny and Sonny, a friend of Edith's, the friend of James's who'd been best man, Mr Turner from the laundry, but she couldn't remember what she'd said to any of them. Ada had told her that Renshaw was away visiting her family but that she and Cook would remain with her; she was not to distress herself further and she had wondered what could possibly 'distress' her further now?

She stared hard at the hands of the clock. Time! Seconds, minutes, hours, days, weeks, months – the future, her future. How long would she feel like this? Numbed, confused, disorientated? She'd suffered shock and grief before, but it had never affected her as badly as this. She looked at her reflection in the black-draped mirror above the ornate marble mantel. She didn't look any different, paler perhaps and with dark circles beneath her eyes, and her pallor was accentuated by her plain black mourning dress. She shook her head as if to try to clear it. It must be the medicine Ada gave her each night on the doctor's instructions that was affecting her like this. It dulled all her senses but it didn't make her sleep, at least not a deep restful sleep. How could she even try to cope with things if her mind was permanently fogged? she wondered. And despite everything she realised that there were things she must *try* to face. She would have to see that both James and Edith were laid to rest in peace and with dignity. Ada couldn't stay here with her indefinitely; she had a family of her own to care for. Lizzie Renshaw couldn't remain with her family either; she needed her job to help them out. Cook needed to work too and there was the laundry that James had worked so hard to make such a success: people's livelihoods depended upon it remaining successful. People depended on her now. And then . . . then there was the ordeal of the trial to face, but she couldn't think of that now, she just wasn't strong enough. Could she remain here in this house that was so filled with memories and a strange, brooding silence? When she'd seen James and Edith laid to rest would she want to return here? The medicine had mercifully blurred the edges of so much. The memory of how she'd rushed up the stairs behind James, the frightening tableau she'd witnessed on the landing, James struggling with Jimmy and . . . Alfie . . . and then the horror of the hours that had followed. She'd not been in the morning room since and she slept in a spare bedroom but this house had been their home: did she want to leave it?

She pressed her hands to her throbbing forehead; the ticking of the clock was grating on her nerves now and she resolved that she would take no more of the sedative. She couldn't go on in this semi-stupefied state. No matter how painful, how heart-breaking the memories and the days ahead would be she must try to face them for not until she confronted her demons could she try to overcome them.

Ada entered quietly and was surprised to find her leaning on the over-mantel with her head in her hands. 'Jane, luv, are you all right? Would you like some tea?'

Jane straightened, turned around and managed a bleak smile. 'Yes, please, Aunty Ada. I've been trying to think . . . and I've decided that I'm not taking any more of that medicine Doctor Treacy left. I . . . I have to try to face . . . things. I can't spend my days and nights in this . . . stupor. It's not going to help me.'

Ada frowned, concerned. 'Do you think that's wise, luv? I mean it's very early days yet . . .'

Jane squared her shoulders and nodded. 'I know it is but . . . but there are things I *have* to think of and prepare myself for. I don't think either James or Edith would want me to . . . to continue like this.'

Ada hurried to her side and put her arm around her. 'Now, don't get upset, luv. Sit down while I go and get some tea.'

Jane sat wearily on the sofa, still trying to dispel the numb feeling from her brain. 'Aunty Ada, I think I'd like Emily to come to see me when she has time.'

Ada smiled. It was the first time Jane had asked to see anyone. 'I think it might do you good, luv, and I'm sure she'll be only too happy to.'

Jane nodded. 'Perhaps then you could go and spend a couple of hours with Uncle Fred and the boys. They must miss you.'

'I might just do that too – see what kind of a mess they've been making of the place, left to their own devices,' Ada replied, thinking that it might indeed be better for Jane if she were to discontinue taking the medicine. Perhaps she was ready to try to face her future. If so, Ada would feel easier leaving her while she went to meet Joe.

Chapter Twenty-Seven

GOING TO LONDON: that had been the biggest mistake he'd made, Alfie thought as he sat in the mail car of the train now travelling through the night to Liverpool, handcuffed, while two uniformed officers of the Liverpool City Police sat opposite him, grim-faced and silent, their contempt for him barely disguised. Like a bloody fool he'd headed straight for Lime Street Station and caught the first train out, but he hadn't been thinking straight; if he had he would have considered his position more carefully. He didn't know London, he'd never been there before, and when he'd reached Euston he'd just wandered the streets that surrounded the station, wondering what to do next.

At length he'd gone into a pub in one of the back streets and had sounded out the barman regarding obtaining lodgings. He should have kept his mouth shut, he thought bitterly.

'You just arrived, mate?' he'd been asked, the man picking up on his accent.

He'd nodded, taking a deep swig of the ale he'd been served.

'And looking for work? Where've you come from then?'

He'd been wary. 'Up north. Manchester, like,' he'd answered, thinking the barman wouldn't know the difference between a Mancunian and Liverpudlian accent. The man had nodded slowly.

'I might be able to help. I'll ask around and if you come back later this evening maybe you'll have somewhere to lay your head tonight. Won't be cheap though, at least not as cheap as . . . er, Manchester.'

'I've got money, I just need a room. I'd be really grateful, mate,' he'd said with relief. He had to get off the streets, give himself time to think. Plan what he would do next. Maybe even get out of the country altogether.

He'd found a cheap café where the food wasn't too bad and when he'd returned he was introduced to a middle-aged, blowsy-looking woman who called herself 'Ma Stebbings', who had an attic room she was prepared to let him rent. After he'd bought her a pint of ale and a large whisky she'd taken him to a house in a street around the corner and shown him the room. It was as cold and depressing as the one he'd rented in Liverpool but he hadn't cared.

He shifted uncomfortably on the hard seat, keeping his eyes averted from the two burly figures who seemed to note his every move. There was absolutely no chance he could escape, he thought dully, not handcuffed, closely watched by those two and locked in the mail car. He'd been at Ma Stebbings's for three days, days fraught with anxiety and fear, trying desperately to try to find a way out of the predicament he found himself in. He was forced to go out for something to eat – she provided no food – and a couple of times he'd called into the pub, but for the rest of the time he'd stayed in that freezing attic, cursing himself.

He'd begun to realise that he should have stayed in Liverpool. He knew the city well and there were enough places he could have hidden until the hue and cry had died down. What money he had wouldn't last much longer and he'd be forced to try to find work of some kind or starve. He dared not risk thieving or any other form of criminal activity.

The following day they'd come for him. When the news and his description had appeared in the papers the barman from the pub had tipped them off. He'd gone cold when he'd heard the heavy footsteps on the stairs; then the door had been kicked open. He'd tried to protest but had been ignored as he'd been forcibly dragged downstairs to the waiting van while Ma Stebbings screeched at the top of her voice that she hadn't known he was a criminal, a wanted man and on the run.

The heavy iron cuffs bit into his flesh and he shivered; there didn't seem to be any heating in the car at all. It was all Richie's fault! Bloody stupid Richie! He'd cursed him over and over ever since that night. He should never have trusted Richie; he'd known he wasn't very keen on doing the job with them. Some stupid superstitious nonsense about that cell in Walton. He'd been frightened and clumsy, woken the old woman and then gone to pieces, making a complete mess of everything! He shivered again but this time involuntarily as he remembered the events of that night. They might all have got away if Jane and her husband hadn't arrived back. What the hell was he supposed to do when Davenport had tried to throttle Jimmy? It had all happened so fast and Richie had run, yelling and gibbering like a madman; he'd spooked them all. Bloody Richie! And now because of him he was being taken back to Liverpool to stand trial. He hoped they'd put Richie back in that bloody cell that he hated so much, he thought venomously. It would serve him right. He'd heard that both his 'accomplices' – as one of the scuffers had called them – had been caught and were back in Walton Jail. It was where he too would end up, he thought, anger and frustration filling him. And it all could have ended so differently if everything had gone to plan, except for bloody Richie!

A bitterly cold wind was driving a mixture of sleet and hail across the expanse of Mann Island next morning and it stung Ada's cheeks like pinpricks and was making her eyes water as she struggled down towards the Landing Stage. The ship had already tied up, the last passengers had departed and the first members of the crew had begun to disembark. As she walked on she searched the small group of men for the familiar face of her eldest son and was relieved to see him making his way towards her, his sea bag slung over his shoulder. She raised a hand to attract his attention; he would be home now for a few days at least.

Joe was surprised to see her and realised instantly that something was wrong. He took her arm. 'Mam, what are you doing here on such a cold and miserable morning? What's wrong?'

'I had to come to meet you, Joe. I didn't want you to hear all kinds of . . . lurid tales or read in the newspapers that—' she started.

'Hang on to my arm; this wind will have you off your feet.

What "lurid tales" and read about what?' he interrupted.

Ada shivered and shook her head sadly. 'It's . . . a terrible tragedy, Joe.'

'Look, we can't stand here in this weather. Come across to the Style House and you can tell me what's happened,' he urged, indicating the waterfront pub frequented by the crews of all the ships that arrived and departed from the Pier Head.

Ada was scandalised. 'I'm not going in *that* place! I'm a respectable woman, Joe Ellis!' she protested.

Joe shook his head impatiently at her protests. 'Mam, we can't stand here, we'll sit in the snug and anyway the place won't be too busy at this time of day.'

The rain was getting heavier so reluctantly Ada agreed and was relieved to find that the pub was indeed reasonably quiet and that a good fire was burning in the snug, which they had to themselves.

Joe ordered a small brandy for her, knowing she must be cold and was obviously upset by whatever events had brought her down here to meet him.

'No arguments, Mam. Drink it, you're frozen. Now, what's the matter? Is it Da or one of the lads? What's happened?'

Ada sipped the drink and felt some warmth returning to her cold limbs. 'No, they're all right, Joe. But something . . . terrible, really terrible has happened.'

Joe was concerned but his expression became far more serious as his mother informed him of the events that had taken place while he had been away. There had been a rumour about someone being murdered in Liverpool: they'd got the news by wireless telegraph, but there had been few details and he'd not given the matter much thought but now . . . he was trying hard to take it all in. James Davenport was dead, killed by Alfie Shaw, and so was his mother and Jane . . . Jane had witnessed it all. Alfie was now in jail and in one night Jane had lost her husband, her mother-in-law and her brother, for Alfie had more or less signed his own death warrant. He wanted to rush to her and take her in his arms and tell her that everything would be all right, that he'd be at her side now to help her through this terrible time. That he loved her and would care for her and help her through the dark days ahead.

He'd had time to think on this last trip for the ship hadn't been busy and he'd determined that after the cruises he would take his chances and try to make a new life for himself in Canada. It was a big country, a young country, he'd liked the places he'd seen when he'd travelled with Mr Ibsen and there were opportunities for people who were prepared to work hard. He'd lost Jane and he'd convinced himself that he would stand a better chance of putting her out of his mind and his heart forever by going to Canada, but now everything had changed. Jane was a widow and she would need the support and love he could give her.

'Oh, Mam! I . . . can hardly believe it! How is she . . . coping? What will she do?'

'It's been a nightmare for her and she's been in a terrible state, but yesterday she . . . she seemed a bit . . . calmer. She said she's not taking that stuff the doctor prescribed because it's not helping her and she has to try to face . . . things. She asked to see our Emily and that's the first time she's wanted to see anyone.'

Joe nodded. He couldn't even begin to try to imagine what she had suffered and what she must be going through now but a wave of anger surged through him as he thought of Alfie. 'What the hell kind of brother is he that he'd try to rob his own sister? Terrify the old lady and then . . . kill . . .! How could he put her through all *that*?' he raged.

Ada sighed heavily. 'I don't know, Joe, I honestly don't. He was never any good but it defies belief that he could be so . . . wicked! Poor Ellen must be turning in her grave. She tried so hard, she worried about that lad so much and all to no avail. But now he's going to pay for what he's done and perhaps the worst aspect of all is that it's poor Jane's testimony that will send him to the gallows. I just don't know how she is going to cope with that on top of everything else.'

Joe shook his head, wondering bitterly why fate had singled Jane out for such malign treatment, Jane who had never done anyone any harm in her life, who was kind, gentle, loyal and trusting. 'Mam, I . . . I'd like to see her.'

Ada sighed. She'd known this would be what he'd want to do but she shook her head. 'I knew you would, Joe, but . . . leave it, lad. She's not up to it yet. Give her a bit more time.'

'But I love her, Mam. I realised that I've always loved her when I thought it was too late,' he pleaded, desperate to see her and try to alleviate some of her suffering. But maybe Mam was right: Jane might need only his friendship for now.

'I know you do and so it's only natural you want to go to her, but if you go telling her you love her now . . . I just don't know how she'll feel, Joe. It might well make things . . . worse. More confusing for her. Leave it, at least until you get back after next trip. The funerals will be over then and there might be some news of the trial,' Ada urged.

'Mam, I've only got a few days! You've forgotten that then

302

I'll be away for three months. I can't leave it *that* long. I can't! What will she think? That I don't care about her at all or about what's happened? I left her once before, to chase my own dreams. I can't . . . I *won't* do it again.'

Ada bit her lip. She had indeed forgotten he'd be away for so long and she could understand his feelings and his reasoning. She finished the brandy. 'No, she won't think that, Joe. I'll . . . I'll tell her you wanted to see her but that I thought it best to leave it.'

'At least *ask* her. Ask her if she wants to see me and if . . . if she doesn't then I'll at least have tried and she'll know that I'm not completely heartless,' Joe begged.

Ada thought about it but she was convinced that a visit from Joe now wouldn't help Jane. Even though she was confident that Joe wouldn't tactlessly blurt out his feelings it was just too soon for the poor girl to cope with. 'No. I feel for you Joe, I really do, but I have to think what's best for that poor girl now. I'll tell her that you wanted to see her, that you're very upset and want to try to help but give her time. Give her time to try to come to terms with her loss. It's for the best, I *know* it is.'

Joe didn't reply. He was bitterly disappointed by her attitude although he realised that she was only thinking of Jane's state of mind.

Ada picked up her bag. 'Right, we'd better get home. I promised Nellie Grimes I wouldn't be long.'

Joe got to his feet. 'When is our Emily going to see Jane?' he asked, wondering if he could enlist his sister's help.

'Tonight and while she's there I'm coming home to spend a few hours with your da,' Ada replied, giving him a sidelong glance. She wasn't convinced that Joe had accepted the situation.

*

It was bitterly cold and frost was already dusting the pavements when Emily got off the tram and walked up Upper Huskisson Street. As she approached Jane's house she shivered involuntarily, thinking of the terrible events that had taken place here. Joe had taken her aside before she'd left her mam's house and had begged her to tell Jane that he dearly wanted to see her but that Ada had advised against it. He'd revealed his love for Jane and had urged her to tell Jane that he was thinking of her constantly and that he was deeply concerned about her but that if she felt she couldn't see him, he would understand and promised he would write to her whilst he was away. To Emily that fact alone had emphasised how much her brother loved Jane.

Renshaw opened the door to her. 'She's in the drawing room, miss. Go on up; there's a good fire so it's nice and warm and just ring when you would like some tea,' she said, taking Emily's coat and hat.

'How is she?' Emily asked for her mam had said she thought Jane was feeling a little better.

'I only got back this morning but she doesn't seem as . . . dazed, miss, but we're all still upset,' the girl answered.

A fire was burning brightly in the hearth, the heavy curtains shut out the dark frosty night and the shaded lamps gave the room a warm, welcoming glow. As she entered Emily was relieved to see that Jane did look much better than on the last time she'd visited her. She smiled and gave her old friend a hug. 'It's freezing cold out there so you're in the best place and you certainly look much . . . brighter, Jane. Are you feeling any better?' she enquired, sitting down on the sofa beside her.

Jane smiled. 'I'm sort of . . . calmer now, Em. I've been sitting here trying to sort things out in my mind.'

'What things?' Emily enquired.

'The priorities really. To start with there are the arrangements to be made for the . . . funerals. I can't just let the days drift by.'

Emily took her hand and squeezed it. 'You know Mam will help you and if there is anything . . . anything at all I can do . . .'

'Thanks, Em. Everyone has been very kind but I'm glad Aunty Ada's gone to spend a few hours at home. It can't have been easy for her being here all the time. I haven't been of much use to anyone. It's all made extra work for you, too.'

'I don't mind, Jane, and I know she's been so worried about you that she felt she couldn't leave you. But I think the lads have been missing her – even though she's always complaining they drive her mad with their antics.'

'I can't expect her to stay indefinitely, Emily. I have to try to make an effort to come to terms with what's . . . happened. I can't take unfair advantage of her.'

'Don't say that, Jane! You're not "taking advantage" and you've got some very difficult days still ahead of you,' Emily reminded her. 'The lads can manage for a bit longer and now that our Joe's home for a bit they'll have him to keep them company.' Emily paused. 'He got home this morning,' she added.

It was the first time Jane had thought about Joe and she nodded slowly. 'Does he know, Em . . . about . . .?'

Emily sighed. 'Yes. Mam went to meet him to tell him.'

So, that's where Ada had gone this morning, Jane mused.

'He told me that as soon as he heard he wanted to come to see you, Jane, but . . . well, Mam told him not to. But he isn't very happy about it; in fact he's very upset as he'll be sailing again in a few days for New York and he doesn't want you to think that he doesn't . . . care.' Again Emily paused, trying to judge Jane's reactions. 'He loves you, Jane. He told me. He said he'd realised that when he came . . . back and he begged me to tell you he's very concerned about you.'

Tears pricked Jane's eyes. 'Oh, Em, I'm so confused.'

Emily bit her lip and squeezed Jane's hand. 'I shouldn't have told you! I've upset you, I'm sorry.'

'No. I think I . . . I think I realised when he came back and I saw him that first time. I tried so hard not to believe that I still loved him. I tried so hard not to let James down in any way. He was my husband and he'd been so good to me and I was very fond of him and wanted desperately to make sure he was happy but I . . . I couldn't help the way I felt about Joe.' She was struggling to put her conflicting emotions into words.

Emily put her arm around her shoulders. 'Oh, Jane, stop tearing yourself apart. If Joe hadn't stayed in America things might have been different, but he did and you married James. None of us can go back and undo parts of our lives; all we can do is try to make the best of the future. You *did* make James happy. No one knew what was going to happen to him and I'm sure he wouldn't want you to be miserable or to mourn him forever.'

'I haven't begun to get used to him not being here. I haven't even . . . buried him, Em!' Jane cried. 'I can't think about anything or anyone else!'

'I know but Joe will be away for a long time and he does

care, Jane. Just before I left to come here he told me how much he loves you and how he wants to make the future happy for you. It's all he seems to be thinking of now. You, and how to make life easier and . . . more joyful for you.' Emily smiled as she remembered how Joe had taken her aside and emphatically impressed this upon her. He'd wanted desperately to come and see Jane himself but as that wasn't possible he'd begged her to tell Jane that he wasn't going to think only of himself now. She was the person he cared most about; her happiness was all that mattered to him.

Jane thought about agreeing to see him but she couldn't shake off the feelings of guilt. James wasn't even buried; she simply couldn't contemplate seeing Joe again so soon. She shook her head. 'No, Em. I . . . can't see him! Not yet. It . . . it's too soon.'

Emily nodded. Mam had been right. 'What shall I tell him?'

Jane twisted her hands together as she tried to think clearly. 'Tell him that when . . . when he comes home things will be . . . better. I'll have . . . sorted myself out. Everything will be behind me and perhaps I'll be able to think about the future.' At this precise moment she didn't know exactly how she felt about Joe and wondered if, after everything that had happened, her feelings had changed? She would only know for certain when she saw him and that wouldn't be for quite a while, which perhaps was for the best.

Emily nodded. 'He promised to write to you and I know he will. He won't forget about you this time, Jane.'

Jane didn't reply but wondered had he received the 'From Liverpool with Love' postcards she'd sent him when he'd first gone cruising. He'd never mentioned them and if he hadn't got them maybe that's why he'd taken the decision to stay in America. A decision that had affected their futures . . . Already she felt she had done the right thing to tell Emily to relay her words – she didn't want to give him any false hopes, but she didn't want to dash them either. When Joe returned home in April she would have had time to come to terms with her loss, the ordeal of the criminal proceedings against Jimmy, Richie and her brother would be over and maybe also the guilt she felt now would have disappeared. She had at the very least to mourn the loss of James, Edith and life she'd shared with them.

Emily stood up to ring for the tea, which she felt they both needed. 'I'll explain everything to him.'

Jane managed a smile. 'Tell him I'll . . . I'll look forward to his letters, Emily. They might help to divert my mind from . . . other things.'

Emily bent and poked the fire vigorously. For Jane's sake she wished the next weeks and months were over, then maybe her friend could start to look forward again without sorrow and trepidation. Jane hadn't mentioned Alfie but Emily knew it must be weighing very heavily on her mind, heart and conscience that her testimony would result in her brother being hanged.

Chapter Twenty-Eight

'Y OU'RE CERTAIN YOU want to do this, Shaw?' the warder
demanded of Alfie.

Alfie nodded determinedly. It was the only thing left for
him to do, the only possible way he could think of to escape his
fate and he was desperate. He understood now why Richie had
hated and feared this place so much. Despair and desolation
seemed to permeate even the cold, bare walls of his cell and
he too had now heard tales about the infamous216: the
condemned cell and its ghosts.

'Even though the governor has given his permission, you
realise she might well refuse to see you? Haven't you caused
her enough grief?' the warder reminded him, thinking he
wouldn't blame the girl if she refused point blank. This one
seemed to have no remorse for what he'd done.

'And she might not. Will you make sure she gets the letter?'
Alfie replied tersely. He had to see Jane, talk to her, try to find
out what she intended to say when he went on trial. Surely she

wouldn't refuse to see him one last time? He was still her brother.

'I'll make sure it's posted,' the warder said, pocketing the letter as he left Alfie, locking the door behind him.

Jane reread the letter that had been delivered that morning. Her heart had sunk as she'd recognised the still-childish handwriting and she'd noted the printed words on the back of the envelope 'H. M. Prison Walton'. Her hands began to tremble as she'd slowly opened it. She'd never thought to hear from her brother again and she wasn't sure she wanted to. As she read she realised that he was asking to see her – just once more, he pleaded.

She folded the letter and laid it on a small side table. Should she see him? What was there to say? James and his mother had only been buried a few weeks ago. She thought sadly of her mother; would Ellen have wanted her to go to see him? Did he now want to beg her forgiveness for what he'd done? He'd said nothing about that in the letter, but should she give him one last chance to try to redeem himself in her eyes? Was it too much to ask of her?

She passed a hand over her forehead; a dull ache had begun over her left temple. Should she ask Ada's advice? she wondered, but then realised that this was one decision she would have to make entirely alone.

At length she got up and went to Edith's little writing bureau and took notepaper and an envelope from one of the drawers. She would go. She would see him: she owed it to her parents' memory; and if he begged her forgiveness then all she could do was try to find it in her heart to be charitable.

It was a cold, misty-grey February day when she was escorted to the governor's office and she had shivered as she'd walked along the silent, austere stone corridors of the century-old building. The warder who was escorting her had treated her with great respect and courtesy and she was grateful for his reassuring presence for this was the most depressing and frightening place she had ever been in. Even her memories of the grim, austere workhouse took on a different aspect by comparison, she thought.

The sparse but infinitely more cheerful interior of the governor's office was a relief.

'Mrs Davenport, you are quite sure you have made the right decision to come here today? There is still time if you wish to change your mind,' Mr Irving, the governor, said quietly after greeting her formally and indicating she should sit down.

Jane managed a polite smile. He was a man of middle height with short grey hair and a clipped moustache. Pale blue eyes regarded her thoughtfully from behind horn-rimmed spectacles. His bearing was almost military, she thought. 'Thank you for your concern, Mr Irving, but . . . but I won't change my mind at this late stage. I . . . I think it is what my . . . our . . . parents would have wished and I feel I should at least hear what he has to say.'

He nodded to the warder, who had remained standing respectfully by the door. 'Mr Marsden, would you bring the prisoner up, please. I myself will escort Mrs Davenport to the room prepared for the interview.'

To hear Alfie referred to simply as 'the prisoner' made Jane shiver at her brother's predicament but she said nothing as she was escorted to a smaller, almost bare room. It contained only a table on either side of which was an uncomfortable looking, upright wooden chair and nothing else. A barred window set high up in the wall let in light and again she shivered as she sat down, clasping her hands tightly in her lap.

When Alfie appeared, dressed in prison uniform and accompanied by Mr Marsden, she stood up, searching her brother's face for some sign of regret.

'Sit down, Shaw,' the warder ordered curtly and Jane realised that she was not going to be allowed to speak to Alfie alone. Mr Marsden took up his position by the door and Alfie sat down opposite her, nervously picking at the skin around his bitten-down nails.

'I didn't know if you'd even reply, Jane,' he started, looking at her closely. He hadn't seen her since that terrible night.

'I . . . I felt I had to come, Alfie. Just . . . just to see what you had to say to me,' Jane replied hesitantly.

'I wanted to ask you what you'll say, Jane? When I go for trial, like,' Alfie said flatly. He'd planned exactly what he was going to say. This was his only chance.

Jane stared at him in some confusion; this wasn't what she had expected. 'I . . . I'll tell them what happened, Alfie. I'll answer all the questions – truthfully.'

He glanced furtively in the warder's direction and lowered his voice. 'If you do that, you know what they'll do to me and it wasn't meant to happen, Jane! I'd only intended to steal stuff.'

She didn't speak for it was slowly dawning on her what he was asking her to do. She shook her head. 'I have to tell the truth, Alfie!'

He leaned forward. 'If you do, they'll hang me. What was I

supposed to do when he went for Jimmy and tried to throttle him? He . . . he didn't leave me much choice. I told you, Jane, it wasn't meant to happen!'

She stared at him hard as she shrank back a little in the chair, a feeling of utter disbelief and disappointment filling her. Surely he wasn't going to try pleading self-defence. James hadn't attacked him. This wasn't what she'd come to hear, that James had given him no choice! Anger filled her eyes and as she replied there was a hard, bitter edge to her voice. 'Maybe you had no intention of attacking anyone, but you lied to me, Alfie! You came to the house and told me you were going to London! And then you came and broke in! You'd planned to rob us – your own flesh and blood! And it all went horribly wrong!'

Alfie could see she wasn't going to help him but he had to try again. 'I know all that, Jane, but it wasn't meant to happen to him – James. You had everything! Money, position, a secure future, a life of luxury. What did I have? What kind of a future did I have? Wasn't I entitled to have a bit of that kind of life? And you'd even disowned me, hadn't even told him about me! You didn't care what happened to me when you left me in that place!' He paused, staring at her, trying to judge her reactions.

'Of course I cared and so did Mam!' she cried, stung by his accusations. He wasn't going to apologise. He wasn't sorry. He was . . . blaming her.

'No you didn't, neither of you!' Alfie's voice rose and his tone was bitter. 'Mam was pathetic; she just gave up and took the easy way out, taking us into the workhouse. And after that she didn't care about what happened to me. Didn't care that I hated every minute I was in there!' he shouted.

'That's enough of that, Shaw! Keep your voice down and at least try to be civil!' the warder interrupted harshly.

'It's not true – any of it, Alfie. You're just using it as an excuse! Trying to gain some sympathy, using it all as some sort of . . . explanation for what you've done! You killed my husband!'

'You see, Jane, you still don't care about me!' Alfie snapped. She wasn't going to do or say anything to help him but now he didn't care. He despised her.

Jane got to her feet. 'I . . . I didn't come here to listen to this, Alfie! I stupidly thought you wanted to say you were sorry for all the lies and deceit, the thieving and for . . . what you did to poor James and Edith.' She turned to the warder, who had remained impassive. 'Mr Marsden, I have nothing more to say. I'd like to leave now, please.'

He nodded and opened the door. 'The governor will escort you out, ma'am, and . . . and I'm sorry he's wasted your time,' he added more kindly.

She was very near to tears and greatly relieved to leave Alfie with Mr Marsden as Mr Irving quietly escorted her back to the small gate set into the huge heavy main gates. He didn't ask her about the interview, he'd hear it all from Marsden, but formally wished her good day as she stepped out into the wide street. She felt a great weight of sorrow and regret settle on her shoulders, wishing she hadn't come at all. Alfie seemed to be incapable of any feelings of remorse or regret. He cared for no one but himself.

As she began to walk up Hornby Road she tried to put the last hour out of her mind. She had enough sorrow to contend with at present.

Spring was at last on its way, she thought as she stood staring out of the window at the trees that lined the street. There were new green buds beginning to appear on their branches, which seemed to have been so bare and skeletal for so many months now. Soon daffodils and then tulips would bring a riot of colour to the gardens and the parks; crocuses and early primroses were already in bloom. Winter had seemed interminably long and the short, cold, dark days had added to her feelings of grief and depression. The only thing she had looked forward to were Joe's letters but it had been a while before she'd been able to reply for her feelings of guilt were slow to diminish.

After Joe had sailed she had thought long and hard about what she should do in the coming months. Slowly she had begun to come to terms with her loss and had confided to both Ada and Emily that she felt she could start to think about her future. Ada had advised her to do nothing drastic until everything was over and done with and Joe returned home and she had agreed, but she had been wondering about the laundry. She would need something to do to fill in the days; she couldn't just idle her time away sitting in this house with her memories. She had never imagined making a career for herself but she did have a good working knowledge of how the business was run and she would have Mr Turner to help her. He'd been very supportive and had kept her informed and she felt that it would be good for her to have something with which to occupy her mind, especially in the weeks to come. It would be another two months before Joe was due home and she would have decisions to make.

She turned away from the window. Her hat and coat and bag lay on the sofa and picking up the black hat trimmed with a short black veil she crossed to the mirror above the fireplace. Plain, austere black had never really suited her, she thought as she secured the hat with a long jet-topped pin. It made her appear very pale and wan. Also, if she were truthful, she had aged in these last few months. She was only twenty-one, still a young woman, but she had endured more than most other women her age and it had taken its toll. She frowned as she turned away and shrugged on the black wool coat with its astrakhan collar and cuffs. At least she hoped today would herald the end of all the traumas she had suffered.

She had fastened the coat and was pulling on her gloves when Ada and Fred arrived.

'Oh, I thought we'd be a bit early but I see you're ready,' Ada greeted her, giving her a peck on the cheek and scrutinising her closely for signs of distress. She looked calm enough, she thought, but today she would have to face giving evidence at Alfie's trial and she knew Jane was dreading it.

'Oh, Aunty Ada, I just wish it was all over. It was bad enough when the other two were tried, I felt ill for days afterwards, and this is far more . . . serious,' Jane confided, feeling her stomach begin to churn, trying not to remember the last time she had seen her brother – in Walton Jail.

'I know, but you just remember what that Mr Hopworth, the barrister, told you, luv. And you won't have to stay after . . .' Ada reminded her.

Jane nodded. She'd been very thankful that after she'd given her evidence at Jimmy and Richie's trial she'd been able to leave the courtroom and she would do so today too. They'd both been very cowed and apprehensive; Richie in particular had looked terrified and she had almost felt sorry for him –

until she'd thought of Edith. She'd learned later that they'd both been sentenced to eight years' hard labour.

'I don't think any of it will take very long,' Fred added. 'It will just be a matter of going through all the formalities. The verdict should be a foregone conclusion.'

Ada nodded her agreement. Oh, he was guilty all right, she thought grimly. Jane had witnessed him attack James. Yes, he had been going to Jimmy Cobham's aid but that wouldn't cut any ice: none of them should have been there in the first place, all were engaged in a criminal act and Alfie certainly hadn't been defending himself. 'Well, let's go and get it all over with,' she stated, gently propelling Jane towards the door. They'd all feel relieved when today was over.

The taxi was waiting to convey them to the Crown Court situated in St George's Hall and they were all silent and preoccupied as they were driven through the city streets. Jane, Nellie and Lizzie had all been thoroughly briefed by Albert Hopworth, K.C., the prosecution barrister, and his legal team but none of them were looking forward to the few next hours. They also knew that everything would be reported in the newspapers and read avidly, which only added to their discomfort and distress. Nellie and Lizzie were being called mainly to corroborate Jane's evidence, having witnessed the aftermath of the murder and robbery, and as character witnesses for their mistress, for it was very unusual for a sister to testify against a brother, a fact the papers hadn't hesitated to point out.

As they drove through the sunlit streets, Jane sat clutching her bag tightly to try to stop her hands from shaking. Oh, she was so glad that Ada and Fred were with her but she wished

Joe were here too. In his last letter, posted in Port au Prince, Haiti, he'd said that he hoped by the time she received it the trial would be over but if not he urged her to try not to get too upset. To try to remember that although Alfie was her brother, to have treated her the way he had he couldn't have any feelings for her. To try to remember that for most of their childhood and youth they'd not been close, and when he'd absconded from Brownlow Hill he'd not tried to get in touch with her but left her to fret and worry. And then he'd only sought her out to extract money from her. Joe wished he could be at her side to give her the support he knew she'd need because he loved her. Everything he'd said was true, she thought now. She'd only ever been close to Alfie when he'd been a small child and even then he'd always seemed to be in trouble. When her poor mam had been so distraught after Da had been killed he hadn't seemed to care: he'd stayed away from school, running the streets with Jimmy and Richie. Then once they'd gone into the workhouse she'd barely seen him and after that it had just got worse until he'd ended up here . . . on trial for murder.

She was brought out of her reverie by the taxi coming to a halt and Fred paid the driver and then ushered the little group into the grand, ornate corridor with its pillars of polished granite where Mr Hopwood, resplendent in his black silk gown and traditional wig, came forward to greet them and usher them into a waiting room.

'There's no need to distress yourself, Mrs Davenport. Just stay calm and remember how I instructed you to reply,' he advised firmly.

Jane nodded. 'Thank you. I'll try to speak as clearly as possible,' she assured him but she felt sick with apprehension.

'Just remember, luv, that it will all be over very soon now and then you'll be able to look forward to . . . better days,' Ada whispered, feeling extremely nervous herself as she and Fred were directed to the public gallery.

The time seemed to drag interminably, Jane thought, and yet she knew she had only waited fifteen minutes until she was called. She followed the usher into the courtroom, took her place in the witness box and swore the oath; she was thankful her voice was clear and steady although her hand resting on the bible shook slightly. Only then did she look up and across to where Alfie stood in the dock flanked by prison officers. She swallowed hard. Of course his appearance was so very familiar to her yet she felt as if she didn't know him. He stared back at her without any expression at all. Not recognition, not shame, not sorrow, not guilt. He was staring at her as if she were a stranger and not his sister. She thought of her parents and then James and Edith and in that moment she felt a deep sense of pity fill her. Her brother's whole life had all been so . . . futile and that was yet another tragedy. Alfie hadn't cared about his mam and da or James and Edith. He didn't care about her. He didn't care about what had happened to Jimmy or Richie, whom he'd called his friends. He didn't appear to even care that he was on trial for his life. He just appeared utterly cold and callous. It saddened her beyond measure and she looked away. Yes, she'd promised her mother she'd try to look after him but Ellen hadn't known how her son would turn out. She could never have envisaged what he was capable of, what he'd done.

She answered both barristers' questions clearly and truthfully. There was nothing she could do or say now that would help him, nor could she forgive him for the terrible crime he'd committed. She'd done the right thing, the only possible thing to ensure that James and Edith received justice.

When it was over and she finally and thankfully stepped down and turned towards the door there was no crushing sense of guilt, no bitterness, no overwhelming feeling of sorrow, just relief that it was finally over. As the door closed behind her she felt as though she was leaving behind her the part of her life in which her brother had featured. With his selfishness and cruelty he had come close to ruining her life. The memory of Alfie would fade in time, as would that of his crimes. He belonged in her past now as did her parents and James and Edith, but she would not mourn for Alfie as she had done for them.

Two weeks later she went back to the laundry for the first time since the day she'd become engaged to James. George Turner had visited her at home the previous week, at her request, and she had thanked him for his loyalty and his hard work in keeping everything running smoothly.

'It was the least I could do, Mrs Davenport, and all the staff send their regards,' he'd replied rather formally.

'Now that . . . everything is over, I have decided that I will take an interest in the business. As you know I worked until I married James and I feel that I need something to occupy me now.'

Mr Turner nodded slowly; he could indeed see her point of view.

'So, I will come in next week to learn more. I realise that there are areas where I have little or no experience so I will continue to depend on you and rely on your advice, but if there are any improvements or changes you feel necessary or would be beneficial I'd like you to discuss them with me. James was always very . . . forward-thinking.'

'He was indeed, Mrs Davenport. It was one of his strengths and why he managed to improve the business so much. In fact there are a few things I would like to discuss with you, regarding new contracts and possible expansion,' he confided. He'd always admired James Davenport's business sense and had been grateful that he'd promoted him to general manager almost as soon as he'd taken over the laundry after the old man's death. Mr Jenkins, the previous manager, had been long due for retirement in his opinion and had been as opposed to change as old Mr Davenport himself had been. George Turner had no objections to her taking an interest for it did not appear that she intended to change the methods and systems of working but was interested in keeping the business profitable. 'Then I'll have Mr Davenport's office spruced up for you, and I know Miss Roberts will pleased to see you,' he'd informed her.

She walked the short distance for it was a bright early March morning and the signs and sounds of spring were all around. It seemed strange to be walking in through the gates again, she thought as she smiled in acknowledgement of Bert Hedges' greeting. George Turner was waiting for her in James's office, which bore all the signs of having been tidied up, and there was even a small vase of daffodils on the top of a filing cabinet, which she suspected had been placed there by Cynthia Roberts.

'I thought we'd start by going over all the contracts, Mrs Davenport, and I can then advise you how perhaps improvements can be made and new ones obtained,' he suggested as she sat down at the desk.

She nodded. She would get used to sitting in here, she thought, for she felt that she owed it to James to try to continue to keep the Empire Laundry a thriving and growing concern.

Mr Turner had certainly given her plenty to think about, Jane mused later that morning when she left the office and went down to seek out Cynthia and thank her for her welcoming gesture. There had been catalogues of new machinery which she'd assured him she would peruse – although stressing that she would leave any final decision to him for she was far from mechanically-minded – and a list of possible new contracts to tender for, mainly from city hotels and catering establishments.

The heat, the dampness and the smells of the vast laundry room reminded her of the days when she'd worked here, she thought as she nodded amiably to Nora Lafferty – still the senior operative – en route to the supervisor's tiny office. How long ago now seemed those times when Maggie Rosbottom and her cronies had tormented her and the day she'd learned of her mam's death.

Cynthia Roberts rose to her feet, a smile of genuine pleasure on her face. 'Mrs Davenport! It really is such a pleasure to see you here again.'

Jane smiled back. 'Thank you. And I've come to thank you for the daffodils. It was a very thoughtful gesture and much appreciated.'

'I thought they'd brighten the room up a bit, Mrs Davenport.'

'Please, Cynthia, call me Jane. I never forgot how you

always looked out for me from the first day I started working here and how kind you were to me the day my mother died, and afterwards.'

'You were so young and so very . . . upset that day and it was not the easiest way to learn such news.' She paused and twisted her hands together a little nervously. 'I . . . We were all terribly shocked and saddened . . .'

Jane nodded. 'Thank you. It was a dreadful time but . . . but now I hope that by returning to work I can find some purpose to my life again.'

'You're going to work with Mr Turner, I understand.'

'I am. While I have some knowledge of the business I still have a great deal to learn. But I'm looking forward to it all.'

'Would you like me to show you the new equipment that was installed during the annual summer holiday last year?' Cynthia Roberts offered, becoming brisk and businesslike. 'The girls don't have to lift or drag the linen with tongs any more, it's fed by a conveyor into the boilers now. Much easier, less mess and far quicker.'

Jane was impressed, remembering how her back and shoulders had often ached from manhandling the linen. 'I'd find that very interesting. I had no idea so much had improved.'

'And I'm sure you'll notice that there are a few new faces too. I found it necessary to dismiss certain *people* who were not exactly the type of worker we wanted or needed. They overstepped the mark once too often.'

Jane knew she meant Maggie and Bertha and wondered if they had managed to find other employment. They were not the brightest and had been vindictive towards her but there was enough poverty and hardship in this city so she hoped they'd found something. 'I'm sure you were right, Cynthia,' she answered as they walked out into the cavernous and still steamy room where she had once suffered their taunting of her for being 'the workhouse girl'. Those days were long gone and she intended to improve conditions for the girls and women who worked in *her* laundry as well as keep the business running so it could provide a wage both for herself and all those other women who worked here.

Chapter Twenty-Nine

H ER DAYS WERE busy and when she returned home each evening she found she was tired – but satisfyingly so – and she was beginning to sleep much better. There was so much she didn't know, so much to learn, but she was managing to grasp most of it and George Turner was indeed very patient. She'd found an ally too in Cynthia Roberts with whom she sometimes spent the lunch break. It had been to Cynthia that she'd first broached the subject of some kind of welfare benefits for the workers.

'What did you have in mind? They earn a reasonable wage comparable to factory work and those with some skills get a higher rate of pay. They all have an annual week's holiday and the usual Bank Holidays and conditions have improved since old Mr Davenport's day,' she reminded Jane.

Jane was aware of all this but she looked thoughtful as she poured them both a cup of tea. They were sitting in her office. 'There are a few minor things that we could introduce which

I'm sure would be appreciated. There are some outbuildings beside the loading bay that could be turned into proper cloak-rooms, somewhere they could hang their coats, leave umbrellas in wet weather, instead of just the pegs on the walls in the laundry rooms. A mirror could be put up on one wall, a couple of washbasins installed and roller towels. There is already a toilet block but wouldn't it be better if they had somewhere to wash and dry their hands and comb their hair? And it wouldn't cost a fortune: there's no building work involved.'

Cynthia had agreed it would be an improvement.

'And then there's the matter of overalls of some kind. Everyone, except of course the maintenance men and drivers who already have them, just comes dressed in old clothes that they don't mind getting messy but if we provided them with an overall and, say, a cap, wouldn't it look much tidier and smarter? We could have "Empire Laundry" printed on the cap,' she'd suggested. 'It would be good for customers to see the name whenever they saw one of our workers.'

'And of course it would cost us virtually nothing to launder them, there would be just the initial outlay,' Cynthia had added. 'And we might get them at a discount seeing as it will be a sizeable order.'

'Also I think there should also be some kind of emergency fund. When my mother died you personally asked James for me to be allowed time off, without pay of course, and I was very grateful. But I propose that in such cases in future pay should be made available. It's never for longer than a few days and often at such times there are extra demands on what money they do earn. Mourning clothes, wreaths, the provisions for the funeral tea, things like that.' She paused. 'I intend to discuss all this with George Turner but I wanted to get your reaction first. I feel that the changes would make the workplace more pleasant and will improve productivity.'

Cynthia had nodded. 'I think all your ideas should be implemented. I'm sure it will make for more loyal and contented workers. I'll impress that on George too.'

Noticing that Cynthia had called him by his Christian name, and reflecting that she seemed friendly with the manager, she went on to settle the matter of the most practical design for an overall until the break was over.

Ada had returned home but visited a couple of evenings a week to satisfy herself that Jane was all right; Emily usually came at the weekend.

'It's a treat for me to come up here for a couple of hours, Jane,' Ada had confided. 'Those lads are always bickering about something or playing that gramophone, which annoys Fred and then he starts complaining and grousing. Sometimes I feel like screaming at the lot of them.'

'That house really is very small, Aunty Ada. Would you not think of moving from Gill Street? I'd be very happy to help financially,' Jane had offered.

Ada had frowned. 'I'll think about it, luv, but I certainly wouldn't want anywhere as big as this. I wouldn't have enough furniture to put in it for a start, it would cost a fortune to heat and I've lived in Gill Street for so long that I wouldn't want to move too far away.'

'There are some nice medium-sized terrace houses around Mount Pleasant, that's not very far from Gill Street or the centre of town,' Jane had urged.

'We'll see. It's quite a big step for me to take, Jane,' Ada had replied. She was relieved and happy that Jane was spending her days at the laundry; Jane seemed to enjoy it, although Ada knew that she didn't have any pressing need to work, for James had left her financially secure. Unlike herself. Fred still wasn't employed on a regular basis – the old system was still adhered to on the docks – neither Danny or Sonny earned a great deal and she knew Danny had hopes of getting engaged in the not too distant future. However, she knew that Fred had his pride and accepting financial help from Jane to move to a bigger and better house wouldn't go down well at all. Still, Ada was grateful for the offer.

By the middle of April Jane felt more far more confident in the role she now played at the laundry. She had never been required to make decisions like this before, to initiate new ideas and take responsibility for her actions, but she got on well with all her staff – George Turner and Cynthia Roberts had been towers of strength – and the business seemed to be doing well. She had been instrumental in securing two new contracts, negotiating them herself, which was something new as such undertakings had always been done by James. One was for the hotel of which Brown's Tea Rooms was a subsidiary – a fact which gave her a real sense of satisfaction. She viewed it as a yardstick with which to measure how successful she was becoming.

Emily called that Saturday afternoon, for Georgie had gone to the football match with his father and Lily sometimes used that as an excuse to visit her daughter-in-law. 'It's not that I don't get on with her but she can be a bit like Mam: set in her ways. She thinks I should spend my time doing housework and cooking or baking, seeing as I'm at work all week. You know what they're like. Monday is wash day, Tuesday it's ironing . . .'

Jane smiled at her. 'And you want some time to yourself?'

Emily nodded as she took off her jacket. 'I wanted to come and see you. Georgie's gone off to Goodison Park and then he'll go for a pint with his da so why should I stay at home? Lily knows I'll be back in time to get him his supper and she can't say he's neglected. He always has clean shirts, there's always a meal ready when he gets in – well, almost ready – and the place is tidy. And if we didn't have my wages we wouldn't have half the furnishings we've got,' she declared emphatically.

'Well, I don't think she's got much to complain about, Em,' Jane assured her, thinking that Emily looked very well, even though she was coping with a job and a home. Her friend had gained a little weight but it suited her and she was always smartly turned out. Her red and black paisley printed rayon dress had a fashionable white Peter Pan collar and a narrow black belt at the waist; she'd let her hair grow a little longer and had recently had a Marcel wave.

'So, you're still quite happy going to work each day? Don't you find it all a bit . . . daunting? ' Emily queried.

'No. Sometimes it can be . . . challenging but I'm enjoying it. George Turner sees to all the machinery side of things; I concentrate on orders, overseeing accounts, collection and delivery and staff matters.'

Emily looked impressed. 'I couldn't manage all that.'

'You could if you didn't have to run a household as well. Cook and Renshaw manage everything here and if there's something that's beyond them we get a handyman in. It's surprising just what you can achieve when you put your mind to it; I've found that. This week we got the contract for all the linen for Brown's Tea Rooms and the Excelsior Hotel and that's something I'm delighted about. I wasn't sure we'd get it, even though they'd become very dissatisfied with their previous laundry service, for there were others competing for it. I worked very hard to impress on that hotel manager that our standards are very high, delivery of clean linen is never late and our costs very competitive.'

Emily laughed delightedly. 'Did you ever think you'd be capable of being such an independent, decisive woman, Jane?'

Jane laughed too. 'Never – not when I was in the workhouse with my every hour accounted for. Independence was the last thing they wanted from you! I'm enjoying it too.'

Emily grinned, her dark eyes dancing with mischief. 'Don't expect Mam to completely approve, Jane. Oh, I know she thinks it's good for you to have something to occupy you, keep you from . . . brooding, but you're not supposed to be *enjoying* it as well.'

Jane returned the grin. 'Well, I am!'

Emily became serious. 'I've got something to tell you but I don't want you to say anything to Mam just yet or she'll start fussing and insisting I give up work.'

Jane looked mystified. 'What?'

'I think I'm going to have a baby,' Emily said a little shyly. 'I've told Georgie but he's sworn to secrecy too until I'm absolutely sure, which I will be by the beginning of next month. Then I'll have to give up work.'

Jane threw her arms around her friend. 'Oh, Em! I'm

delighted for you! I really am! What did Georgie say? Is he pleased?'

'I think he was a bit . . . stunned at first but once he sort of took it in, he was over the moon. He's so proud you'd think no one had ever been a father before.'

'Just think, Em, this time next year you'll be a family! Georgie, you and . . . baby Taverner!'

Emily smiled happily. 'We will. I'm really happy, Jane. Oh, we haven't got much saved but we'll manage.'

'You'll have to take care of yourself now, Em, rest more,' Jane urged.

'Don't you start!' Emily laughed before looking at Jane questioningly. 'I know it's a bit early but will you be god-mother, Jane?'

Jane flushed with pleasure. 'Of course I will. I'll be honoured. Who will you have as godfather?'

'Our Joe, of course, and while we're on that subject, you do realise he'll be home soon. Will you go with Mam to meet him when the ship docks?'

Jane felt her heart turn over. 'I know when he'll be home but . . . but I'm not sure about going to meet him, Emily. It's all so public!'

Emily understood. After being away from their home port for three months there were always crowds of relatives and friends waiting for the crew members when the ship docked. It was something of an occasion and was indeed a very public homecoming. She nodded. 'It can all get a bit like a three-ringed circus.'

Jane looked thoughtful. 'And if I'm totally honest, Em, I'm . . . I'm a bit apprehensive about it. I haven't seen him –

actually *seen* him for nearly eight months. The last time was when I went to visit your mam, not long after he'd come back from America.'

Emily frowned. 'But you do still care, Jane? You know he loves you. He's written to you.'

Jane nodded. 'Yes, I know he loves me and I do care. I care a great deal but, Em, I know I've changed—'

'Of course you've changed, Jane,' Emily interrupted. 'It would be a miracle if you hadn't but I think you're letting your nerves get the better of you. Would it be better if he came to see you here or, if you're worried about gossip, maybe at Mam's?'

'No, I'm not worried about gossip, but I'm . . . anxious about just how I'll feel.'

Emily took her hands and looked her squarely in the eyes. 'You've loved him for years, Jane, and all the unhappiness, the tragedy is behind you now.'

Jane nodded and smiled. 'Tell your Mam that I'd much prefer to see Joe here, perhaps the evening he gets home.'

'That will give her a few hours with him to hear all his news,' Emily agreed. 'But don't be surprised if she has something to say about it. She might still want to protect you from upset, you know.'

It would also give her time to think about just what she would say to him, Jane thought. She was excited and looking forward to seeing him yet she knew she shouldn't allow herself to fall into his arms. By Society's standards she was still recently a widow and added to that was the fact that this was the home she had shared with James. She wouldn't be surprised if those were points that Ada would be swift to raise.

Chapter Thirty

———◆———

THE DAY THE *Empress of Scotland* arrived back in her home port had been a busy one for Jane. The new cloakrooms were finished and duly inspected by Jane, Cynthia and George Turner and then declared 'fit for use'. There had been great interest in the project and when finally the girls and women, all now wearing the dark blue overalls and caps with the words 'Empire Laundry' printed on them in red and white lettering, went to view the new facilities there was some excitement and unanimous approval.

A couple of the younger girls giggled as they'd viewed their reflections in the large mirror on the wall, tucking stray wisps of hair under caps, much to Jane's amusement. Nora Lafferty, who had worked there for years, just smiled and shook her head at their antics.

'You'd think they'd never seen a mirror before,' she commented.

'What do you think, Mrs Lafferty? Is it an improvement?' Jane asked her.

'Aye, it's that, Mrs Davenport. And so are the overalls; quite smart we all look now. Gives us a bit of pride in our appearance it does. Mr Davenport, God rest his soul, was a good employer but he'd never have thought of things like this. And we hear there's to be financial help, like, in times of bereavement or sickness.'

'There is. They are difficult times without the added worry of losing pay. I hope these things might help to make life a bit easier for you all,' she explained.

Nora nodded her agreement. 'As I said, he was a decent man but you . . . you understand what life is like for us and always has been. You've worked and suffered hardship the way we have and we're grateful for your . . . thoughtfulness.' It was one of the longest speeches Nora had ever made in her life.

'I take that as a great compliment, Mrs Lafferty, thank you,' Jane replied, touched by the woman's sentiments.

She thought about Nora's words as she got changed that evening. She had really not done very much – they were only small gestures in the greater pattern of things – but she'd experienced a real sense of satisfaction that she had been able to provide some measures to help her employees and glad that she was now in a position to be able to do so. It boded well for the future, but what did that future hold? She wanted to spend it with Joe and hoped he would help her to run the business and in time expand it. Surely he wouldn't want to spend his life going away to sea, working those long hours in often difficult conditions and being away from home when she could now offer him a comfortable life and financial security? She was sure he would quickly fit in as she had and then she would spend less time at the laundry.

She'd asked Ada to invite him to come for some supper and Ada had felt it prudent to include herself in the invitation.

'I know it's not exactly the way you'd like your meeting to be, luv, but well . . . you have a position to maintain, you know, you're the widow of a prominent businessman and a respected employer and you know how people love to gossip, shaking their heads and saying you should wait the prescribed time. I'll spend some time downstairs with Nellie in the kitchen to give you time alone,' she'd promised.

Jane brushed her hair slowly, sitting before the mirror of her dressing table. For the first time since James's death she had abandoned her austere black clothing. Her wool crêpe dress was of a lilac shade trimmed with purple braid, still official mourning colours but she felt that it was time to put aside full mourning and the colours suited her better. Around her neck she wore a single strand of matched pearls which had belonged to Edith. She hoped she looked attractive as well as confident and calm, rather than nervous, which was how she felt. She got to her feet, glancing at her watch. She'd said seven o'clock and it was five minutes to. She *was* strangely nervous – there were butterflies dancing in the pit of her stomach – but she mentally shook herself. In heaven's name, why? She'd known Joe all her life, they'd grown up together, he loved her and she loved him: what was there to be nervous about? What on earth was wrong with her? They had a future together now – wasn't that what she'd always wanted, even before she'd met James?

*

Joe stood on the top step, flanked by the two tall columns, waiting for the door to be opened, Ada beside him. He twisted his hat around between his fingers by its brim, feeling a bit apprehensive. He'd waited so long for this moment and his mind was full of plans and ideas. He'd had months to formulate them and he was longing to see her and tell her about them. He'd been very disappointed that she hadn't accompanied his mam to the Pier Head to meet him when they'd docked that morning but Ada had explained that Jane hadn't wanted their first meeting to be somewhere so public, hemmed in and jostled by crowds of excited friends and relations of the crew. She'd also told him that these days Jane was very involved at the laundry and in fact there'd been something quite significant happening there today, so she'd asked them to go for supper at seven that evening. No, it wasn't the homecoming he'd envisaged at all. He'd been expecting to see her waving and smiling like everyone else, delighted to see him and rushing to greet him, but his mam had reminded him that there were still certain constraints placed upon a young widow with a prominent position. And of course she was a wealthy young woman in her own right too now and the realisation of that had made him wonder if it would change things between them. He sincerely hoped not.

'Good evening, Mrs Ellis. Come in, you're both expected,' Renshaw greeted them smiling, shooting Joe a quick, appraising glance. Cook had mentioned that she thought it was all a 'bit too soon' but she hadn't agreed. Cook's ideas about mourning were rather old-fashioned and hadn't poor Mrs Davenport had enough sorrow in her life up to now?

'Will you tell Nellie that I'll be down to have a bit of a chat with her after we've eaten, Lizzie? I don't mind giving you both a bit of a hand to clear up. I'm not one to be sitting around doing nothing, you know that,' Ada said firmly.

Lizzie Renshaw nodded and smiled again. Or to be playing gooseberry either, she thought.

As soon as Jane saw him in the doorway of the drawing room all her nervousness fell away. 'Oh, Joe! I'm so glad you're home at last!'

'So am I, Jane!' he replied, thinking she looked so lovely and so poised. He crossed and took her in his arms and kissed her on the cheek, bearing in mind Ada's instructions not to 'lose the run of himself completely'.

She held him tightly and as she looked up into his eyes she knew her feelings for him hadn't changed. She loved him; she'd always loved him. Emily had been right; she could admit it to herself now and would no longer tear herself apart with feelings of guilt.

'He's been like a cat on hot bricks all afternoon and only the fact that you were up at the laundry kept him at home,' Ada stated, sitting down in an armchair.

Joe sat on the sofa opposite his mother, feeling a little resentful of her presence while Jane poured the drinks. It was a far cry from his mam's kitchen, he thought as he glanced around, a bit old-fashioned but grandly furnished.

'We've got something to celebrate, Joe. You've been away for so long,' Jane explained, handing him a glass of whisky.

He smiled up at her. He just wanted to take her in his arms and tell her all the plans he had for their future together, an exciting adventurous future, but knew that would have to wait.

At least his mam intended to let them have some time alone after they'd eaten. 'Well, I'm home now, Jane.'

'For how long?' she asked, hoping they could see each other every day while he was on leave.

'I'm not sure. While a ship is in port it's not making any money so they won't hang around long, but . . . we'll have plenty of time to talk,' he promised. If his plans went well he wouldn't be sailing on the *Empress of Scotland* again – well, at least not as part of the crew.

'How did it all go today, luv? The new cloakrooms?' Ada enquired, hoping Renshaw would soon appear to inform them that the meal was ready to be served for she could see they just wanted time alone together.

Jane explained to Joe about her ideas and improvements and then went on to enlighten Ada about the day's events.

Joe listened closely. He knew that she spent a lot of time now at the laundry but he hadn't been aware of the extent of her involvement. But he realised that it was now *her* business. It was becoming evident to him that she took a close interest in everything about its running, something he hadn't gleaned from her letters, and that she genuinely cared about the girls and women she employed. He felt a frisson of doubt run through him as he sipped his drink. Was what he intended going to be too much for him to ask of her? he wondered. But at least being involved in the business was far better than her sitting at home all day with all those memories to contend with. It had certainly taken her mind off James Davenport's death and more recently that of her brother for Emily had written to inform him that Alfie Shaw had gone to his death in Walton Jail in March. Jane had naturally been upset then,

Emily had written, and she had offered to accompany Jane to church should she wish to go to pray for her brother, but Jane had told her it wouldn't be necessary. She'd prayed in private that Alfie would be forgiven. At least it was all behind Jane now, Joe thought.

As soon as they'd finished eating it was Ada herself who stood up and began to stack the dishes while Jane rang for Lizzie Renshaw. Joe leaned back in his chair thinking his mam seemed far more at ease here than he did.

'Right, Lizzie, I'll give you a hand,' Ada informed a rather bemused Renshaw, who had arrived carrying a large tray.

'Thank you. Cook's got the kettle on, Mrs Ellis,' she answered, heading for the door, followed by Ada.

As soon as the door closed behind them Joe was on his feet. 'At last I've got you to myself, Jane.'

She smiled. 'I know she meant well but I really don't think I need a chaperone.'

Joe took her in his arms. 'Oh, Jane, it seems so long since I saw you last and so much has happened. I wish I'd been here to help you through everything. You know I wanted to come to see you before we sailed but Mam said to leave it, that you were in a state of shock and I'd only make it worse but I've regretted it so much ever since. There must have been something I could have to done to help. Was it very bad?'

She rested her head against his shoulder. 'Yes, but somehow I . . . got through it all. I've put it all behind me now. The first time I really felt that I could at last start to look forward was when I left the court at Alfie's trial. I couldn't do anything to help him, Joe, and it was obvious that he didn't care about . . . anything. I think that day I stopped thinking of him as my brother; it was as if I'd lost him years ago. After that I started back at the laundry and it really has helped me to put everything into perspective.'

He kissed her gently on the forehead. 'My poor Jane, you've suffered terribly and I love you so much.'

'I've missed you, Joe, and I do love you. At first I felt guilty about it, I felt I had no right to love you, but it was Emily who made me see that I couldn't mourn James forever, nor would he have wanted me to, and that I had to make a new life for myself.' He loved her, she thought happily as she rested her head on his shoulder. He'd always looked out for her and she remembered how he'd protected her all those years ago when Maggie and her friends had mocked and threatened her. Yes, Joe really did care for her and she felt safe in his arms, safe and more emotionally secure than she'd felt for months.

He drew her down on the sofa beside him, his arms around her. '*We'll* make a new life together, Jane, and it will be a better life I promise. I lost you to James because I decided to stay in America. I didn't realise then how you felt . . .'

She looked up at him, perturbed. 'But I sent you postcards, Joe. Didn't you get them? I thought they'd get to you quicker than letters. I chose them because they had "From Liverpool with Love" printed on them. I thought that would . . . tell you how I felt about you.'

Joe shook his head ruefully. 'Oh, Jane, postcards take longer and get lost much more easily than letters. Maybe they arrived after the ship had left port and the agents forgot about them. I got your birthday card though . . . but let's not dwell on all that now. I've had so much time to think about our future. You will marry me, Jane? I'll get down on my knees if you want me to?'

'Oh, Joe! I don't want you to do any such thing and of course I'll marry you,' she replied, her eyes shining with joy.

'Then before Mam comes back I want to tell you what I've been planning for us.'

She nestled close to him, filled with happiness and eager to hear of his plans for their future.

'You've had so many unhappy experiences over the years, Jane, that I want your life to be happy now. All the memories you have of Liverpool are tinged with sadness and hardship and some are just . . . tragic. You've suffered the way no one should suffer. You know I've always wanted a better life than Mam and Da. I want us to get married, Jane, as soon as it's . . . decent and then go out and start a new life in Canada. It's a wonderful country for young people, Jane. It's a big country, there's so much space, so many opportunities; I noticed that when I travelled with Mr Ibsen. People of our age were doing well; they had good lives. We could start afresh, both of us. I'd thought of starting a business of my own – be my own boss for a change. Maybe I'll open a garage; I've had some experience with cars. I always took care of the maintenance of Mr Ibsen's car as well as driving it. We could have a house and a business of our own and in time a family. I've got a bit of money saved . . .'

At first she listened eagerly but as he outlined his plans for their future she felt the first niggling doubts. She wanted to marry him, she loved him, but she wasn't at all sure that she wanted to leave Liverpool and make a new life in Canada. He was right: a lot of her memories were tingled with sadness, but not all of them. She now looked on Ada and her family as *her* family and indeed when she married Joe they would be but . . . but then she would have to leave them. She'd never lived outside Liverpool in her life and she loved her native city even with its faults. Would she be able to settle three thousand miles away across the Atlantic Ocean? And what about her business – the laundry – and this house?'

Joe's voice broke into her thoughts. 'Jane, you've not said a word. What's wrong?'

'I was just thinking about . . . having to leave your mam and da – they've been so good to me, Joe – and the boys and Emily . . . and . . . the laundry.'

Joe was surprised even though it had crossed his mind earlier that he might be asking too much of her to give up everything. He'd hoped she would have been as enthusiastic as he was. He was trying to make the years ahead happy for her by taking her away from all the dreadful memories. 'Think about *our* future, Jane. We can have a great life together out there with no painful or bitter memories, no workhouses, no slums, no class system.'

'Oh, Joe! You always wanted to travel, that's why you left the laundry all those years ago. You wanted to live and work somewhere new. Your da said it was a "wanderlust". But I'm not like that. I've been content to stay here where I have friends, good friends who have been so supportive when I needed them most, and . . . now people depend on me. The laundry provides much-needed jobs, Joe, and I care about my business and my workers.'

He drew away from her, feeling hurt and disappointed, his euphoria slowly draining away. All he wanted to do was make her happy. 'I know you do but let someone else worry about it, Jane. It's a successful business; you'll have no trouble finding a buyer for it. I love you. I want to *care* for you. I want to take you away from this life to something better.'

She felt a little shocked that he obviously wanted her to sell the business. 'I know you care, Joe, but . . . but I didn't think of our future as being somewhere so far away,' she pleaded.

He couldn't hide the burgeoning sense of disappointment he felt. It was as if she was flinging his love, his hopes and dreams for their future back in his face. 'You mean you don't want to give up the life you have now!' His tone was harsh.

'Joe, please try to understand. I just didn't think you'd want to leave Liverpool, it's all so . . . sudden. If you'd mentioned it in your letters I'd have had time to think about it . . . all. Working in the laundry has been my salvation. It's made me realise certain things about myself . . . and I'd hoped that you would help me, become my business partner as well as my husband, that eventually I could leave the running of the business to you.'

His disappointment turned to anger. 'You mean you're prepared to put it all before me?'

'No! No! Oh, Joe, I didn't mean it to sound like that,' she cried, upset now.

He got to his feet. 'Well, that's what it sounds like to me, Jane! You're not the girl I once knew. You've become used to all . . . this and don't want anything to change!' He flung out his arm to encompass the large room.

Jane was wounded and resented his accusations. She felt he was being unfair. 'Is that so wrong? Yes, I have changed, Joe. I'm not the "workhouse girl" now. I've grown up and I've had to contend with so many things that I *couldn't* have remained the same person. But I *do* love you!'

'But not enough to want to make a new life with me! You're quite content to stay here in this big house, run your precious laundry and expect me to help you. Well, that's not enough for me, Jane. I've got my pride and I've got ambitions too; I told you that years ago. I'm going to Canada, with or without you!' he stated impetuously, too hurt to realise the implications of his words.

She caught his arm. 'Joe, please, give me time to think about it all,' she pleaded. 'I *know* you've got ambitions but . . . but so have I. Please let's talk about it?'

He flung off her arm. 'There's nothing to talk about, Jane. You prefer to stay here, that's plain enough.' He turned away and stormed out of the room, leaving the door wide open.

She sank down on to the sofa, shocked and bitterly upset. Had she misjudged him? Did he really love her or did she in fact take second place to his ambitions? He had obviously decided that she would sell up and invest everything in a new business in a new country and hadn't really thought about what she would want to do. And what of her own ambition, her plans to increase and improve her business? He hadn't even considered that. He hadn't thought about how she would feel leaving everything and everyone behind. She covered her face with her hands. Oh, it was all such a mess and it wasn't supposed to have ended like this. She loved him, she'd waited so long for him and she'd wanted to marry him. She began to sob, feeling utterly miserable.

'Jane, what's the matter? I heard the front door slam.

344

Where's our Joe?' Ada cried, panting a little for she'd rushed upstairs.

'He's . . . gone. We . . . we had a row, Aunty Ada. He's going to Canada and he wants me to sell up and go with him but . . .' She broke down.

Ada shook her head as she put her arm around Jane. 'What's the matter with that lad! Will he never learn? He always thinks the grass is flaming well greener on the other side of the hill or in this case the ocean!'

'I begged him to give me time to think, begged that we talk about it, but . . . he thinks I don't love him.'

'Take no notice, Jane. I'll have a few words to say to him when I get home, I can tell you,' Ada promised grimly. This was the first she'd heard of his schemes but surely he could see that a good life awaited him here in Liverpool? He'd sworn he loved Jane and wanted to marry her and she was sure the girl had agreed: wasn't that enough for him? Why go and risk everything in a country he'd only ever visited? And after all Jane had been through she didn't need him to run off and leave her to chase his dreams.

Chapter Thirty-One

———◆———

ADA HAD PLEADED with Joe in vain and in the end she had lost her temper. He was determined to go, he'd said emphatically. Jane had changed, she wasn't the girl he'd wanted to take away from all the sadness and misery she'd suffered and care for forever. Now she was more interested in her damned business than she was in him.

'That's just not true, Joe Ellis! She loves you, she's always loved you and wanted to be with you but no, off you went and accepted that job in America without thinking how she would feel or how it would affect her! She was so . . . distraught that she hardly knew what she was doing and James Davenport was kind to her and I for one didn't blame her when she accepted his proposal. You never showed any sign of coming back. The rest you know, but you're a bigger fool than I thought you were if you go and leave her again and turn down the opportunity of the kind of life she's willing to give you!'

'That's part of the problem! I don't want that kind of a life!

I want to be my own boss, to be able to support my own family, and it's quite clear that it's not what she wants at all. I've got my pride, Mam. I'm going and that's the end of it!' Joe had replied angrily, his anger hiding the deep hurt he felt. Yes, his mam was partly right when she'd said he'd hurt Jane by taking that job with Mr Ibsen but he hadn't realised then that she really did love him. But his mother didn't know he hadn't received those postcards from her. When he'd had no word from her all the time he'd been away he'd assumed her feelings had been more shallow than he'd believed. If he had known things might have been so different . . . but now he felt he had completely thrown away any chance of happiness with Jane. He'd told her she'd changed, and she had, yet he still loved her . . . but he wouldn't change his mind now. It was too late. He was miserable but he still had his pride. He'd try to make the dream of a new life come true even though he knew in his heart that it wouldn't be the same without her.

When Emily heard what had happened she was upset for both Jane and her brother. 'Oh, Mam, what a mess! I thought everything would be just fine for them both now but . . .'

'He should have at least given her some idea of what he was planning to do, Emily. He shouldn't have just sprung it on the poor girl like that. In fact he should have given us all some inkling of what he was thinking. And I'm not exactly delighted that he wants to go and make a life for himself so far away,' Ada fumed.

'What does Da say?' Emily asked.

'Not a great deal. He says he's old enough to make his own decisions and his own mistakes and believe me, Emily, he is making a mistake. A very big mistake indeed.'

Emily sighed heavily. 'And he's insistent that he's going?'

Ada nodded. 'Adamant! He says he's got his pride! He's taken what savings he's got out of the post office and been and booked his passage. He's going on the next ship out, the *Empress of France*. He's told your da he'll find lodgings and look for work in Montreal to start with. I just don't know what he's thinking of, Emily. I don't know why he wants to drag that poor girl off to another country, away from all her friends and the life she's used to.'

Emily was very concerned. 'Mam, we can't let this happen. We can't let them separate like this, not again.'

'There's nothing we can do about it. He won't change his mind.'

Emily made up her mind. 'Mam, I'm going to see Jane to see if there's anything—'

Ada shook her head. 'Stay out of it, Emily. It's between them.'

'But does she know he's booked his passage?'

'I haven't told her that yet. I don't want to be the one to tell her that he really is leaving her – again. She's so upset, hurt and bewildered,' Ada replied sadly.

Emily didn't reply but Jane should know, she thought, even if she was going to have to be the one to break the news to her.

In the time that had elapsed since Joe stormed out Jane had got through the days in a daze. She'd forced herself to go into work but she hadn't really been able to concentrate; she couldn't sleep and had no appetite. She was so miserable and dejected, just the way she had felt when he'd written to say he was staying in America all those years ago: abandoned and bereft. But this time it was worse because he wouldn't even talk to her about it. In her heart of hearts she'd hoped that when his anger had cooled he would come back to see her and they could try to sort it all out. She loved him and she wanted to be with him and she'd begun to ask herself was she being unreasonable? But as the days passed and there had been no word from him her despair had deepened.

Emily called that evening, hoping she could start to sort things out between Jane and her brother for there wasn't much time. 'How is she, Lizzie?' she asked when the girl opened the door to her.

Lizzie raised her eyes to the ceiling and shook her head. 'She's not herself at all, Mrs Taverner. She's very upset,' she confided.

Emily bit her lip. This wasn't going to be easy, she thought, but someone had to try to reconcile them.

Jane was sitting staring dejectedly at the empty hearth but she managed a smile when Emily gave her a hug. 'Oh, Em, I'm so glad to see you.'

Emily sat beside her and took her hand. She decided to get straight to the point. 'What's gone wrong between you and our Joe? Mam's told me the gist of it but . . .'

Tears welled up in Jane's eyes. 'He wants me to marry him and go to Canada and start a new life together but . . . I told him I didn't know if I wanted to go and he . . . got upset and then . . . really angry. He said I thought more of the business than I did of him and he wouldn't even wait to discuss it with me. He stormed out and I've not seen or heard from him since. I'm so miserable and . . . confused, Em! I've been trying to work things out in my mind, trying to think what a new life in

349

a new country would be like. If I could settle and be happy there or would I miss everyone so much that it wouldn't work and I'd end up miserable and blaming Joe.'

'I hate to be the one who has to tell you this Jane, but . . . but he's going. He's booked his passage on the *Empress of France*. She sails tomorrow morning.' Emily felt awful but if there was to be any chance of a reconciliation Jane had to know how little time there was left.

Jane dashed away the tears from her cheeks with the back of her hand. 'So, he really is going.'

'He is. Of course he may hate it but I don't think his pride will let him admit that or let him come back. Oh, Jane, don't throw away your chance of a happy future! Despite everything I know he loves you, he's just bitterly hurt and disappointed that you don't share his dream. And will you be happy if you stay here? Will your involvement in the business and your life here be enough?' she pleaded.

'But I'll be leaving everything and everyone I love,' Jane replied.

'You love *him*, Jane, and it's breaking your heart to lose him, I can see that.'

Jane nodded. She really shouldn't be thinking about Ada or anyone else. It was her life, not theirs. 'I do love him and I do want to marry him but—'

'Then don't let anything stop you from spending the rest of your life with him. He loves you deeply, underneath all the . . . anger and resentment and . . . stupid pride, it's breaking his heart. He wants to spend his life with you, Jane, he wants to make you happy and he thought that by going to a new country you could forget the past and be just that: happy!'

350

Jane nodded again.

'Give it a try, Jane. You might love it. If you don't go what will happen? You'll go on working but for what? Georgie and I don't have much money but we're happy and I wouldn't change that. What do money and position matter in the end if you're not happy?' Everything she was saying was true, she thought, remembering how Joe had begged her to impress upon Jane how much he loved her and wanted to care for her the night he'd got home and learned of James's death.

'Your mam said something similar to me once,' Jane said sadly.

'And she was right. Oh, Jane, you're my oldest and dearest friend, you're like a sister to me and I hate to see you so miserable. You deserve to be loved. After all you've been through you deserve to have a wonderful future, you deserve to be happy . . . and what about children?'

Her words reminded Jane that Emily was pregnant and the tears started again. If she let the chance of marriage to Joe slip from her grasp would she ever love another man? Would she ever have children of her own? She'd hoped for children when she'd married James but their time together had been short and it hadn't happened.

Emily squeezed her hand in sympathy. 'Maybe it's not my place to say such things, Jane, Mam told me not to interfere, but I hate to see you both throwing away the chance of a good life together. Please, please just think about it all. Promise me that?'

Jane nodded. 'I will, Em. I promise' She'd put the past behind her, she thought. The future was the most important thing now in her life.

'They don't sail until mid-morning so . . .' Emily left the rest unsaid as she got to her feet. She'd tried; that's all she could do.

When she'd gone Jane crossed and stood at the window looking out at the fresh green leaves on the trees in the familiar street outside. She had to make up her mind; she couldn't let the hours slip by. Everything Emily had said was true, she thought. Joe did have his pride and if he went she knew this time he wouldn't return. Was she really prepared to give up the chance of happiness, marriage and children to remain here? Yes, she was financially secure and she did enjoy working but would that compensate? Was she just clinging to money and position and did they make her happy? Would they be enough?

Her emotions were in turmoil as she turned away from the window and sank down on the sofa. She'd taken Ellen's advice about 'choosing wisely' for a secure future when she'd decided to marry James but now it was different. Whatever happened to her she would not be left penniless and struggling but would she always wonder 'what if'? Would she always regret letting him go?

At length, exhausted by her deliberations, she decided to go to bed, though she doubted she'd sleep. She had before her a decision that would affect the rest of her life.

Chapter Thirty-Two

⚜

J OE STARED AROUND the small cabin that he was sharing with someone else. Just who that would be he didn't know yet because apart from himself it was empty but there was a battered case on the bunk opposite. He put his sea bag down on the vacant bunk; his other luggage had been taken to the baggage room. He sat down next to his bag and stared around. The bunks took up most of the cabin's space, together with two small lockers, a tiny wardrobe and a washbasin. He hadn't expected much else and from his days in the crew mess he was used to cramped conditions.

He'd said his goodbyes early that morning and that hadn't been easy. His da had wished him luck and told him to be careful with his money and the company he kept. His mam had hugged him and told him to look after himself and to write regularly but he knew she was far from happy that he was going, and going without Jane. His brothers had shaken his hand, awkward and upset, and Emily had called in on her way to work; she'd hugged him with tears in her eyes and made him promise faithfully to write. He ran his hands through his hair. This wasn't how he had envisaged starting out on a new adventure. He felt miserable, apprehensive about a future that had once excited him so much, and heart-broken that he would never see Jane again. He had no inclination to unpack or to go up on deck for the last sight of his native city, to see below on the Landing Stage friends and relations calling and waving. There was no one there to wave him farewell; he'd not wanted them to be there. 'It's not too late,' a small voice in his head reminded him. He could just pick up his bag and walk off the ship and go back to Gill Street. Is that what he should do? Give up his dreams and go back to Jane? He loved her, he couldn't deny that, and he wanted to be with her. There was still time . . . but no, he'd made the decision, he'd made the break. Jane didn't love him enough to come with him and he'd just have to accept that and get on with life without her. It would be hard, possibly the hardest thing he'd have to do in the years ahead, but there was no help for it. There was no going back.

He stood up and began to unpack his bag, trying to ignore the increasing noise in the companionway outside and the adjacent cabins as other passengers arrived accompanied by family and friends and proceeded to hold their own small 'Bon Voyage' parties. He was also trying to ignore the feeling of loneliness that was creeping over him.

Jane hadn't slept well – her mind was still in turmoil – but when she got up she'd at last decided what she had to do.

She dressed quickly, pulling on a pale grey skirt and a white silk blouse trimmed with grey ribbon for she had resolved to try to look her best. She carried the matching jacket, her hat, gloves and bag into the dining room with her.

'You're early this morning, Mrs Davenport,' Lizzie Renshaw remarked as she carried in the tea tray.

'I'm going out, Lizzie. When I've finished do you think you could see if you can find a taxi cab outside?'

The girl nodded but she was perplexed. If the weather was fine her mistress tended to walk to the laundry and she usually wasn't dressed quite as smartly either. Lizzie wondered where she was going but was glad that at least she looked a lot better this morning than she had of late.

Jane looked impatiently at her watch as she waited in the hall for Lizzie to return. Why did time always seem to race by when you didn't want it to? Emily had said mid-morning but she didn't know the exact time; she didn't even know if visitors were allowed on board before the ship sailed. If not, then she would have to somehow get a message to him. Oh, she prayed she wouldn't be too late. Of course she could write to him later but that wouldn't be the same. She wanted to see him, wanted him to see that his love was all that mattered to her now. Because that was what she had decided. She wanted to be with him and have a life, a future with him.

She'd stopped worrying about leaving behind all that was familiar: she knew that with Joe beside her she would cope. She'd even had an idea of what she could do for work over there: there had to be hundreds of women like her who'd left their homes for a new life. Women who felt lonely or perhaps needed advice or practical help. Who needed somewhere to go to make friends or just have someone to talk to who understood

355

their fears and worries. She could set up a group for them, a 'Women's Immigration Society'.

In the taxi her heart began to race and not for the first time she wondered was she mad? But no, she wouldn't let herself think along those lines now. She'd made her decision; she wouldn't change her mind.

But would Joe still want her? Would *he* have changed his mind— No. She wouldn't even contemplate that. She forced herself to stop thinking as the driver stopped at the top of the floating roadway that led down to the Landing Stage and as she paid him she got her first sight of the huge white-painted vessel. It was still tied up although grey smoke was issuing from its three mustard-coloured funnels, a sign of its impending departure.

She quickened her steps as she walked down the roadway and when she reached the Landing Stage she pushed her way through the crowd as politely as she could until she caught sight of a gangway and hastened towards it.

'Excuse me. I'm looking for a passenger: Mr Joe Ellis. Will I be able to come aboard to see him?' she asked the uniformed officer who stood with a clipboard at the foot of the gangway.

'You will, madam. Is the gentleman travelling first class?'

Jane was relieved she would be allowed on board but a little confused. She had no idea in what class he was travelling. 'No, no, I don't think so. In fact I'm not sure what kind of . . . accommodation he booked.'

'Try one of the other gangways then, madam. This is for first-class passengers only, and I'd hurry if I were you, all visitors will be leaving shortly,' he instructed, pointing down the side of the ship.

Her heart began to thud sickeningly as she ran towards the next gangway; it seemed so far away. She hadn't realised just how big this ship was and time was running out. Nor did she know whether he'd booked a second- or third-class passage. She was slightly out of breath when she reached the next gangway and was directed aboard but with the same warning about time. With a feeling of rising panic she realised that she didn't have a clue where she was going. Ahead of her stretched a seemingly endless corridor crowded with people. She caught the arm of one and ascertained that this was the second-class accommodation and pressed on. There were stairs ahead of her going down and at the bottom she was relieved to see a lad in the white uniform jacket of a steward.

'Oh, please, can you help me? I'm looking for a Mr Joe Ellis?'

He grinned at her. 'What's his cabin number, miss?'

'Oh, Lord! I don't know! I think he might be in second class but I'm not sure of that either! But I have to find him and I know I've not got much time. Please, please help me! It's so important. *Everything* depends on me seeing him!' she begged.

'Bit like a needle in a haystack, miss, but follow me and we'll try,' he promised cheerily.

She pressed a pound note into his hand and then kept close behind him as they went down seemingly endless passageways full of people and luggage, while the boy shouted Joe's name aloud.

'Can't move for "Bon Voyage" parties down here, miss. It's always like this on sailing day,' he called to her.

She peered into every cabin they passed but was beginning to realise how impossible it was to find him without even a number. When they at last came to a large open area he stopped.

'You go that way, miss, I'll go this way, but hurry. If I find him I'll call you,' he instructed before turning away.

She began to run down the corridor trying to avoid the pieces of baggage outside doors and began to call his name as loudly as she could. What if she couldn't find him? What if the steward couldn't find him?

'JOE ELLIS! JOE! IT'S JANE! OH, JOE, WHERE ARE YOU?' she shouted, near to tears, her voice full of despair. And then she heard the steward's voice calling her. She turned and uttered a cry of relief as she saw him hurrying towards her followed by a bewildered Joe.

'Oh, Joe! I thought I'd never find you! Oh, thank you, thank you!' she cried.

The steward grinned. 'Better get a move on, the pair of you,' he advised, winking at Joe.

'Jane! Jane, I can't believe it's you!' Joe cried.

She flung herself into his arms, her eyes bright with tears. 'Joe, I've made up my mind. I'll come with you, if you still want me to. I love you and I don't want to spend the rest of my life without you! I've even thought of what I could do out there: I could set up a sort of "Women's Immigration Society". But most of all I just want to be with you! '

He held her tightly, waves of pure happiness and relief washing over him. 'Oh, Jane, my love, of course I still want you! I was so miserable, I really didn't want to go without you. I love you so much!'

'ALL ASHORE THAT'S GOING ASHORE!' The words were bellowed down the companionway, accompanied by the loud clanging of a hand bell.

'Joe, what will we do?' Jane begged.

'You'll have to go, Jane, but will you follow me? I'll find somewhere for us to live, I'll make all the arrangements for us to get married and I'll write to let you know about everything. And when you come I'll meet you,' Joe promised, still hardly able to believe that she had come to find him.

She kissed him passionately as the sound of the warning bell became louder. 'Of course I'll follow you, as soon as I can. I'll sell the house and the business and book my passage.'

'We won't be apart for long and then we'll start a new life and we'll be so happy,' Joe promised. 'Now, I'd better take you to the nearest gangway or you'll get lost, then I'll go up on deck.'

'And I'll stand and wave, Joe. I'll wave until the ship is out of sight but you'll know that I'll be following you soon. And I'll be coming from Liverpool with love, with all the love in my heart.'

Meet

Lyn Andrews

Read on to hear about Lyn's own childhood
growing up in Liverpool, her inspiration for the novel
and the real Brownlow Hill Workhouse . . .

Q & A with Lyn Andrews

It's fascinating to think that the Brownlow Hill Workhouse actually existed. Can you tell us a little more about its history and how it inspired you when writing FROM LIVERPOOL WITH LOVE?

It was built in 1772 as the 'New House of Industry' in a part of the city which was still quite rural, but the city and port grew with the Industrial Revolution – which brought thousands more people in to work – so it was enlarged in 1842 and at maximum capacity could house five thousand inmates. In 1865 local pharmacist William Rathbone paid for twelve nurses from the Nightingale School to staff the Infirmary, plus eighteen probationers and fifty-four inmates who helped out, all under Superintendent Agnes Jones. This was at a time when cholera and typhoid frequently raged through the Liverpool slum areas and Brownlow Hill was the first workhouse in the country to have such an infirmary. Although the workhouse buildings had been demolished by the time I was a child (the demolition happened in the mid-1930s I think, for the site the

Catholic Cathedral of Christ the King was built on), people of my parents' and grandparents' age remembered it well and it was through those memories that I became interested, although none of them had ever been inside the place – mercifully.

It is very moving in the novel to see how the Ellises do all they can to help the Shaw family, even though they have very little themselves. What examples did you find of the ways neighbours rallied to support each other through hard times in poorer communities?

People in Liverpool traditionally helped each other in hard times, particularly as no one had very much. I remember when a young woman with small children moved into a house three doors away from us (on a council estate) and her husband was in hospital dying from TB he'd contracted in the Navy during the war, my parents and other neighbours did whatever they could to help her. They remained good friends and neighbours for many years. I still sometimes see one of those 'small' children – of course she's almost my age.

At the beginning of the novel Ellen is surprised to find that, although she feels desperate and humiliated when she has to take her family into the workhouse, she also feels relief. When you were researching workhouses, what did you think of the conditions? What improvements had been made since Victorian times?

When I started researching the workhouse I found that conditions had greatly improved by the 1900s, although life was still harsh and very restricted. The sexes were still segregated and inmates had to work long hours at very tedious jobs and had to wear a hideous 'uniform'. However food had greatly improved since the days of Dickens' *Oliver Twist* and Christmas was far from a frugal and cheerless occasion. In the reign of Queen Victoria the conditions really were very, very grim indeed as attitudes to the poor were along the lines of 'it was usually their own fault and therefore they deserved little sympathy and definitely nothing that could be deemed a luxury', but in the 1920s and 30s thankfully that kind of attitude had disappeared and emphasis was placed on teaching skills which would secure jobs and therefore a better, more independent life.

It was exciting to read about the opportunities that opened up for Joe as a result of his job on the Empress of Scotland. How easy was it for boys like Joe to build a better life for themselves through travelling or emigrating to places like America and Canada?

In the Liverpool of the 1920s, 30s, 40s and 50s very many men and boys 'went away to sea' – I think every single family had at least one member who did, myself included. For jobs connected with engineering etc. of course you had to have experience, but there were plenty of positions where it wasn't necessary and so young men (and women as stewardesses) had the opportunity to travel and to meet people often in a far wealthier position than themselves and some, like Joe Ellis, were offered jobs in other countries ensuring them a new and often better life.

One of the most joyful scenes in the novel is when Joe, Emily, Jane and Georgie welcome in the New Year with crowds of fellow revellers to the sounds of Liverpool's ships sounding off their whistles. Can you tell us how you and your family celebrated New Year when you were growing up in Liverpool?

New Year's Eve in Liverpool when I was growing up was exactly as I've described it in the book. There was always a party in someone's house, often three or four, and people would wander in and out of them all. Just before midnight, everyone would go out into the street, regardless of the weather, and then you would hear the bells, ships' whistles, car horns – it was magical!

Jane suffers a lot of sadness in the novel, loosing people dear to her in traumatic circumstances. How difficult do you find it to write distressing scenes for your characters and do you ever wish you could always give them happy storylines?

Distressing scenes are always difficult to write because you are actually trying to put yourself into your character's 'skin' and imagine how they are feeling, and it can be quite draining emotionally. Sometimes I do wish I could give them happy storylines but then that wouldn't be very realistic. Everyone has some tragedy and setbacks in life.

Despite being brother and sister, Alfie and Jane are complete opposites. Alfie chooses a life of crime while Jane works hard to forge a bright future for herself. In what ways do you think their paths would have differed had they not experienced living in the workhouse?

I didn't envisage Jane and Alfie's paths being very different had they not gone into the workhouse. Alfie was always going to turn out 'a bad un' and Jane was always going to work hard for a better life.

Jane and Alfie lose both their mother and father to an accident and illness that today's health and safety standards could have prevented. What examples have you found of situations where people protested about conditions?

When I worked as a secretary, before I had my children, one of the duties I really dreaded was taking the minutes at the monthly Works Committee Meeting. I worked in the offices of a factory that made washing machines, this was in the 1960s, and the representatives of the workers were still trying to improve conditions for them. Those meetings went on for hours with innumerable arguments between them and the 'Management', all of which had to be noted down and typed up! My late mother-in-law was a union shop steward and so was at the forefront of trying to obtain better conditions – even though she voted Conservative all her life and shop stewards were traditionally Labour!

Do you think Jane could have lived contentedly as James' wife, in such wealthy surroundings, or do you think she would always have yearned for Joe and the familiarity of her Gill Street roots, despite the hardships they brought?

I think Jane would have tried to be content as the wife of a wealthy man – she is very aware of things like loyalty – yet I think her heart would always have been in Gill Street with Joe. So of course I had to do something to bring that about.

It is wonderful when Jane gets her happy ending with the man she loves, however it is sad that she has to give up her role at The Empire Laundry. How difficult do you think you would have found it to make that choice if you were in Jane's position?

I don't think I would have found it too difficult because I'm of a generation that took it for granted that when you got married and had a family you gave up working. Mine was probably the last generation who did so. Very few of us ordinary working-class girls expected to become 'career women' – at least not until our children were much older. The fact that I've had a thirty-year-long career as an author is something that still amazes me.

Read on for a sneak peek at Lyn's
captivating next novel

Heart and Home

Chapter One

1933

'Mam, I won't do it! I won't!' As she faced her mother Kitty Kinrade's cheeks were flushed and her dark eyes flashed with mutinous determination. She was small and slight for her age – she had just turned fifteen – and the faded paisley print dress, being two years old now and too short for her, added to the illusion that she was still only a child. That was something Kitty herself would have realised was no longer true even if both her parents had not impressed upon her that, having left school, her childhood was behind her and from now on she must earn a living and contribute to the household.

Lizzie Kinrade sighed heavily and looked up from the kitchen table where she had just finished rolling out the pastry for the pie she was making for supper. She wiped her hands on her stained cotton apron and looked with annoyance at her eldest daughter. 'Kitty, don't start on that again! You have to get work, and what else is there here in Ramsey for the likes of us?' Her gaze strayed around her small kitchen, which, apart from the tiny scullery, was the only room on the ground floor of the stone cottage where she and Barney had lived all their married life. It opened directly on to the street and was both kitchen and living room. They had only the essentials in the way of furniture – which was just as well, she thought; when they were all at home you could barely move. Upstairs there were two small bedrooms; the minuscule yard at the back contained the ramshackle privy, a tin bath hanging on a nail in the wall and her washing tub. It was all they could afford and although with six children it was definitely overcrowded she considered herself fortunate that she had a good, hard-working husband, a roof over her head, food for the table, fuel for the fire and that she had not lost any of her children to hunger, disease, war or the sea as many women had on this small island.

Kitty clenched her hands tightly and pursed her lips, shaking her dark curly hair around her oval face; this was one battle she was determined to win no matter how much friction it caused. She had thought long and hard over this decision and was not going to give up on it.

'I know I've got to get work, Mam, and I will, but I'm not going to gut fish!' Inwardly she shuddered at the very thought of standing on the quay all day in all weathers, up to her elbows in the blood and guts of herrings, which would then go to be smoked or pickled, or mackerel or bass or cod or any other fish. All her life she'd witnessed the women and girls in their filthy, blood-stained aprons, wielding long sharp gutting knives as they worked by the Fish Steps in the Market Square beside Ramsey's outer harbour, which was where the fishing fleet tied up. They all looked hard and weather-beaten and they stank of fish. It was a pervasive odour that seemed to get into the very pores of your skin and no amount of washing, even with carbolic soap, could eliminate it. No, she'd decided that she wanted something better. Ever since she'd been a small child she'd been fascinated by the shops in Parliament Street, Ramsey's main thoroughfare, establishments that were far beyond the reach of her mother's very limited budget. She'd loved to stand and gaze at the displays of fashionable dresses, jackets and coats in rich fabrics and the magnificent hats and soft leather gloves and handbags. Of course she'd soon realised that she would never be able to afford to buy clothes like that. Indeed she'd come to understand that she'd never even be able to get work in such shops. Girls of her class and education could only expect to be employed in very menial jobs, but that didn't stop her dreaming and hoping that one day she might in fact achieve something better; something that would help to contribute to their standard of living, for her father and brothers worked very hard for little reward.

Lizzie sat down in her old, scarred, bentwood rocker and looked wearily at Kitty. In appearance the girl resembled her; with her dark hair and eyes and small but sturdy stature, she bore all the traits of her Celtic ancestors, like many people from the south of the island. However, in nature Kitty took after her father. Bernard – Barney – Kinrade was tall and well built, with blue eyes and fair hair – although now there was more silver in his hair than gold – attributes that harked back to the Viking heritage of the people of the north. He was a rather taciturn man and could be stubborn, but he didn't gamble or drink. Any man who went out to sea with a belly full of ale was a fool, he often remarked. He was superstitious, but then all fishermen were, she conceded. His was a hard and dangerous life – the sea had claimed many lives – but he never complained.

'Kitty, we've argued this down to the bone and there's nothing more to be said. You've to work, and that's an end to it. Do you think Jack and Jacob *wanted* to go out on the boat with your da? Do you not think they wanted an easier, safer way of earning a living? Of course they did but what else is there for us? It's fishing or farming and we've no land to work. We're not fortunate enough to have a shop, a business or a house big and grand enough to take in paying summer visitors. The lads couldn't get an apprenticeship and for most other types of decent employment in this town you'd need a better education than any of you have had. I'll have a word with Madge Gelling tomorrow and see if you can start at the Fish Steps on Monday. There'll be no more arguments.'

Tears of anger and frustration pricked Kitty's eyes but before she had time to utter another word her younger sister Ella piped up.

'*I* won't mind working with Mrs Gelling and the others, Mam, when I leave school. I heard their Nora saying it's great getting your money at the end of a long week. It makes it all worthwhile.' From beneath her heavy fringe of dark hair she shot a surreptitious but triumphant glance at Kitty, who glared back at her. Ella shrugged. Kitty was just plain stupid if she thought she could get a good job.

'Oh, shut up, Ella! You just want to cause trouble; it's all you ever do!' Kitty cried, knowing full well that her sibling delighted in goading her. Fenella – called 'Ella' by the family

– was almost thirteen and had been a torment to her for as long as she could remember.

'Don't speak to your sister like that!' Lizzie snapped as she got to her feet, trying to head off a squabble. Those two fought like cat and dog and always had done. Her head had begun to ache and she still had a day of chores ahead of her before she could rest for a few hours by the fire after supper. Tomorrow was Sunday and they would all attend St Paul's Church in the Market Square, for Barney insisted they 'keep the Sabbath'. Tonight they would all take their weekly bath here in the kitchen, which meant hours of heating up water on the range. She would have to make sure that their clothes were clean and pressed and any rips or tears were neatly mended and their boots and shoes polished, ready for church in the morning.

'Ella, take little Hal and go and see if there's any sign of your da and the lads yet, while I put on the porridge – they'll be starving,' she instructed, and then turned to ten-year-old Meggie. 'You start to peg out the washing in the yard for me, girl. I'll come out as soon as I can to help and to make sure that there's not a wind getting up that may bring the rain.' Preoccupied by a seemingly endless list of tasks, she turned to five-year-old Harold – Hal – the baby of the family, and, despite his protests, bundled him into an old cut-down jacket of Jacob's to keep out the chill March wind.

While her mother was preoccupied Ella pulled a face at Kitty and hissed, 'You'll have to gut fish and then you'll stink of them and no one will want to come near you!'

Snatching her cardigan from the back of a chair, Kitty slammed out before she too could be instructed to undertake some job. She wanted a bit of time on her own, away from her mam and Ella and Meggie and Hal, and before her da and her brothers came home and the kitchen filled to bursting. Then it would be hard to hear yourself speak, let alone think.

She shivered as she stepped out into Collins Lane and pulled her cardigan more closely around her. The narrow lane seemed to act like a funnel for the wind coming in off the harbour. Collins Lane ran between the West Quay and Parliament Street, Ramsey's main thoroughfare where all the best shops were located. But Collins Lane, at its widest point opposite the cottages, was barely three feet in width. It was so narrow and crooked that the sunlight hardly ever managed to penetrate to brighten or warm it. They lived in the middle of a block of three stone cottages which were overlooked by the wall of the warehouse on the opposite side. She stood for a few seconds debating which way to go; then she turned left and headed down towards the quay.

It didn't take her long to reach the end of the lane: ahead of her lay the harbour, divided by the swing bridge. In the outer harbour the fishing boats were already tying up, the boat her da and brothers worked on amongst them. They didn't own it; if they did they would be considerably better off. She shivered in the wind; she had no wish to see her da just yet – he'd only ask where she was going – nor had she any intention of heading towards the Market Square where the fish would already be being unloaded and the women gathered on the steps ready to start the gutting.

She crossed the harbour by the iron swing bridge which divided it into an 'inner' and 'outer' and could be 'swung' open to allow boats to pass through. She intended to head out towards the sea front along the promenade, away from the town, but she'd only gone a few yards when she heard her name being called and she turned to see her brother Jacob hastening across the bridge towards her, a grin on his face.

'Where are you off to, Kitty? What's the matter? Have you escaped Mam and the Saturday chores?' He fell into step beside her and despite her desire to be alone she couldn't help but grin up at him. They got on well and had always been close.

'I've come out to escape the lot of them! Our Ella's being a torment – as usual,' she replied.

Jacob tutted in mock disapproval. Like his father he was tall, well built and fair and at eighteen was considered by quite a few girls to be handsome. 'Squabbling again? What over now?'

'Oh, she was just being hateful, sucking up to Mam and saying she won't mind working with Mrs Gelling when she finishes school, and then taunting me that I'll stink of fish!'

Jacob frowned. He was aware of the arguments. He could understand Kitty wanting a better job but he also knew that for his sisters there wasn't much else on offer.

They walked in silence for a while until they reached the wide promenade that faced the sea and led out towards Mooragh Park, Jacob seemingly oblivious to the sharp edge to the wind, although Kitty now wished she'd put something warmer on. The sea looked choppy, its surface broken by white-topped wavelets. However, the sun was struggling to break through the clouds so she hoped it might get a bit warmer as the morning wore on. Overhead the gulls wheeled and dived, their strident cries grating on her nerves.

It was Jacob who broke the silence. 'So, you're still

determined not to gut fish.' It was more a statement than a question.

Kitty nodded. 'There's *got* to be something else, Jacob. I worked hard at my lessons. I can read and write and do my sums well enough and Miss Costain said I have a "pleasant way" with folk and should look to "improve" myself. Surely I can do something better than gut fish?'

'All that's not enough, Kitty. I know it's hard but, well, you know we need every penny.'

She stared out across the wide sweep of the bay, her gaze settling on the half-mile-long Victoria Pier at the end of which a ferry boat was tied up. There were regular sailings to England, Scotland and Ireland, and in the summer months the ferries brought hundreds of visitors and day trippers to the island. Across the sea was England and . . . Liverpool. Oh, she'd heard such tales of that city and its magnificent buildings, its huge ocean liners, its wide streets full of shops. Shops that were enormous compared to those here in Ramsey and even Douglas. She'd only ever visited the island's capital once and had never been off the island. 'There's a whole world out there, Jacob, full of chances and opportunities. Why shouldn't I go to Liverpool? I'd get a decent job there. Why shouldn't I make something of my life, "improve" myself, like Miss Costain said? I might even get a job in one of the big shops there, something I've always dreamed of! I have to try, Jacob!' Impatiently she pushed a few wisps of dark hair, tousled by the wind, away from her forehead. 'I don't want to be poor all my life. I don't want to be like Mam, always tired, always worried. Why can't I have hopes and dreams and a better life?'

He smiled down at her a little sadly. He was very fond of

her and knew he was the only one she'd confide in. But she was still so young and didn't realise that for the likes of them hopes and dreams were a luxury which seldom became reality. You had to take whatever hand life dealt you; no use raging against it. 'Why can't you have hopes and dreams? Because for us, Kitty, they're like circles drawn in the sand. When the tide comes in it washes them away.' He paused. 'I . . . I didn't want to follow Da into fishing but . . .' He shrugged. 'I got used to it and most of the time it's not too bad. We have to be grateful for what we've got; isn't that what Mam's always telling us?' If he'd had a choice he would have liked to have become a carpenter. He enjoyed working with his hands – he often fixed things around the house, and the boat too – but to have become a tradesman he would have had to serve an apprenticeship. His parents didn't have the money to pay for his indentures and so no one had been prepared to take him on.

Kitty bit her lip. It seemed as if there was no escape for her and yet she wanted so much more from life. But maybe Jacob was right. Maybe her wishes and dreams were simply circles in the sand.

READING CORNER

PHONICS

In the Shed

Written by
Clare De Marco

Illustrated by
Anna C. Leplar

Practising phonemes of more than one letter and
simple polysyllabic words
+ and / the / to / I / he

First published in 2009 by
Franklin Watts
338 Euston Road
London NW1 3BH

Franklin Watts Australia
Hachette Children's Books
Level 17/207 Kent Street
Sydney NSW 2000

Text © Clare De Marco 2009
Illustration © Anna C. Leplar 2009

A CIP catalogue record for this book
is available from the British Library.

ISBN: 978 0 7496 9155 4 (hbk)
ISBN: 978 0 7496 9164 6 (pbk)

Series Editor: Jackie Hamley
Series Advisors: Dr Barrie Wade,
 Dr Hilary Minns
Series Designer: Jonathan Hair

Printed in China

Franklin Watts is a division of
Hachette Children's Books,
an Hachette UK company
www.hachette.co.uk

There is a puzzle at the end of this book.
Here are the answers for you to check later!

The matching words are:

jacket packet

Jack back, lack, rack, sack

pocket docket, locket, socket

shed bed, fed, red, wed

2

Jack is in the shed.
It is thick with cobwebs.

He picks up a ring ...

a doll ...

and a ship.

Then Jack kicks a red,
velvet jacket off its rung.

6

"Yuck! Moths!" he yells.

7

Jack picks up the jacket
and checks in a pocket.

9

"Mum, is this cash?"
Jack yells, and he runs
back to Mum.

11

"Yes," Mum tells him.
"Nan got that jacket
to visit the king."

13

"I put that in the pocket for luck," Nan tells Jack.

15

"I am rich!" Jack yells.

"Rich, but such a mess!"
Mum tells Jack.

"Get that jacket off and get in the bath!"

"I am king of
the bath!"
Jack tells Nan.

Puzzle Time!

Match the words that rhyme
to the pictures!

jacket

sack

locket

fed

Jack

rack

socket

bed

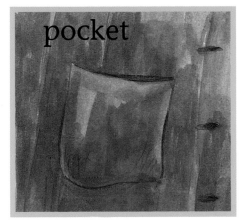

pocket

docket

lack

wed

packet

back

red

shed

See page 2 for answers!

Notes for parents and teachers

READING CORNER PHONICS has been structured to provide maximum support for children learning to read through synthetic phonics. The stories are designed for independent reading but may also be used by adults for sharing with young children.

The teaching of early reading through synthetic phonics focuses on the 44 sounds in the English language, and how these sounds correspond to their written form in the 26 letters of the alphabet. Carefully controlled vocabulary makes these books accessible for children at different stages of phonics teaching, progressing from simple CVC (consonant-vowel-consonant) words such as "top" (t-o-p) to trisyllabic words such as "messenger" (mess-en-ger). READING CORNER PHONICS allows children to read words in context, and also provides visual clues and repetition to further support their reading. These books will help develop the all important confidence in the new reader, and encourage a love of reading that will last a lifetime!

If you are reading this book with a child, here are a few tips:

1. Talk about the story before you start reading. Look at the cover and the title. What might the story be about? Why might the child like it?

2. Encourage the child to reread the story, and to retell the story in their own words, using the illustrations to remind them what has happened.

3. Discuss the story and see if the child can relate it to their own experience, or perhaps compare it to another story they know.

4. Give praise! Small mistakes need not always be corrected. If a child is stuck on a word, ask them to try and sound it out and then blend it together again, or model this yourself. For example "wish" w-i-sh "wish".

READING CORNER PHONICS covers two grades of synthetic phonics teaching, with three levels at each grade. Each level has a certain number of words per story, indicated by the number of bars on the spine of the book:

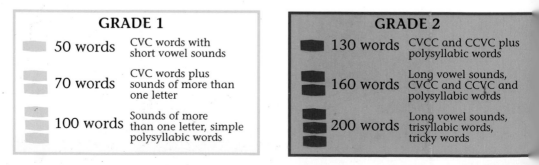

GRADE 1	
50 words	CVC words with short vowel sounds
70 words	CVC words plus sounds of more than one letter
100 words	Sounds of more than one letter, simple polysyllabic words

GRADE 2	
130 words	CVCC and CCVC plus polysyllabic words
160 words	Long vowel sounds, CVCC and CCVC and polysyllabic words
200 words	Long vowel sounds, trisyllabic words, tricky words